NICE DOGGIE . . .

Cerberus turned its Snarly head, and the giant, jaundiced eye unblinkingly trained itself on my frozen form. The dog's eye narrowed, and I knew without anyone saying anything out loud that I was only one slo-mo minute from getting digested.

The other two heads stopped their obsessive licking and raised themselves in line with Snarly head. They didn't look nearly as mean as Snarly, but as I watched, something much worse began to register in their eyes: excitement. The big hellhound's tail started thumping more quickly against the gate.

Then, without warning, Snarly head swooped forward, teeth bared, giant eyeball trained in one direction . . . *mine*. Frozen in shock, I could do nothing but stare as Cerberus, the guardian of the North Gate to Hell, prepared to make me its lunch . . .

Ace Books by Amber Benson

DEATH'S DAUGHTER
CAT'S CLAW

death's daughter

AMBER BENSON

THE BERKLEY PUBLISHING GROUP
Published by the Penguin Group
Penguin Group (USA) Inc.
375 Hudson Street, New York, New York 10014, USA
Penguin Group (Canada), 90 Eglinton Avenue East, Suite 700, Toronto, Ontario M4P 2Y3, Canada
(a division of Pearson Penguin Canada Inc.)
Penguin Books Ltd., 80 Strand, London WC2R 0RL, England
Penguin Group Ireland, 25 St. Stephen's Green, Dublin 2, Ireland (a division of Penguin Books Ltd.)
Penguin Group (Australia), 250 Camberwell Road, Camberwell, Victoria 3124, Australia
(a division of Pearson Australia Group Pty. Ltd.)
Penguin Books India Pvt. Ltd., 11 Community Centre, Panchsheel Park, New Delhi—110 017, India
Penguin Group (NZ), 67 Apollo Drive, Rosedale, North Shore 0632, New Zealand
(a division of Pearson New Zealand Ltd.)
Penguin Books (South Africa) (Pty.) Ltd., 24 Sturdee Avenue, Rosebank, Johannesburg 2196,
South Africa

Penguin Books Ltd., Registered Offices: 80 Strand, London WC2R 0RL, England

DEATH'S DAUGHTER

An Ace Book / published by arrangement with Benson Entertainment, Inc.

PRINTING HISTORY
Ace mass-market edition / March 2009

Cover art by Spiral Studio.
Cover design by Judith Lagerman.
Interior text design by Kristin Del Rosario.

ISBN: 978-0-441-01694-5

ACE
Ace Books are published by The Berkley Publishing Group,
a division of Penguin Group (USA) Inc.,
375 Hudson Street, New York, New York 10014.
ACE and the "A" design are trademarks of Penguin Group (USA) Inc.

PRINTED IN THE UNITED STATES OF AMERICA

10 9 8 7 6 5 4 3 2 1

For the two special men in my life:
Dad and Adam

Acknowledgments

There are three people integral to the creation of this book: my awesome literary manager, Brendan Deneen; my equally fantastic editor, Ginjer Buchanan; and the man who started it all, my frequent collaborator and good friend Christopher Golden. Without their encouragement and support, Calliope Reaper-Jones would never have seen the light of day. I also want to send a shout-out to the singer-songwriter Angela Correa, whose album *Correatown* furnished the sound track for the writing of this book.

one

My name is Calliope Reaper-Jones, and I think I'm losing my mind.

Okay, maybe I was being a *touch* melodramatic. I *wasn't* completely losing my mind, but things were definitely getting a little screwy in my neck of the woods.

It was like the universe couldn't help itself. It had to mess with you every once in a while—you know, just to make sure you were paying attention. I guess it reasoned that since we were all so busy being anal little worker ants, its job was to step in occasionally and shatter whatever carefully constructed illusions of normalcy we had created for ourselves.

Just to shake things up a little . . . for our sakes, of course.

Because, unlike us, the universe knew that illusions were just that: illusionary—and they could be destroyed with one well-placed roundhouse kick.

* * *

my kick in the pants came last Saturday: the day of my most recent blind date.

My next-door neighbor, Patience, had decided she was sick and tired of my sad ass feeling all sorry for itself—her words, not mine, but the sentiment was definitely correct. I mean, I hadn't had a real date in, well . . . It was so pathetic an expanse of time that I didn't even want to talk about it.

You see, my not-so "dream job" job had totally precluded me from having any kind of social life. Period. I spent all week working my butt off, so that when Saturday finally *did* roll around, I was too dead to the world to enjoy it. Plus which, my few pathetic attempts to "hook up" through craigslist were just that—pathetic.

I usually ended up in zombie mode until Sunday when—somehow mildly recharged—I'd get up, do my laundry, run a few necessary errands, then meet some girlfriends at whatever new "happening" breakfast place they'd decided we were going to have brunch at that weekend. They never bothered asking for my foodie opinion, just e-mailed me the address—for reference only, since I wouldn't know a "happening" place if it hit me over the head with a shovel and whispered into my ear: "I'm a hot spot!"

Anyway, that's enough about my pathetic excuse for a social life. Let's go back to the blind date, and the day everything in my life went to hell in a handbasket.

Said blind-date guy was one of Patience's office mates at Brown, Stimple, and Brown, Esquire, a big law firm uptown. I wasn't exactly sure what she did there, but she had a really big television hanging on her wall, so it must've been something very important and unbelievably exciting—*not*. The legal world was nothing if not nail-bitingly . . . *tedious*.

Anyway, the guy she'd decided was my soul mate worked in a different department, but since they had mutual friends, she said it would be as "easy as pie"—her words again—to get him to take me out on the town one Saturday night in the near future, ending my fantastically *long* dating dry spell—*hurrah!*

Well, it turns out the "near future" was only two days after she'd told me about the idea in the first place. There wasn't even enough time to get freaked-out about the whole thing. All I could do was take my Friday lunch break at Saks, and pray there was something on the designer sale rack that fit.

Unfortunately, the one dress I fell in love with at first sight, a beautiful DKNY silk number that was marked down to a ridiculous forty-three bucks, was way too big. No matter how I tried to cinch the waist, it looked like I was wearing a mumu. Empty-handed, I went back to work feeling—for the first time in my life—slightly perturbed that I wasn't twenty pounds *heavier*.

That night, I was stuck in the office until eight thirty collating four copies of my boss's son's book report, by which time all the stores were closed, or getting ready to close. I knew right then and there it was gonna be Saturday afternoon or nothing.

When I got home, I set my alarm for nine thirty, determined to get up, brush my teeth, and go find something slinky, sultry, and cheap to wear on the blind date. I had decided that even if the guy was a total dog—which he probably *would* be, with my luck—*I* was gonna look hot, and take *somebody* yummy home, even if it only turned out to be my old standby: Ben and Jerry.

That night, all tucked up in my little Battery Park

City bedroom, I fell asleep with visions of department stores in my head, more excited about a Saturday than I'd been in a long, long time.

Had I known what the next day was going to have in store for me, I don't think I would've slept a wink. Needless to say, I was completely clueless, so I slept like a baby . . . on Ambien.

the day did not even *start* well.

First, my alarm decided to not go off.

I'd set that sucker, checked it twice—I can be a bit OCD when I feel like it—and even made sure the alarm was set to *buzzer* rather than *radio.* I knew it was going to have to be one of those screaming "alarm only" mornings if I was going to make myself crawl out of bed at a quasireasonable hour, so I took, like, extra, *extra* precaution.

So, of course, no alarm meant no wakey-wakey on time. Which in plain English meant that when I finally did get up, it was one (!) in the afternoon.

The next thing I discovered was that *all* the water from every tap in my apartment was boiling hot. The scalding water made it almost impossible to brush my teeth, let alone take a shower or wash my hair, so now I was stuck stinking my way into what was supposed to be a brilliant Barney's shopping-excursion day.

Weird, but not unheard of.

In fact, only six months earlier the entire building had been without water for two days, in which time I learned the true meaning of the term "Irish bath." Take it from me, not the best way to make friends on the subway.

In retrospect, I guess I should have seen all the above

weirdness as a sign. But at the time—and you have to believe me here—it did not seem like a big deal, definitely not strange enough to warrant an exorcism of the old homestead.

It wasn't until I got to the front hall of my building that I realized I might very shortly be in the market for the phone number of the local Catholic church.

The monster was blocking the whole length of the entranceway to my building. His back was to me, his front facing the window-paneled door. (I guess so he could watch the traffic?) I say it was a *he*, but that was only a hypothesis. I just could not imagine any self-respecting female—monster or not—ever getting as pudgy as this thing was.

Strangely, I wasn't frightened of the big guy, not even as I was getting my first glance of its tremendous bulk. I don't know how to explain that other than to say that there was something about the creature that was . . . soothing.

At the time, I had no idea what kind of monster the thing was, but if I really think back on it, I'd have to guess it was probably, at least, *part* dragon. I mean, it had a long, scaly brown tail, huge brown haunches, and a row of blue triangular-shaped flaps of skin that ran the length of its back. So, it was either a medium-sized dragon, or a smallish dinosaur. Take your pick.

Luckily, it didn't appear to notice my arrival—which I took as a good thing—but I played it safe by standing still as a statue on the bottom step of the stairwell, trying not even to breathe if I could help it. I was a lot of things, but *super idiot* wasn't one of them. If the dragon/monster thing wanted to sit in my front hall and watch the traffic go by out the window, like a dog, I wasn't gonna be the dum-dum who disturbed it.

As quietly as I could, I backed my way up the front stairs until I hit the second-floor landing. Then I high-tailed it up the next four flights until I was back in the relative safety of my own apartment.

After taking a moment to catch my breath, and have a shot of the Bailey's I'd had in the back of my fridge since Christmas, I sat down on my couch and made my plans: I was gonna go next door, get a witness, and then go back downstairs. Patience would see the dragon/monster and freak out, verifying the fact that I was not losing my mind.

There was just one slight hitch in my plans: She wasn't home.

I thought about knocking on some random person's door and trying to get them to go see the dragon/monster with me, but I was too scared it might have gotten bored in the interim and left—which would've made me look like a real nut job—so I put an ix-nay on that one.

After taking another calming sip of Bailey's, I did the only rational thing a person could do in my situation: I called Animal Control.

"I'm making this complaint anonymously," I said tersely. "There's a big monster dog in my front entranceway, and I need you to send someone out to get it!"

The woman on the other end of the line kept asking me for my name, but I wasn't stupid. If I gave it to her, then everyone would know *I* was the weirdo caller, and I might *actually* end up in Bellevue before my blind date could save me.

Finally, sick of her wheedling for more information, I blurted out the address and hung up. Then, I raced to my bathroom, which was home to the only window in my whole apartment that looked out onto the street in front of the building, and rolled up the shade, ready to watch and wait for the man with a big net to come and catch my monster.

I waited a long time. I called again. I ate some peanut butter out of the jar, returned to the bathroom, and waited some more.

At six thirty my buzzer sounded. I was sitting hunched over the lip of the bathtub, furiously filing my nails with a weather-beaten emery board. I quickly sat up straighter, so I had a better view out the window, and craned my neck to see who was at the front door.

I could just make out a man-sized shape on the stoop, and my heart began to beat inside my chest like a nasty little ball-peen hammer.

Damn, had Animal Control traced my phone number to my apartment?

It was only when I peered closer that I saw that the Animal Control guy was carrying a bouquet of . . . *flowers*?

Crap! It wasn't Animal Control . . . it was my *blind date*! I had totally forgotten about him!

I had always thought of myself as a normal kinda gal, and normal gals—even if they saw a giant dragon/monster in their front hall—did not let said monster interfere with a possible encounter with Mr. Right. I was gonna have to pull it together, stop being a wuss, and answer the door.

I ran to the living room and pushed the button on the intercom.

"Shit! I mean, hello . . . ?"

"Uhm, is this Calliope?" a dreamy voice said, sounding uncertain.

Maybe this date won't be such a dud after all. The guy is definitely in possession of one helluva sexy voice.

I nodded, pleased with Patience, then realized that the guy wasn't standing in front of me and probably thought I hadn't heard him.

"Definitely! This is, uh, definitely Calliope Reaper-Jones!" I said in an overloud voice.

There was silence as the blind date digested what I'd said.

I couldn't believe what an idiot I sounded like. He must've thought I was one of Patience's *slow* friends. I don't know what it is with the opposite sex, but I just can't seem to keep an intelligent thought in my head when there's an attractive man in my vicinity.

"I'm Brian. I work with your friend Patience," he finally replied.

"That's my neighbor," I burbled back at him like a ninny.

Once again, radio silence from Brian, the blind date.

"Okay, yeah, your neighbor." He cleared his throat. "Uhm, I don't mean to be rude, but can I come up?"

"Come up?" I asked smartly.

"Yeah, uh, come up to your apartment?"

"I don't know if you want to do that," I said. "There's a big, fat dragon/monster thing in the front hall."

I clapped my hand over my mouth, almost jarring my front teeth loose in the process.

"Just kidding! Just kidding!" I screeched through my fingers. "Come on up!"

I buzzed him in immediately so I wouldn't have to hear the sound of his shoes hitting the pavement at a terrified run.

"Crap!" I said out loud.

Then I caught sight of myself in the mirror that hung above the living room couch.

"Crap!" I said again, this time in reference to the fact that I looked like a homeless woman.

I couldn't believe what a rat's nest my hair was. I had on absolutely *no makeup*, and I was wearing an old, comfortable pair of Juicy sweats. Good for an intense shopping expedition. Not so good for a blind date.

Not knowing which mess to address first, I nearly sat down on the couch and gave up, but instead, my brain thankfully switched into autopilot and sent my body on a fact-finding mission to the bedroom.

Figuring, with the five flights of stairs Brian, the blind date, would have to traverse to get to my door, I'd have seven minutes to get myself together, or forever hold my peace.

Tripping my way across my messy bedroom floor, I threw open the closet door and grabbed the first thing that caught my eye: an adorable little jumpsuit I'd gotten on sale at Saks. It was made of organic white linen and felt just like butter on my skin.

Even though it had been kinda scrunched in the corner of the closet floor when I picked it up, it didn't look that wrinkled in hand, so I gave it the sniff test, which it passed with flying colors—*yea!* I yanked off my sweats and slipped on the jumpsuit, zipping it up so quickly I caught a little piece of my boob in the zip's teeth.

"Ahhhhh!" I screamed, trying not to rip skin, as I yanked the zipper back down. There was a huge red welt on my left breast, but I ignored it, this time being a little more careful with the zip as I reworked it back up into position.

Digging my way through the messy pile of dirty clothing that surrounded my bed, I found my favorite pair of cream kitten heels under a crumpled skirt and slipped them on, silently cursing myself for not having gotten a pedicure recently. The bright purple nail polish I'd loved when I'd had the girl put it on three weeks ago looked like toe fungus now, all old and chipped.

There was nothing I could do about the would-be fungus, so I ignored it, making a run for the bathroom to slap on as much makeup as I could in the space of sixty seconds. Makeup done, I grabbed an elastic band from one of the crappy cultured-marble vanity drawers and scraped my rat's nest into what I hoped was some semblance of a ponytail, praying Brian, the blind-date guy, wouldn't notice a few errant pieces of hair sticking out here and there.

The doorbell rang just as I was putting on the finishing touch, something I used only for *special* occasions: a spritz of Chanel No. 5.

And voilà! I was ready to rumble . . . or at least have dinner. As unbelievable as it seemed, I had gotten ready for an important date in less than seven minutes. A bloody miracle.

I threw open the door, hoping against hope that Brian, the blind date, looked like Clive Owen. I knew in my soul that with a voice like that, the body had to match.

"Is Brian here yet?"

Patience stood in my doorway, holding a thick manila folder in her hand. She looked amazing, as always, her thick blond hair hanging loose and curly around her angelic little face. She was like a miniature version of that doe-eyed French actress Julie Delpy. If she weren't so nice, I would've totally hated her.

I mean, the little bitch was wearing a tank top and *bicycle shorts*—and her butt looked good in them. *So* not *fair!*

"Hello . . . ? Earth to Callie? Is your date here yet?"

"Not yet," I stuttered.

"Did he stand you up?!" she said incredulously, ready to go beat him up for me, bicycle shorts and all.

I shook my head, trying to reconnect to reality.

"No, I mean, he's not here yet because I just buzzed him in, and you know, there are five flights of stairs, so . . ." I trailed off.

Patience raised an eyebrow at me, then rolled her eyes.

"Here," she said, thrusting the manila folder into my hands. "Make sure you give him this."

I nodded vigorously.

"It's important, Callie. For work."

It was like she didn't trust me to give the guy a stupid manila folder. Jeez, I wasn't a total screwup . . . was I? The look on her face gave me pause, but I brushed it away. Of course Patience didn't think I was a screwup. You didn't introduce screwup friends to hot guys from work. It just wasn't done.

"I will give him this manila folder if it's the last thing I do," I said.

"Make it the *first* thing you do, and I'll be happy," she called over her shoulder as she walked to her door and let herself in, leaving me alone in the hall.

Something niggled at the back of my mind. I tried to ignore it, push it to the nether regions of memory where the bogeyman and the My Little Pony Universe still resided from childhood, but suddenly the thought would not be laid to rest.

"Oh, Jesus!" I choked out, making a desperate run for the stairs.

What was I thinking!! I let the blind-date guy come

right into the building, even though the big, scary monster might still be in the lobby! And all because I wanted to look hot! I am *a screwup, after all!*

I took the stairs two at a time, my kitten heels double clacking so loudly behind me that it sounded like the Easy Spirit basketball team was overrunning the stairwell.

"Shit," I said under my breath as I almost went down the third flight headfirst.

I reached the bottom of the last set of stairs after what seemed like an eternity. My hair was in my face, and my cheeks were red from exertion, but I had made it. I was almost in the lobby, and I was gonna save my blind date if it killed me.

"Get away, foul beastie!" I screamed, brandishing the folder Patience had given me as I leapt off the last step, my velocity pushing me toward the front doors. I felt a sudden lurch, and I was falling face forward, the cool, green marble tile of the front lobby coming toward my unprotected face at amazing speed.

I felt two strong hands grab me from behind, and instead of hitting the floor face-first like I had predicted, I was suddenly on my feet, kitten heels making one loud, final clack as I caught my balance.

"Thank you," I said as I looked up into the face of my savior. My blind date . . . Brian.

"You're welcome," he said, smiling. "That was almost a bloodbath."

He was shorter than me. That was the first thing I noticed. Shorter and fatter than me, with a large head, and small round John Lennon glasses perched low on his long nose. If he had been maybe seven inches taller, I might have been thanking Patience, instead of cursing her heartily in my head.

"You're . . . Brian?" I said weakly. He nodded happily.

Oh, God, I thought to myself.

"This is for you," I said, thrusting the folder into his chubby hands. He took it, flipping through it before smiling back up at me. It was obvious that he was smitten. I was probably the most attractive female he'd ever touched.

"You didn't see that big dinosaur-looking monster I mentioned down here when you first came in, did you?"

I looked around the lobby. Nothing. And then it hit me—if there had been something here, it would have eaten Patience when she came home. I couldn't believe I had spent the entire afternoon hidden in the bathroom waiting for Animal Control because I was losing my mind, seeing things that were obviously *not* real.

Brian gave me a quizzical look, but shook his head. "Sorry, no dinosaurs. But I did see a cowboy in his underwear playing a guitar in Times Square."

since brian had saved me from certain facial disfigurement, I went to dinner with him. He was a nice guy. Short, but nice.

I was gonna kill Patience . . . right before I checked into Bellevue.

two

If I had any doubts about my sanity, they were not assuaged during the rest of the weekend. I spent all of Sunday hiding in my apartment, afraid to so much as turn on my television for fear of seeing more freaky things that would confirm my diagnosis of insanity. Feeling a little bit better when I crawled into bed that night, I said a quick thank-you in my head and closed my eyes, hoping Monday morning would put the weekend craziness into perspective.

I woke up late. So, instead of walking to work—which is the only exercise I get these days—I decided to take the subway. Now, I love the trains, but taking them in the mornings, and after work, is like willingly cramming yourself into a tin can of sardines—and smelly sardines at that.

Not something I enjoyed doing even on mornings when I was running late. Still, I really didn't have a choice—the only other option was to take a cab, which would cost a small fortune, and probably make me even later.

So, that was how I found myself standing in a rickety subway car, holding on to a sweaty pole and praying someone would get off at the next stop so I could finally grab a seat.

I was totally minding my own business—trying to find my iPod headphones that somehow always ended up at the bottom of my purse wrapped around a tampon—when, suddenly, a homeless man was standing in front of me, staring at me with dark, hollow eyes.

Now, normally, I would just throw some change a few feet in the other direction, causing a homeless person free-for-all, but this guy didn't even blink when I tossed a handful of quarters at the heavyset Hispanic lady who was taking up the whole row of handicap seats behind me. I felt a little bad about sending Mr. Homeless in her direction, but then I figured she *was* taking up *all* the handicap seats so she was fair game.

But instead of freeing myself from the Homeless Man's eye-embrace, something strange happened. Something I had never experienced in my two years of Manhattan living—living that had exposed to me to lots of unseemly things which were rather scarring to my delicate countenance.

Instead of chasing the coins I'd thrown, the homeless man dropped to his knees—in a crowded subway car no less—and, looking up from his position of supplication on the dirty subway car floor, he wiggled his greasy eyebrows seductively at me, his eyes full of awe, and blew me a kiss.

That was not the bad part.

Here's the bad part: As the car came to the next

stop . . . Mr. Homeless leaned forward, *and tried to kiss my feet through my Marc Jacob sandals!*

Ewwww!

The only way I could get the dude to cease and desist was to throw myself out the subway car doors right before they slid shut. Needless to say, I ended up engulfed in morning-rush-hour commuter traffic. I was lucky a gaggle of Wall Street number crunchers didn't trample me and my knock-off Kate Spade bag right there on the subway platform.

All of this alone was heart-attack-inducing enough, but the worst part was yet to come. As I was free-falling out the subway doors, I actually thought I heard Mr. Homeless say:

"You're next in line, Mistress Calliope."

Double ewwww!!

How the hell did Homeless Man know my name! I mean, I understand the guy intuitively sensing that I was a lovely thing of exquisite beauty that needed her feet kissed every once in a while, but c'mon, this was no idle beauty worship hit. This guy had some kind of agenda, and it probably included stalking me all day, then following me home to my sixth-floor walk-up and putting all my underwear on his head before murdering me in my bed.

Triple ewwww!!!

So much for good, old Monday-morning perspective, I thought miserably.

when i got to work, immediately all my own worries were forgotten in favor of my boss's needs.

I started the morning in what was turning out to be a fruitless search of the Internet for a restaurant that did organic dim sum. Easier said than done. I mean, have *you* ever eaten organic dim sum? Well, I hadn't, but my boss, Hyacinth Stewart, had.

She had gone to some hoity-toity party on the Upper East Side the night before, and the hostess had bragged for hours about the organic dim sum she had served, and how Jennifer Aniston *only* ordered from the place whenever she was in town.

Now, I'm no star whore, but even I had to admit that whatever Jennifer Aniston was eating to stay that thin must be worth the rest of us at least *trying* a taste. So, I couldn't fault Hy for wanting Jennifer Aniston's organic dim sum.

And Hy definitely needed all the diet help she could get. I mean, she *did* have that glandular problem . . . at least that was what she said it was.

Unhappily for me, I was having absolutely no luck, and it was starting to really piss me off. Usually I'm a whiz at finding things on the Internet, but I was starting to get this funny feeling that Hy had made the whole thing up just to screw with my day. She was probably sitting in her office right now, snickering into the nonfat decaf latte I'd gotten her this morning.

Why the woman wanted a nonfat decaf latte was beyond me. The whole office knew it was ordered for appearances only, that she probably dumped the whole thing in the potted plant behind her desk as soon as I had closed her office door in favor of whatever calorie-laden goodies she had stashed in her desk drawer. But hey, I was only her assistant. I didn't care *what* the hell she did with her coffee.

Deciding to give the computer a break and get back to the rest of the crap I had to deal with for the day, I looked down at the overflow of phone messages I'd accumulated since this morning and had to really hold myself back from chucking the whole mess of them out the window.

Too bad we were only on the second floor, and they wouldn't go very far.

Being the assistant to the Vice President of Sales at House and Yard, Inc.—fine purveyors of any and every gadget you could ever want for your house and yard (you've probably seen many of our *amazing* (!) products on the Home Shopping Network)—looked like a great starter job . . . before I took it. To be absolutely honest, I always thought I'd have a glamorous life in fashion or publishing or something. I mean, a career that was *at least* exciting enough to brag about at cocktail parties and weddings.

Instead, I found myself sitting behind a messy cubicle desk eight hours a day, quietly watching my tan fade underneath the fluorescent lights, too busy rolling calls, picking up laundry, sending e-mails, and ordering dim sum to have any kind of "glamorous" New York existence.

Having discovered early on that I *hated* home and garden crap, it had been a hellacious year and a half since I'd taken the job, but I was determined to stick it out. I only hoped I got headhunted before I dumped Hy's nonfat decaf latte on her head.

I mean, it wasn't that she was a total dominatrix—quite the opposite, actually. It was just that, regardless of points off for good behavior, I was on the verge of having some kind of midtwenties crisis, and I had decided I was *not* prepared to spend the best years of my life toiling in the home and garden sector.

All I needed was for Hy to put in a friendly call to

one of her publishing friends, and I'd be rolling down the fashion runway. Yet, try as I might, she would just not take the hint. I decided that all I could do was try my best to please her, and pray she'd want to reward me with some kind of promotion.

Then, to my absolute horror, three months ago I discovered through one of the other assistants, Geneva, that Hy had told everyone she was so happy with my work that she was determined to keep me for her own, locked in House and Yard hell . . . *her assistant forever!*

"Callie, I'm going out. Hold all my calls," a voice said from behind me.

I turned to find Hy standing in the doorway of her office wearing a rather large Diane von Furstenberg knock-off wrap dress and pointy little black boots. She had her long honey blond hair pulled back off her face, accentuating her large blue eyes and pouty, cupid-bow mouth.

She was a gorgeous size twenty, and reasonably proud of it.

"Will do, Hy," I glowered, hoping she'd stride out of the office to the elevator lobby and leave me alone. With every day, it got harder and harder not to feel resentful toward her for selfishly restricting my career growth.

"Any luck with the dim sum?" she asked, her voice annoyingly chirpy.

I cringed internally but plastered a smile on my face as I turned around in my chair and nodded.

"Looks good," I said, hoping I sounded more confident than I felt. "The outcome definitely looks good."

I was beginning to sound like an uncooperative Magic 8 Ball even to myself.

Hy, sensing my disquiet, tilted her head to one side, appraising me. I knew she was aware that I wasn't happy, but for the life of her, I don't think she could figure out why.

Before she could spend any more time speculating, Hy left. After what seemed like an eternity, I heard the elevator come and the doors close.

As much as I hated to do it, I was just going to suck it up and tell Hy exactly what was wrong with me. If she fired me, so be it.

Gulp.

Boy, am I off my game today or what? I thought to myself as I took a moment to lean my head against the cool metallic edge of my desk.

I hated the cubicle almost as much as I hated the job. I just couldn't get used to the complete lack of privacy cubicle life imposed upon you. It made it much harder to slack off during the day if at any moment your boss could walk by and see you playing solitaire on your Mac.

I sat up, my eye catching the overflowing incoming-messages box on the computer screen—they were all e-mails I had to return on Hy's behalf, usually with bad news for whoever was on the receiving end. It was the Vice President of Sales's job to make sure that the whole Sales Department ran smoothly, and that usually required lots of saying the word "no."

"Uh-uh, no way am I in the mood for this . . ." I said out loud. This bought me a look from Geneva, the occupant of the cubicle next door.

"You doing okay, Cal?" Geneva said, returning to the pages of the new *Vogue* magazine she was reading. "You look kinda stressed out."

Geneva had the cool boss, the one every would-be assistant wants to have her first time at bat, the one who was so low maintenance that she practically took care of herself.

Thus, Geneva had time to read whatever magazine tickled her fancy that day, and do her nails, and talk to her football player boyfriend . . . so *not* fair.

"Organic dim sum," I said cryptically. Geneva raised an eyebrow, her eyes still on her magazine.

"Sounds like it's time for a trip to the kitchen," Geneva said, looking up. "I think Robert brought in some vegan chocolate cupcakes. Grab me one, will ya?"

Immediately, my day was looking up. The kitchen was my favorite thing in the whole world. I could spend hours in there, munching my way through all the crap the office manager bought to keep the peons in an unending state of sugar high. It was my oasis in the storm that had become my life.

"Good idea," I said, standing up and shutting off my computer. Hy wouldn't be back for at least an hour. That meant I could spend thirty minutes in the kitchen before I had to return to the drudgery of office work.

Geneva, her long, lean body gracefully folded into one of the uncomfortably small cubicle desk chairs, gave me a wave as I sauntered out of the office and headed toward the kitchen. And—though I couldn't have known it then—my *destiny* . . .

there was no one there when I stepped out of the fluorescent-lit corridor, just an empty stretch of hallway that led to the brightly lit doorway that had sadly become the key to my sanity.

The Kitchen. A six-foot-by-three-foot bastion of goodness that was mine all mine. I stepped inside and immediately found myself perusing the vegan chocolate cupcakes our newest little intern, Robert, had brought from home this morning. Robert had never claimed such, but I was almost positive he was some kind of PETA spy who had been sent to House and Yard to make sure we weren't condoning any products that cut short the lives of the beasties that roamed the suburban landscape.

I took the recycled paper towel off the top of the cupcakes and reached for one of the little nasties.

"Yummy, my dear. I have always been *partial* to chocolate myself."

The *voice*. I *knew* that snooty British accent. But from *where*? Damn it, I couldn't place it.

I whipped around so fast the Alice band I was wearing to keep my hair in check nearly went flying off my head. To my surprise, there was nobody there.

I was really losing it, and now it had seeped into the workplace, too. Bellevue was closer than I had imagined, what with disembodied voices—wasn't that a sign of schizophrenia?—talking to me out of nowhere.

I took a quick support bite of the cupcake, but for some reason it didn't sit well in my stomach. I felt a strange tingling inside, and my whole body went cold, then hot. There was an explosion of intense pain in my brain, and a flood of images filled my head.

Suddenly I found myself sprinting back down the corridor toward the unisex bathroom and praying that (1) there was no one in there, and (2) I made it before I threw up vegan stuff all over the floor.

I pushed open the door to the bathroom and rushed inside, holding back the vomit that threatened to explode before I made it to a stall.

Luckily, my first prayer was answered, and the place was completely empty. I got into one of the white laminate stalls and fell to my knees, tightly clutching at the porcelain god with shaking hands as I threw up.

"My poor dear. Sorry about the cupcake, but it was the only way to reverse the spell."

There it was again, that stupid disembodied voice, *commenting* on my misfortune no less, and talking about *spells*! I wiped at my mouth with a swatch of toilet paper I'd yanked off the holder and glared wildly around, trying to see where the hell the voice was coming from.

"Leave me alone!" I almost shrieked, dragging myself to my feet and stumbling out of the stall toward the bank of sinks on the far wall. I caught sight of my reflection in the long wall mirror and nearly choked. I looked like Death warmed over. My light brown hair was in disarray, and there were dark circles underneath my large brown eyes. I even had this weird pinched look on my normally reasonably attractive face.

Without warning, more images—memories really—streamed into my brain, and I ran back to the stall to throw up bile, the only thing left in my stomach.

"It's hard-core food poisoning. That's all it is," I said to myself as I sat back on my heels and held the toilet seat for support. Yet even before the words were out of my mouth, I knew they were wrong. It wasn't food poisoning; it was something far worse than getting a minor dose of salmonella and upchucking organic, gluten-free baked goods all over the place.

I was in full possession of my memory again, and that was why my insides had tried to run away screaming. The Forgetting Charm I'd placed on myself three years before so that I could lead a normal existence for the first time in twenty-four years had been reversed.

And it was all because of a *goddamned enchanted cupcake*!

I plucked up my courage and said the name that had

instantly come into my head when I had finally acknowledged the truth of the situation to myself.

"Jarvis . . . ?" I said, letting the name float in the ether. When no one responded immediately, I looked around, hoping I had gotten lucky, that maybe I had really only imagined this whole thing after all.

But I knew it wasn't the case. All the weird experiences I'd been having recently finally made sense now. It sucked because I actually found myself wishing I were losing my mind instead of the alternative.

"Show yourself!" I said without hesitation. If this was what I *thought* it was, then I was going to nip it right in the bud before Jarvis could even get started.

I guess he must have gotten held up somewhere along the line because it took him thirty more seconds before he finally materialized in the room.

"Oh my God . . . it *is* you!" I squealed as I tried not to faint from shock. Leaning against the wall for support, I took lots of deep, calming breaths to stave off the faintness, so I could take a good look at the man staring at me from across the bank of sinks.

Jarvis was small—no more than four-eleven on a good day—and now, as he appeared in the corner of the unisex bathroom, he was exactly as I remembered him: *miniature*. Still, he looked impeccable in a dark double-breasted jacket that matched perfectly with his cream-colored dress shirt and cravat.

"In the flesh," he said as he took a careful bow, bending as low to the ground as his goat-shaped haunches would allow. You see, Jarvis was actually, by birth, a faun. And one of the proudest I've ever met. The word "goat" was anathema to him. If you ever want your teeth knocked out for free, just call Jarvis a "goat-boy."

"Shit! Shit, shit, shit," I said.

Lovely, I already have a great *start on the whole nipping it in the bud thing,* I thought sarcastically to myself.

"What're you doing here?" I squeaked, trying to pull myself together but failing miserably. "Father and I had a rule! As long as I was under the Forgetting Charm, you guys had to leave me alone!"

Jarvis held up his hand warningly.

"Talk to the hand."

Well, that stopped me in my tracks. I mean, it had been more than a decade since someone pulled a Fran Drescher on me.

"Excuse me, Jarvis, but I'm gonna have to stop you right there," I said, my voice beginning to return to its normal pitch. "Because that is *so* 1995."

He pursed his lips, his mouth pink and plump underneath the thick black mustache he always wore. Then he wiggled his large, hawkish nose unhappily at me. He obviously did not like me calling out his little faux pas like that, but I felt it was my duty as a member of the pop culture police to maintain the sanctity of twenty-first-century pop culture everywhere.

"That is neither here nor there, Mistress Calliope—"

"Nah-uh-uh!" I said, cutting him off midsentence and nearly poking him in the nose with an angrily pointed index finger. "There will be none of that 'mistress' stuff around here."

Jarvis sighed, running a well-manicured hand through the thick, pomaded black hair.

"Fine, Mistress—I mean, *Miss* Calliope, but if you would just listen for a moment without taking exception . . ."

But I didn't *want* to hear what Jarvis had to say. It had taken years of work—and the use of a heavy-duty Forgetting Charm—to extricate myself from my family, and there was no way in hell I was gonna let goat-boy drag me back into that *insanity* without a fight.

"I think you should just disapparate back to wherever you came from, *Jarvis*," I said, turning on my heel and storming toward the door.

"And you can tell my father that I have nothing to say to him that I haven't already said before!" I added, turning back around to glare. "So, there's no use calling in his Executive Assistant or any other tricks of the trade to get me to change my mind!"

I put my hands on the bathroom door, and a wave of happiness flooded through my body as I felt the door begin to inch forward.

Behind me, I heard the sound of a small *sniffle*.

Well, that stopped me cold. It wasn't like my father's Executive Assistant to lose his composure or, in fact, to show any emotion at all besides displeasure.

"I can't tell him," Jarvis said, his voice pinched and funny-sounding.

I turned back to face him, the blood running like liquid nitrogen in my veins.

"What do you mean . . . *you can't tell him*," I said quietly.

Jarvis, now having lost his stiff upper lip, was sniffling loudly into a pale cream hankie. He waved his hand at me, indicating that he was unable to talk.

"What do you mean, Jarvis?" I said again, this time grabbing the poor little man by the shoulders and giving him a good shake.

Whenever I'm truly, utterly terrified, my body goes all funny, and suddenly I find myself grabbing something or somebody and shaking 'em. Not a great fight-or-flight response, but it's just the way I was built. That day in the unisex bathroom with Jarvis was no exception.

He shrieked like a little schoolgirl and tried to cover his head with his hankie. If I hadn't been so freaked-out, the image of my father's right-hand man cowering from *me*—under a piece of flimsy cream silk, no less—would have made me wet myself with laughter.

Instead, I released the little faun and watched as he tried, in vain, to keep his balance. His small hooven feet were no match for gravity, and he tumbled into a heap on the tile floor.

He glared up at me, his eyes like two smoldering coals in his handsome face. I could almost see the steam trying to escape out his ears.

"I shouldn't have told your mother I'd do this. It was a waste, waste, waste of time," he whispered angrily under his breath as he tried to use a sink to pull himself back onto his hooves. I offered him my hand, but he snorted and refused to take it.

"My *mother* sent you?" I stammered.

This bit of information was almost unimaginable. My mother never spoke to Jarvis. Not because she didn't like him, or was mean-hearted or anything. It just wasn't *done.* Jarvis was my father's boy, taking his orders directly from the man on high himself.

"Why would my *mother* send you?"

Jarvis ignored me, focusing instead on brushing bits of lint from the bathroom floor off his suit coat. I began to pace, trying to work out what the hell was going on.

This visit was highly abnormal. As much as I liked to think that I was still a thorn in my father's side, I had to admit that he'd pretty much left me alone since I'd decamped to Sarah Lawrence six years ago. There had been that dramatic plea from my mother to come home to Rhode Island for the holidays during my junior year, but after I'd finally confronted my father about not wanting to go into the family business, and used the Forgetting Charm, there'd been nothing . . . nada, zip, zero.

And now this.

"Look, I'm sorry I freaked out on you, Jarvis," I began.

He looked at me coldly.

"Yes . . . ? Go on."

It was obvious he wanted me to grovel.

"And I'm sorry that I was rude and that I shook you—"

"And that bit about the hand! Apologize for that, too."

I took a deep breath. This was gonna be a hard one.

"And I'm sorry I made fun of your Fran Drescher hand thing . . ."

This seemed to satisfy him, and he smiled, victory his for a fleeting moment. Then he shook his head, clearing the glee from his eyes. When he looked up again, there was something else there, something very much like *fear.*

"It's your father, Miss Calliope. He's been . . . He's been . . . *kidnapped.*"

I heard a sharp intake of breath and realized it had come from me.

"But that's impossible," I said, the words rushing from my lips faster than I could think them into life. "It doesn't make any sense . . . Who in their right mind would want to kidnap Death?"

three

Okay, so I lied. I'm *not* just a regular girl with a mom, dad, siblings, and dog waving in front of a two-story suburban Colonial enclosed on all sides by a perfect little white picket fence. Nope, that's not my life at all.

In counterpoint to all that, I was raised in Newport, Rhode Island, in a disgustingly large, old mansion called Sea Verge, which—even though it could have housed *seven* families to our *one*—I adored with all my heart. Commissioned in 1875 by the shipping heiress Sophia Miles-Stanton to be the jewel of Bellevue Avenue, Sea Verge had fourteen bedrooms, nine bathrooms, a ballroom, a formal dining room, a gourmet kitchen, a swimming pool, and a twelve-car garage. All of which were surrounded by the most stunning views of the Rhode Island Sound that ever existed.

Growing up, I spent my summers and school vacations at Sea Verge, while the rest of the year I attended the New Newbridge Academy, a prestigious boarding school in Connecticut. I didn't mind going back to New

Newbridge at the start of every school year—it was as interesting a place as any to spend my childhood, full of eccentric teachers and even stranger students. It's also where I met my best friend, Noh, whom I still consider to be the greatest girl in all of New England.

From afar, my life seems privileged but relatively normal. My father is the President and CEO of a multinational conglomerate. My mom is a socialite who spends the majority of her time arranging fund-raisers for all manner of charitable organizations. My older sister, Thalia, is a Senior Vice President in my father's company. My younger sister, Clio, is still in high school, and I, as you know, am a peon in the home and garden industry.

What you don't know is that behind all this supposed normalcy is a deep, dark secret—a secret I had tried to erase with a Forgetting Charm. But I guess you can't ever really run away from your past no matter how many charms you put on yourself. It's a secret I discovered one hot summer afternoon while playing a game of hide-and-seek down in the cellar at Sea Verge with Clio.

We had chosen to play in the cellar—a place neither one of us had, up until that day, spent much time in—because the cellar, being firmly underground, was about ten degrees cooler than anywhere else in the house. I don't have much memory of that day, just a vague recollection of spending the vast majority of the game pretending not to see five-year-old Clio hiding behind a heap of moldering coal left in the cellar since electricity had been brought to Newport.

The whole cellar thing had been my bright idea, so I guess it was only fitting that I would be the one to find the door. It was small, with a thick oak frame and a strange, rough-hewn wrought-iron handle in the shape of an evil eye stuck in the middle of its heavy wooden body.

What's so amazing about a door? I bet you're asking yourself. What could possibly be behind its wooden frame—short of a dozen dead bodies, and/or a herd of elephants—that would change my perception of the world forever?

You see, what was behind this particular doorway was something very special. A magical wormhole, if you will, that led to a place that immediately topped anything my adolescent mind had ever imagined.

A place we'll call, for lack of a better name . . . Hell.

i think the door handle was hot when I touched it that first time, but I don't know for sure. I might only have imagined it, but I know the door *did* give way easily as I turned the handle, opening inward, so I was able to see what lay behind it only after it had been opened all the way. At first, my mind couldn't grasp the idea of a wide, open desert lying just behind. I knew for a fact the cellar was underground, that the only thing the door should open onto was another room. Yet, there, right before my eyes, was a whole other world waiting for me to explore.

Confusion quickly gave way to wonder, and I found myself stepping over the threshold into the strange, new realm. A little voice inside my head told me to close the door, that this was something for my eyes only and it would be a mistake for Clio to follow me there.

Just like that, as soon as I felt the door shut, I knew I'd made a mistake. I swung back around, frantic to get back into the cellar, but of course, the door was gone, empty air filling the void where it had once been.

I don't think I'd ever *really* been scared before that moment. My life had been pretty average. I'd had nightmares, and once when I was six, I'd been thrown headfirst off a pony I was riding, but that was it. Now fear, the real deal thing, began to creep up my spine, settle in my stomach, and fill my head with images of the family and friends I would never get to see ever again.

I'd like to say I was a tough little kid, who told fear where to shove it, but I can't. Instead, the truth is much more pathetic. I sat down right there on the ground and began to sob. Not just tears, but great heaving breaths that filled my aching lungs and made the veins in my head throb. I must have sat like that for a good twenty minutes before I was finally able to collect myself and stop crying. Wiping my eyes and nose on the back of my hand, I crawled onto my knees, determined to find my way home, even if it killed me.

As the fear receded, the first thing I noticed about my new environs was how hot it was. Not just "Newport in the summer hot," but, like, really, really, *really* hot. I looked down at my bare arm and saw a strange sheen on my skin. It suddenly dawned on me that it was so hot the sweat was literally *evaporating* from my skin before it could form, leaving a thin coating of salt instead. Thank God I was only wearing a thin pink tank top and shorts, or I would've been roasting.

The heat also made it harder to breathe, and I found myself wheezing a bit as I stood up and looked around. About five hundred feet in front of me there was what seemed to be a small oasis in the middle of the empty landscape. I hadn't noticed it before, which was strange, but I *had* been pretty preoccupied.

I was too far away to make out anything other than a droopy palm tree shading the pool, and the gleam of water reflecting back the harsh desert sunlight, but I moved toward it anyway. There didn't seem to be much else for me to do, my options being to stay where I was and roast, or to head to the oasis and try to get a drink.

When I was a few feet from the water, I noticed a disheveled man in a ragged robe hiding behind the palm tree. He was just thin enough so that the only thing I saw of him at first was his beak of a nose, shoes, and a bit of dirty white robe.

As I reached the water, he stepped out from behind the tree and bowed. He had squinty gray eyes that looked like marbles in his sun-browned face and a greasy mop of dark-colored hair. He lifted himself out of the bow and smiled, revealing two rows of mismatched yellow teeth. All I could think about was what my dentist would say if he ever saw my teeth looking like that.

"Hello, madame. What a fine day it is, no?"

His voice was high and squeaky with a trace of a French accent. His words surprised me, and I took a step backward, not wanting to get too close to him.

"I guess so . . ." I said, my tone uncertain. I mean, it was a sweltering day with no end to the heat in sight, but if he wanted to ignore that and stick to pleasantries, I wasn't going to argue with him.

"My name is Marcel, madame, but you may call me Monsieur D," he said, his lips snaking up to reveal pinched pink gums. It was a horrible rictus of a smile. He bowed again quickly, his head immediately snapping back up to stare at me.

"I'm Calliope."

He spoke my name quietly under his breath, letting the *l*'s trill in his mouth like a hiss. While he was committing my name to his memory, I was taking a closer look at him.

It was only upon this second inspection that I realized he was tethered to the palm tree by what looked like a sheer nylon string. It was almost invisible against the sand, but occasionally the line caught a bit of sunlight and reflected it. As soon as I noticed this, I was entranced.

Why was this strange man tied to the palm tree?

"Why are you tied to the palm tree?" I asked, blunt in my innocence. Monsieur D immediately blanched, the air expelling from his lungs like he'd been punched in the gut.

"I do not know what you mean," he replied.

"That," I said. I pointed at the nylon string for extra emphasis.

"This?" he said, reaching down and tweaking the nylon string with his long fingers. *"This* is *nothing."*

He tried to laugh—to show how *in control* of the situation he was, I guess—but the laughter came out like a bark, then the bark became a choked sob. I watched as the ragged-looking wretch threw himself down in the sand and cried.

I didn't really want to touch him, but something inside of me—pity, I think—made me close the gap between us. I kneeled down beside him, noticing for the first time how much larger than me he was. He had seemed small, dwarfed by the palm tree, but now, in such close proximity, I noted the long, skinny arms and legs and the large, shapely head and hands.

"It's okay," I said, thumping him on the back with the palm of my right hand. It was the closest thing to consoling Monsieur D I could make myself do. I didn't know the guy, so I was *not* going to give him a hug.

"You don't understand," he said, looking up at me with baleful but drying eyes. "And I am not allowed to talk about my *situation*, so I am afraid we find ourselves at an impasse, Calliope."

I nodded as if I understood, but I really had no idea what Monsieur D was talking about.

"Please, be a good girl," he said, "and fetch me some water."

I felt pretty sorry for him, lying there in the cornmeal-colored sand like a sad sack of potatoes. I stood up and looked around. There had to be something to put the water in besides my own two hands, because the idea of his lips touching my skin was repugnant.

I almost stepped on it before I saw it. Half-buried in the sand, only inches from the edge of the water, was a small silver cup. I picked it up—it looked like it had been made for someone just my size—and let its weight rest heavy in my hand. This was no silver-plated trinket; this was made of one solid chunk of metal.

I wondered who had left it in the middle of the desert for Monsieur D to use.

Suddenly, my fingers felt frozen where I grasped the cup, the interlocking circles that decorated the surface of the thing biting into my skin, leaving their outline in my palm.

"Please, hurry!" Monsieur D urged, his voice pinched.

Nervous now, I looked over at him, noting the strange gleam in his eyes. There was something wrong about this scenario, even if I couldn't quite put my finger on it.

Body ignoring the mind's misgivings, I took a step forward, unconsciously moving toward Monsieur D. I was unprepared for the shooting pain that ran up my arm, through my neck, and into my head. A small gasp escaped my lips as pain seared my insides, my brain sizzling like a fajita combo plate.

I dropped the cup—instinctively sensing it was the cause of my pain—and my hands flew to my head, cradling it against another onslaught of sizzle. But the pain was gone the moment the cup left my fingertips.

I looked up, my head still throbbing with the aftershocks of the attack, and saw the cup begin to roll toward Monsieur D almost, it seemed, of its own volition. I watched, transfixed by the cup's progression, as it slowly snaked its way through the sand, closer and closer, until it was just within reach of the desperate prisoner.

Prisoner.

The word echoed in my brain until it germinated a new thought.

Monsieur D was a prisoner. And he wasn't supposed to have that cup!

I didn't even have to think. I ran for it. Stepping hard on my left heel, my right foot shot out, instantly connecting with the gleaming silver vessel. The cup flew into the air, Monsieur D's fingers only millimeters from grasping it.

He let out the most horrific howl I'd ever heard from another human being, like his very soul had been wrenched from his body, which it might well have been for all I knew.

"You imbecile! What have you done!?"

Still on his knees, he made a grab for my ankle, but I jumped back just out of his reach. He was sobbing now, crocodile tears sliding down his withered cheeks. He picked up a handful of sand and lobbed it at me. I was so shocked that an adult would behave this way that I stood there, staring at him, openmouthed.

Then, as suddenly as it had begun, Monsieur D's attack faltered. His eyes left my face, coming to rest on something just behind my shoulder. I nearly screamed when I felt a heavy hand clasp my shoulder and wrench me backward.

"*Callie,*" the voice said, deep and resonant in my ears.

I looked up, my body relaxing instantly as I recognized my father's face. He was in his tennis whites, a headband holding back the lion's mane of golden brown hair that encircled his handsome, chiseled face. He looked more worried than I'd ever seen him.

"Daddy!"

I grabbed him around the waist and squeezed. I was very happy to see him.

"We have to go, Callie," he said, gently pulling me off him like a barnacle from the belly of a ship. "Time is of the essence."

He took my hand and, without a second glance back at Monsieur D, began to drag me away. But I was stubborn. I wanted him to know what had happened.

"That man there," I said loudly, pointing with my free arm back to Monsieur D. "He tried to trick me into giving him this weird silver cup."

Monsieur D gave me a nasty look, which I ignored.

"We'll talk about this later, sweetheart," my father said, keeping hold of my arm so that I couldn't escape.

"But Dad . . ." I whined.

"Later, Callie."

This time his words were more than just an order; they were magic, and to my consternation I found my lips glued shut. They remained that way for almost three hours.

Much longer than it took us to find the cellar door and get back home.

four

That was the memory of my father that came back to me first as I tried to wrap my mind around the fact that he was in danger.

Mother had sent Jarvis to bring me home, and he wanted to leave for Newport immediately—just open a wormhole right there in the bathroom and hit the road—but I put a kibosh on that one. I mean, I *had* to let someone know I was going home, or I'd never work in New York again—and there was no way I was gonna let that happen after all I'd suffered to get where I was in the first place. I decided I'd tell Geneva my father was sick, and then I'd let Jarvis take me to Newport.

I just hoped Hy wasn't going to have a coronary when she realized I was gone. Okay, I knew she'd have a coronary—but I hoped it wouldn't do her irreparable harm. As much of a pain-in-the-butt boss as she could be, I actually had a soft spot for the woman. She may have been hard to work for, but I admired her tenacity and ability to get stuff done, no matter what problems appeared in her path.

"Wait here, don't talk to anyone, and I'll be right back," I said to the testy little faun, who promptly glared at me. Jarvis liked to give orders, not take them.

I took a moment to smooth out my clothes and run my fingers through my hair before pushing the door open and stepping into the corridor.

I looked both ways to make sure I was alone in the hall, then let the door close. I only hoped Jarvis wouldn't be tempted to come out and cause a scene. It was one thing to introduce your work colleagues to your father's Executive Assistant—it was another if said Executive Assistant was in possession of *hooves*.

I took a deep, calming breath and started down the hallway toward my desk.

"Hey, Callie," a voice called from behind me, the words flowing in a slow Louisiana drawl I recognized as belonging to Robert, the cupcake baker.

I stifled the nervous shriek that had been forming in my throat and turned, smiling brightly. Robert stopped and smiled strangely at me. It was the first time we'd had a conversation of any real length, but I was definitely groovin' on his amazing Southern accent.

"Did you find the organic baked goods I left in the kitchen?" Robert said, the strange smile still plastered on his face.

We stood in silence for a moment. I was starting to get a wee bit paranoid. The intraoffice gossip *was* that he was some kind of spy from PETA. Maybe he was here to bust me for harboring a faun without a license.

"What?" I said. "Nothing's going on."

"I didn't ask you if anything was going on—" he started, then immediately stopped. "Did I?"

He looked utterly confused.

"With the cupcakes. I didn't eat them all or anything," I said cagily, not sure what the hell *I* was talking about, either.

"You ate all the baked goods?" he asked, his cute little blue eyes all scrunched up with uncertainty.

The idea that I would eat *all* the cupcakes was so absurd I snorted. As a side note: When I find something particularly funny, I tend to laugh so hard I snort. It's an embarrassing habit I try not to share with men until at least the fourth date. Anyway . . .

Robert shook his head as if to clear it, sending a sheaf of longish dark brown hair flopping into his face. It was a pretty charming move, and I found myself really looking at him, checking him out, even. It seemed that I was kind of attracted to the cute, granola-eating, hemp-wearing PETA spy.

And from the strange smile Robert still had on his face, I could tell he kind of liked me, too.

"Well, glad you liked them," he said as he fidgeted with something in his back pocket. A second later, he dragged an old, taped-together cell phone out and flipped it open.

"Hey, maybe we could go get food sometime?"

"I would love to," I said, fluttering my eyelashes at him. This was too good to be true. I was standing right in front of a guy I kinda liked, and I hadn't hit him over the head with anything . . . yet.

With bated breath, I waited while he put my phone number into his cell.

"Awesome," he said as he flipped the top of the phone

back into place and pocketed it. "Well, I gotta hit the head."

I nodded, then smiled dreamily as he passed me and headed for the bathroom.

The bathroom!

"No!" I cried as I realized what he was about to do.

From across the hall, all I saw was the back of his DEATH CAB FOR CUTIE T-shirt and the butt of his ripped jeans as he pushed open the door to the bathroom and stepped inside.

"Please, don't!" I yelled, but I knew it was too late. There was no way Jarvis was gonna be hiding in one of the stalls. I could hear Robert give a muffled "Sorry" from where I had been standing across the hall. Then I heard him say:

"Hey, is it bring your kids to work day or something?"

Those were all the words he got out of his mouth before he realized Jarvis was anything but someone's kid.

Robert stepped back, out of the bathroom, his face bone white and his eyes almost bulging out of his head.

"It's okay—" I began, trying to calm him, but Robert started shrieking like a little girl, cutting me off.

"Please! Don't scream," Jarvis said as he stepped into the hallway. "There is absolutely no reason for this kind of behavior."

Robert turned to look at me, his brain not even registering Jarvis's words. He just lifted his arm and pointed at the faun in the bathroom doorway, then promptly passed out on the floor, his head hitting the speckled carpet with a hard *thwump.*

I stood, frozen, beside Robert's prostrate body, unsure of what to do next.

"He'll be fine once the shock dissipates," Jarvis said

as he stepped out of the doorway and into the green-toned fluorescent light.

This is insane, I thought to myself. *This cannot be happening to me.*

"Close your mouth, Mistress Calliope," Jarvis said. "You look like a codfish."

I instantly shut my mouth, but hated myself for doing it.

"What're you? Mary Poppins?"

Jarvis shrugged.

"And what are we going to do with Robert?" I almost wailed. "He saw you!"

Another thought slammed into my brain, filling me with horror.

"Oh my God, what if someone *else* sees you?" I immediately started scanning the hallway, praying no one else decided to leave their cubicle and investigate what all the screaming was about.

"He won't remember a thing when he wakes up," Jarvis said, his voice calm and without the least bit of worry. "The human brain tends to ignore what it cannot understand."

"Oh, and you know this how?" I spat back at him.

"Experience. Centuries of it."

You just can't argue with someone who's lived long enough to remember the Battle of Waterloo like it was last Tuesday.

"What're we gonna do with him?" I asked, choosing not to continue the argument.

"We shall put him in the bathroom—"

"In one of the stalls?" I said incredulously.

"Yes, of course, one of the stalls," Jarvis said, rolling his eyes. "You get his legs, Mistress Calliope, and we shall leave the door cracked slightly so that someone will notice and offer assistance." Jarvis reached down and grasped Robert under the arms, his hands wrapping around the scrawny chest with a viselike grip.

I nodded, taking ahold of Robert's thick calves and lifting.

"Jesus," I gasped. "He weighs a ton for someone with only, like, twelve percent body fat."

Jarvis only grunted in reply.

Together, we were able to carry Robert's limp body into the bathroom and put him inside the cleanest stall I could find. Surveying our handiwork, I was satisfied that Robert was really no more worse for wear than if he'd had one too many lagers out with the boys. He was probably going to wake up with one hell of a headache, but that was it.

"Shall we go now? Before there are any more mishaps?" Jarvis said testily. I had forgotten how bossy the little faun could be.

"I told you," I said, "I have to let someone know I'm leaving. Don't you even listen to what I say? Now, stay in the bathroom and I'll be right back."

I turned and started down the hall toward my desk, but not before I heard Jarvis mumble the word "impertinent" under his breath.

"I heard that," I said, not even bothering to turn around. I could feel his glare burning a hole in my back; I didn't need to see it.

geneva was still sitting at her desk, the glossy pages of *Vogue* reflecting the fluorescent light from the ceiling back at her.

"Geneva, something terrible has happened," I said huskily, perching on the edge of my desk.

She instantly dropped the end of the dreadlock she'd been twisting around her finger and looked up.

"What's wrong? Lord, Hy didn't fire you, did she?"

I shook my head, trying to compose my face into the most depressed-looking expression I could muster. I was even able to manage a little bit of tear action by opening my eyelids unnaturally wide and not blinking.

"Are you okay?" Geneva asked. "Your eyes look kinda funny—"

I held out my hand to stop her.

"Trying not to cry," I said, my voice still as husky as I could make it.

"Oh, sorry."

I shook my head.

"My father is really . . . *ill*, and I need to go home. Can you let Hy know?"

Geneva nodded, her face scrunched up tight with empathy.

"Of course. Oh, jeez, Cal, I'm sorry. That's so awful."

She reached over and gave me a tentative, one-armed hug. It was sweet of her since I knew she was not a public-display-of-affection kind of person.

"Is there anything I can do?" she added.

"Just tell Hy it was an emergency."

She nodded, then her eyes lit up.

"Oh, I'll call HR, so they can make sure there's someone to fill in for you while you're gone," Geneva said helpfully.

I gave her a weak smile full of gratitude.

"You just get on home before anything happens," Geneva said, giving my arm a commiserative pat.

"I will," I said. Boy, this whole thing was starting to make me feel like a total jerk. I hated to lie to Geneva, especially when she was being so nice, but it really couldn't be helped.

I packed what little I needed from my desk into the Kate Spade knock-off shoulder bag—twenty bucks in Times Square—and with a wave to Geneva, who was already on the phone with HR, headed back down the hall to where I knew Jarvis would be eagerly waiting.

using a wormhole to jump from one place to another is an efficient way to travel, but not the most comfortable as far as I'm concerned.

How do I describe the sensation? Kind of like Alice falling down the Rabbit Hole, I guess, but let me tell you, Lewis Carroll never said anything about your stomach jumping up into your throat, or your head throbbing like it was being squeezed in a vise.

I had almost made Jarvis call the house and order a helicopter—I hated wormholes so much. Instead, I'd taken a deep breath and followed him through the swirling mass of black nothingness he'd called up inside the bathroom while I was back at my desk.

It was as bad as I'd remembered. My head ached, my stomach knotted, and I was pummeled on all sides by bursts of strong, hot air. Then, it was over, and I fell hard to the floor, my body so unused to the experience that it couldn't hold me up on my feet.

"Crap!"

I opened my eyes and found myself in the middle of my father's dark, wood-paneled library.

As far as I could tell, the room was just as I remembered it: two tasteful brown leather wingback chairs and a matching couch, holding court in front of the massive mahogany fireplace; a bloodred-and-cream Oriental rug laid out across the dark patterned parquet floor; the wet bar where my father kept his cognac and other after-dinner liquors.

My sisters and I had spent many an afternoon playing hide-and-seek here, one or the other of us shut up in the wooden belly of the tall grandfather clock that stood majestically by the large bay window that looked out onto the water. Sometimes it was hours before someone found your hiding place and released you, legs and back sore from the long stretch of inactivity. That was the problem with having such a big house—too many good hiding places.

As much as I hated to admit it, even to myself, being back at Sea Verge made me realize how much I'd missed the place—and my family.

"Are you all right down there?" a masculine voice called from the doorway. I looked up, expecting to see Jarvis, but instead found a tall, scrumptious-looking *man* standing there staring at me, one of my father's books in his hand.

Embarrassed, I stood up. *Of course I make an ass out of myself in front of the only member of the opposite sex in the room—typical Callie,* I thought miserably to myself.

"I'm fine," I said, trying to compose myself. *Damn it!* I could feel a nervous grin starting to take over my face.

Another thing you should know about me is I tend to grin like an idiot when I'm nervous—and hot guys make me *extremely* nervous. I can't help it. I'm just not good when it comes to interacting with good-looking men. I always say the wrong thing or fall over a chair or something. *It's so embarrassing.*

"Yes, you *are* a fine little girl, aren't you," he said, giving me a wry, knowing grin as he appraised my face and the figure underneath my clothes, which today consisted of a really adorable flowered tank dress from Anthropologie.

His gaze was very penetrating, and suddenly, I realized the guy was, like, *mentally undressing me*! Who did he think I was? *Dial-a-call-girl?*

Not sure at all how to respond, I glared at him. The one thing I've found that can combat nervousness is anger. And this guy with his *so cool* attitude was starting to make me really angry . . . and, I hated to admit it, kinda horny at the same time.

"In fact, you look as hot as a four-alarm fire in Hell," he said in response to my silence. Shocked, I took a step back. *Is the guy talking about how angry I look,* I thought, *or is he just—*

"Are you making a pass at me?" I blurted out before I could stop myself.

This made the guy laugh, and for the first time I noticed how incredibly blue his eyes were. They had to be the palest ice blue eyes I'd ever seen outside of a Paul Newman movie. He also had nice, shiny white teeth and a head of curly, ebony hair that made his pale skin look almost translucent in the sunlight.

"You're a funny little thing, aren't you?" he said, putting the book back on the bookshelf-lined wall. "I haven't heard the term 'making a pass' at someone in a very, very long time."

He took a step toward me, and I took a halting step back, trying to keep as much distance between our bodies as I could—fat lot of good that did me. He closed the gap between us in two quick steps, the warmth from his tall, lean body almost palpable as he stood mere inches away. I swallowed hard, not liking the way my body was instinctively reacting to his. Part of me even wanted to reach out and touch him, play with the soft curl of hair that escaped from the top of his button-down shirt, but I fought hard to keep that part of me firmly in check.

"Who are you?" I asked, my voice thick in my throat. This was going very badly. A few more minutes, and I'd be ripping the shirt right off his chest, my body was getting *that* excited by his nearness. I hadn't felt this way about a guy in years. In fact, I didn't think I'd *ever* felt this physically attracted to another human being in my life.

Suddenly, he reached out, his fingers gently grazing my cheek as he slipped a stray lock of hair back behind my ear. The way he did it was so sensual I almost choked on my own breath.

Oh, God, I thought, my legs as weak as a newborn lamb's, my mouth dry with anticipation. *He's gonna ravage me right here on my father's Oriental rug . . . and I am so gonna let him!*

He leaned in close—close enough to feel his breath hot against my ear, to smell the woodsy bouquet of his cologne. I closed my eyes, my heart thumping erratically in my chest with all the horny enthusiasm it could muster.

I was so *not* ready for what was obviously gonna come next: *sex.*

I mean, I wasn't on the pill, there were no diaphragms magically waiting to be spermicided in my purse, and I definitely didn't think my father was the kinda guy to keep a pack of condoms tucked away in his desk drawer.

Screw it! I thought to myself. *You only live once.*

Having made peace with my dubious situation, I licked my lips, prayed my breath wasn't too terrible from the double espresso I'd had that morning, and let my mouth go slack with anticipation.

"Go ahead," I said. "Do your worst."

I closed my eyes and waited. I didn't have to wait too long. He came closer, his lips only a hairbreadth from mine.

"I am . . ." he said, then he paused.

I swallowed hard, trying to becalm my struggling pulse and the throbbing between my legs.

"I am the Devil's protégé."

five

I opened one eye, then the other, and stared at him.

"Oh . . ." I said, hoping the "Devil's protégé" couldn't see how disappointed I was we weren't fornicating on the floor already. "Is that all?"

He looked surprised (or maybe "upset" was a better word) that I wasn't shocked by his pronouncement, scared of him even. He frowned and cocked his head, obviously trying to reconcile some incorrect vision of me he had in his mind.

"You're not surprised?" he said, his brow furrowed. "But I don't understand. I was told you were the *normal* member of your family—"

"Who told you that?" I demanded.

"Common knowledge," he said, skirting my question.

"And I guess you just took that to mean I didn't have a clue as to what went on around here?" I sniffed. *"Please."*

He took a step back, and I felt a sharp pain in my chest. *Am I experiencing "Devil's protégé" withdrawal?*

I shook my head, trying to clear it, and the guy took another few steps backward until he had put a good "couch and wing chair" between us. It was the strangest thing, but the farther he got away from me, the more I wanted to jump him. It was actually becoming a struggle to keep from leaping over the couch and attacking.

I put my hands on the back of the leather couch and dug my nails in. This was getting ridiculous.

"I, uhm . . ." I began, but couldn't seem to think beyond how attractive I found him, how much I wanted to screw his brains out right there on the floor.

"God! Stop it!" I said to myself, holding on to the couch for dear life.

"Is something wrong?" the Devil's protégé asked, but I only shook my head.

"Get. Out," I finally said through clenched teeth.

"What?"

He didn't seem to understand we were a reaching crisis point. He just stood there looking at me. Obviously he had no experience with hormonal women.

"Get out before I do something we'll both regret," I almost screamed at him.

He jumped, my words like a cattle prod.

"I don't understand—" he began, but I didn't let him finish. With both hands, I picked up one of the red accent pillows on the couch and lobbed it at him.

Shocked, he just stood there.

"Get out! Get out! Get out! If you value your life, get out!"

This seemed to penetrate, and he looked a little terrified at my outburst. He quickly turned on his heel and departed, shutting the door firmly behind him.

The moment the door closed, I felt a tremendous

release—and not the *orgasmic* kind. Up until that moment, I hadn't realized how physically tense I was. My jaw ached horribly, and I noticed I was still in the middle of quietly grinding my teeth. I stopped grinding immediately and put two fingers on both sides of my jaw, rubbing the sore spots.

"Ow," I said under my breath. "That really hurts . . ."

Suddenly, there was a knock on the door, and I instinctively reached for the other accent pillow.

"Mistress Calliope . . . ?"

"Stop calling me that," I said, dropping the pillow back on the couch as Jarvis tentatively opened the door.

"Pardon me, Mistress . . . I mean, *Miss* Calliope," Jarvis intoned. You could see it was just killing him to do what I told him to.

"Where were you!" I yelled at him. "There was almost an *incident* in here, Jarvis."

"Excuse me?" he replied. "An incident?"

I shook my head, a dull headache creeping up my neck and settling in my temples.

"Forget it," I said, flopping into one of the wing chairs and closing my eyes.

"I've been looking for you throughout the house, Mistress—" He stopped, annoyed with himself. "*Miss* Callie, I expected you to come with me to your mother's sitting room. She's very anxious to see you, as is your sister."

"Hey, I didn't *choose* to make a stop in the library. It just happened!"

"Shall I take you to your mother?" Jarvis asked, ignoring my rudeness.

"All right," I said, dragging myself out of the wing chair. I followed him out of the library and through a long hallway that led to the main foyer.

"Jarvis," I said, "who was the guy waiting in here?"

"What 'guy' are you referring to?" Jarvis said, turning to look at me with a puzzled expression.

I followed him up a wide set of marble stairs, the focal point of the foyer, and down another long hallway. When we were kids, my sisters and I would slide down the cool length of the banister, our butts black and blue from landing hard on the marble floor at the end of each ride.

"Look, there was a guy in the library—tall, dark hair, blue eyes, kinda hunky."

Jarvis snorted at the word "hunky."

"I'm not kidding," I said. "There was a guy here. Who was he? He said he was the Devil's protégé. What does that mean?"

Jarvis shook his head, frowning.

"I haven't the foggiest. There is no one here today but the immediate family and your father's lawyer, Father McGee. I'll have to look into this."

He pushed open the gilded door to my mother's bedroom and went inside. I stopped at the doorway, my mind reeling from what Jarvis had just told me.

"Callie?!" a tremulous voice called from inside the bedroom. I could smell Chanel No. 5, my mother's favorite perfume, leaking out of her boudoir and into the hallway.

Oh, God, I thought. *This is* not *gonna be pretty.*

I took a deep breath and stepped inside.

my mother and father hadn't slept in the same bedroom since my sister Thalia was born. This did not mean my parents hated each other, or only *tolerated* each other's presence *for the children.* It was quite the opposite, actually. My parents not only tolerated each other's presence, but also were, in fact, madly, deeply, passionately in love with one another.

The truth is that they would *have* to be all gooey-eyed over each other for my father to petition both God and the Devil to make my mother immortal, and my mother to renounce her mortality to stand by my father's side for eternity. If that sounds like pretty heavy stuff, believe me, it was.

Anyway, the reason they slept apart was entirely my father's doing, even though he didn't know why it was his fault until *much* later.

After Thalia was born, my mother stopped sleeping. Everyone thought it was the stress of new motherhood, but after two months of insomnia, it was apparent the cause was more than just being overwhelmed by torrential floods of breast milk and dirty nappies.

If you look at pictures of my mother from that time, she's almost skeletal—her bones poke out at odd angles from strangely translucent skin, and dark smudges encircle her eyes like rain clouds.

She looks almost haunted.

My father was beside himself as he watched his new bride wither on the vine right in front of him. He brought specialists from all around the world to see her, but not one of them could figure out what was wrong.

Meanwhile, my mother continued to care for Thalia with a sleep-deprived, almost-obsessive attention to detail. My sister never went for more than ten seconds in dirty diapers or without being fed when she was hungry—I think that's the reason Thalia's the uptight, anal retentive, paper-pushing neat freak that she is. She can't even pass a tie without wanting to straighten it, which, from experience, can be a really weird and annoying thing when you're riding on the subway with her.

So, my mother doted on her new baby, my father fretted over my mother's health—and also doted on the new baby, contributing to Thalia's already fast-growing sense of self-importance—and no one could figure out why my mother was turning into a ghost. Finally, in sheer desperation, my father called in an aura specialist, hoping someone from the spiritual community would be able to figure the mystery out.

Madame Papillon, a small woman with a pinhead and a large, protuberant nose that looked more like a muzzle than a human olfactory organ, took one look at my mother's aura, sighed heavily, and announced that my mother was dying. Then she added that she knew how to save her.

It seems that every immortal has one *thing* in existence that can destroy them—kinda like Superman and Kryptonite. Sadly, no immortal is born knowing what their weakness is, so they spend a lot of time worrying about it. But once their weakness has been made known—and they've survived the encounter—then it's a pretty easy task to avoid the offending thing. But it just sucks if it turns out that the very *thing* is intimately tied up with something you love.

Turns out my mother's weakness was . . .

Snoring.

Since my mother's immortality hadn't been granted until right after Thalia's birth, the whole time my parents had lived together—and slept together—she'd been mortal, and my father's snoring hadn't affected her one little bit. And since no one had suspected her weakness would be quite so . . . domestic . . . it took an out-of-town aura specialist to put the whole thing together.

In the end, my parents—regardless of their death-defying love—found themselves nocturnally separated for all of eternity.

I have only two words for that story.

Total bummer.

Anyway, because of her *weakness*, my mother had her own set of rooms right down the hall from my father. As much as she might have wished to sleep beside her husband, I think she was grateful for her own space. My father's personality could be a bit *overwhelming* at times—I mean, he *was* Death.

As I stepped into her sitting room, I saw her—her usually placid face tense and streaked with tears—seated in one of the pair of delicate Gothic tracery-backed Chippendale chairs that had been in her rooms for as long as I had been alive. They reminded me of her, actually: neat and delicate, but strong enough to manage the heaviest of asses.

"Callie," my mother said again as she stood and closed the gap between us.

Chanel No. 5 pierced my nostrils, not unpleasantly, and I could feel her heart hammering in her chest like a tiny woodpecker. She seemed even smaller and more delicate than I remembered, or maybe it was just that it had been a long time and people always seem larger than life in our memories, their strengths somehow exaggerated in their absence.

She pulled back out of the hug and looked me over. I took the moment to do the same, noting the light pink silk kimono, which was obviously her dressing gown, and probably a gift from my father. It seemed like his taste. Her pale golden hair was held back out of her face with a mother-of-pearl clip, and she was wearing no makeup to speak of.

She didn't look a day over thirty.

She bit her lip, then took my hand, squeezing it hard.

"I'm so happy you came. I was afraid . . . afraid that . . ." she stammered, then forced a pinched smile. "I was afraid you wouldn't come."

I swallowed, not sure how to respond. On one hand, I understood my mother's worry, but on the other . . . *how could she think I wouldn't come?* He was my *father* after all, wasn't he?

"Of course I came. You're my family. It's like the law or something that we have to stick together in times of crisis, right?"

"I'm glad you see it that way," a voice called out from behind me.

I turned and saw an old man in a long cleric's robe closing the door that led into my mother's bathroom. I could hear the last flushing of the toilet as the door latch slid into place.

"Father McGee."

My father's human lawyer gave me a wink before grabbing me—one only hoped he had washed his hands—in a big bear hug and nearly lifting me off my feet. He had always been a small man, but since he did calisthenics every day of his life, he was a small, *well-muscled* man. It made me happy somehow that I could still feel all those ropey muscles underneath the long black robes he wore.

He gave me another wink as he let me go, and I noticed immediately how much he had aged since I saw him last.

God, he has to be close to eighty-five by now, I thought, my heart going out to him. *I wonder how he copes with being so old?*

As he crossed the soft cream carpet to sit in the

Chippendale chair nearest my mother, I was happy to see there was still *some* spryness in his step.

After the distraction of his entrance had passed, it took only a few moments for the weight of what he'd just said to register in my consciousness, and I found myself blurting out:

"Wait a minute here, you guys. Don't get me wrong; it's great to have the whole family reunion thing and all, but what the hell did you mean when you said you were *glad that I see things that way*?"

My mother and Father McGee exchanged glances, then Father McGee cleared his throat.

"Well, Callie, my dear. You see, we're in a bit of a bind here—"

I raised an eyebrow.

"A bit of a bind?"

My mother stood, wringing her hands as she began to pace.

"You see, sweetheart, it seems that—"

Father McGee cut her off.

"With your father missing, and no heirs at the age of consent to take his place, the Devil wants a recall."

My mother began to cry.

"They want to kick us out of Sea Verge, Callie. Strip us of our immortality, and let your father rot, or worse, in whatever cesspool his captors have thrown him into," she sobbed.

Father McGee patted her on the back. I didn't want to seem impertinent, but I had no idea how any of this "bind stuff" applied to yours truly. It seemed totally clear to me who my mother needed to call.

My older sister, Thalia, would probably wet herself to take over the top spot at Death, Inc. I knew for a fact that she totally resented being *just* the Vice President in

Charge of Passage. I, personally, had no sympathy for her, since I was *just* a lowly assistant at a home and garden supply company with no title to speak of at all.

"What about Thalia? She's way past the age of consent and I'm sure she's just salivating to take the reigns while they look for Father," I said with only the slightest trace of bitterness in my voice.

Strangely, my words only seemed to make my mother sob even harder.

"Your sister and all twelve of the company's key Executives were taken along with your father. The act was perpetrated right in the middle of the annual Solstice Meeting. As far as the Board is concerned, the company has been totally devastated."

"What?!" I almost shrieked. "Why didn't Jarvis say anything to me about Thalia before?!"

"I asked Jarvis not to tell you about your sister," my mother said, taking a silk handkerchief from her kimono sleeve and dabbing at her nose with it. "I didn't want to upset you any more than I had to."

"It's not an easy decision you must make, Callie. We know that . . ."

My mother nodded hopefully.

"But we *know* you will make the *right* decision . . ." Father McGee added soberly.

"The right decision . . . ?" I squeaked. *Oh, shit. He is so not pulling a guilt trip on me right now! Isn't there a commandment or something against priests manipulating members of their flock?* I thought miserably to myself.

"Yes, Calliope. The *right* decision," Father McGee chirped. "Only you have the power . . . *to save your family from certain doom.*"

six

"No."

Neither my mother nor Father McGee seemed to understand what I was saying, so I said it again with more emphasis.

"No. No, no, no, no, no, and no into infinity . . ."

"But Calliope—" my mother began, obviously sizing up the situation and recognizing immediately that a good defense meant having an even better offense.

Nipping her attack in the bud, I stuffed my fingers in my ears and began to hum the theme song to the *Smurfs* cartoon like some passive-aggressive two-year-old. I thought this tactic might be just shocking enough to shut her up, and I was right. She closed her mouth and stared at me with pursed lips, a very disapproving look on her beautiful face.

Oh, and when I say beautiful, I mean *beautiful.*

My mother didn't entice the Grim Reaper into her bed for nothing. She was a direct descendant of Helen of Troy, and she lived up to the lineage. She had smooth porcelain skin and the kind of aristocratic nose that people pay good money for.

She was like Brigitte Bardot . . . *ad infinitum.*

Ignoring her disapproval, I said through clenched teeth, "What part of the word 'no' do you not understand?"

I couldn't believe we were dealing with all this business stuff when we should be formulating some kind of plan to get my father and sister back in one piece. So I said as much:

"Besides, I want to know what the hell is being done to get Father and Thalia back. I really think that should've been our first order of business—"

"We won't have any say in what attempts are made to rescue your sister and your father if we've been thrown out of the spiritual community, Calliope," my mother said testily. "I can't imagine the new Grim Reaper would deign to consult with his predecessor's family, can you? Especially if he has gotten his commission through chicanery."

I was starting to feel just a *teensy* little bit overwhelmed by the whole situation, and my mind was quickly trolling for happy, calming memories to keep me from totally freaking out. I let the image of my messy but extremely *normal* apartment in Battery Park City fill my head. If I could just get everyone to realize I was so *not* the person for the job, I'd be back there before I could say "enchanted cupcake."

Thus equipped, I continued:

"I worked too hard for too many years to keep myself out of the family business, and I am *not* gonna let you two guilt-trip me into it! There must be another way we can get them to let us stay here. Couldn't we just petition God or something?"

I could hear my voice rising, but I tried to stay as focused as I could on my old, normal life.

"Impossible," Father McGee said. "There is no other way. You're the only answer your mother and I could come up with. Believe me, if Clio was of age, I would have barred your mother from contacting you at all."

"Excuse me?!" I exclaimed. "Not even *contact* me? About my own father and sister being kidnapped? What kind of priest are you?"

"You were the one who put a Forgetting Charm on yourself . . ." Father McGee began.

"Please, Calliope. It's just until we find your father . . ." my mother added, hoping to stave off a fight.

"Nothing's ever that simple," I said acidly. "It's nice to know, Mother, that the only reason you're dealing with me, period, is that you *need* something from me."

Father McGee stood up, and I could see the vein that ran across his forehead pulsing furiously. I could tell that he was two seconds away from imploding, and if he hadn't been an old man who seemed to have a serious jonesin' for a stroke, I might have laughed at the absurdity of the situation.

Here I was, in my mother's palatial, coffee-and-cream-palette, wall-to-wall-Berber-carpeted rooms, having a screaming match with a half-dressed Goddess runner-up and a priest.

And this *is exactly why I didn't want to go into the family business,* I thought angrily.

I watched as my mother's face crumpled. She sat back down in the Chippendale chair and did not move. She seemed to be channeling all of her energy into not crying. I could see the effort on her face, the strain in her eyes, and I started to feel like a major-league jerk.

"I'm sorry, Mom."

I moved to her side, crouching so that we were level, and wrapped my arms around her shoulders. She let me squeeze, and I took that as a good sign. I looked over at Father McGee, who nodded, the anger seemingly having drained out of him when I started behaving like a *good* daughter.

"I know this is hard on you, Mom," I began. "I really do understand. I'm sorry I was being such an ass. You guys just . . . *surprised* me with all this 'company man' stuff."

My mother didn't reply, but I could feel some of the tension easing out of her.

"If this is really what you want me to do, Mom, then I guess I can . . . *think about it*."

She glanced over at me hopefully, and the look on her face was so pathetic that I did a really, really, *really* stupid thing . . .

I agreed to take the job.

"Okay, I'll do it, but only *temporarily*. You have to start looking for someone else to take over, like ASAP. That's my only stipulation."

My mother nodded, relief flooding her features.

"Thank you, sweetheart," she said, squeezing my arm with affection. "I knew I could count on you to come through in the end."

As much as I wanted to be positive about my good daughter behavior, I couldn't help but feel like I'd just gotten myself into a very precarious position. One that I wouldn't be able to so easily extract myself from, no matter how hard I tried.

* * *

"boy, they *so* totally conned you. I knew they were up to something when they put you on twenty-four-hour watch."

"Twenty-four-hour watch?" I said.

"Yeah, they wanted to make sure that no one kidnapped you, so they sent the Death Guardianship to your apartment."

So, that was who the giant dinosaur/monster thing and the homeless guy were, I mused thoughtfully. *Death Guardians.*

I was lying on my sister Clio's bed, staring at the purple lava lamp that sat like a talisman on her nightstand. There was something just so *pleasant* about watching the fat blobs of whatever the hell was inside a lava lamp glide fluidly up and down the length of their glass enclosure. It was easy to get sucked into the lava lamp blob world.

"Callie, you're not listening to anything I'm saying, are you?" my sister said loudly in my ear. She had flopped down onto the plush, purple, hypoallergenic duvet–covered bed beside me while I was busy staring at the lava lamp blobs, so I didn't notice her until her words nearly punched out my eardrum.

"Ow, Clio," I said, rubbing my ear. "That really hurt."

"Sorry," she said, but she didn't really mean it.

"Why can't you let me slide into lava lamp oblivion in peace, huh? Leave me to contemplate my misery like any other good younger sister would if she were smart, and valued her life."

Clio laughed as she poked me in the arm with one of her purple-nail-polished fingers.

"Are you sure being someone's assistant is where it's

at for you, Cal? 'Cause I think melodrama is your true calling."

I glared at her, but only for a minute. It was hard to be mad at someone as adorable as Clio.

Even with her shaved head and black-framed Buddy Holly glasses, she couldn't hide how breathtakingly beautiful she was. She had been the only one to really inherit our mother's beauty—but somehow that beauty had been convoluted by our father's genes, so that instead of the blond Goddess features of our mother, Clio sported the tiny visage of a pixie child.

Her pale skin and pitch-black eyes and hair made such a shockingly gorgeous combination that Clio, in her infinite seventeen-year-old wisdom, had decided to shave her head to make herself look more normal.

It hadn't worked as well as she had hoped, but at least it did stop grown men from asking for her hand in marriage. Something that can be kind of embarrassing when you're a freshman in high school and the "grown man" is your totally hot twentysomething substitute biology teacher.

I was pretty certain, though no one else in the family agreed with me, that Clio had Siren blood in her somewhere. My mother insisted that it was completely impossible, but I didn't think she'd own up to it even if it was true. No one in their right mind would want the Sirens associated with *their* family tree.

I hadn't seen her in three years, and I realized that she was the one member of the family that I'd have missed most—if I'd remembered that she existed.

"So, did they pull good cop, bad cop on you?" Clio asked.

"Huh?"

"Did one of them cry and the other yell? That's about as simple as I can put it for ya, sis."

Ignoring the insulting part of the question, I said, "I don't know. I guess so."

Clio rolled her eyes.

"How are you gonna run Death if you can't even tell when you're being manipulated by your own mother?"

"I know when I'm being manipulated, Clio. I'm not a complete idiot."

"Are you sure about that?" she said teasingly, then added, "Just kidding, Cal."

"I wish you were the age of consent," I said miserably. "You're much better suited for the job."

"That may be true," Clio agreed, "but I would hate to have Dad's job. It *sucks*. He was always looking over his shoulder, worried someone was after his job. The stress alone was a killer."

She was right. I wouldn't wish being the Grim Reaper on anyone. The job *did* suck, even if the benefits were pretty great.

Damn it!

The memory of my probably impending firing came flooding back with a vengeance. Because of all this bullshit, I would lose my job at House and Yard, and that would spell the end of any kind of New York–based career period if Hy had anything to say about it.

Double suckage.

Just thinking about the sad prospect of never being allowed inside the world of high fashion—no matter *how* far away I was from it at the moment over at House and Yard—made me want to cry.

"I can't believe I'm gonna lose everything I've struggled for all these years just because a bunch of jerks decided to steal Father and Thalia. I mean, they're immortal, aren't they? It's not like they can kill them or anything."

Clio didn't say a word, but the look on her face made me suddenly feel like my rhetorical questions might actually need answering after all.

"Uhm, Callie, weren't you listening to what Mom and Father McGee were saying? The Board wanted to strip the family of their immortality—and that included Dad, too."

"What?" I almost shrieked.

"If they took his immortality . . . well, I don't think it'd be pretty."

What kind of deal had *I gotten myself into here?* I thought miserably.

"But you said yes," Clio continued. "So, as long as you don't get fired, or quit, Dad's safe."

I was terrible under pressure. All I had to do was think about getting fired, and somehow I'd make it happen.

Oh, shit, this was so not *good.*

"Earth to Callie," Clio said, rolling her eyes at me.

"Sorry. I was just . . . I mean, I can't believe Mother didn't tell me any of this."

Clio shrugged.

"Probably didn't want to make you freak, 'cause we all know you're the queen of psyching yourself out."

"Great," I said, feeling like the weight of the world had descended not only on my shoulders, but on my head, too. I had a *terrible* migraine, and I knew that it would only get worse as the day wore on.

"Okay," I said calmly. "I just have to suck it up for a few days, and then when they find Father, I'm outta here."

Clio watched me as I stood up and began to pace around her room.

"That's exactly what I'll do," I mumbled to myself. "When it's all over, I'll go and beg Hy for my job back. I'll have to get on my hands and knees, but I can handle it . . ."

"I cannot believe you just said that. That is *seriously* sad." Clio sighed, then hopped off the bed and moved to the desk, where her laptop sat.

I forgot to mention that Clio is a math and science genius. In her free time, she likes to play with algorithms and dissect any little critters that are crazy enough to cross her path.

Flipping up the top, she sat down at the computer and began to type.

"What're you doing?" I asked. "I'm in the middle of a crisis here, and you're playing Tetris."

"Tetris is so last millennium," she said. "Anyway, I'm just checking something."

"Checking what?"

I seriously wanted to know what could be more important than my own personal crisis.

She didn't look up.

"Checking the probability of success."

"The success of what?" I asked. Getting an answer out of Clio was like pulling wisdom teeth.

"Of you running Death, and not getting thrown into Purgatory your first day on the job," she said breezily.

"Gee, thanks for the vote of confidence, Clio."

She finished typing, then turned around in her seat to give me a big smile.

"Better odds than I would've thought," she said, her perfect white teeth glinting in the purple lava lamplight.

"Yeah?" I said, waiting on pins and needles for her to give me the data.

"The computer gives you a seventy-two percent chance—"

That's not so bad, I thought.

"—of failure."

"A seventy-two percent chance of *failure*?" I yelped, nearly having a heart attack right there on Clio's floor.

"I thought you said it was better than you figured?"

She shrugged.

"I gave you a ninety percent chance of failure. Guess the computer's just a sap."

after i left my younger sister happily punching keys on her computer—probably trying to get the stupid thing to up its ratio of failure to success, the little witch—I went downstairs to find Jarvis.

Now that I was the new President and CEO of Death, Inc., Jarvis had become *my* Executive Assistant.

I'm sure he'd already heard the *good news* and was trying to shove himself down the garbage disposal that very minute.

"Jarvis?!" I called as I walked down the long hallway that led from my sister's room to the front staircase. I had the vague recollection that the little guy had to come whenever my father called him, so I was hoping the perk had transferred over to me.

A moment later, Jarvis appeared right in front of me, nearly making me trip down the last two steps of the stairwell.

"Damn it, Jarvis! Don't sneak up on me like that!"

"Yes, mist—"

Jarvis stopped himself midsentence and glared at me. He had almost called me "mistress" again, and it made him fume.

Hee hee hee, well, at least this part of the job is gonna be fun, I thought to myself, feeling the migraine I'd been working on starting to disappear.

"You called for me, Miss Calliope?" he said through gritted teeth as he followed me through the front foyer.

"Just Callie to you, my little friend."

He pursed his lips and shook his head in consternation.

"You know, you are expected at the offices in thirty minutes for a meeting with the Board," Jarvis began, but I ignored what he was saying in favor of my own question.

"Hey, just curiosity here, but aren't you supposed to do whatever I say?" I asked.

His face blanched like an egg. I could see his mind scrambling for some kind of answer that would save him from a fate worse than death, but happily, there was no respite.

"Isn't that part of the job? Like if I ask you to get me organic dim sum, you have to, like . . . do it. Right?"

Jarvis swallowed hard, and I could see that it was a strain for him to answer.

"Anything within reason—" he began, but I cut him off.

"No, I don't think that's what I remember, Jarvis. I think you gotta do whatever I ask. And I mean, like, *everything*."

"Yes, Miss Calliope. You have me. I *must* do your bidding, but your father did not abuse—"

"I want organic dim sum on Hy's desk within the next ten minutes, no excuses. I also want a note from the President of Home and Yard, Inc., telling Hy that I've been sent on special assignment—your choice, just make it exciting—and my position must be held open for me, no matter when my return is."

"But—"

"No buts, Jarvis."

He closed his mouth, a pained expression on his face as we reached the door to my father's study.

"Yes, *Callie*. Is that all you will be requiring of me?" he said, nearly spitting the words at me.

"Yep, I think that'll do it. Spit spot on the double now, Jarvi," I said, adding my perky little nickname to the end of the sentence before closing the door on Jarvis's shocked face.

seven

I had never wanted immortality. It was not something that appealed to me in the least. I would've been perfectly happy to live a good eighty to ninety years in mortal obscurity, then croak in my big, old, four-poster bed surrounded by an adoring extended family—preferably my own.

I guess the grass is always greener on the other side. I was just going to have to accept the fact that I was immortal, and there wasn't a damn thing I could do about it.

When I was sixteen, I was in a car accident. I was on the way back from a trip to New York City with my Newport friends—Jessie and Davia—both townies that I'd hung out with every summer since I was nine.

We'd spent the past two days seeing every Broadway show we could get tickets for (my treat), and we were only fifty or so miles from home when some irresponsible idiot in a tractor-trailer fell asleep at the wheel and crossed over the grass divider into our lane.

We were in Davia's mother's burgundy Volvo station wagon—which we all know is, like, one of the safest cars on the road, hence the reason we were willing to be, quite literally, caught dead in it—but even the Volvo couldn't stop fate from taking its due.

The tractor-trailer hit us head-on, crunching the front of the station wagon like an accordion. At first, I couldn't believe it was happening, I was in total shock, but as the bright yellow headlights bore down on us like Devil's eyes, I knew it was real, and the outcome was not going to be a good one.

Having lost shotgun to Jessie, I'd been relegated to the backseat of the car. It was from this lofty vantage point that I sat, screaming my head off while I watched my two friends getting squished like human bugs in between a ton of steel and carbon fiber. I think it was the utter surrealness of the situation that brought on what some would call an epiphany, but what I just refer to as "the big wake-up call." I realized then and there that there're many things worse than death in this life, and what I saw that day rated as one of them. Being immortal had just as many drawbacks as being mortal.

The following week, I sat—completely unscathed by the accident—at the double memorial service for my two friends, and I knew then that being immortal was a curse, not a boon.

It was like I was somehow being punished for a crime that I didn't even know I had committed. And the sentence was for eternity.

After that, I pretty much gave up on the supernatural side of my life. I had never hated what I was before that day—in fact, I'd always thought what my father did for a living was kinda cool, actually—but after that, I found myself loathing anything to do with the family business.

Now, here I was, eight years later, working for the very "corporation" that I loathed. I knew the whole thing was a necessary evil, but that didn't mean I had to like it.

There was a knock on the study door, and I sat up, stretching my neck against the cool leather back of my father's desk chair. I looked down and saw that I had been absentmindedly doodling all over the desk set. He was so gonna kick my ass when he came home and saw the half-drawn faces and swirling mandalas of pen ink everywhere.

"Come in," I said, grabbing a couple of thick tomes from the bookshelf behind the desk and artfully arranging them so that no one would see the mess I'd made.

The door opened, and Jarvis stepped inside, followed by a very tall man in an ill-fitting suit and tie. If my guess was correct, and I was pretty sure it was, he had pulled the suit right off the rack at The Men's Wearhouse.

He hadn't even had the good sense to let out the pants' hem so that it at least covered the tops of his shoes, hiding the mismatched brown argyle and black cotton socks he had put on that morning.

On the utter patheticness of the man's suit, Jarvis and I were in complete agreement. I raised an eyebrow in question, but Jarvis merely shuddered, then, remembering we were at war, glared haughtily back at me.

"Miss Reaper-Jones, this is Detective Davenport from the Psychical Bureau of Investigations. He's here to speak with you about the kidnappings."

I nodded, and gestured to the chair in front of my father's desk.

"Hi. I'm Callie Reaper-Jones. Please have a seat."

Detective Davenport walked across the threshold, his hand outstretched. As we shook, I found my small hand nearly engulfed in his larger one. He gave me a cool, formal nod, but you could tell by his stiffness that he thought being shunted off to one of Death's kids was some kind of joke. I didn't mind his snooty attitude, though. I was quite enjoying the view his handsome, angular face presented. If I squinted just the teensiest bit, he kinda looked a little like a younger, less British version of Daniel Craig.

Not bad at all, I thought happily, imagining Daniel Jr. throwing himself across the desk and grabbing me in an erotic bear hug.

Yummy.

As my imagination took off, I found myself ignoring the bad clothing in favor of the longish lighter brown hair that curled a little around the nape of his neck, and the pale gold irises surrounded by thick fringes of dark brown lashes. I noted his slim, athletic build, and decided there were definitely muscles hidden underneath the ill-fitting cotton-polyester blend.

Jarvis turned to go, but not before mouthing the words, "You're not his type," under his breath.

I shot Jarvis a nasty look in return, but only managed to get his retreating back.

Damn, he is a little bitch.

The detective took a seat in one of the leather-upholstered armchairs in front of me, and took out one of those cute little leather police notebooks and a pen.

"How can I help you, Mr. Davenport?" I began, but he stopped me.

"It's *Detective,* ma'am."

Ma'am? He has, like, ten years on me, and he is calling me ma'am? I steamed.

"Okay, *Detective,*" I purred, but underneath the pleasantry, all I wanted to do was pinch him. He may have looked like Daniel Craig, but he was almost as smarmy as Jarvis.

"Yes, ma'am—"

"You know," I said, interrupting him now, "why don't you just call me Miss Reaper-Jones. The whole 'ma'am' thing is like nails on chalkboard, if you know what I mean."

He looked at me strangely, but nodded.

"All right, Miss Reaper-Jones."

We smiled tightly at each other, and even though he was cute, he was fast losing his appeal.

"The reason I'm here," he began, "is to gather as much information as I can from the family. Now, can you tell me where you were when the kidnapping occurred?"

"What am I? A suspect?' I said, nearly falling out of my chair.

"We just need the most complete picture of the family we can get—"

I glared at him. "So, you accuse me of kidnapping my own sister and father? That is so rude."

He looked taken aback. I'm not sure he'd ever come across a subject that was quite as combative as I was being.

"Please, Miss Reaper-Jones—"

"Don't 'Miss Reaper-Jones' me! You can just go back to the 'ma'am' thing, as far as I'm concerned," I said, continuing to glare at him.

He sighed, and put his notebook down on his thigh.

"Look, I'm not accusing you of anything—"

"You better not be," I said menacingly.

He closed his eyes, obviously counting to ten under his breath.

"I just need you to tell me where and what you've

been doing during the past two days so that I can get a clearer picture of the time line. I promise I'm not accusing you, or your family, of any wrongdoing . . ." he added, holding up his hands in submission.

"Okay," I said after a minute. "I'll tell you what you want to know, then."

"Thank you," he said, picking up the notebook again. I was really exasperating him, and it was *so much* fun!

I told him about House and Yard—embellishing my job description only just the teensiest bit—and how I hadn't spent much quality *family time* at Sea Verge over the past few years because of school, and then the job. He took copious notes, looking up only when I told him about Jarvis, the bathroom, and the comatose granola boy.

I found that I was enjoying the way Mr. Detective hung on my every word, listening to me in a way no other man had ever deigned to. It was kinda sexy in a strange way. Who knew a good set of ears could be so enticing?

"So, your father's Executive Assistant came to escort you home?"

I nodded.

"Yeah, and now he's my Executive Assistant. Pretty crazy, huh?"

Detective Davenport gave me a sharp look.

"Excuse me, I'm sorry. Did you just say that he's *your* assistant now?"

I nodded again.

"Yep, the faun's mine, all mine."

Detective Davenport's brow furrowed, and I could tell he had just figured out that *yours truly* was the new head honcho in charge.

"Yep, I'm The Man."

He swallowed hard, and I noticed that he had begun to sweat, beads of perspiration sitting like pearls on his upper lip.

"You're . . . you're . . . *Death*?"

I gave him a cold smile, and for the first time I felt the power that went along with the title surging through my veins. It was an unbelievable rush, one that was hard to ignore, no matter how much I tried.

"I didn't know. I'm sorry . . ." He swallowed hard again, then licked his lips nervously. "Please, *forgive me.* Had I realized . . ." Davenport said, his voice high and squeaky inside his throat.

"Forget it," I said, waving a hand. "It's no biggie. You *were* being a putz before, but you're nicer now."

I realized with a start that the detective was shaking. Not just a little hand quiver, but a full-fledged body tremor.

"A putz?" he said through clenched teeth.

"Yeah, a putz. You know, a jerk, an ass, an . . . Hey, are you okay?" I said, realizing that he *wasn't.*

He tried to nod, but his body stiffened, belying the gesture.

"Detective?" I said again, kinda worried now.

He didn't answer, but as his eyes rolled back into his head, and he slid onto the floor, I did hear the faintest of *gasps.*

Uh-oh.

"you can't just go around scaring people to Death," Jarvis said angrily. "You have to learn to control yourself, Callie."

The moment Davenport fainted, I'd screamed for Jarvis, who'd burst through the study door like an avenging angel. It took him only a second to realize what'd happened, and start working on the prostrate detective, checking his pulse, etc.

"Thank God you haven't received all your powers from the Board yet, or this man would be deader than dead. That's all I have to say about the matter."

I nodded mutely as I watched Jarvis waft some smelling salts he'd magically produced from his pocket under Detective Davenport's nose.

How the hell am I supposed to know what I'm doing? I thought to myself. *It's not like there's a book on the subject.*

"Hey, you don't have to yell at me. It's not like anyone gave me an instruction manual—"

"Second desk drawer on the right," Jarvis said, pointing to my father's desk before returning to his ministrations.

Damn it.

"Oh," I said, getting up off the floor where I had been crouching beside the detective and going over to rummage through the desk. I found the book Jarvis was referring to almost immediately and opened it, reading the first words that my eyes fell upon.

"*Death, An Annotated Rule Book,*" I read aloud. I put the book down, giving Jarvis a withering glare. "Gee, thanks for telling me sooner, Jarvi."

Jarvis ignored my bad attitude in favor of his handsome patient's needs. Detective Davenport had started to stir, and Jarvis was helping him to sit up. I looked over and caught his golden eyes open, alert, and trained in my direction. I could instantly see the lingering edge of fear behind his gaze, but I also sensed a newfound respect.

I walked around the desk, coming to stand above him. I reached out a hand, and Davenport took it. With

Jarvis's help, we were able to hoist him back onto his feet, where he swayed unsteadily for a few moments before finally regaining his equilibrium.

Jarvis inclined his head in the detective's direction as he telepathically imparted information in my direction. I knew what the little goat was thinking, and as much as I hated to admit it, he was right. Under Jarvis's watchful gaze, I somehow felt compelled to apologize.

I looked down at my feet.

"I'msorryIalmostkilledyoubackthere."

The words came out in a jumbled flood, and I grimaced at how they felt on my tongue: slimy and gross. There was just something about the sound of my own stupidity that made me nauseous.

Davenport nodded, accepting my apology without question. He looked like he just wanted to get the hell out of my way as soon as possible without offending me in the process.

"I should probably go and speak to your mother and sister before I head back to the office," he stammered, picking up his notebook and pen off the floor and shoving them into his coat pocket.

"Yeah, that would probably be a good idea, I guess."

He gave me another nod, and then one for Jarvis, before hightailing it out of my father's study as fast as his muscular thighs could carry him.

"I think he was kinda attracted to me," I said as Jarvis and I watched the door slam loudly on the detective's retreating back. "At least a little in the end there. I think the whole Death thing kinda turned him on."

"If you're even the slightest bit serious . . ." Jarvis said, rolling his eyes heavenward.

"I may be dumb, but I'm not oblivious," I said, knowing full well that Mr. Handsome Detective would rather eat leeches than squire me on a date.

Suddenly, a flicker of happiness flared in Jarvis's eyes as he remembered something he was obviously going to relish telling me. Something I was *not* going to relish hearing.

"By the by," he said, his voice full of pleasure, "you wouldn't believe it, but I found the cutest little organic dim sum place in the East Village. Took me ten minutes—"

"I looked online, like, *forever*!" I blurted out, interrupting him.

Jarvis giggled.

"I know you did. That's why telling you about it gives me such complete and utter pleasure."

the lobby was cold.

Not in the sterile, hospital-like definition of the word, but in the "I need two sweaters, a scarf, and a pair of those little earmuff-thingies just to sit in here, period" way. Luckily, I had—at the insistence of Jarvis—changed into more "businesslike attire" (his words) for this meeting. A very well-cut dark blue Ann Taylor pantsuit. I didn't know where Jarvis had magicked it from, but I was glad he had. Otherwise, I'd be freezing.

I leaned back in the stylish steel and leather chair I was perched on—one of four that occupied the small vestibule Jarvis and I were waiting in near the bank of elevators that led to the Penthouse—and began to leaf through a dog-eared copy of *Elle* I'd found underneath a stack of *Wall Street Journal*s on the glass-topped coffee table in front of me.

Teeth chattering, I tried to focus on the article, but instead found my eyes drawn inextricably across the coffee table to where Jarvis sat twiddling his thumbs, an expectant look on his face.

I had immediately realized upon our arrival that Jarvis was not supposed to have come with me. The receptionist at the front desk had given him a very pointed look, almost a glare even, but he had stood his ground, refusing to be intimidated by the pretty sentry. I wasn't sure if he was doing this because he felt sorry for me, or if he just liked his job too much to let me screw it up for him. Either way, I had unwittingly enlisted the faun as my de-facto chaperone.

"Hey, Jarvi," I whispered across the table at him. He looked up, and I only barely caught the strained expression in his eyes before he hid any emotion behind his usual poised visage.

After a pregnant pause, he sighed heavily. "Yes . . . ?"

I looked around to make sure we weren't being overheard, then leaned forward in my chair.

"I have to pee."

The glare he gave me was so intense I kinda wished I hadn't been a smart-ass after all.

"Just kidding," I said quickly, hoping to escape his wrath. "Seriously, I was wondering who I was gonna be dealing with upstairs, and secondly, why the hell is it so bloody cold in this stupid building?"

Jarvis nodded, taking in my questions.

"When the office of Death was first created at the beginning of time, God gave its commission to one of the seraphim, but after the Christian Fall—"

"You mean Adam and Eve?" I said helpfully.

Jarvis shook his head.

"No, the Fall when Lucifer decided to wage war

against his God, lost, and was sent down to Hell. That Fall."

"Oh," I added unhelpfully.

"So, after *that Fall*, God decided it would be better to have an impartial creature running Death. So, instead of an angel or demon having dominion over this plane, he appointed an earthly being to the office. Someone impartial, who could govern Death without favoring one side over the other," Jarvis finished.

"Okay, but that still doesn't answer my question. Who's upstairs?"

Jarvis smiled.

"God's not an idiot. He knew that no matter how impartial a human, or other earthly being, could be, they could still be swayed. So, he created a Board to keep the office of Death in check. That is who must bequeath the power of the office on you so you can run the business properly."

"So, I'll just pop in, say hi, get bequeathed, and then I can go home."

Jarvis shook his head.

"It's nothing as easy as that. You have to prove your worth to the Board—"

"Excuse me," I interrupted. "I have to prove my *what* to the *who*?"

"There are three tests. Only the next in line for the job can pass them."

"You didn't say anything about any tests," I said, standing up. "I do *not* do tests. No way, josé! I am *so* out of here."

"You're lucky," Jarvis added, ignoring my protests. "There *used* to be twelve tasks, actually—"

"I don't care if it's half a task," I yelled over my shoulder as I stormed over to the exit. "It isn't happening!"

I grabbed the *Elle*—I wasn't gonna leave it behind to be mauled by every ignoramus who sat down—and started for the front door.

Suddenly, the elevator doors slid open and two large jackal-headed men in very expensive black suits stepped out. They turned their heads in unison, fixing their coffee-colored eyes in my direction. As if commanded by unseen forces, my feet stopped dead in their tracks, refusing to continue forward no matter how hard I willed them to.

"You are summoned," they said in tandem.

"Damn it," I said under my breath as my feet did a do-si-do and turned me back around. All I could do was follow the Jackal Brothers back to the elevator, still holding the magazine tightly to my chest.

As the elevator doors closed in front of me, the last thing I saw was Jarvis standing by his chair, fiercely clutching his hands together in something that strangely resembled prayer.

eight

The ride in the elevator was pretty uneventful. I spent the two plus minutes admiring the powerfully muscled backsides of the Jackal Brothers—now there were two guys who knew how to work a suit, even if they didn't have the kind of heads I usually saw on my favorite catwalkers.

I tried to make conversation, but they were having none of it. They kept their large jaws clamped shut no matter what tack I tried. To Jackal Brother Number One:

"So, you come here often?"

Silence.

To both of them:

"I really dig your muscles. Do you guys work out?"

Double silence.

Finally, the elevator chimed twice, and the doors opened, revealing a well-appointed foyer.

"The Penthouse," Jackal Brother Number One said, not even looking in my direction as he and his twin stepped out of the elevator and beckoned me forward.

For a moment, I was tempted not to follow them, just to piss them off, but one look from Jackal Brother Number Two convinced me that it was in my best interest to get out of the elevator—and I mean, like, *now*.

I crossed the threshold into the foyer, noting the elegance of my surroundings. There had obviously been an interior decorator at work here. The place was absolutely gorgeous—like something out of *Architectural Digest*. I mean, the room had, like, twenty-foot ceilings and a budget that probably exceeded my yearly salary at House and Yard by three hundred thousand dollars.

Whoever had done this room was a true Master. Dark cherry wood–paneled walls framed crème brûlée–colored marble floors, all of this offset by a gorgeous oxblood-and-rust antique Oriental carpet and two sumptuous burgundy velveteen couches. I could have lived in that foyer for the rest of my life and been happy.

Jackal Brother Number One gestured for me to follow them through the gorgeous room—which I did hesitantly because the Jackal Brothers were starting to kind of give me the creeps.

They led me toward a pair of heavy wooden double doors that were set into the far wall, stopping just in front of them. Jackal Brother Number One knocked three times on the right-hand door, then waited as the knock was returned in kind. Suddenly, there was a loud hissing sound—like when you let a balloon go and it whooshes all over the room—and the double doors creaked open, bathing the dark foyer in light.

I have to admit that I gasped. I didn't mean to, but the strangeness of going from that immaculate foyer to . . . what I saw next was, well, surreal.

"Welcome to Atlantis," Jackal Brother Number Two said, stepping out into the light.

When I was a little kid, I liked to read about faraway places. Usually, they were real places that you could go to if your parents had the time and inclination to take you there, but sometimes they were magical places, places that belonged to imagination alone. One of my favorite *magical* places was the submerged continent of Atlantis.

I had devoured every book I could find on the subject, lovingly tracing the artistically rendered seascapes and citied pavilions, engorging myself on fantasies of the awesome family holidays we could have had there if the stupid place hadn't "gotten lost."

Now, here it was in all its glory, better than anything I'd ever found in a book, realer than my imagination had ever managed.

"Jesus Christ," I whispered under my breath.

Jackal Brother Number Two turned in my direction. "Where?"

I rolled my eyes.

"Jeez, it was just a figure of speech," I muttered.

Obviously the Jackal Brothers were of the *literal* persuasion. Absolutely no sense of humor whatsoever.

I followed them down a rocky outcropping, glad that I was wearing "sensible shoes" with my "business attire," toward a white marble and mother-of-pearl open-air pagoda that had an unbelievable view of the ocean below us. I could feel the rush of the surf in my ears, my skin prickling at the touch of sea spray on my face. It was way warmer here. I slipped off my jacket, and my body instantly relaxed as the rays from the dazzling summer sun seeped into my skin.

We walked closer, and I saw that set deep inside the pagoda was a large marble banquet table. One man and two women sat behind it, waiting.

For *me*, it dawned on my brain slowly.

This is a hell of a lot more overwhelming than Jarvis even intimated.

We crossed the last group of rocks, and then we were there. The two Jackal Brothers bowed deeply to the assemblage.

"We have brought the one you requested."

The older man seated at the middle of the table bowed his head in return.

"Thank you, Brothers Anubis. You may go back to your own business."

The old man's accent was hard to place, but something inside of me voted for Scandinavian. He had a head of thick gray hair with streaks of black still threaded though it and a bushy beard to match.

The Jackal Brothers bowed again. Then before I could say, "Boo," they both vanished.

"Please, have a seat." The old man gestured to a wooden stool that had magically appeared behind me.

"Thank you," I said, sitting down. The seat was a little hard on the rear, but I ignored it for the sake of politeness.

I looked at the rest of the Board. The two women were both wearing dresses of draped fabric—an orange sari and an off-white toga—but that was where the similarities ended.

The one in the sari was a bit younger with dark hair that roped around her head like a frame for her handsome, aristocratic face. I would have said she was beautiful if I hadn't noticed the hint of cruelty lying just beneath her even features and honeyed skin. As my gaze came to rest on her face, she gave me a devilish smile and a quick wink.

Cheeky little bitch, I thought to myself before turning my attention to the other woman.

She was older than the girl in the sari, but she had a much more welcoming face. Her bone-colored toga hugged her voluptuous curves in a way I would've killed for, and her perfect white teeth beamed out at me like headlights. Her long blond hair hung thick and curling to her shoulder blades, and her skin was a milky white, maybe even alabaster; it was hard to tell which—mostly because her skin, hair, and even her teeth were reflecting the sunlight so intensely that it was like it was their job in life to blind anyone who came in contact with her.

Having internally summed up my first impressions of the group—the good and the bad—I decided to get the ball rolling, keeping things on my terms as long as I could, so they couldn't force me into taking any stupid and/or pointless tests. I was gonna take charge, lay my cards on the table, and tell them what *I* would and wouldn't do to get their stupid job.

"Let me just start off by saying that I am so *not* gonna be taking any written tests here. I took the stupid SATs twice, and that was more than enough suffering for one lifetime—" I began, but the woman in the sari snorted, stopping me midsentence.

"What?" I said, totally annoyed at being snorted at.

She shook her head, her eyes lively beneath the fringe of her cinnamon lashes. When she spoke, her voice was deep and mellifluous, a hint of the East belying her obviously Indian origin.

"Nothing," she said smoothly. But I could tell that wasn't what she *really* thought.

"No, seriously. That was, like, totally weird and kinda

rude," I said, feeling justified in my reaction. She *was* being rude, and I was *so* gonna call her on it.

"It is just that . . . for the daughter of such a great man, you speak like an idiot."

I gaped at her. *Did she just call me an* idiot*?*

"Excuse me?" I countered, my voice starting to get all high and whiny. I knew I was dangerously close to throwing the magazine I'd rescued from the lobby at her—sari or no sari.

"You heard what I said," she replied. I could tell she was enjoying my agitation profusely, and it pissed me off even more.

I rolled up the *Elle*, threatening to lob it at her if she so much as opened her mouth again.

"Ladies," the old man said, standing up and putting a restraining hand on the Indian girl's arm.

"She started it," I said, still holding the magazine above my head like a weapon. Before the old man could restrain her, the girl in the sari leaned forward, almost crawling over the table at me.

"I totally did not, you dumb white girl!"

"Bitch!"

She glared at me and spat her next curse at me.

"Dipwad!"

Somehow the world "dipwad" broke the animosity I felt toward her, and I giggled.

"Dipwad?" I said, checking to make sure I'd heard her right. "Where'd you get *that* one?"

She shrugged, but there was a sheepish smile lurking at the corners of her mouth.

"It seemed good at the time—"

The old man interrupted her before she could finish.

"Ladies, please, we haven't the time for trivialities.

There is much to discuss before Miss Reaper-Jones leaves us."

The girl nodded, and I felt like maybe she wasn't such a bitch after all. I decided she was probably just annoyed about having to sit there in the sun for so long, and had taken it out on me.

"It sounds as if you have already been informed of the tasks, Miss Reaper-Jones, so I will begin there," the old man continued. "I am Wodin of the North. Myself, and the rest of the Board, Persephone and Kali—"

Persephone inclined her head when her name was called, but the girl in the sari only raised an eyebrow.

"I'm Kali," she said importantly, as if I hadn't already figured it out for myself.

No duh, I mouthed back at her. She rolled her eyes in return.

It was strange, but I got the feeling Kali actually liked me, and this was only her twisted way of trying to make friends.

"As I was saying," Wodin of the North interjected, interrupting my thoughts. "The Board cannot grant you the powers of your father's office until you have completed the three tasks I will now set forth."

Before he could launch into an explanation of the dreaded tasks, I raised my hand. There was a pause as Wodin of the North was obviously confounded by my action.

"Yes, Miss Reaper-Jones," he said finally.

"Can't we just pretend I'm, like . . . you know, a substitute teacher, and you're gonna, like, give me my emergency teaching credentials 'cause it's, like, you know, an *emergency*?"

I knew there was a perfect analogy out there for my

situation, but somehow I didn't think the one I'd just pulled out of my ass was it—especially given the snickering it elicited from Kali.

"I don't think you understand the gravity of the office," Wodin said sternly. "Your father—"

"Is missing," I said. "I understand. Let's just get on with it."

Kali gave me another covert wink. Obviously, she appreciated my lack of subservience when it came to Wodin of the North.

"Very well," Wodin said, looking nonplussed. "The tasks are as follows . . ."

He nodded to Persephone, who opened her mouth and spoke for the first time.

"Your first task . . ." she began, but I immediately lost the thread of what she was saying because her voice was so incredibly beautiful.

The only way I can describe it is to say that her timbre must have been the very one that inspired Edgar Allan Poe to coin the word "tintinnabulation." Each syllable sounded like a thousand tiny bells ringing in beautiful synchronicity.

As I listened uncomprehendingly to her words, I felt so full of emotion that tears started to roll down my cheeks. Kali made a face and elbowed Persephone in the side. Persephone closed her mouth, giving Kali a questioning look.

"Knock it off, Seph; you're making her cry like the baby she is."

Persephone shrugged, and cleared her throat roughly. "Sorry about that," she said to me in a much more human tone. "Forgot I was using my Goddess voice."

"It's okay," I said, shaking my head. Then, without

thinking, I added under my breath, "Where's Jarvis with the Kleenex when you need him?"

There was a small popping sound, and suddenly Jarvis was standing there beside me, holding a Kleenex in his outstretched hand.

"You called for me?" he squeaked, confused.

Actually, he looked more than confused. He looked *shocked.*

"What in the name of all that's holy . . ." Wodin began, but let the sentence trail off into nothingness.

I'd obviously committed some sort of terrible Death faux pas by asking for a Kleenex. Maybe the underworld had a thing against name brands. Maybe they preferred I ask for a *tissue* instead . . .

"I promise I'll ask for a tissue next time," I said, taking Jarvis's proffered Kleenex and blowing my nose.

Kali stared at me, her eyes wide.

"How'd you do that?" she said.

"How'd I do what? Blow my nose?" I countered.

"Call your servant into this realm, dipwad?"

There she goes calling me dipwad again. Does the girl not learn?

"I told you to stop calling me names." I stood up and lobbed the *Elle* in her direction. She ducked, the magazine missing her head by a mile.

"You missed," she taunted me.

What she didn't know was that if I had *really* wanted to hit her, there'd be a big red welt on her forehead.

"Enough!" Wodin shouted. "I will not have any more fighting! Do you understand me?!"

We both nodded begrudgingly. I was totally happy to leave her alone just as long as she left *me* alone.

Wodin continued to glare at both of us.

"Like schoolchildren," he muttered under his breath. I let the comment slide, but I was so *not* above sending a shoe in Wodin's direction if he decided to get bitchy on me, too.

"Now," Wodin continued, "I will ask the same question Kali asked you a moment ago. How did you call your servant into this realm?"

"You're not mad about the Kleenex?" I said. Kali rolled her eyes, but didn't open her mouth.

"No, of course not," Wodin said patiently. "We would just like to know how you summoned your man there."

He pointed to Jarvis, who still looked too shocked to speak. I would have to remember this one for the future. It was nice to know that I could shock the little goat into silence when he really got annoying.

"I don't know," I replied. "I wanted a Kleenex, so I said that I wished Jarvis would bring me one."

"She's so full of it," Kali said. "No one just summons people into other realms like that."

"Well, I guess I do," I said, shrugging. Something about the way Kali said that no one else could do it made my chest puff a little.

"I have to concur with Kali," Persephone added in her non-Goddess voice. "The girl must have someone helping her."

"Excuse me, but I did *not* have anyone 'helping me,' thank you very much."

"She really didn't."

I looked over at Jarvis—who had finally found his tongue, thank God—and gave him what I thought was an encouraging smile. He cocked his head curiously at me—so I guess it might've been more of a grimace than a smile—before turning his attention back to the Board.

"May I have leave to address the esteemed Board?" Jarvis began.

Wodin nodded regally.

"I have known my mistress since she was but small—"

"What am I? Fat now?" I muttered at Jarvis under my breath. He took the opportunity to grind his hoof into my foot. I nearly cried out, but his warning glance shut me up instantly.

"And she has foresworn all magic until—"

But it was another voice that finished Jarvis's sentence.

"Until now."

nine

The look on Kali's face was priceless—I wish I'd had a camera to catch it. She turned red, then pink, then white, then chartreuse—all in the space of about twenty seconds. She had the strangled look of a woman who had just seen an exceptionally handsome ex-lover that she still hadn't one hundred percent gotten over yet.

Oh boy, this is gonna be a good one, I thought, mentally rubbing my hands together with glee.

"Daniel?!?"

Persephone's Goddess voice cut like a knife through the air. Immediately I started to get furious, anger coursing through me like a river. She had stood up beside Kali, and her beautiful patrician features were clouded by rage.

"How dare you come here!" she said.

With these furious words, I clenched my fists and turned around, ready to beat the crap out of the bastard standing behind me, who had somehow royally pissed *me* off without me even knowing who he was.

But the strange thing was that I *did* know the guy. I didn't know why I was so angry with him—probably had something to do with channeling Persephone's Goddess voice, I reasoned to myself—but I definitely knew him.

"The Devil's protégé?" I said before drawing back my fist and slamming it into his nose. He didn't drop like the ton of bricks I'd expected. Instead he calmly put a hand to his nose, felt for any blood, then cracked the offending appendage back into place with his bare hand.

"Nice seeing you again, too," he said as he reached out, took hold of the same hand that had broken his nose, and gave it a lingering kiss.

He looked exactly like I remembered him from my father's study: a yummy, yummy studboy. Trying not to let the curve of his sexy lips drive me to distraction, I looked over at Jarvis, who shrugged.

"I'm charmed," I said sarcastically, keeping my libido in check but *wishing* my self-control would take a flying leap off the piece of rock we were standing on.

"Daniel, you bastard," Kali said. I turned to see her planted behind the mother-of-pearl conference table, looking like she wanted to leap over it and give Daniel a piece of her mind.

With her bare hands.

Daniel took that opportunity to give her a wink, which only seemed to further infuriate her. Persephone opened her mouth to speak again, but Daniel put a finger to his lips. Looked in my direction.

Damn, he is hot, I thought wantonly.

"Seph, please, you're gonna make the poor girl break a nail," he said firmly.

I looked down at my nails. *Damn it, he's right. One*

is already starting to look kinda wonky, all bent back and cracked.

"No nail breaking," I said warningly to Persephone. "Use the indoor voice, or else."

She had the good sense to look slightly ashamed at using me like a human battering ram to beat up the Devil's protégé.

"To what do we owe the pleasure of your company, Daniel?" Wodin said crossly. Only he and Jarvis seemed to be immune to Daniel's charm.

Of course, I thought, realizing what was going on. *The guy has some kind of weird power over women. Myself included. Probably Siren blood, like Clio.*

Which totally explained the sexual craziness I had experienced before. I hadn't been just a miserable horndog; I'd been charmed by magic. And by the looks of it, so had Kali and Persephone.

At least I was in good company.

"I have come here in protest," Daniel said. "The Board knows that by all rights I should be the next Death. And here you are, giving some mortal wannabe a chance at my job?"

"Mortal wannabe? *Your* job? What the hell does that mean?"

Daniel turned on me.

"The whole underworld knows you've been estranged from your family for years, that you spend your days in the pathetic pursuit of ingratiating yourself into the mortal world. That, in fact, your greatest heart's desire is to be *mortal* yourself." He said the last sentence with a derisive snort. "What kind of recommendation is that for the job?"

"What's wrong with being a mortal?" I parried. "I

mean, if you're gonna be Death, Mr. Smarty Pants, don't you have to have an interest in the mortal world? Since you're the one who's kind of in charge of all those silly *mortals* after they die?"

"Couldn't have said it better myself, sister," Kali said from behind the table.

Wodin gave Daniel a shrug.

"The girl does seem to have a point. And she is a blood member of—"

"I don't care," Daniel said. "It's *my* job, and I want it! The Devil promised it to me!"

"Look," I said to the Board, ignoring him. "I don't know if I'm the best person in the world for this job, but I do know that I owe it to my father and my family to give it a try. Please, just tell me what you want me to do, and I'll do it."

Jarvis shot me a surprised smile.

"Please?" I added. I wasn't above kissing a little ass. I did it every day at House and Yard, for God's sake.

"I'm just giving her the frickin' parchment, Wodin," Kali said, reaching into her sari and pulling out what looked like a faded piece of leather, but upon closer inspection turned out to be papyrus. I nodded to Jarvis, who reached out to take it from Kali.

"No!" Daniel said, going for the parchment himself.

Lucky for me, Jarvis was not only my father's Executive Assistant, but his bodyguard as well. My little goat-at-arms gave Daniel's shin a fierce kick with one of his hooves. I heard a loud cracking sound, saw Daniel's teeth clench, and knew from experience how unpleasant the pain he was gonna be in felt.

"Ow!" Daniel squealed, grabbing his shin and starting to hop around the front of the table like an idiot.

The two women behind the table each wore a satisfied smile, and I guessed Jarvis had just eternally endeared himself to them.

"God, can you be more of a baby?" Kali said to Daniel mischievously, before giving me a quick thumbs-up gesture.

Daniel glared at me, his face red with rage. I tried to stay out of his way while Jarvis rolled up the parchment and put it neatly into his front coat pocket.

"You're toast—" Daniel said as he hobbled in my direction.

"Let's blow this joint, Jarvi," I said, grabbing my protector's arm. Daniel had a mean look in his eye, and I didn't want to be on the receiving end of whatever he was thinking of doing in retaliation.

"As you wish," Jarvis said rakishly, snapping his fingers and transporting us away.

jarvis looked a little perturbed to be sitting in a Starbucks in the middle of downtown Peoria. I had suggested Peoria for two reasons. One, because I'd never been there before, and two, because I figured it was one of the last places in the world anyone would think to look for us.

"But a Starbucks . . . ?" Jarvis whined. "Could we not just find a pleasant little café that serves fair trade coffee and loose leaf tea? Maybe an organic scone or two for good measure?"

I rolled my eyes.

"Precisely why we're here," I said, taking an exploratory sip of my nonfat double latte with no foam. "The place you just described is exactly where they'd *think* we would go."

"Rrrrreally . . . ?" Jarvis said, rolling his *r*'s with this sarcastic little lilt that I found extremely annoying. "You think so, do you?"

"I know so," I said, pulling the lid off my cup to add three packets of sugar to the brew.

The corner we were in was small with only two other tables in the quasinear vicinity and a large plate-glass window behind us. Jarvis had chosen it precisely for this reason: We would be able to see everyone who came in or out of the place, and no one could sneak up on us from the back.

After I had finished incorporating the sugar into my coffee mixture, I leaned forward in my seat, gently resting my elbows on the slightly sticky surface of our two-seater table. I was ready to start figuring this crazy mess out.

"So, hit me. What do we have to do to wrap this whole Death thing up?"

Jarvis pulled the parchment out of his jacket.

"I'm not putting this on a sticky tabletop," he said, pointing to a stack of napkins someone had left on the table nearest to ours. Begrudgingly, I grabbed them and mopped up the table as best I could.

"There. All happy now?"

Jarvis nodded, then pulled a handkerchief from another pocket and draped it over the table.

"Why'd you make me clean it, if you were only gonna do that?" I glared.

"Because it made me happy, and that is *always* reason enough."

I sighed as I watched Jarvis spread the parchment out on the handkerchief. No matter what we went through, Jarvis and I were always going to have a testy relationship, I decided.

"What's it say?" I said, craning my neck to get a better look. Trying to read it upside down, all I could make out was the word "pup" before Jarvis suddenly tsked to himself and quickly rolled the parchment back up.

"Why'd you do that?" I demanded.

Jarvis motioned to the left with his eyes.

Oh my God, we've been found, I thought to myself as I looked in the direction he'd just indicated.

"Don't look *now,*" he started to say through clenched teeth, but he was way too late. I had already turned my head.

I realized that at some point in our conversation the table farthest to our left had become occupied. Jarvis had noticed, but I guess I was just too new to the whole cloak-and-dagger thing and had missed it.

Damn it, I thought to myself, *one more thing for Jarvis to feel superior about.*

"Sorry," I offered to Jarvis, who didn't seem in the least bit excited about accepting my apology. Instead, he kept the sour expression on his face, while I took the opportunity I'd bungled into to appraise our enemy.

A harried-looking woman with frizzy brown hair and a cell phone glued to her ear was busy overstirring her Americano while a small child sat in the chair across from her. The woman was completely engrossed in her phone conversation, but the kid was openly staring at Jarvis and me with wide, curious eyes.

When the kid saw that I had caught him in the act, he didn't look away with the practiced nonchalance of adulthood, but instead stared at us even harder. He was probably no more than seven, but there was a stark intelligence behind his pretty blue eyes.

I did the only thing I could think to do in the situation.

I waved.

"Oh, Lord, I told you *not* to look!" Jarvis hissed. "And now you're *waving*? Cavorting with the enemy? What would your father say?!"

I rolled my eyes.

"The kid's not a spy, Jarvi. I just don't think he's ever seen a man with *hooves* before."

Jarvis quickly shoved his hooves under his chair, but it was too late. The kid was already entranced. He ignored the chocolate milk box in front of him in favor of something more entertaining . . . us.

"I told you we shouldn't have come here," Jarvis said miserably.

"Well, if you'd put some *shoes* on, maybe no one would be staring at you," I spat back.

We'd made a quick stop off at Sea Verge to gather some supplies, and get Jarvis a pair of pants, but he'd drawn the line at shoes. He said human beings were so oblivious that if the hem of his pants were long enough, no one would even notice his hooves.

I, on the other hand, had done a full outfit change, borrowing a pair of black, white, and gray camouflage pants and the cutest little white tank from Clio that had BE MY BITCH emblazoned across the front of it. I'd also traded the sensible shoes for a pair of black Converse All Stars.

Jarvis had *almost* been right about the shoes. It was just too bad we had to run into a minor. I decided kids were just like that: smarter than the rest of us oblivious adults. Here we sat in the hustle and bustle of a popular Midwest Starbucks, and no adult had even paid the least bit of attention to Jarvis and me. Yet, within the space of about two seconds, we'd been completely *made* by a seven-year-old.

"I think we should leave now," Jarvis said tensely.

"What if he sounds the alarm?" I replied.

Jarvis looked pale.

"Oh my God, you're right." He looked around the room, quickly trying to detail our options.

"Stop that," I said. "I was totally kidding. That little guy's not gonna say a word. He's not stupid. He knows no one would believe him anyway."

Jarvis took a moment to digest what I'd said, then nodded. He scowled at the kid—who was no dummy—and the boy quickly turned back to his superexciting box of chocolate milk. Satisfied, Jarvis turned back to me.

"I suppose you're right. Besides, I know what your first task is."

I sat up straighter in my chair.

"You do?"

He smiled weakly.

"You have to go to Hades and get one of Cerberus's pups."

Silence.

Jarvis just stared at me like I was supposed to know what the hell he was talking about. I was at a total loss. I mean, I'm a fashionista, for God's sake. Ask me about Hermès and I could tell you a thing or two, but Hades? I knew it was Greek for *Hell*, but otherwise, I had absolutely no idea.

"Okay, I know what Hades is, but what the heck's a Cerberus?" I asked.

Jarvis rolled his eyes. I could tell by the look on his face that he thought I was an idiot. Well, like I said before, there were some things I knew well—like what designer's bags were more popular with the celebrity set: Prada or Kate Spade. Prada, *like, no duh*—and then there were things I was completely oblivious to—like what the hell a *Cerberus* was.

"You know who Cerberus is!" Jarvis said testily. "You're not brain-dead . . . *are you*?" This last bit was said hopefully.

"Oh, *it's* a *who*. That's helpful, Jarvi." I glared. "Please, just tell me who this Cerberus character is before I *die* of curiosity."

Jarvis sighed heavily, then shook his head.

"Are you really your father's daughter, or just some changeling child someone stuck in the family bassinet?"

From Jarvis's tone, I could tell he was only *half* joking, which made me snort.

"Was that a joke at my expense, Jarvi? I think I'm rubbing off on you."

"If only I *were* joking," Jarvis said wistfully. "You seriously haven't a clue who Cerberus is . . . ?"

I shook my head.

"All right, then," he said, clearing his throat. "Well, Cerberus is the three-headed dog who stands guard at the gates of Hell. Originally, there were—"

I could tell he was gearing up for a hard-core "ways of the underworld" lesson, so I decided to nip it in the bud by interrupting him.

"And I have to get one of whateveritis's puppies?" I said. *"Why?"*

"Because *that* is what the parchment says," Jarvis shot back. He was getting annoyed with me, with my bad attitude, my whining. "And if you want to help your family and keep the balance between Heaven and Hell equal for all mankind's sake, then you will just have to . . . *endure*."

"Look, I don't mean to be a total bitch, but I don't

understand why all of this has to be so *hard*," I said. "Why can't I just sign a piece of paper or something, and voilà! I'm Death?"

Jarvis let out a long sigh, then wouldn't meet my gaze as he spoke, the words soft and whispery so that at first I wasn't sure he was speaking to me.

"I don't know, Mistress Calliope."

For a moment, I thought I detected a note of pity in his tone, but it was gone before I could get a handle on it. Well, the one thing I did not want from Jarvis was pity. I would accept annoyance, hatred even, but I was not gonna let him feel sorry for me. I was *not* Paris Hilton, damn it. I could take a little heat, a little purgatorial jail time. I wasn't some wilting flower who fainted at the first sign of trouble.

Slowly, it dawned on me that against my better judgment I was going to see this thing through. And if that *were* the case, then there would be no more whining—well, at least not *much* whining—because I was going to have to take Jarvis at his word. I was going to have to suck it up.

I was going to have to—Lord, help me—*endure*.

ten

Hell is hot.

That was the first thing I discovered when I got there. The second thing I discovered was that Hell was bound and determined to turn me into lunchmeat.

We had left the temperate environment of the Starbucks through a wormhole Jarvis opened up in the one-stall bathroom. We'd had to wait for at least twenty minutes for it to be empty, but once we were inside, Jarvis was a quick hand with the wormhole summoning.

Jarvis worked it so we didn't come out in Hell proper, but on the outskirts, near the River Styx. It turned out this wasn't far from where Cerberus spent most of the time, guarding the North Gates of Hell. As we took a well-worn path that ran in tandem with the river, Jarvis explained Hell's inner workings.

Jarvis wasn't a bad teacher at all. In fact, he seemed to really enjoy the topic of Hell, so it was only *kinda* mind-numbing to listen to him. His voice rose and fell with such metered rhythm that after a while the tension was sort of lulled out of my being, and I began to enjoy myself for the first time since the whole crazy hero quest had begun.

What I gathered from Jarvis's minilecture was that Hell had been set up as a collection point for evil souls when they departed from Earth—or in plain English, it's the place where the bad guys go when they die. Depending upon what part of the world you came from, and what your belief system was while you were alive, you were sent to whatever part of Hell had been especially created for you and your kind.

For example, let's say you were a fundamentalist Evangelical pastor who had preached all about the sanctity of marriage, but in your own life you'd been screwing as many coked-out man-whores as you could get your mitts on.

When you died, you were judged by Death and (rightly) sent to Hell for your hypocrisy. But you weren't just let out into the bullpen with all the other sinners; instead, you were sent to your special "Lake of Fire," where you, and the other Evangelical Christian sinners, would spend your days of punishment sewing sequins on all the gaffs for the Devil's favorite cabaret, The Gay Minority Demons' Drag Show. (And for the uninformed, a gaff is an undergarment used to conceal a drag queen's private parts. I didn't know that, but Jarvis did.) Some other tasks you might have the opportunity to enjoy: cleaning three football fields' worth of pagan statuary with your tongue; learning the lyrics and melodies to every Barbra Streisand, Britney Spears, ABBA, and Judy Garland tune ever sang, then performing said songs for the demon in charge of your sector of Hell; and reading all the Harry Potter books out loud to a roomful of deaf-mutes.

After you were sufficiently punished—and hopefully learned your lesson—you were then recycled back into the soul pool for reassignment. If you were a really stubborn case who wouldn't learn from your mistakes, more often than not you ended up being reborn as a fly. Don't ask me why, but there was something about shit and flies that appealed to the guys in charge of Hell tremendously—or at least that was what Jarvis said.

After a few reincarnations as a fly, most souls got the idea.

The most interesting thing I learned about Hell from Jarvis was that as humanity changed, so did the Afterlife. Human beings were forever denouncing their religions, deciding that this God, or that Goddess, was out of favor, and anyone who believed in them would be killed, or castrated. That didn't mean those Gods and Goddesses ceased to exist when their religions faded. Quite the contrary, in fact. Rather, they became part of the larger framework of the Afterlife, working to maintain the steady flow of souls in and out of Heaven and Hell. Some of them worked for Death directly, like the Anubis Brothers; others took on a more managerial position in the company, like Wodin and the two Goddesses I'd encountered in Atlantis.

Following the curve of the river, Jarvis listed off a waterfall of facts about Hell like he was some kind of paid tour guide, and I took my first real look at the place.

Only three weeks before, I'd been in Los Angeles for the weekend visiting a friend from college. Since it was my first trip to the city, we'd done the usual tourist stuff—Venice Beach, the Third Street Promenade, The Grove, Rodeo Drive, Kitson. (Okay, you *might* be sensing a pattern of conspicuous consumption here. I *was* in

L.A.—the West Coast shopping Mecca of the nation—and I *was* allowed to window-shop, wasn't I?)

When my brain was stuffed from too much window-shopping, my friend had suggested we go to a local gallery she was doing a piece on for *LA Weekly*, and check out the Mark Ryden exhibit they were hosting.

Now, I've always been a fan of the deer-eyed little girls that people his work, but the stuff we saw at the gallery was even creepier than usual. There was kind of a "camping with the folks circa 1950s Americana" quality crossed with an "empty forest, bears are gonna eat you" thing. Even the frames that held the artwork had been created with the same theme in mind. I felt strangely unsettled as I walked among the paintings, my skin crawling with the bugs of unease.

It was this very same feeling that settled around me as I walked the path of the River Styx through the Valley of Death. The forest grew thick around us—full of oak, birch, and tall pine—crowding almost right up to the banks of the river in some places. There didn't seem to be anyone else on our path, but every so often I could hear the crunch of someone—or something—in the shadowy underbrush.

The thin stretch of valley we walked through seemed like the only treeless space of land for miles around. Damn, the forest really had a way of making me feel small, like I was just an inconspicuous little ant in the grand scheme of things.

I didn't like that feeling at all.

"So, exactly how big a dog are we talking about here, Jarvi?" I asked after the main part of his travelogue had finally petered out.

Since Jarvis was so much smaller than me—did I

say I was five-six in socks and maybe still growing?—he almost had to jog to keep up. He was in such good shape, though, that he didn't even break a sweat. It was totally annoying. I mean, I really tried to make myself go to the gym. I yelled, threatened, cajoled . . . even bribed myself to hit the treadmill, but as I mentioned before, by the time I got home from Hy Hell every day, I was just too damned emotionally exhausted to do anything but potato out in front of the television.

When I first got to New York, I tried to fit in with my "burn it at both ends" coworkers, but the lifestyle is extremely punishing, and since I'm such a wuss, I decided early on that I needed to keep to a quasinormal schedule if I was going to survive my first job.

I knew lots of other "office girls" who sucked it up, went out every night, partied like it was 1999—and spent every morning in the bathroom throwing up all the "fun" they were having. I admired their tenacity, but found that it was a way of life that just didn't suit me.

". . . gargantuan."

Apparently the whole time I'd been fixating on Jarvis's musculature, he'd been answering my question.

I really should learn to pay more attention to people when they're talking to me, I thought absentmindedly.

"I'm sorry. Can you say that again?"

Jarvis gave me a nasty look.

"I said that you are not dealing with some canine mongrel. This is a demon that we are referring to. A very large—dare I say 'gargantuan'—demon with *three* heads and *three* sets of very large, very sharp teeth."

"How am I supposed to steal one of something like that's pups?" I wailed miserably.

"Finally, the girl shows a smidgen of interest in her

present situation," Jarvis said under his breath. "If you would like to inquire as to what my advice would be, then I would more than happily tell it to you."

I didn't like what Jarvis was saying at all. Somehow, I knew in my gut that asking Jarvis for his advice was tantamount to telling him he was the new boss of me. I realized that I didn't have a choice. I was going to have to give Jarvis the satisfaction he was fishing for.

"Okay, you win. Tell me, O great sage on high, what do you recommend I do to soothe the savage beast and steal one of its pups?"

Jarvis was silent for a moment—probably internally rejoicing in the conquest of my will—then he spoke, his words measured.

"Take it for a walk."

"Take it for a walk?" I repeated, incredulous. It was so hot, sweat was already starting to soak through the cute tank Clio had loaned me, and my underwear was sticking to my butt like a second skin. How the hell was I supposed to convince a demon dog to go for a walk in this sauna?

And with this *sound* advice bouncing around in my head, I headed inexorably toward my "walking" date with the three-headed guardian of Hell.

As we went on, I realized that even though I didn't know it at the time, I had been in preparation for this task for the last six months. Now, you say, how could I have possibly prepared myself for a walk with Cerberus, the three-headed guardian of Hell, without even knowing it?

Well, I had a secret weapon. As it happens, I am an acolyte of the *Dog Whisperer* show on the National Geographic channel. And if you've never heard of Cesar Millan, then you are seriously uninformed. He's a genius with dogs, *and* with the people who own them. Let's just say he can soothe even the most savage pet owner . . . I mean, *beast.* It's, like, total psychological entertainment. It's so great . . . *I even watch the repeats.*

Now I was going to put Cesar's theories to a big test.

On first glimpse, I noted that Cerberus had two cute heads (I use the word "cute" relatively) and one really nasty, Snarly one. The two cute ones spent their time cleaning and licking the monster's black coat and nether regions while the nasty, Snarly one kept watch with its one large yellow eye—kinda like a big, unblinking lamp stuck in the top of a lighthouse.

I had a clear view of my prey from where Jarvis and I sat crouching behind a big, green bush. Cerberus stood guard a few hundred yards away, blocking the entrance to the towering stone gates that led to the North entrance of Hell.

Under the Snarly one's watchful gaze, a few of the recently departed trooped down the winding dirt path that led to Hell and disappeared through the gates. It was only a trickle at the moment, so I figured there hadn't been any major earthquakes or tsunamis in the last few hours. (I found out later that the North Gate was where all the Pagans, Satanists, and Atheists entered Hell, so that was why there wasn't a stampede.)

I wasn't sure if I should consider Cerberus as one dog or as a *pack.* I opted for *pack,* since there was more than one slavering mouth that could bite my head off.

I watched my pack, looking for signs of "calm submission"—I didn't think ball licking counted, and Snarly head was anything but calm, the way he twisted his head all around looking for something to snack on.

"Where are the puppies?" I said under my breath at

Jarvis. "I'm pretty sure those are dog balls between its legs, so how does it have kids?"

Jarvis gritted his teeth, and I swear I could almost see him counting to ten in his head before answering.

"The male of its species watches the young, while the female hunts for food."

Jarvis seemed to know an awful lot about the big, ugly dog. I guess I was lucky that Jarvis was a font of useless—unless you're out to take a giant three-headed hellhound for a walk—information.

"Nice," I said, wiping away the sweat that had accumulated above my lip. "When's Momma coming home?"

Jarvis shrugged.

"What good *are* you?" I whined, my eyes drawn back to the massive dog in the near distance. It was still sitting back on its haunches, its tail rhythmically thumping against the bottom of the gate.

"All right, here goes nothing," I said, standing up from my crouch and starting forward toward my three-headed task.

"No, wait!" Jarvis grabbed my arm and yanked me back down behind the bush.

"What?!" He'd pulled me back with such force I had ended up on my butt, and now the seat of my pants was dirt smeared. "Look what you did to my pants," I wailed. "It looks like I had an accident or something!"

Jarvis ignored my complaints.

"You cannot just go out there without a plan."

"I have a plan," I replied, rolling my eyes. "I'm not an idiot."

Total silence.

"I'm not! Whatever . . ."

I stood back up, wiped my backside to get some of the dirt off, and glared at Jarvis. "I have powers, don't I?"

Jarvis nodded.

"If I want something, all I have to do is ask and the ether will supply, right?"

Jarvis nodded again.

"Good. See, I did have a plan," I said smugly. "Do I have to ask out loud?"

Before Jarvis could answer, there was a quick *snapping* sound, and suddenly I was lying underneath the coil of a humongous dog harness and leash. Jarvis snickered at me as I tried to extract myself from the bright red halter.

"I guess that answers that," I answered myself, getting to my feet.

Jarvis wiggled an eyebrow at me, his eyes alight with laughter.

"And how do you plan on getting *this* harness on *that* dog?" he said, pointing at Cerberus, who was vigorously double-licking his crotch.

Crap, I hadn't thought of that.

"Just watch and see, smarty pants," I replied haughtily, grabbing the top of the halter and dragging it behind me as I left the safety of the bush and trudged toward my prey.

Am I insane? I have no plan, I thought, panicking.

"I guess I'll just wing it," I said to myself with a cheerfulness I did not possess. I hoped Jarvis hadn't heard me muttering to myself. No need for the smug-head to know about my little dilemma.

It took me only a few seconds to cross the divide between the bush and Cerberus.

I'm not doing too badly, I thought to myself. *I'm not even really all that scared . . . well, not really.*

Suddenly, I heard a *crunch* . . . and then time slowed down. I mean, like, *way* down.

In slow motion, I could feel the sharp edge of the rock I'd accidentally stepped on trying to dig through the stiff rubber of my Converse All Stars, while a drop of sweat took what seemed like forever to bead up at the back of my neck and then follow a long, tortuous trail down my back and into my pants.

Cerberus turned its Snarly head, and the giant, jaundiced eye unblinkingly trained itself on my frozen form. The dog's eye narrowed, and I knew without anyone saying anything out loud that I was only one slo-mo minute from getting digested.

The other two heads stopped their obsessive licking and raised themselves in line with Snarly head. They didn't look nearly as mean as Snarly, but as I watched, something much worse began to register in their eyes: excitement. The big hellhound's tail started thumping more quickly against the gate.

Uh-oh, I thought to myself, *so much for* winging *it.*

I was sure Jarvis was totally freaking out back behind the bush. I guess he was right to think I was an idiot. It was obvious from the mess I'd gotten myself into that his unfavorable impression of me was *definitely* on the money.

Then, without warning, Snarly head swooped forward, teeth bared, giant eyeball trained in one direction . . . *mine.* Frozen in shock, I could do nothing but stare as Cerberus, the guardian of the North Gate to Hell, prepared to make me its lunch.

eleven

Snarly head stopped two inches from my face, its one jaundiced eyeball staring hard at me. I hadn't moved; I hadn't blinked . . . I hadn't even really breathed. I just stood there, minding my own business, trying to *feel* as nonchalant as I hoped I looked.

You see, the most important thing I'd learned from my *Dog Whisperer* training was that you had to ignore the animal until it was in a calm, submissive state—even if you *were* terrified it was going to make you its lunch. Obviously, Cesar Millan didn't deal with giant, three-headed, human meat–munching monsters, but I figured his teachings would still apply, no matter what size the dog. I just had to ignore the mutt until it decided that *I* was the master of the pack, not him—which I hoped was going to be sooner rather than later because my heart was totally beating in triple time, and I so did not want to have a heart attack while I was visiting Hell.

I'd heard the medical response time there was abysmal.

Anyway, while Snarly head stared, the other two heads quickly moved forward, their great heaving nostrils inhaling my scent like it was ambrosia. Up close, they looked like your average twin black Labs—if you didn't count the razor-sharp teeth. They each had a set of burning yellowish green eyes, black heart-shaped noses, and they both stank like wet dog. One of them even went for a crotch sniff (a typical dog move), but I lifted up my knee, blocking its path—and getting slobber all over myself in the process. I let the two dumb heads do their sniffing, but I was careful to always keep Snarly head in my peripheral vision. Getting Snarly head to submit to me was the key; the dumb heads would do whatever the smart one wanted. Of that I was (hopefully) pretty sure.

Just as I had suspected, after getting their fill of my scent, the two benign heads fell back, deferring to Snarly head. It was gonna be up to him to make the decision if I was friend or foe. I had my fingers crossed it was gonna be friend, but you just never knew with this kinda stuff—I was wholly prepared to make a quick run for it if things headed south in a hurry.

My fingers grasped hard at the rippled bit of canvas I had tucked inside my palm, making sure I still had a firm grip on the halter I'd called up from the ether. I didn't quite know how I was gonna get the thing on Cerberus, but at least I knew it was there and ready the minute I needed it.

Snarly head continued to stare at me, its one eye an unblinking beacon of bad attitude. It hadn't made up its mind to eat me, I thought, but it didn't seem to want me to give it a belly rub, either. I swallowed hard, willing myself the patience to get through this, my first—and quite possibly last if I couldn't get my crap together—task.

As the seconds slowly ticked away, I closed my eyes, saying a silent prayer for Cerberus to decide it was nap time and pass out right there and then. Realizing that this was just wishful thinking—not something to actually pray over—I opened my eyes again, but found that Snarly head had moved away from me. Its head was still trained in my direction, but its eye was staring off at a completely different angle. Suddenly, it made a weird snuffling sound in the back of its throat, which immediately drew my concern, and then its eye started spinning around in its socket like Linda Blair's head in *The Exorcist*—or at least like one of those little round roulette balls in Atlantic City.

"That's weird," I heard myself saying as I stood transfixed by the sight.

Before I could get another word out, the three-headed Guardian of Hell was suddenly barreling toward me—all three of its giant tongues lolling like bright puce slugs in its mouths as its monstrous bulk came nearer and nearer to my delicate, unprotected human form. I started to scream—the extremely large dry-cleaning bill I was gonna have for getting human-remain stains out of my borrowed togs flashing before my eyes—but instead of making roadkill out of my wussy ass, Cerberus galloped past me and made a sharp right, knocking me onto my butt in its wake.

I went down hard—I swear, I could feel a big purple bruise start forming on my left butt check—and as I just sat there, letting my brain reboot after its near pocketbook-destroying experience, all I could think was that I was lucky a bruise on my butt was *all* I got from my Cerberus experience.

From somewhere behind me, I heard a low growling sound. Cerberus must've found heartier prey—maybe a runaway soul that had decided he didn't want to enter the gates of Hell *after all.* Yet, as I listened for the telltale signs of someone being torn limb from limb, all I heard was a whole lot of nothing. Then, out of nowhere, I heard a man's voice.

"Good boy, get down now."

The voice was familiar, so familiar in fact that I knew exactly whom it belonged to. Something weird was going on, and I was going to have to pick myself up off the ground and find out what it was.

I stood, brushing the dirt off my butt, and turned around, hands on hips, ready to let my anger rip.

"Stop following me!" I screamed at the top of my lungs as I stared at Daniel, the Devil's protégé, frolicking in the dirt with Cerberus, the three-headed Guardian of the North Gate of Hell. They were doing this whole "rolling around together, mock fighting/boy-dog cavorting" thing that just made me want to spit.

This is so not *fair!* I thought miserably as I picked up the halter and started walking toward them.

"This is my task, you jerk!" I snarled. "So stop trying to show me up!"

Daniel looked up, and my heart lurched.

"I'm sorry," he drawled. "Is this *your* task? I didn't know. By all means, be my guest." He gestured for me to get down on my knees in the dirt with him and rub the big three-headed dog's stomach.

"You want to calm the savage beast? I recommend a belly rub every time."

I could just imagine what that dog smelled like, and

I was *not* gonna walk around—for God knows how long—smelling like wet fur and dog breath. *But Daniel, on the other hand . . . I'd give* that *savage beast a belly rub anytime he wanted.*

"Screw you!" I grumbled, hating myself for even *thinking* something like that. I dropped the halter on the ground, wanting to cry—*no, wanting to rut wildly in the dirt with the Devil's protégé!*

Ugh! I said to myself. *This has got to stop!*

I closed my eyes and shook my head aggressively, trying to clear the lust that seemed to be clouding my brain like a shroud. I was so *not* gonna let this guy trick me, seduce me, or entice me into having sex with him in any way, shape, or form.

Not gonna happen, I said to myself while I felt my body starting to get all hot and bothered just by his *stupid* "mere presence." This attraction to the Devil's protégé was getting a *tad* bit ridiculous.

Daniel raised an eyebrow while, at the same time, continuing to rub Cerberus's heavy belly with both his hands. The three-headed traitor—begging for Daniel's attention like the bitch it wasn't—was almost four times bigger than the Devil's protégé, but Daniel just treated the mutt like an overeager Labrador retriever. He obviously had the pack-leader thing down pat.

Who the hell was I kidding when I thought I could pull a Cesar Millan and get Cerberus under my sway? What a joke, I thought angrily as I watched the three dumb old dog heads drool happily all over my rival.

"You know damn well I'm supposed to be getting one of that three-headed mutt's pups! And you are consciously trying to stop me!" I almost yelled, hearing the shrillness in my voice, and feeling only slightly bad for being such a bitch about the whole thing.

Daniel stopped patting the dog and gave me his full attention.

"By all means, go get one of the puppies, then," he said, indicating with his head over to where four small cuddly-looking puppies were huddling together over by the right-hand side of the gate.

"I'll just keep Cerb in a state of doggie relaxation so you can steal from him," he said with only the merest hint of sarcasm. I glowered at him, then I started toward the adorable mound of puppyness, my heart in my mouth.

"Oh my God, they're sooooo cute!" I said as I got closer to the little guys. They really were cuter than the cutest thing I'd ever seen—I mean, cuter, even, than those cavorting puppy, kitten, bunny, and duckling calendars you find in earnest around Easter time.

"Wait!" I heard a frantic voice calling behind me. I turned back around to find Jarvis cantering right for me. Actually, he was half cantering, half lurching, his mouth set in a firm line. As he got closer, I saw that he didn't look well at all. His face was the color of the faux marble vanity in my bathroom—nicotine stain yellow with hints of moldy green veining. Truth be told, he actually looked worse than my bathroom vanity—more like a big, faun-shaped piece of Gorgonzola cheese that was trying desperately not to pass out.

"You can't trust him," Jarvis said as he caught up to me, giving Daniel a disdainful scowl. "Look what he did to me! He wanted to keep you from completing your task, so he jinxed me!"

"Are you okay?" I yelped, taking a step back from Jarvis and glaring at Daniel. "What did you do to him, you big bully?"

Daniel opened his mouth to answer me, but I stopped him before he could get a word out.

"No, on second thought, I don't want to know *what* you did. I just want you to undo it!" I growled. "And I mean *now*!"

Daniel stood up, leaving Cerberus on the ground all drunk with affection, and walked over to where Jarvis and I waited only a few feet away from the puppies.

"It was a festering curse if you were curious."

I didn't say a word, just pointed to Jarvis, my mouth set in a firm line. Without a word, Daniel sighed and mumbled a word under his breath, lifting the curse. Immediately, Jarvis was back to normal, glaring daggers at the Devil's protégé.

It was amazing, but if I hadn't just seen Jarvis looking like fermented cow's milk, I wouldn't have known he'd been spelled at all . . . and I had to admit Daniel's prowess with the whole magic thing was pretty sexy. My curiosity almost had me asking Daniel for an instant replay—just for fun—but Jarvis's scowl held my tongue.

"That was amazing," I said huskily.

Jarvis turned his glare in my direction, but I ignored him, instead focusing my attention on Daniel, who shrugged, very aware of the note of interest lingering in my voice.

"It's only magic, babe. Easy as pie. I bet you could cast that one yourself without batting an eyelash."

I giggled.

"It's like two adolescent cats in heat," Jarvis said under his breath, looking heavenward.

"No, not really," I replied, still ignoring Jarvis and his snide little comments. I was getting tired of his crass remarks about my behavior. It was obvious he thought his character was way beyond reproach—and that *mine* was at the *perfect* level to be mocked.

"My father was dead set against any of us using magic in the house, so my magical training was pretty limited—"

I figured this would drive Jarvis nutty, mentioning my father, and I was right—he instantly hissed at me to shut up. I knew I shouldn't be giving Daniel any ammunition against me, but it was weird . . . for the first time I found myself *wanting* to talk about what it was like to grow up as Death's Daughter. I couldn't help myself. I was suddenly desperate to talk to someone, anyone, to spill out my whole life story to whoever was willing to listen . . . especially this *very* engaging, *very* handsome stranger.

"Go on," Daniel said, watching me intently.

"Mistress Calliope, I must insist—"

"Be quiet, Jarvis," I said. "I don't care who he is. He asked me a question, and you can't make me not answer it."

Daniel gave Jarvis a smug look, but the faun didn't immediately respond with the pissed-off look my waywardness usually provoked. Instead, when I looked over at him, his face was a study in utter disappointment.

"As you wish, mistress."

He turned around, and started to walk back toward the outcrop of rocks we'd originally been hiding behind.

"Jarvis?" I called after him, but he didn't turn around or stop walking. He kept slowly putting distance between us, each footstep like a lead mallet beating on my heart, making me feel like a total jerkoid.

"He'll get over it," Daniel said, taking a step forward

and reaching for my hand. His lips were warm when they pressed themselves against the skin of my knuckles, and I couldn't help but forget Jarvis in the rush of "sexual healing" that overwhelmed me. I looked up into Daniel's eyes, letting those two chips of Antarctic ice suck me in. He leaned forward, and I could smell his pepperminty breath as his face inched forward, his lips moving closer and closer, the anticipation dragging on so long I was gonna scream if he didn't bloody kiss me already.

His mouth was warm when it touched mine, and after the first initial panic of bad breath worry, I relaxed into the kiss, letting his tongue find its way inside my mouth.

That was when I started to gag.

Instead of yummy man saliva, my mouth was suddenly filled with the nasty, peculiarly bitter flavor that I can *only* associate with earwax. I pushed Daniel away with both hands, trying desperately to clear my mouth of the horrible taste.

"That's disgusting," I spat, stepping away from him.

Speechless, Daniel blinked, and that was when I saw him for what he truly was: a creep. Somehow that kiss had broken whatever spell Daniel seemed to have over me. I could stand right next to him, staring into his eyes, and feel absolutely . . . nothing.

"Yes!" I said out loud, raising my fist in triumph. "You got nothing on me, buddy!" I stuck my tongue out at him, then turned and walked right over to the mound of squirming puppies. Daniel stared at me, his mouth open, but no sound escaping from his handsome maw.

"I'm getting a pup, and then I am *so* out of here."

I knelt down beside the pups, and looked them over.

There were four of them, and not a one had three heads. I decided to take the runt of the litter, who was about half the size of its larger siblings—or roughly the size of a suckling pig.

"C'mere, Runt," I said, scooping up the puppy in my arms and letting it lick my face happily. "Why's it only got one head?" I said, looking back at Daniel for an answer.

He hesitated, then finally spoke, his eyes uncertain when they looked into mine.

"They're all females."

"Cool," I replied. "Two bitches to drive Jarvis crazy."

I snapped my fingers, and suddenly the oversized Cerberus halter was gone, and in its place a small pink halter with silver rhinestones appeared in my hand. I put Runt down, slipping the halter over her tiny neck. She was so cute with her pink eyes, pink halter, and shiny black coat. I didn't think I could've come up with a more perfect dog for myself if I'd tried.

"I guess the whole magic thing *is* easy as pie, babe," I said, giving Daniel a wink.

I looked over to where Cerberus was still rolling around in the dirt, and shook my head.

"Who knew all you Hell boys were such pushovers?" I said, shrugging as I led Runt past Daniel—who still didn't seem to grasp that I was a free agent—and followed the path I had last seen Jarvis take.

"Wait a minute," Daniel said as I passed him. "Calliope Reaper-Jones, you will do what I say right now."

The look on his face was priceless, so full of egoistic arrogance. He was so totally convinced that I was gonna turn right back around and start kissing his toes that it was kinda sad.

"I don't think so, Mr. Devil's protégé," I answered over my shoulder, not even stopping to rub it in his face. "But thanks for the thought."

I couldn't believe how well that had gone. I'd gotten one of Cerberus's pups, kicked Daniel to the curb, and was well on my way to becoming the head honcho of Death, Inc. *Life is sweet.*

No sooner were those words a thought bubble above my head than I heard a low, menacing growl directly behind me.

"Crap," I said under my breath, not wanting to turn around but knowing I was going to have to.

"Good doggie," I said as I found myself staring right into Cerberus's giant, unblinking eye. Snarly head looked superpissed, and the two other heads were just . . . drooling. Probably fantasizing about how yummy my flesh was gonna taste when they were crunching it between their teeth.

I looked for Daniel, hoping he would call the monster doggie off, but he was gone. He'd obviously left in a snit to let me face my own fate.

"Jarvis!" I squeaked, hoping he was still close enough to come to my rescue, but I got no reply. I was gonna have to deal with the situation all by my lonely. Smiling stiffly at my pup's perturbed daddies, I swallowed hard and tried to regain my composure.

"Look, Mr. Cerberus, sir," I said as calmly as I could manage. "I really need to borrow your little girl, here, so I can save my father and sister from certain doom. I know this isn't your problem, and I'm not asking you to even understand, but trust me when I say that I'll be back with Runt as soon as I can."

The last words came in a rush, but I was pretty sure

I'd said my piece, and said it reasonably well. I waited, hoping that Cerberus understood enough English not to bite my one and only head off.

"Well, why didn't you just ask? Take whatever you need to help your father."

I nearly peed on myself when those words came out of old Snarly's mouth.

"Excuse me?" I said, not sure I was hearing and seeing what I thought I was hearing and seeing.

Snarly head sighed, then closed its eye in disdain.

"Look," it began, opening its eye again and fixing me with a hard stare. "The intelligent thing would have been to ask me first, rather than wasting all of our time with your pointless subterfuge."

"Oh," I stammered. *I guess it* is *always best to be honest about what you want.*

"Just bring Giselda back as soon as you've completed your business, and I will consider you to be in my favor," Snarly head continued.

"You mean . . . I'll owe you."

Snarly head smiled, and it was a nasty one.

"Precisely."

"And if I'd just asked in the first place, I wouldn't owe you?" I asked.

The big dog shrugged.

"Damn," I said under my breath. "Okay, two more things."

I looked down at Runt, who happily wagged her tail. "So . . . her name's Giselda and can she talk the way you do?"

"Not for a few more months," Snarly head replied. "Now does that answer all of your questions? Because I have a gate to guard, and it ain't gonna guard itself."

"Yes. Thank you, sir."

"And be careful. You have precious cargo with you," Snarly head said as he turned tail and sauntered back to his rightful place in front of the North Gate of Hell.

"Well, that was craziness," I said, shaking my head in wonder at Runt, who just looked up at me with those wise pink eyes. "Let's go find Jarvis and get out of here."

We started forward, Runt almost dragging me behind her, she was so excited to be out on her own for the first time.

"Okay, Giselda," I said. "You won't mind really if I just call you Runt—"

Without warning, something cool and firm encircled my left wrist, and I heard the sharp metallic click of that something being snapped into place. Next, I was twisted backward, so that Runt's lead was pulled taut around my legs, wrapping so tightly around my ankles that I fell forward, my face almost slamming into the hard-packed dirt.

Behind me, my poor little doggie companion gave one low growl, which was instantly silenced.

"If you hurt her—" I yelled, my mouth tasting clay and grit as a pair of strong arms wrapped viselike around me and pushed my face deep down into the dirt, shutting me up in the process.

I shuddered with fear, my heart beating wildly in my throat as I felt my attacker's hot breath on my neck. Then a calm, male voice sounded right into my ear:

"You're coming downtown with me, Miss Reaper-Jones."

twelve

"Let me go, you jerkoid!" I yelled as I was roughly hauled up onto my feet and shoved forward.

While I had still been pinned to the ground, my assailant had pulled my free hand behind my back and secured it alongside my already tethered one, making it impossible for me to pinch, punch, slap, or scratch my way out of the situation. Since my feet were still free (unlike my hands), I had to do what the bastard wanted: namely putting one foot in front of the other.

I totally felt like one of those poor declawed cats you sometimes saw sitting morosely in apartment windows forever imprisoned by their human masters for "their own safety."

Well, if they hadn't been declawed in the first place, I thought angrily, *they wouldn't need saving, now would they?*

Okay, I desperately wanted my claws back.

As we went along, my attacker kept one hand firmly on my back, while the other hand was mysteriously missing in action. I just hoped the missing hand was in possession of Runt's leash, or there would be some serious hell to pay when I got out of this mess.

"Come on, let me go! You're *hurting* me," I moaned miserably.

I hated to act all girly and whiny, but I figured it was worth a shot.

Sadly, my protestations got no response, so I twisted my body around, trying to get a better look at my captor and to see if Runt was still with us. I immediately saw the little puppy happily trotting beside me, no more than a foot or so away. Her coat was covered in a fine layer of dust and her tongue was hanging out of her mouth from exertion and heat, but other than that, she seemed to be fine. Her leash trailed behind her, dust eddying around it as it snaked through the dirt—which accounted for her having gotten so dirty in such a short amount of time. It was obvious she was following me of her own volition, which made my heart kind of leap in my chest with happiness.

"Good girl," I said under my breath, sending good vibes in her direction. She must have felt them because she looked up at me and wagged her tail.

Turning my head as far as it would go to the right, I was finally able to get a good look at my attacker.

"You . . . ?" I gasped.

I couldn't believe what I was seeing. My brain got all muddled as I tried to process why the detective from the Psychical Bureau of Investigations would be holding a gun to my back.

"But you're supposed to be one of the good guys!" I stammered.

"I *am* one of the good guys," he said tersely.

Whether he was a good guy or bad guy, it was kind

of impressive that he'd been able to track me down into Hell—even if he *had* cuffed me, thrown me down on the ground, and totally humiliated me in the process.

"Hey, wait a minute," I said as I felt the beginnings of a muscle cramp starting in my neck. Poor Runt must've thought I was trying out some weird yoga move, the way my head was turned at such an odd angle for so long.

"There's something different about you, other than the gun."

It took me a minute, but then it hit me with the velocity of a sucker punch to the nose. Detective Davenport was dressed exactly like a male supermodel. I noted the long gray trench coat worn over the well-tailored charcoal suit—a suit so different from the Men's Wearhouse joke he'd been wearing when I first met him that I couldn't believe the same guy had picked them both out.

His shoes were soft, buttery gray Italian leather, and they looked handmade. They must have cost him a small fortune. I had no idea the PBI paid their operatives so well. I decided that when the whole Death thing was over, maybe I would look into joining up.

"Are you, like, a supermodel in hiding or something?" I asked curiously. "Because those are some fine-looking threads you've got there, Detective."

Ignoring my fashion commentary, Davenport ushered me forward, continuing to guide me toward some destination that only he had the map to. He was definitely pissed about something—*probably me,* I thought—so I decided that asking him what designer he was wearing perhaps wasn't the smartest of ideas. There was a distinct possibility that he might even yell at me for being impertinent.

"Are you aware, Miss Reaper-Jones, that you are not

in possession of an alibi for the time of your father's kidnapping?" he said quietly, brandishing the gun at my back for emphasis.

My eyes widened as I realized what he was inferring. I was so annoyed that I stopped in my tracks and turned to glare at him. Gun or no gun, I was not gonna take this bullshit lying down.

"Are you trying to tell me that you actually think I kidnapped my father, my sister, and, like, twenty other people? I mean, *come on*, do I look like I could've come up with that kind of Machiavellian plan all by myself, buddy?" I said angrily. "I work for a home and garden supply company, for God's sake."

"No, but—"

"Thank you!" I interrupted, glad that he was finally starting to see things from my point of view.

"Now, just hold on a minute. Let me finish," he said testily as he took me by the arm and led me forward.

"What I was going to say is that, no, I don't think you planned this yourself. But I *do* think you planned this with someone else, someone who knew your father intimately. Someone who spent every day with him, who knew his schedule, his interests . . . his secrets, even."

"My mother?" I said. God, I hoped it wasn't my mother. The therapy bill on that one would be astronomical, and my insurance plan with House and Yard barely covered the basics . . . like checkups and Band-Aids.

The detective gave me a withering look.

"Sorry," I muttered under my breath as I tried to keep up with him. He was starting to walk faster, and since he had about a foot on me, his stride was just a wee bit longer than mine. Runt didn't seem to have any problems with our pace. In fact, she seemed quite happy to be clocking along at a steady jog.

"What I am trying to say, Miss Reaper-Jones, is that we are talking about someone close to your father, but not from the immediate family. Someone exactly like your father's Executive Assistant . . . Jarvis de Poupsy."

Ignoring the implications of what the detective had just said, I asked, "Uhm, excuse me, but did you just say Jarvis's last name was '*de Poupsy*'?"

"Yes, your father's Executive Assistant is named Jarvis de Poupsy. What of it?" the detective said without a note of irony.

"Nothing" I replied. If Davenport didn't get the hilarity factor of Jarvis's last name, well, then it was his loss.

As far as I was concerned, the whole thing—including Jarvis being a criminal mastermind—was totally absurd. Jarvis might've annoyed the crap out of me at times, but I was *not* gonna let some dumb detective—no matter how cute or well dressed he was—say anything bad about *my* Executive Assistant.

"You're crazy if you think Jarvis had anything to do with this," I said, but the look on the detective's face told me otherwise.

I decided to try a different tack.

"Seriously, Mr. Davenport—"

"It's *Detective*," he said quietly.

"Fine. Look, *Detective*, Jarvis worshipped the ground my father walked on. I mean, I think he even loves him, actually. I mean, not in a gay way—which would be totally okay in my book—but in a kind of worshipful, loving . . ."

I paused as I realized that this was not coming out right at all.

"Okay, let me start over—"

It took the detective yanking me back by the scruff of my tank top to make me realize we were standing in front of a great, big, gaping pit. I'd been concentrating so hard on what I was saying that I hadn't even noticed when we'd hit the end of the line.

I turned around, trying to gauge his intentions.

"Okay, Detective Davenport, I'll do whatever you want," I said, hoping my words had come out as sweetly as I had intended them to. I even tried to bat my eyelashes at him, but eyelash batting was never one of my strong suits. "Just explain to me what the hell this *thing* is."

I motioned to the giant pit in the ground.

"Just as I said before, Miss Reaper-Jones. You're going *downtown*."

I looked back at the gaping hole, my heart lurching when I saw that it had no bottom. I didn't know what this thing was, but I was determined not to get any closer to it until Davenport explained what the hell "downtown" meant.

"All right, but when you say the word 'downtown,'" I asked, "what does that *really* mean?"

The detective didn't *seem* to glean any pleasure from his next words, though I wouldn't have been surprised if he had.

"This is the temporary Hellhole that leads to a holding cell in Purgatory, where you will be banished until your trial."

I looked down at his hand, the one that was holding the gun pointed directly at my belly. I noticed for the first time that he had long, delicate pianist's fingers, and I imagined, under different circumstances, they could've made me feel real nice, but right now they just looked like the last thing I'd see before the beginning of the end of the rest of my life . . . *in Purgatory.*

From what I'd heard, no one escaped from Purgatory. And I mean *no one.*

"I'm sorry," he said, not looking me in the eye. And it almost seemed like he *was* kind of sorry to be the one who had to do this to me.

He reached out with his free hand, his fingers arcing toward my solar plexus, but before he could touch me, I stepped backward into the abyss. If I was gonna go *downtown*, then I was gonna go of my own volition, not his.

Somewhere in the distance, like it was coming from twenty thousand miles away, I heard Runt bark. As my eyes instinctively flew in her direction, I saw something that totally blew my mind: Not more than ten feet away from me, my Executive Assistant—my knight in shining armor, really—Jarvis de Poupsy, was coming to my rescue.

He was like a little locomotive the way he propelled himself forward, launching himself at the detective. Davenport didn't seem to realize what was happening until they were both sailing through the air toward the ragged mouth of the Hellhole, Jarvis's arms holding on to his prey's waist for all they were worth.

My right foot hit air, and then I felt the ground slide out from beneath my left foot. I started to fall backward, the cool hands of nothingness embracing me.

"Jarvis! No!" I screamed, the words burning my throat as I started my descent into the Hellhole. Since I was in free fall myself, there wasn't much I could do but watch as Jarvis and the detective cleared the lip of the Hellhole and fell straight down into the nothingness.

I felt a sharp tug on my ankle, and suddenly, I stopped

falling, my head slamming back into the side of the pit. While I hung upside down inside the Hellhole, my head aching and tender, I could feel its pull working on me, enticing my body into its vortex. I was terrified that no matter what happened next, I was destined for Purgatory. That whatever had stopped my fall was gonna realize its mistake and let me drop.

"Please don't let me go," I cried, tears starting to course down backward across my temples and into my hairline.

I heard a long, low growl, and then suddenly I found myself being dragged up and over the edge of the Hellhole to safety.

I lay there in the dirt for a long time after Runt let go of my ankle. There would probably be a nasty bruise where her teeth had gripped me, but she had taken care not to break any skin, so there was no blood, thank God. Blood and I were not on the best of terms. Usually when it was anywhere near me, I just kinda passed out.

I'm a total jerk, I thought to myself. I had been so rude and thoughtless when it came to Jarvis, and now he'd gone and saved my life and I couldn't even tell him I was sorry. If it'd been me, I'd probably have just left me to my fate after the way I'd treated him. Instead, he'd risked life and limb to make sure I was okay.

"I deserve to be a fly in my next life," I said to Runt. The little puppy looked up at me from where she'd been rolling happily in the dirt a few feet away and wagged her tail.

"I'm glad you agree."

I sat up and sighed, not even caring anymore if my clothes were a dirty mess or if my makeup was caked. I'd been a selfish idiot for too long, and I was getting really tired of my bad attitude. From this day forward, I pledged, I was gonna be nicer to everyone—especially Jarvis . . . *if* I ever saw him again, that was.

"Well, what do I do now?" I said to no one in particular.

Jarvis, the only person in the whole universe who could help me, was gone, along with the piece of parchment that held the particulars of my last two tasks. I was dirty, tired, extremely hungry, and I had no way of getting out of Hell and assuaging any of these needs because I couldn't open my own wormhole without help.

"This sucks," I said miserably. "I wish you could talk, Runt. Then you could tell me what to do for my next trick."

With these words, Runt's eyes lit up, and she started to wag her tail even more vigorously. She picked herself up out of the dirt and started to trot back the way we'd come.

"Where're you going?" I asked. She turned to look at me askance, as if urging me to follow her.

"You want me to follow you?" I asked, knowing that even if I *did* say it out loud, it was still an entirely rhetorical question. She picked up her pace as I started after her. Every so often she'd stop and sniff the ground; then, when she was satisfied by what she'd smelled, she'd continue on.

Finally, we came to a clump of bushes, and Runt stopped, her head erect, her right paw up in the air, pointing at the greenery.

"Is there something in there you want?" I asked. Runt gave me what I could only call an "are you really such a dope" look, then went back to staring at the bushes.

"Okay, but if there's something nasty in there that you're not telling me about, I am so not gonna be a happy camper," I said to her before I stuck my hands into the top of the foliage, my eyes firmly shut in protest.

The foliage immediately gave way under my touch, and then, after only a few moments of searching around, my fingers found what Runt had somehow known was there.

"You're a genius," I said to the puppy, who wagged her tail again playfully, proud of her amazing olfactory work. As I pulled Jarvis's monogrammed handkerchief out of its green hiding place, I noted that it was rolled up into a neat-looking little spyglass. Upon my touch, it instantly began to unroll, revealing the missing parchment inside.

"Thank you, Jarvis!" I almost yelled. "He must've seen the detective kidnap me and rolled the parchment up in the handkerchief for safekeeping before shoving it into the bushes," I said to Runt, who only cocked her head at me as if to let me know I was stating the obvious.

"Okay, let's take a look and see what exciting task the Board has for us next."

I sat down on the ground beside Runt and spread the parchment out on my lap. Runt moved closer to me, flopping down just within ear-scratching distance. I absently reached out, patting her silken head as I turned the parchment over and had my first look at the document. It took me only a minute of perusing to see why Jarvis hadn't let me near the stupid thing earlier.

"What the Hell?" I said out loud, my voice escalating to a nearly hysterical pitch. "I can't read this! This is in Greek!"

I felt the first stirrings of a very black depression descending on me. It reminded me of the time I'd gone to a Barney's sale without realizing I'd forgotten to bring my credit cards and then had to watch as all the stuff I'd painstakingly picked out was immediately put back out on the floor for someone else to buy.

"I hate me," I said, my voice cracking as I put my head down in my hands and began to cry.

thirteen

I don't know how long I sat in Hell sobbing my heart out, but when the tears finally did subside, my head felt like someone had put it in a vise and was slowly squeezing the life out of it. I didn't have a mirror, but I knew my eyes were probably rabbit pink, the whites hiding behind a web of very bloodshot capillaries.

Runt had stayed by my side the whole time I was incapacitated, her wet little nose pressed up against my neck, nuzzling me like a tiny four-legged mother. My own mother had never been very affectionate—at least not in the physical kind of way—so it was strange to have Runt comfort me with her own body like that. It made me wish my sisters and I'd had a dog while we were growing up.

Hell is a very strange place, I thought to myself as I wiped the last bit of crunchy, smeared mascara—it was so hot, the tears had turned to salt almost as soon as they had slid down my cheeks—from under my eyes and sighed loudly. I didn't really know what the next step was going to be, but I had decided one thing while I was crying: The minute I was out of Hell, I was going back to Sea Verge and enlisting Clio's help. She would probably be able to translate the parchment for me, and if I was lucky, she could also help me figure out who had kidnapped our father and sister so we could save them and spring Jarvis from Purgatory at the same time.

I hadn't really given much thought to the kidnapping until now because I'd been so intent on completing the tasks, but with Jarvis in custody, I was going to have to get on a stick and play detective. Otherwise, the jerk from the Psychical Bureau of Investigations was going to totally screw my whole life up.

Ugh, being in charge totally sucks. Can't I just be, like, the sidekick or something?

Oh well, I was just gonna have to put my thinking cap on and figure this mess out. I turned to Runt and gave her a nice scratch under the chin.

"Okay, Runt, now . . . what would Nancy Drew do?" I said to her cute little puppy face. She didn't answer, just cocked her head and licked my hand. Now, I know that Nancy Drew is a little juvenile, but I'd never really read any Sherlock Holmes or watched *CSI* or anything, so the teenage detective from my childhood was going to have to suffice.

The only thing I really remembered from my "under the covers with a flashlight" reading years was that Nancy Drew liked to throw herself right into the thick of a mystery and then follow the clues to see who the bad guys were. But the sad thing was that I didn't even know *what* the whole "thick" of this mystery was. I mean, I did know *who* had been kidnapped—my father, my sister, and twelve other Executives—but I had no idea *why*.

"Nancy Drew isn't helping," I said to Runt, giving her another scratch.

Okay, then follow the proverbial money, I said to myself.

There was only one person I could see who stood to gain by my father's kidnapping. Only one person could then claim the title of President and CEO of Death, Inc.—that is, if I, the dark horse daughter, could be discouraged out of the job, of course.

And that one person is none other than Daniel . . . the Devil's protégé.

it took five hours of trekking through Hell to find an exit.

If I'd been smart, I'd have gone back to Cerberus and asked him for help, but I was so scared he wouldn't let me keep Runt that I just threw us blindly into Hell and hoped against hope we'd find our own way out.

I wish I could say the trek had been eventful, that I'd magically taught myself to read Greek, or that I'd found Daniel and beaten the whereabouts of my missing family members out of his handsome hide, but alas, all I did was walk and bitch about the heat. Poor Runt must've wanted to run away screaming after all my whining, but she stayed beside me, her cute heart-shaped nose pressed into the dirt, catching every scent we passed by.

She was the one who actually discovered the doorway first. I would've walked right by it, but she did that crazy pointer thing again, so I had to stop and investigate.

We had left the dirt and forests of the North Gate long behind us. Now, we were in empty brown desert, the heat reflecting up off the sand, half blinding me and making Runt pant even harder. I think I was bitching about not bringing any sunglasses with me when she stopped walking and lifted her paw.

"Jeez louise, Runt, how'd you find *that*?" I said.

The doorway, if you could even really call it that, was set into the very ether. Any normal person would have completely missed it, but Runt, having a supernatural nose—and also being much smarter than me—picked up on it immediately. I had to kind of squint and walk counterclockwise to see it. Even then, it was just kind of a shimmering outline in the air.

"Where do you think it goes?" I asked Runt. Obviously, I wasn't expecting an answer, but as the day had progressed, I'd found myself talking out loud to the puppy more and more. Runt gave a sharp bark, then sat down on her haunches and stared at me.

"You think I should touch it? See if it'll open?"

She gave me another bark and wagged her tail, kicking up the sand behind her.

"Okay. Here goes nothing."

I walked up to where the shimmering seemed to be the most intense, my fingers wrapped securely around Runt's leash—I didn't want her to get left behind—and reached out my hand. I heard a sharp *crack*, then a wave of light exploded out of the doorway, enveloping Runt and me and beckoning us inside.

The doorway wasn't like a wormhole. It didn't suck you in, shake you around, and make you want to throw up. For which I was grateful because I really hated the feeling of nausea that traveling by wormhole always engendered in me.

Instead, the doorway overwhelmed me with a feeling of lightness and warmth. It was a little bit like stepping into Heaven. I could only imagine butterflies felt something like it when they were released from their cocoons for their maiden voyages, their newly born wings unfurling for the first time to capture the sunlight and wind and take flight.

The other thing about the doorway was that it made me feel, well . . . *happy.* I don't know how else to describe it. My thoughts were all mushy, full of butterflies, babies, and ice cream cakes. Intellectually, I understood that this had to be some kind of illusion because I *never* felt like this in real life, but no matter what I did, I just couldn't shake all the giddiness I was experiencing.

And then it was gone, a big, gaping hole left in its wake. And if that wasn't bad enough, all the emptiness was immediately replaced with misery. It was like having a whole week of PMS crammed inside you in one whack.

Yuck!

Finally, after the misery subsided, I opened my eyes and looked around at my surroundings. With my heart hammering a staccato beat inside my rib cage, I looked over at Runt, whose leash was still gripped tightly in my hand, and gave a quick *whoop* of joy.

I couldn't believe it. It had to be a miracle. For some unfathomable reason, I was back at Sea Verge . . . safe in my old bedroom. I immediately registered that the room looked exactly as I had left it: deep rose comforter tucked neatly into the corners of the double bed, white wicker desk, nightstand, and dresser, all neatly arranged. The dusty rose carpet was newly vacuumed, and the cream-colored walls looked like they had recently been repainted. It was like stepping back into my adolescence, only a lot tidier.

It was the first good thing that had happened since Jarvis had been taken into custody. In fact, being back home, safely tucked into my old room and completely disconnected from my adult reality—*Dirty Harry* PBI detectives, three-headed dogs, and missing-in-action family members—made me so happy that I wanted to cry.

So I did.

That was how Clio found me, standing in the middle of my old room, holding one of the throw pillows I'd pulled off the bed tight to my chest, tears running down my face, giddy with happiness. Maybe the doorway's magic hadn't completely left me after all, I decided.

"What're you doing?" Clio whispered as she eased open the door and stepped inside. "You're gonna get caught if you don't shut up, and I mean, like, *right now.*" Her tone made me stop burbling like a baby.

"Huh?" was the best I could manage, but Clio just put a finger to her lips, indicating silence. I nodded, so she would know that I'd understood her.

She mouthed the words "nice dog," her head tilting in Runt's direction, then she gestured for me to follow her across the room, where she stopped in front of my old closet door. She quietly turned the knob, eased open the door, and stepped inside, silently motioning for me to follow her.

Once we were inside the closet, which was totally bare since I'd taken every piece of clothing with me when I'd made my escape to New York, Clio clapped her hands twice and smiled. Instantly, the closet was draped in silence. It was like we'd stepped inside a soundproofed recording studio or something.

"How'd you do that?" I demanded. I didn't know Clio could do any magic at all.

Clio shrugged.

"You really think I listen when Dad tells me no magic in the house?"

"I did," I said, which only made Clio snort.

"Exactly my point. And now see what's happened to you?"

She looked so cute and young with her adorable pixie face and serious expression that it made me want to grab her up in a big bear hug and never let go.

"Stop it," she said as she fended me off like I was a bear bent on mauling her.

"Just one hug," I whined. "I really need one. It's been a terrible day . . ."

She rolled her eyes, then stood still so I could give her one of my patented bear hugs. When I was done squeezing her almost to unconsciousness, she laughed and stepped away. Things must've been pretty bad if my rebellious teenage sister was willing to placate me like that.

"Sorry," I said. "But this has truly been a crappy day."

She gave me a serious look.

"I believe you," she said finally. "Because it's been pretty crazy around here, too. The retarded detective from the Psychical Bureau of Investigations told Mom and Father McGee that you and Jarvis kidnapped Dad and Thalia."

"Did they believe him?" I asked, fear crawling up my neck like a hungry boa constrictor. Clio didn't say anything for a long moment. That said it all as far as I was concerned.

"Damn," I wailed. I couldn't believe my own mother would think something so terrible about one of her daughters. Clio tentatively reached out and patted my shoulder.

"He got Jarvis," I said miserably, leaning against the closet door for support.

"Poor Jarvis," Clio said. "They've probably got him locked up in Purgatory by now. I heard it's like the worst thing ever."

"Poor Jarvis" is right. Damn, this day is only getting worse again.

Sensing I was close to my breaking point, Clio changed the subject.

"Who's the dog?" she asked as she squatted down beside Runt to pet her. The puppy instantly warmed to my little sister, lying down on her back and exposing her tiny puppy belly for more scratching.

"What a cutie," Clio said, obliging Runt's scratching request.

"She's one of Cerberus's puppies. I call her Runt, but I think her real name is Giselda—" I began.

"No way!" Clio said, her eyes wide with intense curiosity. "No offense, but how in the hell did *you* get one of Cerberus's puppies?"

I shrugged nonchalantly.

"It was pretty easy, I guess."

Clio narrowed her eyes at me.

"You're such a liar, Calliope Reaper-Jones. Right, Runt?"

Runt gave a quick bark, like she was concurring with my sister.

"You both suck," I said, not at all liking this little alliance Runt was making with Clio. Ignoring Clio's knowing gaze, I decided that now was the time—if there was *ever* going to be a time—to ask for her help.

"Sorry to change the subject back to the problem at hand—and away from my status as a liar—but you don't happen to know Greek, do you?" I asked.

"I can read a little, but I don't speak it or anything," she answered.

"That's good enough for me," I said, pulling the handkerchief-wrapped parchment out of my back pocket, where I'd stuck it earlier for safekeeping. I offered it to her, and she took it eagerly.

"What *is* this?" she said as she unwrapped it and held it up to the light. I went to stand beside her, hoping some of her intelligence would rub off on me for once in my life.

"It's from the Board. Supposedly, it contains three tasks I have to complete before I can be appointed to Father's job."

"Why do you always call him 'Father'?" Clio asked suddenly. Her eyes held a strange light that I'd never seen in them before.

"I don't know." I shrugged. "Old habit?"

"It's weird," she said. "You should just call him 'Dad.' That's what I do."

"Okay, Dad's job, then. Does that make you happy?"

She nodded.

"I guess so. Kind of."

She went back to the parchment, her eyes scanning the rows of Greek characters. She mouthed a couple of the words, feeling for the right pronunciation, then gave her head one decisive shake before turning to meet my gaze.

"Okay, you've completed the first task. Your next task is to find Indra and get him to give you the Sea Foam he used to kill the demon Vritra. Then the third task is something about collecting the Cup of Jamshid—"

"Forget the Cup of Jam, or whatever," I said in disbelief. "Did you, or did you not, just say the words 'Sea Foam'?"

"I *think* that's what they're saying, Callie," Clio said defensively. "God, you don't have to be such a megabitch about it. I mean, do you want my help or not?"

I sighed. "Yes, I definitely want your help, but I don't even know who this Indra guy is, and *Sea Foam*? C'mon, that's totally silly!"

"I don't know," Clio said. "It's your parchment, not mine."

I plucked the parchment from Clio's fingers and held it up to the light.

"What do you want from me?" I yelled at it. The parchment didn't reply—not that I really expected it to.

I handed the thing back to Clio, who stared at me like I needed to be hospitalized for a case of fast-growing insanity.

"I'm not crazy. I mean it," I said to her. "At least, not yet."

"Look, Cal, I don't know anything about Sea Foam, but I do know who Indra is."

"Well, who is he, then?"

"Aside from being a pretty powerful Hindu God . . . ?" she asked.

"Aside from that," I echoed.

"God, Cal, you're so out of the loop."

Runt barked in agreement.

"Okay, I'm out of the loop. So, fill me in already."

Clio gave me a *knowing* look.

"He was voted *People*'s sexiest bachelor last year, Cal. Do the words 'Mr. Sex on a Stick' ring any bells?"

My mind drew a blank. I had no idea what the heck she was talking about. Then Clio smiled, and it was the element of unbridled lust behind that smile—which was *not* the kind of thing any parent *ever* wanted to see on the face of their teenage daughter—that knocked the answer into my brain.

"Oh my God, *that's* the Indra you are talking about? The incredibly hot—*like mouth-burningly hot*—Bollywood superstar?"

Clio looked like she was about to drool.

"The one and only."

I closed my eyes. The whole thing was so absurd that I started to laugh.

"You mean, I gotta go get *Sea Foam* from *Mr. Sex on a Stick*?"

Clio's smile only widened.

"Can I come with you?"

"No," I said immediately. "Not after the look I just saw on *your* face, kiddo."

"Please!" she begged. "Pretty please with sugar on top, and I won't rat you out to Mom."

"You wouldn't dare," I said, sensing the danger behind her words.

"Oh, I wouldn't?" she answered coyly. My baby sister knew she had me cornered, and she was enjoying it.

"*If* I take you, and that's a *very* big if, you gotta be quiet, do what I say, and watch Runt."

"Okay."

Nothing else, no whining about being quiet or doing what I said—she knew I was at her mercy.

"All right, then," I said, acting like the whole thing had been my idea in the first place. "So, how the hell do we get to Bollywood?"

Clio rolled her eyes as she picked up Runt's leash.

"Duh, through the TV, dummy."

It had taken us only a few minutes to get from my old room to Clio's, but when you had to play the silent game while you tiptoed down the hallway of a rickety old mansion that had, like, twenty zillion squeaky floorboards, it was a little intense.

I had wanted Clio to put another silencing spell on us, but she seemed to think the less magic done in the house, the better. I didn't agree with her, but since she was the one in charge of my safe passage through the house, I didn't argue.

When we reached her room, she closed the door behind us, checking to make sure that Runt hadn't gotten left in the hallway in our haste. Then, while I stood there watching, she threw three dead bolts and a chain lock into place.

I stared at all the locks on her door. I hadn't noticed them before—probably because I'd been too busy feeling sorry for myself.

"What's with all the locks?" I asked nonchalantly. I didn't want to put her on the defensive, but all the security definitely caught my interest. She shrugged and sat down on the floor next to Runt, who happily sidled up to her for an ear scratch.

"I installed them three months ago after I noticed someone had broken into my room," she said with a sigh. I looked around her room, at all the computer gadgetry strewn across the floor, taking up space on her desk, and probably even spawning baby computer gadgetry under her bed, and couldn't fathom in the least how she'd been able to guess someone had gone through her stuff.

"I know it looks like a mess to you, but to me . . . not even a little bit. I know where everything is, and I know when someone has been in here," she continued.

"Okay," I said, "I believe you. But why would anyone want to go through your room?"

If I hadn't been watching Clio so intently, I'd have totally missed it. That spark of fear in her eyes that caught fire for only the briefest of moments, then was gone . . . completely extinguished like it had never existed at all.

"That's the weird part," she said carefully. "I don't *know* why."

fourteen

My little sister, Clio, had an incredibly high IQ—which was why I'd decided that securing her help was paramount to my getting through the tasks and rescuing Father, Thalia, and Jarvis—so if *she* was freaked-out about someone tossing her room, well, then I should pay the event special attention.

"They weren't looking for drugs or anything?" I asked suddenly, the idea springing fully formed into my brain. *Better to be thorough than PC when all you have are suspicions,* I thought to myself, knowing full well that Clio was totally gonna take offense at the question.

It *was* a long shot, but my mother could be a little hysterical at times, and Drugs—with a capital *D*—were a well-known Caroline Reaper-Jones hysteria catalyst. When I was a sophomore in high school, she'd once made me pee on a stick to prove I wasn't smoking pot, and another time she'd accused me of drinking all the vodka in the living room liquor cabinet and replacing it with water. Even though the idea would've never occurred to me, I still felt as guilty as if I'd been the one who'd done it. It was just terrible.

Clio glared at me, the peeved look on her face more than sufficient to make me want to retract what I'd said.

"It was just a thought . . ." I began.

"I don't need drugs, Cal. I have my computer. That and the Internet is enough of an addiction for *any* person, don't you think?"

I had no idea. I didn't own a computer, *but* the one at work did have me slightly addicted to solitaire, so I guess she had a point. We all had our own addictions, no matter how weird they seemed to everyone else.

Does anyone want to talk about her shopping addiction? a little voice in the back of my head said, and I started to feel a bit guilty about my love-hate relationship with clothing. The hate part coming from my inability to afford all the scrumptious designer stuff I coveted.

"Did you ask anyone about it?"

Clio groaned. "You mean Mom?"

I nodded.

"She told me I was being ridiculous," Clio said. "Even Thalia thought I was 'blowing things out of proportion.' "

"You told Thalia?" I asked, curious now. I hadn't realized that Clio and Thalia were that close. Actually, I'd thought Clio and *I* were the tight ones, but I guess when you're not around to listen to your baby sister's problems, she finds someone else to talk to.

"Yeah, she was here, helping Dad with some meeting thing, and I wouldn't have said anything to her because she gets that know-it-all tone in her voice which just pisses me off, but Mom thought my complaint was a ploy for attention and decided to tell Dad and Thalia about it," Clio said angrily. "Like embarrassing me was going to discourage me from being a pain in her butt or something. Yeah, right."

For some reason, the fact that Clio thought Thalia was as snooty as I did made me feel extremely pleased.

"Well, I don't blame you for getting the locks, then. I hate it when anyone even *looks* at my stuff," I said helpfully.

Clio gave me a big smile, and Runt thumped her tail on the carpet.

"So, on to more pressing business," I said. "How do we do this TV thing you're talking about?"

I still didn't quite see how we were going to travel through a television set, but I was willing to give it a shot if Clio said it would work.

"I thought you'd never ask," she said with an impish gleam in her eye.

where my sister got the forty-two-inch plasma-screen TV was beyond me. I had a dinky old twenty-one-inch picture tube that cast a green pallor over all the shows I watched on it, so that everything just ended up looking like an *Incredible Hulk* rerun. Clio's, on the other hand, was a crisp, HD-ready baby, the kind I'd seen proudly displayed in every electronics store window over the past few months.

"Nice," I said as I ran a finger down the shiny black edge of the TV. It hung on the wall across from her bed, but I would've never even known it was there if Clio hadn't shown it to me. For some unknown-to-me reason, she had decided to hide her little plasma baby behind a long black drape that hung from the ceiling.

True, all she had to do was move the fabric aside to watch the television, but I still found the whole thing odd, regardless.

There was a lot more to Clio than met the eye. I was definitely glad she was on my side, or I'd have long since been caught and thrown into Purgatory with Jarvis.

"Explain the whole thing to me one more time," I said as Clio slid a DVD into the DVD player and turned on the TV.

"It's really quite simple, Cal. Although I don't think me explaining it twenty times is gonna make you understand the concept any better."

"Just hit me again," I said, annoyed. She reached back her hand to slap me, but I took three steps back.

"Not literally, God, Clio!"

"Just kidding," she said, pressing the play button. "You're *so* gullible."

Immediately, the screen was filled with that really annoying FBI warning that says YOU'RE GOING TO JAIL in huge block letters, but then only explains *why* in a really tiny font that you can't read unless you're standing an inch from the screen.

"Basically, Cal, it all comes down to quantum physics," Clio said as the FBI warning seemed to go on into perpetuity. "Magic and all that stuff is really very scientific, although, if you read all the big science journals, they're still trying to agree on whether or not quantum physics is even real."

I must've looked like I was drawing a blank, because Clio instantly clammed up.

"Go on," I said. "Physics is fake. I get it. Whatever."

Clio rolled her eyes and looked down at Runt.

"Hard to believe we're related, huh?"

Runt flicked her eyes in my direction, then back at

Clio before giving a short bark, which I could only take as an affirmation.

Fair-weather friend, I thought bitterly, but then Runt padded over to me and nuzzled my hand, and all was forgiven.

"Don't worry, Runt. We all know Clio's the genius in the family," I said, patting her head.

The DVD menu finally came up on the screen, but Clio ignored it, still trying to find a way to make me understand all the science stuff she loved so much.

"In layman's terms, Cal, quantum physics is all about the tiniest particles in the universe and how they interact. For some reason, some beings can tap into these tiny particles and manipulate them, basically bending matter to their will. That's what *magic* really is. And that's how we're gonna take a trip into the TV."

"So, I'm a matter bender?" I said, confused.

Clio took a deep breath. She must've thought I was a complete idiot, but it wasn't my fault that math and science had just never come as easily to me as art and English had.

Although, if any of my science teachers had been as cool as Clio, I thought to myself, *I might've liked science a whole lot better.*

"Okay, Cal, let's just say quantum physics is a lot like baking."

Now baking wasn't exactly my strong suit, but I *did* know how to boil an egg, make mac and cheese, and heat up a can of soup, so this was at least a good jumping-off point.

"When you bake a cake, you have lots of different ingredients that you use, right?" Clio said, and I nodded. "So, you could say that a cook was a 'matter bender' because they could take lots of little things and magically make them into something else."

"Like a cake," I said, and Clio nodded.

"Like a cake. Exactly. And to someone who'd never seen anyone bake a cake, it would seem like magic—"

"Because they'd never experienced anything like it before!"

"You got it!" Clio said, pleased with herself.

"I do. I totally get it now," I said, and for the first time in my life I understood what it felt like to be a science geek or a mathlete.

Smiling, Clio picked up Runt's leash, then pressed the play button on the remote control.

Suddenly, the room was filled with the melancholy strains of a lone sitar, and on the screen, a neon-colored Palace scene burst into life with what appeared to be bundles of brightly colored fabric writhing all over the place. The music picked up purposefully—and, like, ten other instruments joined the fray—as the camera zoomed in closer, revealing that the writhing bundles of fabric were actually a bevy of gorgeous Indian women in pink and orange neon saris lip-syncing their little lips off like Ashlee Simpson.

Damn, this is crazy stuff on the TV!

I took a deep breath.

"Let's go bake a cake," I said, taking Clio's hand and closing my eyes.

my nose was instantly assailed by a mouthwatering bouquet of cardamom and cinnamon wafting in on the tail end of a dry, hot wind. As the pungent scents and hot air encircled me, enveloping me in their heady embrace, the bottom suddenly dropped out of my stomach, and I started to scream. It was like being on one of those horrible carnival rides where they send you fifty feet up into the air at a slow crawl, then drop you back to the earth in the space of three seconds.

We hit the ground hard, and I found myself lying in a ball, my face pressed against the cold, hard cement floor. I almost gagged when I tasted blood, thick and salty, in my mouth. Somewhere, like a distant echo in the ether around me, I heard a muted *knocking*, but I decided that it would have to wait since I was too busy trying not to pass out right then.

After a few seconds of deep breathing, I opened my eyes and sat up, letting the dizziness dissipate before feeling for the place where I'd cut my lip. It wasn't bad, but I was definitely going to have the "Lisa Rinna on a Restalyn binge" smile for a while. She paid good money for the fat-lip look so I probably shouldn't complain since mine came *très* cheap.

The place was poorly lit, but I could see that I was in a janitor's supply closet, totally *not* the place I'd intended to find myself in.

"You okay?" Clio said from somewhere behind me. I turned around and nodded, pointing like a triumphant child to my war wound.

"Fat lip," I mumbled, nauseated as a fresh flow of blood dribbled into my mouth. *Yuck!*

"Why are we in a broom closet?" Clio said, looking around, her pretty face scrunched thoughtfully.

"I don't know, but I'm gonna find out," I said, crawling over on my hands and knees to the doorway. I motioned for Clio and Runt to stay back as I turned the doorknob, easing the door open half an inch.

"Oh my God!" I squeaked, scuttling backward like a crab, my ears ringing from the loud music and the rush of Day-Glo orange and rhinestone-covered fabric that had almost blinded me. I'd processed enough in those few seconds of voyeurism to realize that the sari-wearing women we'd been watching on television were now whirling like dervishes right outside our janitor's closet.

"Stay back," I said as Clio crawled up behind me to look over my shoulder through the crack in the doorway.

"Wow, it's like a Skittles commercial out there."

She was right. The colors were so intense they were almost unnatural.

Runt whined, hoping we'd take pity on her and let her climb up next to us. I figured she deserved to see as much as we did, so I picked up her leash and guided her toward my lap.

Bad idea.

Something about the colors, or the way the rhinestones reflected in the bright klieg lights, freaked Runt out. She crawled right up to the doorway, barking like a maniac, and nosed the door open. I pulled on her leash, trying to drag her back, but it was like playing tug-of-war with a very strong, very obstinate baby elephant.

Suddenly, the leash went taut, and Runt was off like a shot. In the space of two seconds, I found myself flat on my stomach—my lungs compressed to the size of empty Ziploc freezer bags—being dragged out of the closet through the doorway and into the melee of swirling saris.

Even though the idea of breaking my face on some hellish version of the doggie Slip 'n Slide terrified me, I refused to let go of the leash. Runt had saved my life, and even if she did insist on behaving like a dog, I wasn't gonna let her get run over by all those dancing girls.

"Callie!" I heard Clio say in a high, reedy voice that was totally unlike her own. For the first time in my remembrance, my little sister sounded scared. If I hadn't been so busy trying not to get my teeth knocked out of my head by the onrushing ground, I might've been moved by the idea that she cared enough about me to be so worried.

For the second time that day, I was literally saved from serious injury by an ankle.

I felt a hard, teeth-jarring tug on my leg, and then I was airborne, my body hovering three inches off the ground, a human suspension bridge between an ecstatic Hell-born pup and my techno-geek teenage sister.

"Ow!" I yelped, my body twisting painfully with Runt's every bark. "Shut up, Runt!"

I looked behind me to see Clio gripping my ankle like it was going out of style.

"Hold on," she said through clenched teeth, her face bright red from the exertion of keeping Runt and me from running headlong into the sea of Bollywood dancers. As it was, a few of the buxom Indian women had already noticed our, *ahem*, "strange appearance," and had stopped whirling in order to gape and point at us with their long, orange and pink lacquered nails. I had to hand it to whoever was running this show, because their "attention to detail" was impeccable.

Suddenly, the music came to a grinding halt, and the dancers ceased their lyrical movements so that, as if by telepathy, they could all turn their heads in unison to stare at us. In the silence that followed, I realized that Runt had stopped barking.

"Oh, crap," I said, my body slamming face-first into the cement as Runt sat back on her haunches, slackening her hold on me. The pain was intense. It actually kind of reminded me of the time when I was ten, and we were on a family vacation at this swanky resort in South Carolina, and I decided to dive off the superhigh dive at the resort pool.

I thought I was just the coolest in my sleek hot pink one-piece Speedo, standing thirty feet up in the air, waving at my sisters, who were chickening it out in the shallow end. I took the board at a run, my body sailing out into the nothingness like I was some kind of seabird Goddess. Then, out of nowhere, the whole thing took a turn for the dark side. I just couldn't get my body to twist the way I wanted, and suddenly, without warning, the ride was over, and I had belly flopped, my nerve endings screaming with the searing hot pain of delicate skin on still water.

Soooo embarrassing.

I was pulled out of my reverie by the sound of sharp heels clicking on cement. My mind still reeling from my three-inch cement belly flop, I looked up, expecting to see a pair of high heels making their way toward me, but instead, I found myself greeted by the sight of two shiny black patent leather men's loafers. They were polished to such a mirrored shine that I could literally see my face reflected back at me, fat lip and all.

When they were no more than five inches away from my face, they stopped, the wearer tapping his left toe with impatience.

Tap shoes? I thought, surprised. *What kind of guy—outside of Gene Kelly, who as far as I was concerned could do no wrong—wears tap shoes in public?*

"What is the meaning of this interruption?" a male

voice said, its East Indian accent clipped by anger. "I do not care for your prostrations before me. Please get up and explain yourself, or I will find myself more upset than usual."

"Ow," I said in response, rubbing my chin where it was throbbing angrily—it was probably as scraped and battered as the rest of me. I closed my eyes, pain drumming itself into my head with every heartbeat. If I kept going at this pace, I was gonna have an ulcer *sooner* rather than *never.* This was really getting to be *way* more trouble than it was worth. Maybe the Devil's protégé *should* just take over Death, Inc., and be done with it.

No, a small voice inside my head said with gusto. *I am gonna find my father and sister, and that is all there is to it. Devil's protégé or no Devil's protégé, this game is on! I am no quitter!*

I closed my eyes, steeling myself for the pain I knew was gonna come slamming itself into my body when I finally got up off my butt and got the party started.

Gritting my teeth, I pushed myself back up onto my knees, and then, with a loud, pained grunt, I hefted myself onto my feet. I opened my eyes and looked directly at the angry man standing before me. He was a few inches taller than me, but extremely skinny—the kind of skinny you get unmercifully teased for in elementary through high school. His well-oiled black hair was stuck to his head like a skullcap, making his long, pointed nose even more pronounced than it already was, and the neon red satin suit he was wearing did nothing at all for his sallow complexion.

And can we talk about the tap shoes again?

"Look," I began. "I'm sorry to interrupt your dance number, sir, but we just want to talk to Indra and then we'll get out of your hair."

"*You* want to talk to *Indra*," one of the dancers said, haughtily tossing her long black hair over her shoulder and giving me a disdainful look. "The Gopi don't like no white bitch messin' with their man."

Hip-hop-speak from a girl in a neon orange sari? This is sweet.

"We're not here to 'mess with your man,' as you so succinctly put it," I said, looking back at Clio, who nodded furiously. "We just want to get some Sea Foam and then we're outta here—"

It took less than two seconds after the words had left my mouth for all hell to break loose.

Suddenly, I found my eyes clouded by a swath of neon pink and orange and black, and I felt a sharp *thunk* in my gut, followed by a wave of nausea so intense I thought I was going to throw up my pancreas. I keeled over onto my knees, my arms wrapped protectively around my stomach, a ward against another sharp jab to the abdomen from my very efficient Gopi attacker.

A scrim of darkness descended around the edges of my peripheral vision, and I had trouble catching even *one* breath—let alone returning myself to a safe and upright position. The pain in my belly was way worse than a thousand split lips, probably more on par with getting a tummy tuck without proper anesthetic.

I looked up, my eyes locking with those of the Gopi standing above me, her face a dark grimace. Chest heaving unproductively, I could feel my body beginning to hyperventilate. My body, the traitor, was just *giving up*, allowing itself to fall into unconsciousness as a cheap effort to stop the pain!

No way am I gonna let that happen on my watch, I thought, trying to think of what you did to stop someone from passing out. The only thing I could come up with was putting my head between my legs, but somehow it just seemed like way too much of an invitation for a Gopi deathblow to the back of the neck.

The Gopi must've sensed what was happening to my body, too, because, without even blinking an eye, she was throwing herself at my back, her manicured fingers making a furious grab for my throat and her legs wrapping themselves around my middle, trying to squeeze the very breakfast—the only meal I'd had today, barring the Starbucks stop with Jarvis—right outta me.

Then, with a well-placed thumb, she found my jugular, and as my oxygen-starved brain began to recede into darkness, a beautiful memory swam to the forefront of my mind—one of my favorites actually—and I almost smiled.

Like the hallucinations of a man trapped in the desert for too long without food and water, I saw a Skyscraper Forest dancing before my mind's eye, beckoning me homeward. Like a lightning bolt to my brain, I suddenly remembered *why* it was so imperative for me to get out of the Gopi's stranglehold. And believe me, it had nothing to do with Sea Foam, or taking over the Presidency of Death, Inc., . . . *or even saving my family.*

It was a far more simple—and selfish—thing that gave me the strength to finally defend myself against my Gopi attacker.

And it could be summed up in eight tiny little words: *I have a life to get back to.*

fifteen

When I first moved to New York City, I couldn't shake the feeling that I was living in a Skyscraper Forest.

Roaming the environs of Midtown, sweat leaking from my body like corrosive battery fluid—it was the height of summer and the City was more humid than a Russian bath—I would spend hours getting lost in its heaving throngs, my eyes invariably straying like magnets to the magnificent chrome and glass buildings that lined the sidewalks.

I found that walking among them was like stepping into one of those New York–centric American Express commercials: Flight to JFK: $350.00; taxi fare to Midtown: $55.00; hot dog and soda at outdoor stand: $4.50 . . . the feeling of belonging somewhere for the first time in your life: priceless.

As I stood at their thick concrete bases, my eyes scanning their peaks, I imagined the skyscrapers were actually giant sentries, guarding the City and its inhabitants against, well, I didn't know what—an attack from

Godzilla and Mothra, or maybe just your standard pigeon uprising. For me, all that really mattered was that, somehow, simply living within their great shadow made me feel all warm and safe inside.

I had lived my entire life never feeling like I fit in anywhere. Sure, I had my family, but aside from Clio, I really didn't have much to say to any of them. And as far as school went, I had a few friends here and there, but only one real friend—my best friend, Noh—whom I would call if I was ever truly in a bind.

So, it was pretty cool to discover another boon companion during my daily—and nightly—explorations. The City itself took me under its wing, culling me from the rest of the masses to give me a big, wet, sloppy Manhattan-style kiss. As far as I was concerned, no matter where I went from then on—whether it was as far flung as Timbuktu or just down the turnpike to New Jersey—I would always have a place to come home to.

How I felt about New York was one of the reasons I finally used the Forgetting Charm on myself.

I knew I wasn't the first person who had ever felt this way, nor did I think I would be the last. This was just the effect New York had on you.

It didn't matter who or what you were—because as far as I could see, *no one* was immune to her charm—you *would* eventually feel the thrum of the City sneaking into your bloodstream, becoming as thick as sludge in your veins, and then without even noticing the transformation, you had become a New Yorker.

And as such, I felt it was my duty to maintain the honor of New Yorkers everywhere by *not* allowing the neon orange and pink sari–wearing bimbo—yep, the selfsame bitch who sucker punched me in the gut and jumped on my back like some screeching banshee—to try to strangle me to death.

Besides, I had a life to get back to. And there was no way I was gonna let this Gopi mercenary take that away from me.

In the end, I did what any sensible New Yorker would do during a would-be attack—one that was *completely* unprovoked, mind you, unless the words "Sea" and "Foam" were some secret Gopi attack trigger that I'd stumbled on by accident—*I kicked the Gopi's ass.*

"Get off of her!" I heard Clio yelling behind me as I slammed my knuckles up into my attacker's nose, then waited for the very nice-smelling, but very unconscious, lady to slide off my shoulders and sink to the floor.

Almost immediately another of her compatriots, this one maybe a tad taller, but for all intents and purposes the exact same model, made a running leap for my chest. I hobbled backward, trying to get out of her way, and tripped, my butt slamming into the concrete floor.

All I could think about as I cowered on the ground, my butt throbbing painfully, was that my gluteus maximus was *not* made for such rough-and-tumble play. Luckily, my fall kept me just low enough to the ground for the neon-garbed dancing girl to sail over my head and body slam another one of her dancing sisters.

"Go, Callie! Kick her ass!" Clio screamed like a one-woman cheerleading squad. I looked back to see her jumping up and down excitedly, her hand gripping Runt's leash with an iron fist. None of the other dancers had attacked Clio and Runt, so I hoped I was the only one the Gopi felt was a threat. If any of them so much as *touched* a hair on their heads, I was *so* not gonna be Miss Nice Death anymore.

"Look, ladies," I said, out of breath, "I don't know what the hell your problem is, but I really think this can be solved *without* violence—"

The words were hardly out of my mouth when *another* lemminglike dancer took aim, slamming her body into my own and knocking us both to the floor. We rolled, our bodies intertwined like the twin snakes on a caduceus, and at the end of the skirmish the Gopi was on top. She flipped me over with the ease of a five-year-old picking up an empty potato chip packet and slipped me into a headlock.

"Uncle!" I yelped, my neck a twist-tie in the dancer's nimble arms. "I call uncle!"

I had no idea if these ladies had ever heard the term "uncle" before—other than in the familial capacity—but I was willing to give it a try.

"We have him!" my attacker said, her arms tight around my throat, choking the life out of me, her words neatly followed by a chorus from the peanut gallery:

"We have captured Vritra for you!"

The Gopi began to ululate in triumph, their voices eerily blending into one as their jubilation echoed around the empty soundstage like buckshot. It was so spooky, and Stepford Wife–like, that I shivered.

"Leave my sister alone!" Clio said as she ran over to the dancer who had me in the chokehold, and started hammering on the girl's back with her fists, Runt barking up a storm in support. The dancer seemed impervious to Clio, weathering her blows without protest.

"My dears! My dears! Please, hold your tongues."

I looked up to see the smarmy guy in the tap shoes and red suit tip-tapping his way through the dancers toward me. His face was pale and the bushy mustache he wore on his upper lip seemed limp under the klieg lights.

He squatted down so that he was directly in front of me and stared deeply into my eyes. All I could do was gasp for breath, and try to glare back at him.

"Make them let her go!" Clio said, instantly ceasing her rain of blows on the Gopi's back and coming around to take her anger out on Mr. Tap Shoes. He ignored Clio, his eyes still searching my own; then his face broke into a crooked smile. He looked up at the Gopi, who instantly let go of my throat and crawled away. I could still feel her arm against my neck, smell the warm, spicy scent of her perfume, which only made me want to gag, but I stifled the bile in my throat and took the man's hand when he offered to help me up. I didn't want to be rude to my savior . . . at least not just yet.

"Who are you?" he asked me, his eyes alight with curiosity.

"She's Death, you jerk!" Clio yelled back at him. The smile dropped from his lips, but to his credit, he didn't run away screaming. Instead, he pulled a thin, silver flask from his inner coat pocket and took a long swallow—I'm not sure what was in the flask, but whatever it was, it sure made the little guy stand up straighter. His drink downed, he capped the silvery body of the flask and slipped it back into its hidden pocket without fanfare. He was so suave about the whole thing it was almost like I had imagined it.

His confidence now restored, Mr. Tap Shoes shook his head in what I took to be a very patronizing way.

"But that cannot be."

Clio came over and took my arm, letting me rest

some of my weight against her skinny shoulder. She was a good kid.

"And why not?" Clio said sagely.

I raised an eyebrow but didn't say a word, my throat still hurting too much to talk.

"Because . . . it just cannot be so," he continued, but he seemed to lose some of the confidence he'd first had. "I have it on good authority that *another* is next in line for the position . . ."

He trailed off, his words even more uncertain than a few seconds before.

"She's Death, and this is one of Cerberus's pups to prove it," Clio said, looking over at Runt, who thumped her tail in agreement.

There was a collective *"Oh"* from the Gopi, and then, with the precision of a drill team, they dropped back Texas Cheerleader–style to form a protective circle around Clio, Runt, Mr. Tap Shoes, and me.

"I think we've explained enough about who we are," I said, my voice coming out like a croak. "Now who the hell are you and where the hell can we find this stupid Indra person?"

I was tired of being Miss Nice Death. I wanted the stupid Sea Foam . . . *and I wanted it now.*

My words got the Gopi all atwitter, and they whispered quietly among themselves like schoolgirls. I couldn't tell if they were impressed by my rudeness, or if they were just planning another attack. I gave Mr. Tap Shoes a sharp look, and he sighed, looking from Clio to Runt and then back to me.

"You would like to speak to Indra, then," he said, resigned.

I nodded.

"So be it."

He snapped his fingers, the crisp sound hanging in the air until it began to quietly vibrate, metamorphosing into a low-register hum. Runt began to howl, her voice melding with the hum, strengthening it until it became a shrill whine. Meanwhile, the Gopi had moved their circle closer, forming a wall of protection around us that was palpable.

Clio leaned over and whispered in my ear, "Can you feel the kinetic energy in the air? It's incredible." Leave it to my little sister to quantify our little adventure in scientific terms.

There was a flash of bluish light, like lightning in an empty sky, and I had to shield my eyes. The air was instantly filled with the acrid smell of burnt flesh and a strange sizzling that charged the ether around us so that you could almost taste it with the tip of your tongue. I opened my eyes to find that Mr. Tap Shoes had disappeared. In his place stood a tall, sinewy Indian man with wild black hair, crème caramel skin, and eyes like melting milk chocolate Hershey Kisses. He looked so yummy that you were tempted to eat him, regardless of all the calories you knew he contained.

Hence the nickname: *Mr. Sex on a Stick.*

You know how you meet some people and they just have this *presence* about them, this ephemeral thing you can't put a name to, but you can feel it emanating off them? The type who would be totally at home commanding an army, leading a violent religious revolt . . . *or spearheading a sex cult,* I thought naughtily.

Well, this was one of those people.

"You wanted to speak to me?" Indra said, his deep voice booming in the silence.

Clio gripped my arm. I really thought she was gonna faint . . . and I honestly couldn't blame her. The red suit that had looked so silly on Mr. Tap Shoes fit Indra's well-muscled body like it had been sewn on to him. The bushy mustache was gone, replaced with a devastatingly handsome, clean-shaven face. You could tell he expected us to swoon at his feet—I was sure every other female he encountered obliged him—so I determined neither of us was gonna give him the satisfaction, and I pinched Clio to keep her from passing out.

"Yes, we wanted to speak to you," I began—having learned from my run-in with Cerberus that honesty was the best policy. "I was given three tasks to complete by the Board before I could take over the Presidency of Death, Inc. And one of those tasks just happens to be getting my hands on the Sea Foam you used to slay the demon Vritra. I know we haven't even been properly introduced, but I really, really, really need to borrow it."

Indra appeared to consider the idea, his dark brows knit together in thought.

"Pretty please with sugar on top, sir?" I said, hoping to sway his decision in my favor. He continued to think on the question, ignoring my blatant brownnosing.

The Gopi retinue—by now it was pretty obvious that they weren't *just* Bollywood dancers—watched our exchange intently, their dark eyes boring holes into my back. Their odd behavior—the way they had instantly sought to protect Indra while he was in his Mr. Tap Shoes disguise and the way they were now scrutinizing Clio, Runt, and me—made me very curious as to what kind of attack Indra was trying to protect himself against.

"I don't think letting you have the Sea Foam would be such a good idea," Indra finally said, his dark eyes serious. "Things are too . . . uncertain."

Damn it, I thought, *why can't any of this ever be easy?*

"Look, Indra, there's obviously something going on here. You're using a spell to hide your identity, you have attack Gopi at your beck and call—"

"Borrowed 'em from Krishna, although they're a bit more intense than I'd expected," he said, grinning. "Not bad to look at, though, really."

"The girls are great," I agreed dryly, "but right now I really need you to focus. There's obviously some stuff happening around here that I'm not privy to, but as the next head of Death, Inc., maybe I could be of help to you."

As he considered my words, I felt a pinch on my upper arm. I turned to find Clio giving me an annoyed look. She blinked furiously in Indra's direction, indicating that she wanted to be introduced to Mr. Sex on a Stick. Out of the corner of my eye as I was turning back around, I caught Indra covertly sliding his silver flask back into his pocket. *Weird.*

"Oh, uhm, by the way, this is my sister Clio," I said, inclining my head in her direction. "She's the one who brought me here to your, uhm, closet . . . *I mean, soundstage.*"

He smiled down at Clio—who was grinning like an idiot—his eyes drinking in her beautiful face and expectant gaze. Suddenly, he took her small hand in his and gave it a slow squeeze before lifting it to his lips and planting a lingering kiss on her knuckles, making her blush the color of a fire hydrant. With a quick wink, he dropped her hand and turned back to me, his face utterly composed.

"Do you like my temple, Madame Death?" he said as he used his arms to indicate the whole of the soundstage. It was obviously a rhetorical question because he didn't wait for me to answer.

"This was built to honor me. My talent, my fame . . . and now, today, I am working on the last scene of my Masterpiece. A film I conceived and am directing and starring in. It is a work of staggering genius the likes of which the world has never known."

I somehow couldn't imagine the man as the next Orson Welles, but who was I to judge?

"Sounds great," I said, but "sounds pretentious" was what I was really thinking.

"What's it about?" Clio asked eagerly, her voice about two octaves higher than it usually was. "Your movie, I mean."

I gave her a look, but she ignored me, her eyes fixed on Indra. *Ugh, he is really starting to get on my last nerve.*

"It's a love story, my dear," he said, his eyes lingering on her face far longer than they should have. Clio turned bright red again and giggled like there wasn't a thought in her head.

Am I really *gonna have to tell the guy she's only seventeen, so he'll back off?*

I tuned back in to find Indra grinning down at me, his eyes literally trying to melt me where I stood.

"In fact, it is the greatest love story of all time . . ."

Jeez, the man has the attention span of a gnat. One minute he's trying to seduce Clio, the next me.

Well, I was having none of his machismo crap.

Instead of falling under his spell, I just fixed him with a withering smile and waited for him to continue, to enlighten us about this work of staggering genius unlike any other.

His silence impressed upon me the fact that he was *not* happy I was showing immunity to his charm. He spun away from me, a mischievous smile on his lips, like he was remembering some private joke that I was the butt of.

What a jerk.

With his Gopi bodyguards and giant soundstage, he really thought he was the King of The World. Well, maybe there was a way to use his giant ego to my advantage. I looked around the massive soundstage (you know what they say about men with big soundstages . . .), my brain sparking the beginnings of—hopefully—an ingenious plan.

"Okay, well, then . . ." I said, smiling stiffly. "I guess since you can't help us, we should probably get going, head back to the Board and tell them I can't complete the tasks."

"Cal, you can't . . ." Clio started to say, pinching my arm again—God, she was gonna leave a bruise—but I gave her a dark look, silencing her. I didn't know how to communicate to her that this was all part of my plan. If I said *anything* out loud, the jig would be up. She was just gonna have to go with it and trust me.

Indra gave me a simpering smile, his dark eyes offering his insincere sorrow at not being able to help us with our predicament.

"I am sorry that I could not be of assistance, but you do realize the stress I am under completing my Masterpiece . . . and there are other things as well," he said, indicating the Gopi. "Serious things."

What a load of hooey, you big, self-involved baby, I thought to myself, but instead, I said out loud:

"Of course, we understand. C'mon, Clio," I said, taking Runt's leash out of her hand. "Bye now and thanks for showing us your cute *little* soundstage."

Suddenly, Indra was behind me, grabbing for my arm.

"Little?" he repeated, uncertain. "What do you mean by that? Have you seen bigger?"

I nodded, turning back around. "Oh, definitely. *Loads bigger.* In fact, if you helped me out with the whole Sea Foam thing, I bet I could get you one double the size."

"*Double* the size, you say?" His eyes flared at the prospect of doubling his square footage. "Hmmm . . ."

"Yes, I really think something bigger would be far more fitting for a genius of your stature," I said, trying to keep my voice nonchalant, even though my throat was raw from nerves and from almost being squeezed to death.

I had no clue how I was gonna get him a soundstage, period, let alone one double the size of this monster. I knew I was being a big, fat liar, but it really seemed like the only way to get the Sea Foam *and* save my family.

"And you can also help me with something else, too?" he said, throwing me a curve ball out of nowhere. *A soundstage* and *something else, too,* I thought miserably.

"Uh, yeah, sure, I guess. What did you have in mind?"

He showed me his straight, pearly white teeth. He was a mongoose and I was his prey. *Damn it, I am really starting to despise this guy.*

"I will tell you, Madame Death," Indra said, "and then we shall see what you can do about it."

sixteen

"I can't do it," I said to Clio, protectively crossing my arms over my chest. "I cannot willingly pimp someone out. Regardless of whether I like them or not—it's just not happening."

Clio and I stood about ten feet away from Indra and the Gopi Guard, huddled in conference. Indra kept giving us covert looks—probably trying to eavesdrop on our conversation, I decided—so I motioned for Clio to lower her voice.

"I can't believe you, Cal. It's only called 'pimping' when sex is involved," Clio stage-whispered. "And by the way . . . who knew you were such a prude?"

"I am *not* a prude!" I rejoined hotly, my voice rising and attracting the attention of the Gopi. I gave them a conciliatory smile before going back to my argument with Clio.

"C'mon. You *really* think he only wants her to sing some song in his stupid movie?" I said earnestly.

"Because I don't buy this whole 'jewel in the crown' thing he keeps babbling about. I really don't."

Clio shrugged.

"How am I supposed to know the guy's true intentions, Cal? Look, whatever *his* deal is, I think *you're* being a little uptight about stuff. I mean, I can't imagine he has trouble in the female department, so I don't think he needs you to procure him any bitches."

"Did you just use the term 'bitches' in reference to another female?" I asked, shocked. Clio sighed. "It was a figure of speech, Cal. Stop acting like a suburban soccer mom."

I couldn't believe my little sister had just accused me of being a soccer mom. Had I really lost my touch? Had I become complacent during my House and Yard tenure? I guessed when all of this Death stuff was over, I was *really* gonna have to do some pop culture soul searching.

"Okay, maybe I *am* being a little soccer mom about the whole thing," I conceded. "You really think he only wants her to come and hang out?"

"I can't say what he *really* wants—"

"Then you *do* think he's a dog!" I whispered.

There was a pause. Clio gritted her teeth.

"Cal, you are *so* predictable."

"What does *that* mean?" I asked, confused. I hated it when Clio got all psychoanalytical on me.

She shook her head in disbelief, and I could tell she was kind of annoyed with me. Sometimes she really made me feel like *I* was the younger sister.

"Look, I think he wants you to do him a favor and then he'll give you the Sea Foam you need. That's what I think," Clio said finally. "And that's *all* I think, so stop trying to get me to dog Indra—because I actually think he's kind of nice."

"He's a jerk, Clio. And you're a minor, so—"

"Stop acting like my mom, Callie," Clio said. "Go call your friend so we can get your stupid Sea Foam and get out of here."

"C'mon, Runt." Clio clicked her tongue, and the puppy followed her over to a low dais built into the Palace set near where the Gopi were standing. The dancers instantly moved away from them, and I realized the Gopi were scared of Runt. They hadn't really paid any attention to her at all until Clio had told them she was one of Cerberus's puppies, and then there *had* been that collective Gopi "Oh."

Interesting. Very interesting, I thought to myself. Something to file away for a later date—in case we ran into any Gopi trouble down the road.

I took a deep breath and turned back around to face Indra. He looked at me expectantly.

"So . . . ? You will do this thing?" he asked.

I nodded. "I can't promise you it's going to happen, but I'll give it a try. How about that?"

He gave me a flash of his pearly whites. "If she agrees to my proposition, you will receive your just reward."

"Okay, then. It's a deal."

Indra clapped his large hands together, rubbing them up and down excitedly.

"Yes, it *is* a deal."

I smiled tightly back at him, but my mind was spinning as it tried to figure out how the hell I was gonna call the Goddess Kali down to do my bidding. Clio had said that doing magic was like baking a cake. I could bake a cake—at least, the kind that came out of a box—so I could do magic, right?

I tried to remember how I had called Jarvis to Atlantis. I couldn't remember if I'd thought his name, or said it out loud. Well, I might as well go for the big finish, I decided after a careful moment of contemplation.

"Here goes nothing," I said.

I cleared my throat, then I closed my eyes.

"Kali, I'm sorry to be a pain in your ass, but I really need you to stop doing whatever you're doing and come to where I am. Please!"

I let the words settle, then I opened my eyes again. The Gopi stared at me, nonplussed. My little SOS to Kali had obviously *not* been as successful as I'd hoped.

"Well, uhm—" I began, but Indra cut me off.

"No deal."

Boy, this was not a guy that liked to be trifled with.

"Look, just let me try one more time."

"No, *she* will not come, and *you* will not get my Foam—"

His words were interrupted by a loud crashing sound that came from the vicinity of the janitor's closet. It sounded like the Tin Man was getting disemboweled in there.

I could hear someone mumbling the words "stupid white girl" over and over like a mantra, then there was another crash and the closet door flew open, shredding the doorframe in the process. If I thought we'd be leaving the way we'd come, I was sadly mistaken. The closet was now compromised.

There was a strangled cry as Kali, a metal bucket stuck on her right foot and a bottle of bleach in her left hand, stumbled into the light, clutching a thick-bristled broom like a crutch. She must've been in the bath when I called her because she'd only had time to wrap herself in a bright yellow duck appliqué–covered shower curtain; otherwise, she was completely naked.

If she hadn't been so pissed, the whole thing would've been kind of funny, but since she looked like she'd take the head off anyone who so much as snickered in her direction, I decided not to tempt fate. I would just laugh harder "on the inside."

Her eyes crackling with anger, she screamed, "White girl! Where are you? I know this is your doing!"

I tentatively raised my hand, and her eyes instantly focused on my face, her mouth set in a grim line. If looks could kill, well, you know the drill . . . I'd be deader than dead.

"I'm gonna make you rue the day, white girl," she said, brandishing the bottle of bleach in my direction, her voice trembling with rage. *"Rue the day!!"*

I should've been a little more concerned about getting bleached, but in her haste Kali had forgotten to take the top off the bottle, so no matter where she shook that thing, the nasty stuff wasn't going anywhere.

"I'm gonna so kick your ass, white girl!"

"Don't blame me," I yelped, backing away from her as the bucket began clanging in my direction. "This was all *his* idea!"

I pointed at Indra, who had already started moving toward the Gopi for protection. Frankly, he looked terrified, which made me much happier than it should have. I didn't know what it was about Indra that rubbed me the wrong way, but there was definitely something.

Maybe the fact that he's such a poseur, I thought to myself, *and a whiny one at that.*

In my peripheral vision, I caught Indra going for his flask again. *Jesus, what the hell is in that thing anyway?*

"I . . . I . . ." Indra stammered, his honeyed voice high and squeaky like a little girl's, his tan face the color of five-day-old pickled cabbage.

Kali turned her rage on him, her eyes glittering malevolently in her beautiful face.

"You . . . you . . . you Soma-holic cry baby! I will rip your entrails out of your belly and make you consume them while I watch," she screamed, advancing on him with ruthlessness and ripping the flask out of his hands. He cowered before her, his eyes locked on the silver flask.

"Please . . ." he whimpered, his gaze focused on the flask like a laser beam. Disgusted, Kali threw the flask back to him, but it slipped through his fingers and landed on the concrete floor with a *ping*, right at his feet. Indra instantly scooped it up and shoved it back into his coat pocket with shaking fingers.

The Gopi, realizing that Kali had transferred her rage from me to Indra, slowly began to move forward in formation, the protection of their master their first priority.

"Ha!" Kali said, glaring at the Gopi. "You think you can best me, you whores of Krishna!"

She opened her mouth, her jaw unhinging like a snake's before it swallowed its prey. A loud, keening wail escaped her lips, rending the air around us and making the hairs on the back of my neck stand at attention. The Gopi, whom I had deemed unstoppable after my earlier battle with them, began to crumple to the ground like paper dolls, their beautifully manicured pink and orange neon hands covering their ears against Kali's wrath.

I looked over, my eyes finding Clio's. She pointed to Kali and mouthed the words "She rocks!"

I had to agree with Clio. Kali was a pretty awesome sight to behold, shower curtain and all. Definitely the kind of Goddess you wanted on *your* side in a fight.

"Do something," Indra pleaded, *"or you will not get your Foam!"* That last bit was said in such a demanding—no, it was downright *rude*—tone, that all I wanted to do was turn around and slug him. I absolutely hate being bossed around (by someone who's not paying me)—and when they try to *manipulate* me at the same time, well, watch out.

"Oh, I'm sorry, are you talking to me?" I asked Indra as he cowered behind one of the set pieces. "Because I didn't hear you. Were you saying something about me 'not getting my Foam'?"

"Yes! You will not get your Foam unless you stop her," he said, the look on his face exactly like that of a spoiled four-year-old child's right before it threw a tantrum on the floor.

"Hey, Kali," I said, turning my back on Indra and finding Kali standing over the Gopi triumphantly, her dark hair wild around her face. She held a handful of black hair extensions in her hand like a prize.

"Hey, white girl, you like my hair?"

I wasn't sure if she meant the hair on her head, or the Gopi hair in her hand, so I just nodded.

"Love the hair."

She smiled at me. "It's not so bad to be summoned out of the bath when I get a nifty prize as a parting gift."

"I am in total agreement," I countered. "So, look, about the whole 'summoning' thing . . ."

She gazed at me expectantly. "Yes?"

"Well, as I'm sure you know since you're the one

who gave me the stupid tasks to complete, I have to get this dumb Sea Foam thing from Indra—"

"Oh, is that what the parchment said?" she asked.

"Excuse me?"

She shrugged. "We never know what the hell is on the thing. The tasks change based on each new seeker. We're only the messengers. The *small fry*."

I guess that makes sense, I thought. *So then why is the thing in Greek when it* knows *I only speak English? Stupid parchment.*

"I wouldn't exactly call you *small fry*," I said, amused by her choice of words. "Anyway, the reason I summoned you is simple—jerkoid over there," I said, pointing to Indra, who was still cowering like a schoolboy behind me, "wouldn't give me the Sea Foam I need unless I promised to get you to do me a favor."

Kali raised an eyebrow.

"And the favor is, uhm . . ." I began, feeling stupid myself. "You see, Indra is making a movie, his Masterpiece, and he thinks you'd be 'the jewel in his crown'—his words, not mine."

Kali turned her attention to Indra. "You want me to be in your movie, Soma-head?"

Indra looked over at me for reassurance, and I gave him an encouraging smile—even though it physically repulsed me to have to help him at all.

"Please, my movie will be a failure if your beauty does not grace its presence," he intoned, crawling onto his knees, his hands clasped at his chest in supplication. He looked around at the unconscious Gopi who were strewn around the soundstage.

"They"—he gestured to the Gopi—"are but mere shades in the wake of your beauty, O Great Goddess of Destruction."

Kali snickered before turning to me, a wicked smile on her face.

"I want you to know, white girl, that if I do this, *if* I prostitute myself to this drug-addled poseur for you, then you are gonna owe me so big that it's not even funny."

I swallowed hard. I knew instinctively that I didn't want to be in debt to Kali—it was bad enough that I already owed Cerberus, and I hated to think my underworld credit was already heading into the "maxed out" zone, but I didn't have a clue how else to get my hands on the jerkoid's Sea Foam.

"She kinda has you by the balls on this one, Cal," Clio said, a protective hand on Runt's cute little head. Neither of them seemed against me accepting Kali's offer—but then they weren't the ones who were gonna owe her big time after all was said and done.

I took a deep breath, trying to release the worry that was tensing up my body, but it was a no go.

"Fine. Okay, I'll owe you big time," I said weakly. "It's worth it to save my father and sister."

"And there will be no backing out at the last minute?" Kali asked.

"No backing out." I nodded.

Barely even noticing the bodies of the unconscious Gopi as she stepped over them, Kali came toward me, her mouth curved in a sickle of a smile. As she passed Indra, he tried to reach out and touch the hem of her shower curtain, but she pulled away from him like he was lower than the lowest Outcast, making him blush with shame.

Ignoring everyone else around us, her eyes focused on mine with the intensity of a high-powered laser beam—giving me a much better understanding of how a deer must feel when it's caught in the glare of an

SUV's high beams. The creepy little smile still etched on her face, she held out her hand for me to take, but instead of shaking on our "deal" like I'd expected, she pulled a tiny pin from somewhere in the depths of her thick mane of dark hair and stuck the tip deep into the meaty flesh of my palm.

"Ow!" I yelped, trying to pull my hand away from her grasp, but she held me tight. Quickly she pricked her own palm, drawing a large bead of blood, then slammed her hand against mine, pressing the flesh of our palms together in some weird blood ritual that was obviously the magical seal to our deal.

"Now we are bound by blood until you have fulfilled your debt to me. After that . . . who knows," she added mysteriously.

She released me, and I grimaced at the long smear of blood that ran across the heel of my hand. I felt lightheaded just looking at all the wasted hemoglobin.

"You do realize how unsanitary that was," I said, pulling a Wet-Nap from my back pocket and using it to wipe away the blood. This only elicited another creepy smile from my benefactress.

"You don't happen to have another one of those on you?" Kali asked, looking at the Wet-Nap I'd bunched together and stuffed into my front pants pocket—as "cool" as Indra's soundstage was, I had yet to see a garbage can anywhere.

I smiled, taking another of the lemon-scented packets from my pocket, and threw it to Kali. "I always travel with a couple of these babies. You never know when you're gonna be touching something yucky."

Kali nodded in agreement as she unwrapped her little moist towelette and daubed at the blood trail on her own hand.

"So does that fulfill my debt?" I asked hopefully, even though I was pretty sure the answer was gonna be "no."

"You wish," Kali said, her dark red lips curling devilishly at the corners. I felt a tug on the hem of my pants and looked down to find Indra, still on his knees, flashing his teeth to me in a semblance of gratitude.

"Thank you, Madame Death."

Okay, I used the word "semblance" because I could tell that behind the glamorous smile he flashed me, Indra absolutely detested having to thank me. He may have been easy on the eyes, but underneath that gorgeous exterior lurked an egotistical little prick who hated to thank *anyone* for *anything*.

"You're welcome," I said, offering him my hand for a shake—which he promptly ignored.

Oh well, I had already kinda figured that Indra and I were never gonna be bosom buddies—no matter how many favors I did, or didn't do, for him. So be it. I mean, with friends like him in your life, why would you ever need enemies anyway?

"So, are we gonna get this show on the road, or what?" Kali said with a yawn. I turned to Indra for instruction, but he was gone. In his place, Mr. Tap Shoes glowered back at me, his weasely little face a mask of irritation as he stood behind the gigantic dolly-mounted film camera, his right eye pressed tight against the viewfinder.

"If you, your sister, and your little hellhound will get out of my frame . . . ?" Mr. Tap Shoes barked at me with impatience.

Fine, be that way, I thought to myself as I motioned for Clio and Runt to follow me off the set. *I didn't want to be in your stupid little movie anyway.*

And the truth was I really didn't.

seventeen

I had never seen a movie being filmed before. I would love to say that it was a superexciting experience, and that tons of cool stuff happened. That it, like, totally changed my life completely and made me want to be a better person.

Not.

Hands down, I have to rate seeing a movie being made as the number-one most boring thing I have ever witnessed in my entire existence. Really, it's on par with watching paint dry, or timing a slug to see how long it takes the slimy little sucker to get across your sidewalk.

I guess it just took more than pretty clothes, bright lights, and a big camera in my face to impress me. I decided that I was probably one of those folks who enjoyed *watching* their TV, not participating in it.

On the other hand, Clio was in geek-girl heaven. Indra let her stand right by him while he guided the camera up and down the long metal dolly track he had magically laid down on the floor. He even let her look through the viewfinder twice—which totally put her over the moon. Even Runt seemed to be enjoying the experience, while it was all I could do not to fall asleep against the wall where I was sitting.

Seriously, they just kept repeating the same stuff over and over again—even though, from what I could tell, each take looked *exactly* like the take before it. For the life of me, I couldn't tell you *what* Indra was accomplishing by making Kali walk down a set of stairs twenty times in a row while the Gopi did their crazy whirling dervish number on the platform below her—unless this was all a carefully planned ruse to make Kali so annoyed she'd go all *Carrie*-insane on us, which was always a possibility anyway with Kali's volatile personality. I'm sure she would've just *loved* an excuse to put on her destructive face and set a few of the Gopi on fire for fun.

The only thing I found even *remotely* interesting—and the word "interesting" was a stretch—was the way Indra used magic to move the lights and the props around the set. Mostly, I was curious about the magic part, but I could see how lighting really was kind of an art form.

For example, there was this one part where Kali was leaning against the stair rail, her long, dark hair like a glorious storm cloud around her face, and Indra got this big light to swoop in real close to her face, giving her features this gorgeous, creamy, sunlit glow. That was kinda neat—*until he did it seven more times*, at which point I stopped paying attention.

Since Indra was the only crew person involved—aside from the now-conscious Gopi, whom he'd had to beg Kali to unspell, which she did begrudgingly—it had taken him only a few minutes to magically get everything set up and running again. Without magic, I got the distinct impression that the crew on a film set would be considerably larger than one person.

Once the Gopi were back on the job—for the rest of the shoot they stayed far out of Kali's orbit, their dark eyes constantly darting here and there, watching for any sign of an impending attack—Indra snapped his fingers, and the door to the janitor's closet flew open to reveal row upon row of beautiful, beaded saris. I reached up and felt my split lip—which was still puffy and painful to the touch—and wished there'd been a closet full of saris to break my fall instead of the janitorial supplies Clio and I'd encountered.

After a heated battle between Indra and Kali over which sari she was going to wear, they finally settled on a bright turquoise one that had little silver-colored beads sewn all over it and strands of silver filigree running through the fabric. It wouldn't have been my choice—I would've put Kali in the fire-engine red number I'd spotted near the back of the closet, but I kept my mouth shut, not wanting to get in the middle of a heated argument between two highly volatile Deities.

Once she'd put on the sari, they'd spent another ten minutes arguing over whether or not Kali needed any makeup—Indra was of the mind that she needed a complete makeover, but Kali insisted on going before the cameras just as she was.

Finally, after Kali threatened to disembowel all the Gopi before adding their skulls to her already renowned collection back home, Indra relented, letting her do the shoot without so much as a smear of gloss on her full lips.

We stood around for what felt like eons until, suddenly, Indra proclaimed the shoot over and Kali *wrapped*.

I had no idea what he meant by the word "wrapped," but if it had something to do with us being done, then I was all for it. As I watched Indra futzing with the camera, I found myself becoming increasingly annoyed with him. Because of his stupid movie, I now owed Kali a huge favor—and all the jerk had wanted her to do was walk down a flight of stairs, lean against a stair rail with a melancholy look on her face, and then sigh deeply.

Maybe I can talk her into reducing my sentence to half *a favor,* I thought hopefully, *since the whole thing was pretty painless in the end.*

The one thing I couldn't figure out was why Indra needed *me* to wrangle Kali into being in his film. I'd have thought since they were both Hindu Deities, all Indra would've had to do was ask for her help. Their strange dynamic made me wonder what the heck the deal was between them, and why Kali seemed to take such an inordinate amount of joy in belittling him in front of us every chance she got.

"Hey, Kali? Can I have a word?" I asked, crooking a finger in her direction after making sure Clio and Runt were otherwise engaged helping the Gopi coil long lengths of electrical cord into bundles for Indra. I wasn't trying to purposely cut my sister out of the loop, but I had a feeling if I wanted any confidences from Kali, then I was going to have to interrogate her in private.

She looked up from where she was still standing on the raised set platform, her chin resting in her hands, a wistful look on her face. At my insistence, she stood up and crossed the platform, taking the stairs two at a time, her long, glossy hair bouncing with every step.

"Yeah?" she said when she'd closed the gap between us.

I wasn't sure how to begin. I didn't want to offend

her, or incur her wrath, but I needed to know what was going on between her and Indra so I didn't find myself without the precious Sea Foam I'd bartered myself into debt for when all of this was over. I'd been voluntarily out of the supernatural world for a long time, but I very much remembered the old adage: *Deal with the Gods at your own discretion.*

It wasn't that they were bad folk, really, but their needs always seemed to take precedence over yours—no matter *what* they'd promised you beforehand. *Like magical Sea Foam, maybe?*

"Uhm, I don't want to be a pain in the neck, but I need to make sure that Indra's really gonna give me that Sea Foam stuff . . . now that I owe you such a huge favor and all," I said meekly.

Kali nodded as if she understood what I was saying, but her next words proved how very much she and I were *not* on the same page.

"You want me to hold the Gopi hostage until he pays up?" she asked, and as nice as the offer was, I was pretty sure that I did *not* want Gopi blood on my hands.

"No, nothing as extreme as that, but maybe you could just fill me in on why this Sea Foam is so important to Indra?" Kali mulled my words over in her head, then nodded.

"So that you are aware of everything? So nothing takes you by surprise?" Kali said, like she was reading my mind. I smiled.

"Exactly."

She considered her words, taking her time, but I could see that she was really stalling so that she could use her peripheral vision to discern Indra's location.

Score one for me for keeping the matter just between us girls.

"Well," she said, "it is a bit of a tale . . ."

"I love a good story."

She laughed. "Of course you do, dipwad."

"Don't call me that." But Kali only gave me a mischievous smile and took my hand.

"Don't worry about your sister. Indra likes her—"

"And that's supposed to make me *not* worry," I mumbled under my breath.

"—and therefore the Gopi will look after her."

Off my look, she laughed. "I have special dispensation from Krishna to kick their asses, but that's a whole 'nother story entirely, dipwad. Just know that the Gopi are highly trained assassins who won't take crap from anyone, let alone an uptight prick from the Psychical Bureau of Investigations."

Nice, I thought, *so does* everyone *in the supernatural universe know my business? What am I? The Angelina Jolie of the underworld?*

Kali, her grip like an industrial-strength steel vise, began to squeeze my hand with a ferocity that quickly yanked me out of my thoughts and back into reality.

As she cranked up the intensity on her very unpleasant hand squeeze, I could feel the little tiny bones in my hand starting to crack—which totally freaked me out.

"Ow!" I cried, trying to yank my hand out of her clutches, but she wasn't having any of it. Just like when she commingled our blood earlier, I was reminded again of how much stronger she was than me—giving me a whole new reason to get my ass to the gym.

"Just one more moment while I sever the cord that binds you to this plane."

"Hey, don't do that! I don't want any part of me severed from any other part of me—" I began, my voice unnaturally high and laced with nervous tension, but

Kali only smiled, increasing the pressure on my fingers until I heard a distinct *pop* and felt a shard of bone slip out of place and pierce my skin from the inside out.

This is disgusting!

I watched in abject horror as a single drop of bright red blood fell from our clasped hands and splattered onto the ground. Between the pain in my hand and the revulsion I felt at seeing my blood out of my body again for, like, the twentieth time that day, I did the only sensible thing I could think to do in the situation.

I passed out.

i knew the whole "severing the cord" thing was a bad idea when I heard it, and this was only confirmed by the fact that I came back to consciousness . . . *without a body!*

I couldn't have been out for more than a few seconds, but those few seconds proved to be more than adequate enough for Kali to sever what she needed to sever and leave me completely floating in space, totally unattached to reality.

I can only describe the sensation as being *sort of* reminiscent of the feeling you get when you're in one of those carnival rides where they spin you at, like, a bazillion miles an hour, so that your whole body is thrown up against the back wall of the ride, and you hang, wriggling like a bug on a pin . . . and that only *kind of* gives you an idea of how bad it was.

I didn't have any eyes, so I couldn't see anything, but I could sort of *perceive* that I was surrounded by a murky darkness that was entirely devoid of any life, except for me.

Suddenly, I felt my bodiless self yanked backward,

dragged out of the murky nothingness, and shoved into something, a body I presumed, that was, like, twenty sizes too big for my soul.

I opened my eyes and instantly closed them again, terrified by what I'd just seen . . . *Indra's face staring back at me.*

i was in a large white pavilion . . . well, it was really more of a tent actually, but it was way nicer than any tent I'd ever been in—including the very large, very drafty one I'd shivered myself silly inside of during the very elegant, very expensive wedding I'd attended as my friend Noh's date four years ago in Montauk, Long Island.

We'd gotten to her cousin's wedding *ten minutes* late due to inclement weather—the worst thunderstorm Long Island had seen in a dozen years—and the stupid ushers hadn't let us sit down even though there were a couple of free chairs only three rows from the back. Instead, we'd had to stand for the whole forty-five-minute ceremony, *and* for the fifteen *more* minutes' worth of dopey homemade vows, our butts getting totally soaked by the downpour that had made us late in the first place.

Seriously, it was the *worst.*

Anyway, *that* was the nicest tent I'd ever stood in, and *this* pavilion made that one look like something you went camping in.

"Wow," I said, my voice low and tremulous and totally *not* my own. I decided to keep my mouth shut until further notice.

The tent was large enough to comfortably hold more than two hundred people under its stretched silk canopy. At first glance, the canopy looked like it was a plain milky white, but when I looked again, I noticed that it wasn't plain at all. The material had been woven by an artist's hand, so that every inch of it was covered with a scene out of Hindu mythology. I looked closer and saw delicate human beings intermixed with the many incarnations of the Gods and Goddesses. It was a living, breathing tapestry of their universe.

I could've spent years looking at it—my eyes discovering something new with each viewing—but instead I found myself drawn to the large, freestanding mirror that rested right in the middle of the otherwise empty pavilion. I reached out my hand to touch its beautifully gilded silver frame, and it shocked me. I took a step back, my fingers tingling as my eyes stuck like glue to the reflection that stared back at me.

I was in Indra's body.

He was dressed in flowing white pants made from the same material as the pavilion, and his gleaming brown chest was gorgeously firm and bare. I lifted the waistband of the pants and saw that, yep, this was definitely a man's body, and that I had been *very* wrong in my estimation of the size of Indra's member.

Jeez, the man was hung like a bloody horse. There was part of me that was *very* tempted to stick my hand down where I shouldn't and see if there really *was* any truth to all the penis fuss, but the idea made me feel a little cheap. Like I was taking advantage of a comatose patient or something. I decided to keep my hands to myself . . . at least for now. But who knew *what* would happen if I got stuck inside Indra's body indefinitely? The guy was a total hunk, and I was pretty affection starved. I bet getting lucky in his body was like shooting fish in a barrel.

I touched the lion's mane of dark hair that framed

his handsome face, and his dark eyes flashed back at me in the mirror.

He seemed full of power and courage.

This is a different man from the one I met back at the soundstage, I thought curiously.

"Yes, he was a different man," Kali said, reading my mind as she magically appeared in the mirror behind me. She was wearing a bright red sari, her dark hair coiled around her head like a snake.

"What happened to him?" I asked in Indra's voice, giving myself the willies. I was definitely gonna have to follow my own advice and keep my mouth shut until I was back in my own body.

"Let him show us, white girl," she said, a strange smile etched on her face. "And by the way, Wodin said to remind you that you only have one more day left."

"What do you mean 'one more day'?" I said incredulously.

She laughed.

"Oops, didn't we tell you? If you haven't completed your tasks before the next sunset—"

"You mean the one after this one?"

She rolled her eyes. "Of course that's what I mean."

"Because technically it's not really sunset yet, so this would be the next—"

"Shut up, white girl." Kali sighed.

Jeez, someone *forgot to take her chill pill again.*

"Okay, whatever. Sorry," I pouted, feeling kind of annoyed by the whole thing. First, she tells me I've got only *one day* to finish my tasks; then she snaps at me just for asking a legitimate question. I might as well concede on the whole thing right here and now and be done with it.

"If you haven't completed your tasks by the next sunset," she continued, oblivious to my inner turmoil, "then the Board will be forced *not* to renew your father's contract, and you and your entire family will become mortal again."

"You know, I heard you, like, the first four times you told me," I moaned. "You guys on the Board are, like, total serial repeaters."

"Well, I can guarantee you haven't heard this part before because Wodin just came up with it," Kali said, getting all smarmy on me. "Know what's going to happen to you if you fail to complete your tasks?"

"What?" I asked, starting to get nervous.

"You die and get reincarnated as a fly."

"Excuse me!?" I nearly shrieked. "I get turned into a what?"

"A fly. And by the way, you *will* still owe me a favor, no matter what form you take in your next life."

"Well, that major-league sucks," I said.

Kali raised an eyebrow.

"Oh, white girl, you have *no idea*."

I turned around to ask her what she meant by *that*, but she wasn't there. When I turned back around, the mirror was empty, too.

Gone again. And just when I was starting to kind of like the sari-wearing bitch, I thought to myself.

Alone again in the pavilion, the afternoon sun had already passed its zenith, and dusk was fast approaching. It was getting cold out, and since I was topless—which was fine for a guy, but still pretty damn chilly—I decided to leave the cover of the pavilion and see if I could find somewhere a little warmer to hang out.

As I looked out at the scene that lay before me right outside the pavilion, I could see nothing but sand for miles in all directions. I didn't know if I was in the middle of the desert or if the sea was just out of my range of vision, but I was sick of standing there, freezing my nipples off, waiting for something to happen.

Best to take the bull by the balls, and see what I can make happen for myself, I thought as I giggled to myself. I mean, *balls*? Come on, how many times in my life would I be able to make a statement like that, and actually have the *balls* to back it up?

God, sometimes I really cracked myself up.

Too bad my laughter was to be so short-lived.

eighteen

As I stepped outside the pavilion, something strange happened . . . I lost control of Indra's body—ending my one and only chance to discover what the heck was so great about owning a penis. Suddenly, I was a passenger inside the great Hindu God, instead of his master. I stopped feeling cold. I stopped feeling anything, actually. It was totally bizarre.

I was the silent partner in this situation, and I didn't like it one bit. I mean, what if Indra did something disgusting—like go to the bathroom or eat an octopus or have sex—and I had to sit there, completely involved but totally without a say in what was happening.

Gross!

I tried to reassert my control over the masculine body I was trapped in by telling its legs to stop moving, but instead I just found myself being carried along inside Indra as he crossed the sands, his large, well-muscled calves carrying us much faster than I could've ever gone in my own body.

He paused once to pull a flask from his pocket and take a long draught of whatever nasty stuff was in it. It was weird because when I had been in control of his body, I hadn't even known there *was* a pocket in his pants, let alone room enough for a flask. I decided that the flask must be magical, and since I hadn't known it was there to find, it had kept itself hidden from me.

More and more, I found myself wishing that I were at least *moderately* magically adept. I couldn't believe I'd actually listened to Father when he'd forbidden magic handling inside Sea Verge. Since Clio had ignored him, I figured Thalia probably had, too—which made me think I was the only dum-dum in the family who ever obeyed our parents' rules. I wondered what other things I had forgone because Father or Mother had told me not to do them.

There were probably lots of other things that I could dredge up from my childhood to piss myself off even more with, but since I was in the middle of nowhere, trapped in someone else's body, I didn't think now was quite the time to be harping on all that.

But I knew *one* thing for sure. I was sick and tired of being Miss Goody Two-shoes. I mean, it's not like anyone—Father and Mother included—ever gave me a pat on the back for being the "nice" girl. I felt completely justified in deciding that the next time someone told me I *couldn't* do something, well, I was just going to do it, and damn the consequences.

While I had been bemoaning my lack of magical ability, Indra had continued with his one-man trek across the sand. He'd stopped one more time to pull another swallow—a long one this time—from his flask, but he very quickly replaced the silvery container and kept going. I only wished I could tap into his brain and find out where we were heading. I would have felt a lot better knowing we weren't about to get eaten by something big and scary—but that was just me.

It was like Indra and I were the main character in the beginning of a video game, totally unsure of where we were going (okay, I guess, *I* was the only one who didn't know where we were going), but armed with the knowledge that as long as we kept moving, we were eventually gonna run into something interesting—hopefully that something would win us lots of points and not kill us in the process.

We were in full twilight, and the emptiness around us seemed to take on a more sinister tone now that the sun was gone. Suddenly, there was a flash of light that split open the sky, illuminating the desert-scape around us for a half second before pitching the world back into semidarkness again. In that split second of illumination I had seen something that chilled my bones down to the very marrow. Not more than five hundred feet away from us was the biggest, scariest-looking castle I had ever seen. It was worse than anything I'd ever dreamed Castle Dracula or Frankenstein would look like in my imagination. And I had dredged up some pretty scary scenery when I was reading those books.

It was maybe 10,000 square feet—give or take a converted basement or two—and it had a main building flanked on either side by two huge, looming wings that both had two turrets topping them like bloated cherries on top of a rancid strawberry sundae. The whole structure of the building was pretty typical castle with cutout windows, and flaming torches stuck here and there for illumination—none of which lent it the frightening air I had encountered upon first glance.

It's the material the castle is made out of that's giving me the willies.

When I think of the word "castle," I imagine big, gray stone blocks piled one on top of another, mortared together to make an impenetrably thick outer wall that no bad guys could ever knock down, no matter how hard they tried.

Well, this sucker was nothing like that.

This castle wasn't made out of stone, or brick, or even wood—I could totally handle a wooden castle, not very practical, but totally fine in my book. No, this *definitely* wasn't built with the kind of stuff you bought down at your local Home Depot . . . this monstrosity was constructed from something that I had never really considered to be building material at all . . . the tortured bodies of thousands of human beings. There were so many of them that by the one-hundredth set of congealed eyeballs I counted, I was ready to throw up my digestive tract. Too bad I didn't have my own body so I could indulge the urge.

The only time I've ever experienced anything that was even *kind of* comparable to the hideous castle that lay before me was when I was dragged to this crazy scientific exhibit in New York by Patience—I don't think she wanted to go by herself, so I was her unsuspecting victim—where some Austrian "scientist" had plasticized the bodies of hundreds of "volunteers" and then put them on display. Imagine a gallery filled with fifty or so plasticized specimens—muscles unbound by skin, eyeballs popping out of unlidded eye sockets, teeth shiny and denuded of lips—splayed in whatever pose best showed off the inner workings of each specimen's physique, and there you had it.

This castle was totally like the "mad scientist's secret hideaway" version of that exhibit: thousands of human bodies split open and weirdly sewn back together to cover every nook and cranny of the place. You could see the mangled appendages, the bloated faces, and the cracked-open rib cages of a small army of victims doomed to spill out their viscera for eternity.

It was so foul, so alien to my sense of what was *right* in the world, that it took me a few moments to fully comprehend the utter evil of the thing.

Indra didn't seem at all phased by it, though. Instead, the insane God picked up his pace so that we would get there *sooner.* The guy was gonna give me a heart attack—body or no body. I wanted to scream at him to turn around and go back to the pavilion, where it was safe, but I had the strange feeling that even if, by some crazy miracle, I got Indra to go back, the pavilion wouldn't be there anymore. In the insane world that I now found myself inhabiting, a missing pavilion would only be par for the course.

Indra walked purposefully toward the castle, stopping when he reached the edge of a very deep, very treacherous-looking moat. The moat was invisible from far away, the edge raked so that you couldn't see the drop-off until you were almost on top of the castle itself. Luckily, Indra seemed to know his way around the place. I got the distinct impression that a lot of visitors—probably in their haste to avoid the exterior horrors of the castle—didn't notice the moat *at all*—and ended up walking right into it, never to be seen again.

Indra stood very close to the edge of the moat, which made me kinda nervous. I so did *not* want to end my life anywhere *near* that disgusting place. Just being in such close proximity made the nonexistent hairs on the back of my neck stand up in terror.

I was really starting to get annoyed about not having my own body. I guess your body is just one of those things you don't really appreciate until it's gone. I don't think I would've nearly minded so much if I were trapped inside someone hot that I *liked*—Johnny Depp or Keanu Reeves, anybody?—but since Indra and I didn't have the greatest relationship to begin with, this body-sharing thing would be intolerable if it lasted too much longer.

The whole time I'd been trapped inside Indra, he'd barely breathed, let alone mumbled any words, but now he spoke, and his voice was like a freight train rumbling through the darkness.

"Vritra, show yourself! I have come through ninety-nine different planes of existence to reach your castle, and I *will* do away with you this night, or die in the trying!"

Luckily, we didn't have to sit around twiddling our thumbs, waiting for whoever owned the place to notice we were there. There was a loud screech from inside, and I had the very distinct impression that whatever was making the racket was *not* human.

Great, now you've gone and done it, you big ass, I thought to myself. *You woke up the monster, and it's gonna eat us!*

The inhuman screech stopped almost as suddenly as it had begun. And the silence was far scarier in my opinion than the creature's call had been.

I felt a tickle somewhere in my brain—did I even have a brain anymore, I wondered? *Vritra?* Where had I heard *that* name before?

Then it hit me. This was the creature Indra was supposed to have slain with the Sea Foam he was guarding so desperately. So, if the creature was still alive, then that meant I was in the past.

I almost laughed when I realized what Kali had done: *She had sent me into Indra's memories.* If this was how she told a story, then I was more than happy never to hear another one out of *her* mouth.

There was a sharp crack, like the tip of a whip striking bare flesh, and suddenly, we weren't alone anymore. The giant drawbridge fell open like a tongue, and what seemed like a thousand men in heavy scarlet and black armor began to stream across its span.

If I had had any control over the situation, I would have turned tail and ran, but Indra had other ideas. He reached inside his pocket—*not another stupid drink out of the flask,* I moaned to myself—but I was wrong in my assumption. Instead of the silvery flask, Indra produced a long, shimmering scepter from his pocket. It was unlike anything I had ever seen before. It was so mesmerizing that even Indra had a hard time dragging his eyes away from its brilliance.

It was no more than three feet long, but slim and pliable in his hands. The length of it had been made from combining two pieces of bone—I was pretty sure they had been some *really* tall guy's femurs in another life—and on either end was a sharp, glittering sickle blade made of a clear, crystallized substance that I couldn't place. It wasn't like I was a small-arms *expert* or anything. As far as *I* knew, metal was the *only* medium of choice when you wanted to decapitate someone special, so what was *this* stuff?

After a moment or two of contemplation, I decided the only thing they could reasonably be made of was diamond—two incredibly *large* diamonds cut into subtle killing blades. Glass or crystal would have shattered instantly in battle, but diamonds were pretty hard little fellows and could take care of themselves—and *these guys* were about as far from Harry Winston as they came anyway.

There was a hypnotizing quality about these diamonds, and I found myself desperately wanting to reach out and touch one of the blades, caress its smooth sharpness with the hollow of my throat . . . *Eww, did I really just think those words? Jeez, the thing* has *to be magic the way it's trying to compel me to kill myself on it.*

Thank God I didn't have a body—or the diamond-bladed monster would've gladly had my blood for lunch. And since I'd already spilled enough of my own platelets that day, I was all for not having a corporeal form so I didn't have to worry about keeping away from the thing.

I watched in awe as Indra raised the weapon high above his head, his body tensing as he waited for the horde of soldiers to envelope him. It was surprising how quickly the armor-clad men gave in to the weapon's siren song. It was amazing to see the men—all of them ashen and mealy eyed underneath their heavy bloodred and midnight armor—rip their breast plates away from their throats and eagerly sacrifice themselves to the call of Indra's twin sickle blades. As each man died, their last prayers for grace gurgling in their throats, the blades would glow white-hot, almost like they were absorbing the souls of their prey.

I had a hard time reconciling the idea of an inanimate object actually *eating*, but that was what was happening—Indra's scepter was scarfing down human souls like a gluttonous little pig. It reminded me of the time

I'd watched a group of Atkins Diet acolytes from work—three middle-aged women in pantsuits—scarf down a whole spit of shawarma at a Middle Eastern–themed Christmas party.

The amount of food consumed was stupefying.

Indra's scepter put them to shame.

I found myself with a much healthier respect for Indra after that. Any man or God that could wield *that* kind of weapon was pretty damn hot in my book. In fact, Indra was starting to take on Fabio-like proportions in my mind. I could imagine Indra's face on the cover of one of those cheesy bodice rippers, his cheek nestled into the swell of my breast as we pretended to be a pirate and a princess, respectively. If I'd had a body . . . well, let's just say I had some very wanton things I wanted to do with Mr. Sex on a Stick.

You know, can I just take a minute to digress here?

It's always really bothered me the way my mind can hate a man one minute and then want to have sex with him the next. Like this whole sexual attraction to Indra thing, it made me feel like a total slut.

I can only imagine it has something to do with this whole love-hate thing we women are conditioned to feel toward sex. It's like we can't love it *too much* because then we're bad girls, but if we "just say no," then we're uptight prudes.

Instead of having all this ambivalence toward sex, I wish society—and my brain—would make up its mind about the whole thing, so I could enjoy getting laid without all the hassle of having my libido—and emotions—smacked around like a Ping-Pong ball.

While I debated sexual politics with myself, Indra finished off the last of the soldiers. The bodies of the dead and dying lay strewn around him, the spoils of a one-God fighting machine. As each corpse expired, its body seemed to shrink in upon itself, its flesh taking on the purplish black hue of rotten meat. It gave new insight into the term "meat puppet." I mean, that was all these soldiers really were in the end . . . just giant rotten globs of meat and sinew. It was kind of sad, all that wasted life, but there was really nothing Indra could do about it. It was either kill or be killed, as far as I could see. And since I was hanging out in Indra's body, it was pretty obvious whose side I was on here.

Indra put the scepter back in his magical pocket—or maybe it was the scepter that was magic, not the pocket—as the last gurgles of life were ebbing away from his victims. He looked back up at the castle as if daring its keeper to send another round of infantry to their deaths.

Suddenly, the ground underneath us began to shake. All I could think of was *earthquake*! I waited for Indra to run away, to duck and cover, *to cluck like a chicken* . . . I didn't care; I wanted him to do *something* other than stand there like a stupid statue. I had a terrible feeling that the whole castle was gonna come down on top of us, and we were gonna be buried under ten tons of dead human body parts until the end of eternity.

But the castle stood firm, and the ground stopped its shaking almost as quickly as it had begun.

"You are a coward, hiding behind your minions!" Indra yelled up to the castle's battlements. *Why are you goading it!* I thought miserably to myself, wishing I had some kind of conduit into Indra's brain so I could give him a good stiff talking-to. I didn't think taunting a monster—no matter *what* kind of magical scepter you had in your pocket—was a very wise choice. Why not just ask the monster to come outside and talk like civilized adults, hmm?

I amended my opinion of our situation when the castle began to belch out flaming fireballs of black goop that rained down on us like a plague from God. I had no clue what the goop balls were *really* made out of, but they smelled suspiciously like burning hair and poop—which definitely gave me pause. I decided that any creature that was partial to flaming balls of shit was *not* civilized. They were just *foul.*

I was also perturbed to find that I could smell again when I was *still* unable to do anything else that required a body. I mean, come on, here I was stuck inside another person, and all I could do was stop and smell the shit . . . so *not* fair!

After a few minutes the deluge of flaming goop balls finally died down, and I found we had been spared their touch—although the rest of the landscape was severely littered with goop-ball carnage, making it look like the *Exxon Valdez II* had decided to explode at our feet.

What next? I thought to myself. *Vomit locust? Snot toads?*

But the goop balls weren't finished with us yet.

The goop ball closest to Indra began to roil and smoke like a just-lit firecracker. Indra, sensing danger, immediately backed away from it, his hand instinctively reaching for his pocket, but before he could get the scepter out and defend himself, the goop ball exploded, covering him in a thick, oozing sludge that stank like an outhouse. Instantly, the sludge began to harden, encasing Indra inside it like a fly in amber. Of course, we were still sharing a body, so I could feel his rage, his mounting frustration at being captured, but sadly I was as impotent to help him as I was to help myself.

While Indra bellowed to be released from his sludgy prison, the remaining goop balls—like they'd each been given an individual all-clear sign—started to smoke and bubble in unison, churning faster and faster as they folded in on themselves until each ball had increased its size by half, so that when they were finally done expanding, they looked just like beached, goop ball–colored puffer fish.

I watched in horror as inside of each "puffer fish" a tiny head and baby-sized fists began to form, pushing their way to the surface, dragging their tar baby–like bodies with them as they burst from their goop-ball chrysalises and took their first, tentative bipedal steps.

When the conversion had been completed, there were more than a hundred of the creatures, each sludge-colored body no taller than a small Saint Bernard, each face devoid of eyes, nose, and mouth, so that every countenance was just a slick of featureless goop. Silent as toddler-sized assassins, they began to move forward en masse until they were surrounding Indra's prostrate form.

They stood like sentries above him, their empty heads tilted down at his writhing form—and even though they had no eyes, I knew that somehow they were seeing right down to his soul . . . and mine.

Then, without warning, the goop-ball creatures swarmed Indra, swallowing him whole. I tried to hold on to consciousness, keep my brain focused and aware, but it was impossible. I felt my very essence rent from me, leaving me an empty shell inside a swirling mass of brown, stinky sludge.

And then I floated away.

nineteen

In the darkness behind my eyelids I heard a voice, one that was not just commanding but seductive, alluring . . . *sexual.*

"Calliope Reaper-Jones, don't be frightened. Open your eyes to the astral plane."

I instantly did what the voice said, only to find myself shivering as I stood naked on the edge of a lapis lazuli–colored ocean, my bare feet tucked deeply into its sandy beach for warmth. As I dug my toes into the kernels of sand, luxuriating in the scratchy feel of sand on skin, I was suddenly compelled to look down at my feet.

I almost screamed.

Wherever Calliope Reaper-Jones was, I was *still* not in her body. I was someone else entirely all over again.

I looked down, taking in the shape of my new ankles—*thin*—and the curve of my calf and thighs—*ripe and sexy and feminine.* Okay, whoever's body I now inhabited had, like, *amazing* legs. That was a given.

I also noticed that my host had a tiny little *star tattoo* just below the talus bone of her right ankle. It seemed strangely familiar to me, like I knew someone in my own life who had gotten that *exact* tattoo. But as much as I strained my memory, I couldn't remember who the hell it was.

Oh, what I wouldn't have done for a mirror. I could only *imagine* the face that belonged to a pair of legs like that, and *hot* probably didn't do it justice.

As almost a second thought, I held up my hand, the one that Kali had squeezed the life out of, but I could see no signs of rupture, no flecks of dried blood. There were just long fingers, a dainty palm, and unpolished, naturally gorgeous nails.

"Look to the water."

There was that sexy voice again. At first, I thought it was a man speaking. Then after I heard it again, I found myself horribly confused . . . Then I found myself leaning ever so slightly toward the voice belonging to someone of the female persuasion. There was kind of a RuPaul quality to it that I hadn't noticed in the beginning, a smoothness to the timbre that almost—but not quite—concealed a gravelly purr underneath. It was this *purr* that totally threw me.

I felt an unearthly compulsion to do exactly what the voice said. It was one of those moments your mother warns you about: the one where she says, "Would you jump off the Empire State Building if your friends told you to?"

All I can say is yes, if the voice had told me to jump off the Empire State Building, that was what I would've done.

"Look to the water, Calliope Reaper-Jones. And remember what you see . . ."

I couldn't see anything at first except the horizon, which seemed to stretch on and on into forever as it sat astride its lover, the Indigo Sea. Air and Water were so intimately enmeshed that I had a hard time telling where pale peach and purple-bruised Sky finished and deep blue Sea began.

I stood, enthralled by the majesty of my surroundings. I had never seen a place like this beach before, neither in reality nor in a book. It was magical, like it had existed since the beginning of time, and would last long after Man and all its creations had been beaten into dust.

"Look," the voice said.

That was when I saw it: the demon Vritra, its long, snakelike body skewering through the lonely ocean. It had the head of dragon—large, pulsating nostrils; a scaly head and throat; wide, almond-shaped eyes—and the body of a serpent. It had to be at least fifty feet long, I judged, as it piloted its way through the water, toward dry land.

I wasn't sure how I knew the demon's name. All I could figure was that the body I was borrowing must have had an intimate knowledge of the creature, and I was picking up on it. I wasn't scared of the demon. In fact, it was quite the opposite: I welcomed it.

It rose with the waves, until it finally beached itself in front of me. I didn't move toward it, or even acknowledge that it was there at all. It crawled toward me on its great belly, until it was only a few feet from me, and stopped, its giant almond eyes glittering in the twilight. I found myself alone in the half-light with only the demon for company.

"You are here."

When it spoke, its voice was like a *hiss*, and I felt the skin on my arms and legs prickle with goose bumps as the last of the daylight strove not to fade away.

I did not speak, only waited for Vritra to continue.

"She comes. I cannot prevent it. She is smarter than you had me believe."

I nodded, and my head felt heavy on my neck, like there was more than one person in my brain.

"But we will conquer them all," Vritra added, and I saw a hint of its forked tongue in the semidarkness—which was totally creepy.

The demon closed its almond eyes in pleasure as I reached out and laid my hand on its bumpy head, rubbing the swollen flesh with the tips of my fingers. The monster was complacent under my hand, and I could feel the thrum of its thoughts vibrating against my palm. They were *dark* thoughts, evil even. The person whose body I was trapped inside of was frightened by those thoughts—even though said person worked very hard to still that fear.

And that was the freakiest thing of all.

Finally, the demon shuddered and opened its eyes again. Without a word, it turned around and slid back into the Sea. I watched its tail disappear into the murky water, then I walked toward the surf, my hand outstretched.

I let the water rush across my hand, and when I lifted it into the air, the water sluiced out between my fingers, leaving only a soapy residue waiting patiently inside my cupped hand.

Sea Foam.

Kali's voice slammed into my head with the force of a ball-peen hammer, making my head ring with pain.

"Remember, white girl, you only have one more day to complete your task, so you'd better get your butt in gear."

The ringing didn't die away with her voice like I'd expected; instead it slowly began to increase until the pain was so intense that I blacked out.

i came back to consciousness with a whimper—not figuratively, but literally. A whimper, and if I have to be completely honest here . . . there was a lick, too.

My head was on fire as I cracked open a very gritty eye to find Runt staring at me, her face not even half an inch from mine. When she realized I was out of Dreamland, she pushed her wet nose into my cheek and licked me right on the mouth.

"Gross," I tried to mumble, but my mouth felt like it was full of marbles. *Double gross,* I thought to myself. *Marbles* and *dog saliva, aren't I the lucky one?*

"Are you okay, Cal?" I heard Clio say as she dropped down into my line of view. Her face was awash with a slew of emotions, the primary ones being: fear, anger, and worry. She reached out and brushed a stray strand of hair out of my eyes, before impulsively leaning forward and giving me a hug.

"I'm fine," I said, but I sure as hell didn't feel fine. I felt like someone was still hammering away at my brainpan but taking breaks every fifteen seconds or so to breathe fire all over my cerebral cortex.

I looked around at my surroundings for the first time since I'd regained consciousness, realizing with a sigh of happiness that we were no longer in Indra's world. Somehow, we had been magically transported back to Clio's messy bedroom at Sea Verge. It was funny to think that before Father had been kidnapped, I had been more than happy never to set foot in Sea Verge again, but here I was, less than forty-eight hours later, counting my blessings to be back in the family fold for, like, the *fourth* time since all the craziness started.

"Look at your hand, Cal," Clio said, her hawk eyes fixed on my fist, which was glowing a strange blue green color. I looked down and instantly felt a strange wetness creeping across the flesh of my palm. I let my fingers open like a blossoming flower, and Clio gasped. The inside of my hand was coated with a bubbly, greenish blue substance that shimmered as it caught the light.

Sea Foam.

My whole experience with Vritra, and the stranger whose body I'd inhabited on the beach, came back to me in vivid detail, and I shivered, remembering how totally creeped out I'd been by the exchange. Still, I was dying to know whose body I'd been in. There was something distinctly familiar about the tattoo I'd seen on her ankle, but for the life of me, I still couldn't place it.

And the thing that was even *more* curious than that was . . . *who* in the hell had been talking to me while I was waiting for Vritra on the beach? I realized that *whoever* it was must've been the one who'd arranged for me to get the Sea Foam—*because Indra, the liar, had never had it to give!*

I was distracted from trying to figure any of it out by a gentle gurgling—kind of like the sound you hear when you let the water out of a full bathtub.

"What the—" I began, but didn't finish because Clio and I were both transfixed by the Sea Foam as it magically started to soak into my skin. The gurgle got quieter, then stopped altogether, when there was only a trace of the Sea Foam left, represented by a shiny residue that coated my palm. Immediately, I could feel the essence of the magical stuff swimming inside my veins, melding with my blood, making me feel strangely invincible.

I gave Clio a long look.

"Well, that was weird . . ." Clio said, her voice trailing off as she indicated my palm. "I wonder what it means?"

I shrugged as nonchalantly as I could muster—considering the situation—but inside, my brain was completely reeling. Clio was right . . . The whole thing *was* major weird, and what *really* freaked me out was how in the dark I was about everything. I mean, I didn't even know if it was *okay* that the Sea Foam was taking up residence in my bloodstream. And assuming *that* part was cool, how the heck was I supposed to show the Board that I had *possession* of the stupid stuff if it was trapped inside me? It wasn't like I could just trot it out like I would Runt—thank God, at least *she* was on a leash.

The whole thing was *way* more than enough to give me a headache—not that my brain wasn't already throbbing from all the memory hopping Kali had forced me into. And speaking of the only wily Hindu Goddess on my shit list . . . boy, was *I* gonna let it rip the next time I saw Kali. I didn't care *how* big a favor I owed her.

"Callie?" Clio said tentatively. "Uhm, someone that we both know just magicked my door off its hinges."

"Huh?" I answered, still too caught up in my anger at Kali to notice the tension in my sister's voice. It was only when Runt started barking like a maniac that I looked up to see Clio pointing at the gaping hole where her bedroom door had once been. Instead of a nice, white, solid core door with a Velvet Underground poster on the back of it . . . there was nothing but an intact white doorframe—with three dead-bolt halves and a half a piece of chain lock dangling from it.

Standing in the doorway were my mother and our lawyer, Father McGee, neither of whom looked very happy to see me.

"Hi, Mother," I said, giving her the biggest, fakest smile I could manage. "Fancy meeting you here."

She glared at me, and I was reminded for, like, the three millionth time in my life just how tough she really was. She may have looked all sweet and dainty, but she was married to Death, for God's sake, so you had to infer *something* from that.

"Calliope Reaper-Jones," she said through clenched, perfectly shaped white teeth, "what have you done with your father and sister?"

"Me?" I said, rising to my feet—and feeling kind of woozy for it. "I'm out there busting my butt to complete these stupid tasks and you have the *balls* to accuse me of being the bad guy? You know what I think? I think you suck."

"Calliope," Father McGee chimed in, his face pinched with anger, "that's more than enough from you."

"Excuse me? But the last time I checked, I wasn't five anymore, so don't talk to me like I'm a child. And that goes for both of you," I added, giving my mother the most meaningful look I could muster.

I couldn't believe they were treating me so badly. Here I was totally putting aside my own life to help *them*, and this was how they treated me? No wonder I put a Forgetting Charm on myself . . . I had known how cruddy being Death's Daughter *really* was.

"The detective from the Psychical Bureau of Investigations told us everything," my mother said finally.

"And I can't say that it *doesn't* make sense, Calliope. You *have* always wanted to be a mortal, so I understand you taking the chance—"

"What?" I interrupted. "You have to be kidding me. You think I planned this whole thing so I could be a stupid human being?"

"We know about the money," Father McGee said, and even though I didn't want to admit it to myself, I could see how painful this was for him. He really didn't want to believe I had anything to do with my father's kidnapping, but someone had obviously shown him—and my mother—some *very* compelling evidence.

"What money?" Clio said, chiming in for the first time. She had ahold of Runt's leash and was keeping the little midnight-colored puppy from attacking Mother and Father McGee.

"The Devil paid Calliope ten million dollars to kidnap your father and sister in a bid to install his protégé as the new head of Death, Inc. We found the money in her bank account."

Well, that's news to me, I thought. *Oh, what shopping damage I could do with a hoard of cash like that. Thank God the Devil hadn't really approached me with his offer. I might have been* way *too tempted to take him up on it.*

My mother lowered her eyes as she finished speaking, and the shame she felt at my "alleged" plot to unseat our family from their immortality was palpable. I hadn't even *done* anything and I still felt like a jerk about the whole thing. It was weird how guilt—even implied guilt like in this situation—was hard to escape once it had been levied at you.

"Callie . . . ?" Clio said, her voice strained with incredulity. "Tell them it's not true."

I swallowed hard. I didn't know if I should be angry and defensive and deny everything, or if I should laugh it off like it was a big joke at their expense. But when I opened my mouth, I found the only thing I was capable of was meekly stammering:

"It's not true."

I should have done something, said something that would gloss over the false accusations, but I couldn't make myself open my mouth again after that.

"Callie . . . ?" she whispered, begging me to explain myself.

Still, I said nothing. It was like my mouth was glued shut.

"Cal . . . ?"

I watched as one lonely tear fell from Clio's eye and slid down her cheek.

"Why . . . ?" she whispered, my heart breaking as I realized that Clio saw only betrayal in my lack of words.

Yet, I still couldn't say anything. It didn't really matter anyway. I didn't have the heart to defend myself after that. If the one person in my family who had staunchly believed in me from the beginning thought I was a bad apple, too, well, then . . . I just didn't care anymore.

"Give yourself up, Calliope, and tell us where you've hidden your father, sister, and the rest of the company's Executives. If you cooperate now, I'm sure we can apply for a lesser punishment," Father McGee said.

I stared at my feet, not sure what to do next. Even if I *did* let them take me in to the Psychical Bureau of Investigations, there was still no way I was gonna be able to show them where my father and sister were being held. I mean, c'mon, it's not like you can tell someone something you don't know, right?

I was between a rock and a hard place, and I didn't know what to do. I was pretty much screwed. I found myself wishing desperately for Jarvis, the amazing little faun who knew exactly what to do in a pinch. He would've figured out a way to convince everyone I was innocent of the charges. I tried to look over at Clio—for help, support . . . anything—but she kept her eyes averted from mine, and I saw that her hands were so tightly wound around Runt's leash that the flesh was bloodless.

I was on my own for the first time since I'd begun this whole adventure, and it was terrifying. I sighed, resigning myself to my fate.

"I'm sorry. I wish there was some way to—Ow!"

I looked down to see Runt attached to my ankle like an oversized, black leg warmer. Her tiny puppy teeth ground into my flesh, making my ankle throb like a son of a bitch—I didn't know what it was that attracted pain to my Achilles tendon area, but whatever it was, it spared me no pity.

"Stop it, Runt!" I heard Clio saying as the pain ratcheted up my leg. "Leave Callie alone!"

But Runt hung on with every ounce of her strength, jaws clamped to my lower leg in a death grip that seemed unbreakable.

Suddenly, I felt a strange lightness race through my being, followed by a pleasant tingling sensation that took over the leg that Runt had been chewing on. Without warning, the feeling spread to the rest of my extremities until it was finally injected into my brain, numbing me. The feeling was so intoxicating that I let it consume me. All I could think about were unicorns and butterflies and how much I would love to take a ride on one, or both, of these magical creatures.

Weirdness.

Then an acute case of vertigo hit me with such gut-wrenching suddenness that I was yanked out of my happy unicorn/butterfly reverie. Clio's room began to swirl around me, faster and faster, until I had to close my eyes, or risk throwing up.

I decided to go with option number one—I *hate* throwing up.

So, with nothing left to lose now but my breakfast, I closed my eyes and let everything disappear.

twenty

When I opened my eyes again, Clio's room and the nausea were gone, and I was sitting alone, a vast desert stretching before me like it was the foyer to the end of time. I looked down at my leg and saw that while there *was* a lot of dog saliva on my pants, there was no blood to be found anywhere on the fabric. I gingerly rolled up the offending pant leg, tentatively poking at the bruised-looking flesh that was revealed underneath the cloth. Runt had been kind enough to restrict the damage to heavy bruising, so I decided my ankle was just gonna be majorly sore the next day, not gangrenous like I'd feared.

Ignoring my leg now that I knew my wounds weren't life threatening, I turned to look at my surroundings. I couldn't put my finger on what it was, but there was something about the place that made my gut twist, bringing the return of the nausea I thought I'd left back at Sea Verge. Then, to my utter amazement, I suddenly began to shiver, my skin breaking out in gooseflesh—

which was *very* odd given that the temperature was hot enough to fry an egg on my shoe.

I had no idea why my body was reacting so strangely to this new place until it dawned on me that I had been there before. Of course, once I realized where I was, I knew why my body was getting all pissed off—it did *not* approve of being returned to a place it disliked without having given its prior consent first.

I guess my body was just weird like that.

And then, like a bolt of lightning illuminating the darkness, the identity of who had saved me from my family suddenly struck me. I realized there was only one logical explanation to the question since *I* couldn't have opened a wormhole in the fabric of time to save my life—I meant that literally—and Jarvis was stuck in the clink, and everyone *else* I knew thought I was a complete family sellout.

And besides that, I had experienced the whole weird "butterfly and unicorn" euphoria *once* before . . . when Runt and I had gone to Sea Verge through the random doorway in Hell that Runt had "found" after Jarvis saved me from the crazy detective from the Psychical Bureau of Investigations.

Now I knew it wasn't just dumb luck that had returned us safely back to Sea Verge that day . . . *It was my hellhound puppy, Runt.*

It only stood to reason that after our day of fruitless wandering in the Devil's dominion, Runt, who was probably trying to kill two birds with one stone, had opened a wormhole in the middle of nowhere to put a kibosh on my whining and save us at the same time.

Unhappiness washing through me, I cursed Runt under my breath—*dumb dog*—as I appreciated *exactly* where my—*dumb dog*—hellhound puppy had sent me: right back to where she'd opened the wormhole in the first place. I mean, I knew I could be annoying at times—and that had definitely been an *annoying at times* kind of experience—but there was no reason for her to send me back to the never-ending deserts of Hell!

What a poor excuse for a supernatural being I'd turned out to be, I thought to myself sadly. *My mother was right: I really* was *just a good-for-nothing mortal wannabe! I was stuck in Hell and I didn't even have enough magical talent to get myself out again.*

"God, I'm pathetic," I said out loud, and before I knew what was happening, I was crying. I felt like a big, fat baby as I let the tears run down my face, but I was helpless to stop them. If anyone had happened upon me at that moment, they would've seen a sniveling, snotty mess of a person curled up in a ball in the sand.

It was true. I really *was* pretty pathetic.

Letting the depression I'd kept at bay until now finally settle over me—and regardless of the really gnarly sunburn I was totally condemning my skin to—I closed my eyes and let myself drift.

I decided I deserved it . . . pathetic or not, the human psyche can handle only so much. Then it needs a break.

I've found that when you deny your body sleep, it invariably gets you into situations where you can't help *but* fall asleep—kind of like some weird sort of "body" payback.

Like you "somehow" find yourself invited to see a really long, really boring, black-and-white foreign film that has crappy subtitles that've been superimposed over the bottom of the picture in a *white* font instead of *yellow,* so that there's no way you can read them even if you wanted to—which you probably don't, but that's beside the point. You can't help yourself. Sleep is just gonna happen whether you want it to or not. It's a given.

I guess that was what my emotional outburst was all about: a way for my body to make me go to sleep so it could restore its energy without me feeling guilty about it.

I have no idea how long I was out, but when I woke up, my nose felt all warm and melty when I touched it, kind of like a quesadilla, and I had a thin layer of salt pasted to my upper lip where all the sweat had evaporated. I wiped off my "salt sweat" mustache and yawned, my mind a blank as I tried to remember where I was and why everything was covered in sand. Then everything came back to me, and instead of feeling refreshed and ready to tackle any obstacle, I just remembered how crappy my family had treated me, and all I wanted to do was stick my head in the sand and hide.

No, I wasn't a *total* coward.

Not.

I guess what I really wanted was something to deaden the empty feeling that had taken up residence in my heart while I slept.

What I wanted, I decided, was a *drink.*

Now, I'm no alcoholic, but I do enjoy a little frou-frou girly cocktail every now and then like any other red-blooded American gal. And after all I'd been through recently, I didn't think it was wrong to want to drown my sorrows in a little grain-alcohol daze.

Even though I knew the likelihood of finding a bar in the middle of the desert section of Hell was nil, I couldn't get the image of something neon green and alcoholic out of my brain. I still don't know what possessed me, but I was suddenly struck with the urge to close my eyes and ask the universe to give me a little "pick-me-up."

So I did.

"I'd like one Midori Sour, please."

It was so quiet in the vast emptiness of Hell that hearing my own voice out loud kind of shocked me. What shocked me even *more* was the ice-cold Midori Sour I suddenly found in my hand.

"Holy crap!" I yelped as I nearly dropped the large, cut-crystal glass of neon green liquid into the sand.

Note that I said "nearly."

Once I was sure the drink was real—and not some weird Hell-born mirage—I drank that melon-flavored concoction down so fast it made my head ache. Needless to say, it took the edge off quite nicely.

Actually, it did a lot more than *just* take the edge off.

Let me preface this by reiterating that I am *not* a big drinker. It usually takes me about a cocktail and a half to get all giddy and slightly wasted, and then I stop drinking so I can just enjoy the buzz. But I guess when the drink consumed is as strong as what I'd just gulped down, well, let's just say a single beverage *more* than sufficed.

"*Eeeerrp* . . ." I burped loudly, a little of the Midori's melony goodness coming back up into my mouth. Luckily, I was able to keep the rest of my beverage of choice down, but it did take a supreme effort of will. My stomach was *not* a happy camper—there was some *definite* hostility coming from my digestive tract.

"*Eeeeeeeeeerrrp!*"

Another burp hit me square in the solar plexus, this one lasting about ten seconds longer than the one before it—and kind of burning my esophagus as it clawed its way up my throat. Coughing, I lay down and closed my eyes, waiting for the waves of nausea to pass.

I had no intention of throwing up if I could help it. I mean, seriously, I'd been through about a dozen wormholes since Jarvis had fetched me from Manhattan, and if they hadn't made me hurl, then there was no way I was gonna let *one* Midori Sour do me in.

It was the principle of the thing.

Besides, I hated throwing up, specifically because of a very visceral memory I had of my sister Thalia throwing up on me in the back of my mother's Volvo Station Wagon when I was ten.

My mother had taken us to a carnival in Providence—Clio and I had had a blast, riding all the rides and eating everything we could stuff in our faces—but Thalia, who was about fourteen at the time, had decided that she was too fat, and hadn't eaten anything the whole day. I think she'd maybe *looked* at a strawberry at breakfast.

Anyway, we'd only *just* piled into the back of the station wagon after a pleasant day of family fun when Thalia leaned over and tapped me on the shoulder. As I turned to ask her what she wanted, she opened her mouth and, her braces glinting like diamond studs in the afternoon sunlight, threw up in my lap.

Wanna talk about nasty? Thalia had absolutely *nothing* in her stomach—which you'd think would be *better* than, like, say a regurgitated Happy Meal—but this was somehow much, much *worse*. The thing everyone likes to forget about throw-up is just how terrible it smells—and pure, undiluted stomach acid is in a category by itself. You can forget about maintaining *any* sense of decorum when someone heaves *that* stuff up in your lap.

When that horrible regurgitated stomach juice smell hit my nostrils, well, there was nothing I could do to stop myself from joining in the fun. Pretty soon it was like an old-school Roman vomitorium right there in our backseat.

Needless to say, my mother was not thrilled. It was a long time before I was allowed back in her car without a plastic bag in my pocket. The weird thing was that everyone thought it was my fault, that I'd eaten too much candy and crap and made myself sick. And no matter what I said to the contrary, no one believed me . . .

I'd forgotten about that part.

It's interesting. When you start counting up all the bad things in your life that you've tried to repress, you find that there are a lot more of them than you realized, and you also discover that they really don't *like* to stay buried—especially the hideous ones. They love to pop back up into your brain when you least expect it, and wreak havoc on your psyche.

As I lay in the sand, my eyes closed firmly against the drunken nausea I'd inflicted on myself, I let my mind reflect on *exactly* how my older sister had lied to my mother that day, letting her think that I'd been the bad kid, the one who couldn't do anything right.

Time and time again it had happened, but instead of remembering it, I'd shoved the bitter feelings so far down into my memory that they'd almost disappeared.

But they've never quite *gone away,* I thought to myself. *They're always there, just below the surface, waiting for an opportunity to be remembered again.*

For some unknown reason my zombified memories had decided that *now* was the perfect time to return from the dead and give me a good memory thrashing.

"What a bitch," I said out loud, my lips moving without my brain telling them to. "My sister was such a—*hiccup*—bitch. Why didn't anyone—*hiccup*—else but Clio ever see that?"

It was like I'd released the memory mother lode, but the only things that wanted to come out were *hiccups*—and the pesky little things were unstoppable. I must've spent the next five minutes trying every trick in the book to make them stop. I held my breath until I almost passed out; I counted from one to ten backward. Nothing worked.

Just as I was getting frustrated enough to stick my head in the sand and suffocate myself in a desperate bid to end my hiccup misery, I felt a hand on my shoulder.

"Argh!!" I screamed, leaping to my feet and thrusting my fists out blindly in front of me in self-defense.

"Hey there! Hold on a minute. I'm not gonna hurt you—"

When I saw who it was, I started punching even harder, hoping I'd knock a nose off or poke an eye out. I was like a wildcat, my hands two taloned weapons looking to rip something apart. My fists found their mark, and I could feel my fingers almost breaking as they tried to pound themselves deep inside my opponent's flesh.

"Ow! That hurts!"

The last person I wanted to see right then was the stupid Devil's protégé, and yet there he was right in front of me, his handsome face close enough to kiss . . . or punch. And the way I was feeling at the moment, it was definitely gonna be closer to the "punch" end of the spectrum.

"You're a jerk!" I screamed, the words coming out much more "slurry" than I'd expected. "I'm gonna beat the crap out of you!"

Okay, I was obviously drunker than I'd realized. Even though I knew it was really the Midori Sour egging me on, there was something very appealing about letting go and saying whatever the hell came into my head. For the first time in a very long time, I felt like I was free. I lifted my fist to hit him in the chest again, but he was much more on his game this time and caught my wrist before my balled fist could do any damage.

"Let me go!" I wailed, the nausea returning with such force that my eyes almost crossed. I could feel my heart hammering like a drumroll in my chest, and for a minute there I really thought it was gonna burst through my chest wall and say, "Hi." I couldn't stop shaking; every part of my body felt like it was being boiled in oil.

"Are you okay?" Daniel asked, his countenance changing from anger to worry as he looked into my wild eyes, felt the tremors that were racing through my body as he held me by my wrists.

"*It . . . hurts . . .*" I was able to get out between tremors. I didn't know what the hell was wrong with me, but I was getting really scared now. The burning had subsided as suddenly as it had begun, but now my whole body had started to go numb, and I was still shaking so hard I could barely think straight.

Daniel's eye caught the faint glint of the crystal tumbler where it now lay moldering in the sand—which was kind of weird because the last time I'd looked at the glass, it was fresh and shiny, not old and moldy gray. Still holding me by the left wrist, he reached down and scooped up the glass, sniffing at it until the smell of what was inside made him recoil in horror.

"Did you drink this?" he said, shaking me. All I could do was nod. I had lost the ability to move my lips, or even swallow. I was slowly being swallowed up, my whole body inexplicably paralyzed.

"How stupid can you be?" he said, sort of under his breath but still loud enough for me to hear every word if I was interested.

Excuse me? I thought to myself. *Who're* you *calling stupid,* stupid*?* I didn't care who Daniel thought he was. I was *not* gonna sit by and let him disparage me like that. Even if I couldn't call him bad names out loud, I could still think them in my head. So, there!

"Look," he said as he laid me down in the sand, "I know you're gonna freak out when I do this, but there's no other way to counteract the poison."

The poison? Is he crazy?

"Just know that this is gonna be harder for me," he continued as he started to unbutton the white cotton dress shirt he was wearing, "than it is for you."

Excuse me, but why are you taking off your shirt? I thought to myself as he reached for his brown leather belt and started tugging on it. *Oh, Lord, are you gonna rape me?*

"This is not sexual," he said as if he were reading my mind. "Believe me, you're the last woman I'd want to have sex with right now." Then, he yanked out his belt and unzipped his pants, revealing his proclivity for boxers, not briefs.

The sad thing was that even though I was glad he wasn't into any kinky quadriplegic sex stuff, it still kind of hurt—and when I say "kind of," I meant it hurt like my soul was being set on fire—that he didn't want to have sex with me. Right here. In the sand. With sand up our butts and the likelihood of a third-degree, full-body sunburn.

"Okay, this is gonna hurt," he said as he lay down on top of me, only a pair of boxers—and all my clothes—between us. I stared up at him, his face only half an inch from mine, and all I could think about was how much it sucked to be me. Even when I was lying prostrate on the ground without the use of any of my limbs, it still wasn't enough to entice a guy to wanna get off with me.

"You are truly a sick and twisted individual, I must say. What a naughty mind you have, Calliope Reaper-Jones."

Damn it, the jerk is reading my mind!

Daniel gave me a devilish smile to let me know that I was right on the money, then he dropped his face even closer to mine, so that our lips were touching. His breath was as sweet as honey as his soft lips pressed firmly against mine. For one single moment my breath caught in my throat, and the world around us ceased to be. Daniel and I were alone in a vacuum that contained only him and me. Then his whole body slid into mine, and it was like I'd been transported bodily up to Paradise. This was the closest I'd ever been to another person—I'm *totally* counting sex here—and it was pure heaven. Just knowing he was inside me, his life force commingling with mine, made me gaga with lust.

Daniel had said that there was nothing sexual about what he was going to do, but this was definitely the most erotic experience *I'd* ever had.

I could've stayed that way forever, Daniel's body magically intermeshed with mine, but it wasn't to be. Suddenly, a deep burning sensation consumed my body from head to toe, searing away all the pleasure I'd just experienced until there was nothing left of me but a writhing ball of pain. A pain that was so intense all I could do was scream.

And scream.

And scream.

twenty-one

"You can stop screaming now."

I looked up to see Daniel, still naked as a jaybird wearing boxers, sitting astride me and grinning like an idiot.

"Stop looking at me like that," I said grumpily as I pushed him off my hips and sat up. The back of my head was caked with sand, and I could feel it leaking from the base of my hairline down into my shirt.

"What? No 'thank you' for saving your life?" Daniel said as he crawled over to where his clothes were lying in a pile on the ground and started to slide his pants on.

"You didn't save my life. You just prolonged the inevitable. God, I feel foul," I continued, lifting the back of my tank top out so the sand could escape. "It's like there's a jackhammer symphony being written in my head—ow, brain spasm."

He raised an eyebrow, but didn't comment. It was weird, but I was having a really hard time concentrating on the jackhammering in my brain because Daniel was so damn yummy looking that it was distracting.

"What did you mean by 'prolonging the inevitable' . . . ?"

I sighed. "My life is worthless. There's no way I'll finish all the tasks; everyone thinks I'm the bad guy—you already know *all* about that." I paused for effect—okay, I was being a bit melodramatic again, but I did feel like my situation *was* pretty darn hopeless—then I finished with, "And I don't even know what a *Jamshid* is, much less *where* it is . . . My family is doomed."

Daniel froze, his shirt only half-buttoned, which again was very distracting for me. He had a totally ripped chest, smooth skin with just a little bit of curly chest hair that started around his nipples, then headed down south in a sexy trail that disappeared into his pants. He was also in possession of the flattest stomach I'd come across in all my varied—I can count them on one hand, so they're not *that* extensive—sexual wanderings. A man should *not* be that good-looking. It just wasn't fair.

"First of all," he began, "I have no idea *what* you're talking about when you say that you're 'the bad guy.' I think it's pretty obvious you're the *good guy* in all this. Your family is lucky to have someone like you to lean on in a situation like this."

If I didn't know what a jerk he normally was, I would've *almost* been touched by what he was saying—it was weird, but I really felt like I was talking to a whole *other* person than the Daniel I'd known up until then.

"Secondly," he continued, "the Cup of Jamshid? *That's* your second task?" He gave me a hard stare that I *suspected* was supposed to be "penetrating," but instead it kinda made him look constipated.

"Third."

"Huh?"

I smiled humbly at him even though it was a total sham; I was *very* proud of what I'd accomplished. "The Cup of Jamshid? It's my *third* task. I already got the stupid Sea Foam."

Daniel swallowed hard, then proceeded to finish buttoning his shirt in silence. When he was done, he took a deep breath, then let it out in one long exhale.

"All right, then."

And that was all he said about the subject. I had expected more, so I was surprised, but not *so* surprised that I stopped babbling at him.

"Look, when you said that what you were gonna do wasn't sexual . . ." I began.

"It wasn't."

I started to roll my eyes, then stopped because it made my head ache more.

"C'mon! That was the most erotic thing I've ever experienced in my entire life, and you're really gonna sit there and tell me it was nothing to you?"

Daniel smiled, showing his teeth like a cat about to launch itself at its prey.

"Nope. It was nothing for me."

"Liar!" I said. "I can tell you're lying by the way you're smiling at me." He shrugged, but didn't say anything—which totally drove me up the wall.

"You were reading my mind. How much more intimate can you be?" I stopped, covering my mouth with my hand—as *if* that could stop him from reading my mind again. "Wait a minute, can you *still* read my mind?"

He laughed.

"You're a riot, kid."

I glared at him and picked up a handful of sand threateningly. I did *not* like being called "kid."

"Truce, wildcat," he said in supplication, but I could still detect a hint of laughter underneath his words. "No, I can't read your mind anymore. It was only because we were *coalescing*."

"Coalescing . . . ?"

"I merged our bodies into one so that we would absorb the poison between us. The effects are less pronounced that way, but we're both gonna have a hell of a headache for the next few hours."

"Oh." So, *that* was why my brain was tuned to *The Jackhammer Symphony Hour.*

I watched Daniel as he put his shoes and socks back on, his head bent so that a little bit of hair fell forward and covered his eyes. Okay, if what he was saying was true, then he had, in fact, just saved my life. Which went against everything I'd been thinking about him up until now. But the burning question was . . . *why?*

Why had he saved my life when letting me get poisoned would've *helped* him get closer to attaining his goal. I mean, with me out of the way, he could usurp Father's job and be done with it. It was almost like he was going *against* what was in his best interest.

I couldn't help myself. I had to know what he was doing.

"Why? Why did you save me if you want my father's job? Aren't I just an obstacle in your way?"

He looked back up at me, shrugged.

"Look, if I hadn't gotten to you in time, you'd have been lost out here, paralyzed for the rest of your existence—or until someone who wasn't nearly as nice as me decided to fix you. And believe it when I say that

that would be a fate much worse than death. I wouldn't wish it on my worst enemy."

I nodded, still not sure that I believed him, but also not sure that I *didn't* believe him. The whole thing was very confusing, and I found myself completely flummoxed by my inability to hate the Devil's protégé for totally screwing up my life and making my family think I was trying to cheat them out of their immortality.

"Thank you for saving me—"

He smiled.

"You can call me Daniel. I promise I won't tell anyone we're on a first-name basis."

"Thank you . . . Daniel. I appreciate you saving me from 'a fate worse than death,' but after what you and the Devil tried to pull, you should've just left me out here to rot."

"After *what*?"

I sighed. I actually liked the big, dumb jerk—even if he was a liar.

"You and the Devil have been conspiring to pin my father's kidnapping on me and have me thrown in jail. And apparently, I have a whole bank account full of cash to prove it."

Daniel looked at me blankly, and once again I wanted to believe that he was *not* guilty as charged. I was starting to develop a soft spot for the guy, and it had absolutely nothing to do with magic. This was *bad*.

"I have no idea what you're talking about," Daniel said crossly. "There may be other things I'm guilty of in this situation, but selling you out isn't one of them. Besides, the Devil's a tight wad who wouldn't spend a penny unless he'd been guaranteed at *least* double on his return."

"Then why are there ten million buckaroos in my bank account? Explain that, buster," I said, my face turning red with anger. "Everyone thinks the Devil paid me to get rid of my father, and it's not fair!"

Before I even realized what was happening, I was crying again, my face all scrunched up and wet with hot tears. It was totally embarrassing.

"Even if I *wanted* to be a mortal, I would *never* do anything to hurt my family like that—*and* I've never been very proactive anyway. It's kind of against my nature; I've always preferred the 'run and hide' option," I wailed, my voice all wonky with emotion.

"I'm a complete and total coward . . . and that's just a fact."

Daniel reached out and took my hand—his was much bigger than mine, and very warm. It was kind of nice that he was trying to comfort me, even if it *was* all a lie intended to disarm and bamboozle me.

"It's gonna be okay, Calliope."

Every now and then I think we need someone to give our hand a squeeze, tell us it's all gonna be okay . . . regardless of whether they're telling us the absolute truth or not. It's like some weird secret that all of humanity—and nonhumanity—share: We *need* other people, plain and simple.

Daniel gave my hand a squeeze, then let it go. My hand felt cold from the loss.

After I'd wiped my nose on the back of my hand for like the fiftieth time, Daniel said, "You're not a coward."

"I'm not?" I replied uncertainly.

"You're anything *but* a coward."

That was a cheering thought. Although I didn't really believe it was true.

"Look," he said, "I have a proposition for you. I know that we don't really know each other very well. Yet."

"Uh-huh." I nodded, wondering where *this* was going.

"But I like you. I think you're smart, and pretty, and . . . nice."

"You make me sound like a horse. Why don't you mention how well I trot," I said. He gave me a weak smile.

"You have a lovely trot."

Which made me laugh out loud, confusing him. I noticed that when he was confused, he wrinkled his brow. *So cute.*

"What I'm trying to say is: Let's partner up. You and I against all the powers of Heaven and Hell—even the Devil—sounds pretty good, huh? I really think we'd make an excellent team, Calliope. What do *you* think?" he finished, a winning smile so etched into his face that I wondered how long he'd been practicing it—and the speech—in the mirror.

Now I was confused.

"Partner up *how*?"

He reached for my hand again, and my stomach lurched. I had less than zero experience with attractive men suddenly grabbing my hand and looking intensely into my eyes at the same time. I felt like a game show contestant who'd just won the big prize only to realize they had to pay taxes on it. It was unsettling.

"Obviously, only *one* of us could be the actual President of Death, Inc., but I promise to take into consideration anything you have to say about the day-to-day running of the company." He continued on like I was a deaf-mute without any kind of opinion at all. "And I also promise to—"

"Wait a minute," I said, yanking my hand out of his grasp. "What're you really saying here? Because it *sounds* like you're saying that we should get—"

Daniel leaned forward and planted his lips on mine, silencing me. He took my shock as a sign that it was a-okay for him to continue mauling me. He wrapped his arms around my shoulders and pulled me closer to him. As nice and heart jarring as the kiss was, I really wasn't in any mood to be molested against my will. I took the next opportunity that came my way to lean forward and slam my fist into his crotch. In less than a minute, I was free of his unsolicited embrace and he was doubled over in fierce pain, holding his nuts protectively.

It was weird how *this* time his kiss wasn't horrible tasting at all. *Just* one *more thing I don't understand.*

"What did you do *that* for?" he yelled at me, his voice half an octave higher than his normal register.

I glared at him, furious. Was he so completely dense that he didn't realize I wasn't in the market for an arranged marriage with the enemy?

"How dare you act like I'm the jerk when you were the one trying to seduce me so you could steal my father's job!" I yelled back.

"I was trying to help you out, you idiot! If we got married, I'd have a legitimate claim to the title *and* your family could keep their immortality," he screamed in return. "You think I *want* to marry you? I'm only trying to do what's best for the world . . . because *you* running Death on your own is a recipe for disaster."

I gasped. How *dare* he suggest that I wasn't capable of doing my father's job?! I'd already completed two of the tasks the Board had assigned me, and the third was probably gonna be a piece of cake, so screw him. I was gonna find that Cup of Jamshid, and then show Daniel exactly where he could stick it!

"I think you'd better go," I said, taking a deep breath and letting it out slowly, calmly. I was *not* gonna let him see how badly what he'd said had rattled me. It was my attempt to instill a bit of restraint into the proceedings, but I wasn't sure how well it was working for me, *or* the proceedings.

"I'm not going anywhere until I make you understand your situation," he said.

"I understand my situation, so you can go now."

"I don't think you do, Calliope," he answered. "Someone powerful took your father—"

"Someone like your boss," I said.

"You really think I'd be down here trying to broker a deal with you if the Devil had anything to do with the kidnapping? Think about it, Calliope. Use your brain, and you'll see the logic in what I'm saying."

"If it wasn't you . . . then who?"

Daniel sighed.

"I don't know. None of it makes any sense. It has to be someone under the radar. Someone that no one would ever suspect."

"Like me," I said through gritted teeth.

"Yes, like you. You were definitely high on our list . . ."

"That's so nice of you to say," I said, letting the sarcasm drip off my tongue. "It makes me feel so incredibly special to know you guys thought I was a *criminal mastermind*."

Daniel shrugged. "We had to look at everyone. And you *are* the black sheep of your family. You ran away to the human world; you abhor anything magical—"

"That's not *entirely* true," I objected.

"You seemed like the weakest link. If anyone was gonna be turned, our money was on you."

"Great," I snorted. "So how do you know this *isn't* some setup, then? That I didn't drink that stuff myself so I could lure you into rescuing me, and then take you hostage along with all the other people I'm holding hostage."

Daniel paused.

"Is that what you're planning to do?"

I punched him in the arm.

"No, it's *not* what I'm planning to do! God." Did so many people really think I was capable of this kind of treachery? Apparently so. If the whole "my family thinks I'm a rat fink" thing hadn't been so annoying, I would've kinda been impressed by my alter-ego selves: mild-mannered executive assistant by day, evildoing criminal mastermind by night!

"Look, let me help you find the Cup of Jamshid, and then we can go to the Board together," Daniel offered helpfully. "I promise to be good, and just help. That's it."

"Really?" I asked skeptically.

"Really," he said without a trace of irony.

I wanted to believe him. I really did, but there was something nagging at the back of my mind, telling me that Daniel, the Devil's protégé, had another agenda that I wasn't privy to—one that was *not* in my best interest.

"That's totally sweet of you. Wanting to help out of the goodness of your own heart, but I don't think it's necessary. I'm pretty sure I can handle this on my own. Thanks, though. And I really mean that," I added as I took a step away from him. "I'm gonna go now. Bye . . ."

Daniel just stood there watching me as I took another

step forward, putting more distance between us. I felt weird just ditching him like that—I mean, he did save my life—but I couldn't stand there grinning at him all day, could I?

"Let me come with you."

"No," I said, "I don't think that's a good idea."

He took a step forward, following me as I tried to move farther away from him. I stopped and gave him a hard look.

"Go away."

He shrugged. "I can't help it that I happen to be going in the same direction you're going in."

I turned on my heel and marched right past him in the opposite direction. I didn't look back to see if he was following me this time. I *knew* without looking that he was. I picked up my pace so that I wasn't walking, but trotting—*yes, I do give good trot.* If he was gonna stalk me, well, I wasn't going to make it easy for him.

After about ten minutes of fast walking through the sand, my body was exhausted. I could feel the sweat pouring down my face into the back of my tank top. My underarms were a stinky mess. Even my butt crack was joining in the sweaty fun. I felt like a human sweat-making machine. If *only* they could harness all that perspiration and use it to irrigate a small third-world country, it would be great. Otherwise, it was just disgusting.

I snuck a quick peek over my shoulder to see what progress Daniel had made, but when I scanned the dune behind me, I realized that he had disappeared. I decided that he just wasn't as excited about sharing the Presidency of Death, Inc., as I'd thought he was—or maybe he'd only gotten sand in his shoe and had to stop to dump it out. I had no idea where the Devil's protégé was, nor did I really care to think about what his motivations were for *anything* he did. He was the enemy as far as I was concerned, and the farther away I got from him, the better.

The only "real" problem I could see in my near future was that I had absolutely *no* idea where I was going. I'd just started off in whatever direction was the *opposite* of where Daniel was supposedly going, and now I was totally lost. Not that I'd really known much about where I was *before* I'd made my escape from my "Midori Sour Savior." I'd been going under the assumption that Runt had shipped me off to whatever place seemed safest at the time—i.e., it was as far away from my irate family as possible.

Now I was lost, and it was totally the hellhound's fault. Well, there was nothing else I could do but keep walking. Maybe I'd find the end of the desert, and someone would give me a prize for "persistence in the face of intense heat."

Not.

I started walking again, leaving a straggly trail of footsteps behind me so any rescue parties—the Devil's protégé's Rescue Party *not* included—could track me down without too much of a fuss. At first, I told myself that I would eventually run into something or someone, but after what seemed like hours, all I had seen was nothing but endless sand in every direction. This made me feel less than positive about my situation. Without blinking an eye, I shifted away from hope and slid right into desperation . . . my favorite of all the human emotions.

I am never going to escape from this desert. I am

gonna spend the remainder of eternity here in this vacuum, making sand castles and getting eaten alive by sand fleas while I slowly turn into a giant human salt lick.

It was just as my mind thought the words "salt lick" that I looked up . . . *and saw the palm tree.*

twenty-two

I was a child again—thin and scraggly in a pink tank top and a pair of shorts—my eyes red from crying as I stared up at the tall, drooping palm tree that stood like a sentinel in the blistering heat. I felt scared and lost . . . and very, very alone.

I had seen the palm tree then, and here it was now, just as skeletal and bent as I remembered it, waiting for me like a phantom nightmare from my childhood.

The oasis had barely changed. The palm tree was still the sole vegetation, still thin as a whip of licorice or a starving dog. The water was still so clear you could see the sandy bottom magnified in its depths.

And sadly, as I stood there remembering my adolescent impressions of the oasis I'd discovered in Hell when I was a kid, I realized that, like this place, I, too, hadn't changed much in the intervening years.

I was still thin and scraggly . . . and very much alone.

I wondered if my "friend" Monsieur D was still here,

too. Or if he had paid whatever penance he'd owed and was now back on the Wheel of Samsara, fulfilling whatever destiny God had in store for him.

I trudged forward in the sand, my hand shading my eyes so I could look for signs of habitation.

"Hello . . . ?" I called, my voice dying quickly in the stillness of the hot, desert day. There was nothing but silence in return.

"Anybody home?" I said less loudly. Suddenly, from behind the scrawny palm tree, I saw a flash of movement, followed by . . . nothing.

"Monsieur D?"

Two extremely thin fingers—the nail beds caked with dirt and grime and God knew what else—poked out from behind the palm tree, followed by two more. In one smooth movement, they wrapped themselves around the tree trunk and pulled. The trunk shifted, and a man stepped out. It wasn't Monsieur D.

It can't *be Monsieur D.*

The little man I had met at the oasis all those years ago had teeth—granted they were yellowing and completely mismatched, but they were still *teeth.* This man had nothing but inflamed red gums where teeth should have been.

Like Monsieur D, the man was wearing a dirty, ragged robe, but unlike my "friend," all this man possessed underneath his robe was bone in a translucent skin sheath. Yes, Monsieur D was thin, but not a walking skeleton, not a rag-and-bone man like this one.

Then he turned so I could get a better look at his face, and my heart stopped.

The nose. This man had Monsieur D's beak of a nose.

"Monsieur D," I said, "do you remember me?"

My heart had started pumping again, but now, with every beat, it hurt. It hurt for my lost childhood; it hurt for this beaten man who stood before me in a dirty white robe; it just really, really *hurt.*

"I remember," he replied. The high, squeaky voice from my memory was gone, the trace of the French accent I remembered almost nonexistent in the harsh whisper Monsieur D now used to communicate with.

"What happened to you?" I asked. It really *was* like I was a kid again, asking every blunt and inappropriate question I could think of. *What is it that makes a kid behave like the world really* does *run on honesty?* I wondered.

Monsieur D didn't reply. He stared at me with big, sad eyes, all the life drained out of them. This wasn't the same callow, indulgent creature I'd met before. Not by a long shot.

"You look like crud," I found myself saying. Monsieur D smiled, and I almost had to avert my eyes from the ravaged red gums. A strange barking sound came out of the back of his throat, and I realized that he was laughing.

"Sorry, that was rude of me."

Monsieur D was still bark-laughing at me, yellowish tears trailing like raindrops from his eyeballs to his chin.

"It really wasn't *that* funny . . ." I said uncertainly. "Was it?"

He shook his head and continued to howl with laughter. I decided to wait for the hysterical mirth to stop before I said anything else—I didn't want to give the man a *stroke.* Finally, after a few minutes, the laughter subsided, and the gaunt man stopped shaking. For the first time since I'd stumbled upon him again, I could see something resembling happiness in his eyes.

"You're not gonna cry like you did the last time, are you?"

This set him off again, and I had to wait another few minutes for him to compose himself. I couldn't understand what the hell was so funny about what I was saying. I mean, I was being blunt, but I wasn't standing on my head and yapping like a dog, was I?

Jeez.

"Okay, enough laughing at me. I know I'm just a *total* riot, but please, I need your help, and you laughing at me isn't gonna make that happen."

Monsieur D narrowed his eyes malevolently, and I took a step back, glad that he was tied to the palm tree and couldn't get any closer. To make sure, I looked down at his leg, reassured to see the nylon string was still attached.

"You *dare* ask for my help? After what you did to me?" he croaked, his consonants soft and round in his toothless mouth.

"What did *I* do?" I said, my indignation trying to match his anger, but failing.

"You were supposed to free me, but instead you left me here to rot!" he moaned, then threw himself down in the sand, sobbing.

It turned out that I hadn't asked him such a pointless question after all. We *were* gonna have a "crying jag" repeat of the last time.

As he cried loudly into the sand, his whole body racked with sobs, I started to feel guilty. I mean, *I* didn't know what the guy was guilty of—maybe he'd given Zarathustra the clap, or he'd accidentally sold his people into slavery in exchange for three measly shekels. Neither of those things was *so* bad, was it?

The man looked like crap, he smelled like crap, and he obviously blamed me for it. The nice thing would be to give him his stupid cup and be done with it. Besides, the sobbing gave no hint of abating in the near future, and it was starting to make my headache worse.

A voice in the back of my mind tried to remind me that I hadn't given Monsieur D his prize back then for a reason, but I ignored it as my eyes began to scan the ground for the silvery glitter of the cup. I wondered distractedly if anyone else had been lured into Monsieur D's service since I'd been here last. If not, then I had a pretty good idea where the cup would be.

I put all my concentration into finding it, scanning the desert floor until suddenly my eyes alighted on its half-buried body. What was once a gleaming, silvery object of beauty had become an ugly, tarnished brown monster—but it was *definitely* Monsieur D's cup.

I walked over to where it lay and gingerly poked at it with my shoe. Given a few more years of neglect, it would've disappeared completely into the sand's embrace. And what the sand steals, it doesn't return.

Remembering the pain I'd felt when I picked it up the first time, I took a moment to think of the best way to touch the thing without turning my brain into a melted orange ice cream Push-Up.

"I wouldn't do that if I were you," a voice called behind me.

I was surprised I could hear *anything* over the sound of Monsieur D's sobbing, but then I realized he wasn't crying anymore. Not sure what I was gonna find behind me, I turned around slowly and saw Daniel standing across the water, his shirt wrapped around his head to staunch the flow of blood—the shirt was soaked red with it—cascading down his face.

"Oh my God," I said, staring at Daniel's pale face. "What *happened* to you?"

"You know *exactly* what happened to me," he said. I heard a low, guttural cackle behind me and trained my gaze over to where Monsieur D was kneeling in the sand, a gleeful, expectant look on his nasty, toothless visage.

Had I really intended to pick up the cup and happily hand it over to that crazy old coot? I had to have been insane—or maybe "spelled" was the more correct theory here—to have even contemplated the idea.

As I stared at his grotesque mask of a face, I knew the latter was true . . . because right at that moment you couldn't have *paid* me to give Monsieur D his beloved little cup. All I felt was disgust for the creature that sat burbling to himself in the sand.

He was gonna have to turn over a whole new leaf—and I'm talking a full-on *My Fair Lady* makeover—before *I* ever did him any favors.

I turned my attention back to Daniel, worried that he was gonna pass out from sheer blood loss before I found out what I was supposed to have done to him.

"Okay, tell me what I'm accused of now—but you should know ahead of time that I'm not apologizing for something you only *think* I did," I said haughtily, trying to pretend that Monsieur D wasn't there, listening to and judging every word I uttered.

Daniel took a step forward, but he lost his footing and ended up falling onto his knees.

"You pulled a switchback," he said through clenched teeth, "and hit me over the head."

"Are you okay?" I asked, ignoring his accusation, trying to focus on his state of being without sounding too defensive.

"You heard me," he coughed, struggling to climb back onto his feet but not succeeding. "You hit me . . . on the back of the head."

"I didn't hit you," I said as I walked around the small pond of water toward him, careful to avoid crossing into Monsieur D's airspace. "I don't even have a baseball bat on me." I gestured with my hands, letting him see they were empty. "See?"

"Then who?" he said as I reached him and grabbed him underneath both armpits.

"Can you stand?"

He nodded as I hoisted him back onto his feet, getting a long smear of blood across the front of my borrowed tank top for all my Good Samaritan efforts.

"Look, I don't know who did this to you, but it wasn't me," I said as he leaned against my shoulder for support. "You saved my life. Why would I hurt you?"

"Because you can—" he said before a great, bellowing cough erupted inside his chest and overwhelmed his ability to finish his sentence.

"That's just plain stupid thinking," I replied. "I don't work that way. Never have and never will."

As the coughing fit subsided, I noted that his breathing was becoming more labored with each passing second. I was kinda starting to really worry about him. Jerk or not, I didn't want anything too bad to happen to him on my watch. Then something really, really screwed up occurred to me. It was so terrible that I tried to push it out of my mind, but it wouldn't go.

"You can't die, can you?" I asked in a low whisper. I didn't want Monsieur D to hear what I was saying. God knew *what* would happen if the wretched man tried to involve himself in our problem.

Daniel looked up at me with big blue eyes clouded with unshed tears.

Oh, crap, I thought, *don't do it! Don't you say what I think you're going to say!*

"I sold my immortality to the Devil. I'm as human as . . ." He looked over at Monsieur D. "As him."

My mind went blank, and then one word popped out of my mouth.

"Shit."

This made Daniel laugh, laughter that quickly turned into a dry, hacking cough that was completely devoid of any of its former mirth.

"I think we better get you out of here and to a hospital," I said quickly. "Can you open a wormhole for us?"

Daniel slowly rolled his eyes at me; the extreme loss of blood was making him loopy.

"You do it," he mumbled. "I'm the one who's dying here . . ."

Great, a real comedian, I thought to myself.

"Uhm, I don't mean to be a pest, but I . . . uh, *don't know how.*"

Daniel didn't respond. When I looked over, I saw that he'd passed out.

"Crap!" I almost shouted as I took the full weight of the unconscious man against my shoulder—and Daniel was much heavier than a grown man had any right to be.

Across the pond Monsieur D cackled at my expense again.

"Shut up!" I screamed at him. "Don't you see I'm in the middle of a crisis here?"

That only made him cackle harder.

"Stupid toothless Frenchman!" I called from across the water.

"Gormless human-being reject!" Monsieur D yelled back at me.

"Don't make me come over there!" I screamed, almost losing my grip on the unconscious Daniel in the process.

"I dare you to try, wannabe!" he shot back.

I was beginning to feel like I was back in elementary school again where "taunting" ruled.

"Your boyfriend is going to die," Monsieur D said, suddenly calm again . . . if you could *ever* term his harsh lisp of a voice as "calm."

I glared at him as I tried to hoist the slowly sliding Daniel back up to a standing position. Finally, tired of fighting a losing battle, I let him go where he wanted—which was into a heap on the sand.

"See what you made me do!" I yelled at the raggedy old man as I poked at Daniel's arm with my shoe.

Monsieur D only snorted at me with disdain as he pulled himself up to a standing position and smiled at me. It was weird, but he seemed taller somehow, less ravaged now.

"Come here," he said finally, raising a skeletal finger and crooking it in my direction.

"Why?" I said, holding my ground. I was hot and stinky and sweaty and miserable. I wasn't going to put all that aside and go trotting over there like a puppy.

"Come here," he intoned.

Without a second thought, I was walking back around the water and right up to where the Frenchman was waiting for me. I hadn't even had time to make my brain tell my feet to stop moving—and I doubt that if there *had* been time, my feet would've listened to my brain anyway.

"What?" I said petulantly.

He leered at me, and I leaned as far back as I could to get away from his *really* foul-breathed clutches.

"It heals," he whispered.

"What does?"

He gave me a knowing smile, then looked over to where the cup was still lying half buried in the sand.

"The cup?"

He didn't say anything, just cocked his head speculatively.

"You can't tell me, huh?"

He shrugged.

"You don't *want* to tell me—"

He rolled his shrunken eyes.

"You *shouldn't* tell me—"

He gritted his gums.

"You think I'm an idiot and you don't like my choice of clothing—"

"Argh! It's an enchantment, you ninny!" The words exploded out of his mouth in a rush.

"Oh," I said. "Okay. Gotcha. It's an enchantment that you're forced upon pain of something or other not to talk about."

Monsieur D gave me a gut-churning smile. Boy, I was so *not* good around toothless people. Something about seeing a mouthful of gums instead of ivory really made me feel nauseous.

"Yesssss, now that you've named it, we can discuss it."

"Why didn't you just say so before?" I asked.

Monsieur D looked like he wanted to give me a tongue-lashing but instead decided to hold his tongue—

which was probably for the best given that he wanted my help . . . and I *needed* his.

"Do you want to help your friend?" he said.

I nodded.

"Then get me the cup . . ."

I took a deep breath and let it out slowly before I spoke my next words.

"It's wrong to give you the cup, isn't it?"

He didn't answer me, just gave me an "are you really *this* stupid" look that I interpreted as a "yes."

I didn't know what to do. I'd never had such an important decision to make in my whole life. If I gave Monsieur D the cup, a lot of bad stuff might possibly go down, but if I didn't . . . well, Daniel was obviously gonna die. I was between a rock and a hard place—and I did *not* like the feeling one little bit.

"Okay. I'll do it." I didn't even think about my decision; I just jogged over to where the cup lay and reached out. The pain was searing—seriously, I could hear my brain sizzling inside my head, and as the pain began to eat away at my consciousness, I immediately cursed myself for making such a painfully stupid decision.

"Ohgodohcrapohpoo," I wailed, the words not even registering as they spilled out of my mouth. I couldn't think, I couldn't see, I couldn't function. All I knew was *pain.*

Luckily for me, it turned out that I didn't need to be in control of my faculties. The cup had a mind of its own. It swung me around, sent me soldier-marching to the edge of the pool of crystalline water, and threw me to my knees. With a loud *hiss,* I thrust the cup into the water, and suddenly I was free again.

I looked around me, blinking back tears of pain. Monsieur D was crouched beside me, tears streaming down his own face. He looked up at me with such profound gratitude that I almost had to avert my eyes. I really didn't feel like I deserved his appreciation. I hadn't done this out of the kindness of my heart, after all. I had had my own selfish reasons for doing his bidding.

"Thank you," he said as, with shaking hands, he reached out and took the brimming cup from my singed fingers. He put the cup to his lips and drank from its depths like a dying man. Instantly, his shoulders relaxed, and his eyes closed happily.

"You're welcome—" I started to say, but the words ceased as I stared at Monsieur D's face. Something strange was happening to him. His skin, which until moments ago had seemed so thin it was almost translucent, was taking on a healthier glow, and the cheekbones that had been so prominent before looked like they were now covered with a layer of fat.

"Monsieur D . . ." I stammered. "Your face . . ."

He swallowed the last drop of water in the cup and sighed contentedly before letting the cup fall to his lap. I was shocked. The man who sat beside me was entirely transformed. Gone was the rag-and-bone skeleton, replaced now by a handsome, patrician-looking man who was probably no older than I was.

"What are you?" I whispered. Was I really having a Cinderella–Snow White moment right here in Hell with Monsieur D? Was the nasty old homeless-looking guy really a handsome prince in disguise? Would wonders ever cease?

God, I hoped so. Because I was having a really hard time reconciling this guy with the crazy creature he'd been no more than two seconds before. This was definitely magic at its weirdest as far as I was concerned.

"You may call me Marcel now," he said as he smiled at me, revealing a handsome set of pearly whites.

Much better, I thought to myself. *No more Mr. Gnarly-mouth.*

"Okay, *Marcel,*" I replied, continuing to goggle at him since I wasn't quite sure what to do next. All I knew was that he was pretty cute, and he did kinda owe me one for helping him out.

Marcel stared deeply into my eyes, his gaze penetrating to my very core. I watched, helpless as he leaned in toward me. *Oh my God,* I thought giddily, *he's totally gonna kiss me. Hmm, maybe this is about to get a lot more interesting than I would've ever imagined.*

With his face now only inches from mine, he pursed his lips and whispered, *"To the shortest Reign of Death that ever was."*

"Excuse me?" I said, not sure if I'd heard what I *thought* I'd heard.

The only answer I got concerned Marcel's hands . . . and how expertly they wrapped themselves around my throat . . .

twenty-three

I don't know if you've ever been properly strangled, but let me tell you, it is *not* fun. It hurts, you can't breathe, and you're having a panic attack all at the same time. It's god-awful.

All I wanted to do was scream at Marcel to let go of my throat, and once he did, I wanted to kick him in the nuts so hard that he was forced to speak in a falsetto for the rest of his life. I wasn't really worried about him killing me straight up, but I was in no mood to deal with any brain damage from lack of oxygen.

The weirdest part about being strangled is that you have absolutely nowhere else to look but into your strangler's eyes. I mean, I tried to look at his nose, or over his shoulder, but it was no use. I was stuck. I *had* to look deep into his eyes—the whole time wondering why in the heck he wanted so badly to "kill" me. Obviously, he had no idea that I was immortal by association—my father *was* Death—and that, while he could render me unconscious, he couldn't do away with me definitely.

Staring into Marcel's dilated pupils, I couldn't help but muse on why someone would want to kill someone else. I understood that Death was a natural part of life, but I couldn't reconcile murder with that scenario. Murder just seemed like the *antithesis* of the Natural Order of Things. Humans and other creatures willfully taking the only thing that their fellow living beings possessed—their life—and squandering it? That did *not* seem like something Mother Nature would condone. Death for food was a-okay in old Mother Nature's book, but death for fun and gain—I just wasn't feeling it.

As the pressure on my trachea increased, I felt the life essence inside me begin to ebb away, and while it didn't scare me—not at first—it definitely didn't feel great, either. I wanted to know why Marcel was doing this to me, but since my throat was kind of in control of my ability to speak, I was at a loss. All I could do was make gurgling sounds deep in my larynx and turn red.

Not the most *flattering* of pictures.

Suddenly, the pressure on my throat relaxed, and I was able to breathe again. I looked over Marcel's head and saw Daniel crouched above us, the cup held tightly in his hands as he prepared to slam it into the back of Marcel's head for what appeared to be the second time. His face was a terrible ashen color, and his lips were nearly bloodless, but he had a determined look in his eyes that would have scared me if it hadn't been directed at my attacker.

"Let her go," he growled as he slammed the cup into the side of Marcel's head. Marcel's eyes rolled back, and he swooned on top of me, his body weight trapping me against the ground. I looked over at Daniel, hoping for some help, but Daniel had passed out, his head only a few inches from the water.

Crap, I thought to myself, *how am I gonna get demented Marcel off me if Daniel isn't gonna help?*

Using every bit of strength I possessed, I shoved at the dead weight resting on top of me. I couldn't even budge him.

"Daniel, a little help here," I croaked, but my hero was out cold, a pool of blood forming near the base of his skull where the shirt tourniquet he'd tied around his head had loosened. I realized that I needed to get Daniel that water soon, or he really *was* going to die.

Damn it! I screamed angrily inside my head.

I had no idea how I was gonna get out of this mess. As it was, speaking was a painful exercise, and between the strangulation and the unconscious body on my chest, I could hardly catch my breath, let alone scream for help.

After a few minutes of careful thought, I decided that my only option was to do the thing I least wanted to do: I was gonna have to call for help. I closed my eyes and pictured my victim's face in my mind's eye.

"Kali, can you help me?" I squeaked the words out, my throat on fire. Behind me, I heard the water in the pool begin to bubble, and then two strong arms reached out and yanked Marcel's body off me.

"You owe me again, white girl," Kali said as she offered me her hand and yanked me back onto my feet.

Damn, the woman is strong.

I gave her a weak smile to tell her "thank you" and was glad to see that, at least this time, I hadn't summoned her while she was in the bathtub. Today, she was wearing a flowing peach and scarlet sari, and the daintiest-looking little diamond-encrusted sandals I'd ever seen.

I am so *gonna have to find out where the woman*

does her shoe shopping, I thought to myself. *Those sandals are awesome.*

Kali, taking in her surroundings, looked past Marcel to Daniel's prostrate body lying in the sand, and for one horrible instant I really thought she was going to kick him right in a very "prone" area with those amazing sandals.

"Don't!" I screeched, the pain in my throat making tears spring to my eyes. *"He saved my life."*

My voice was all scratchy and thick, making me feel like I'd smoked a whole carton of unfiltered cigarettes in one sitting.

"You look and sound like crap," Kali said as she turned away from Daniel's body and raised an eyebrow at my disheveled appearance. I shrugged, wanting to talk as little as possible.

Besides, she *was* right. I could see my reflection in the pool of water that rippled happily below me, and I *did* look like the Bride of Frankenstein. My hair was standing up straight, my throat was a mass of red and white finger marks, and my split lip was caked in blood—the wound had probably reopened when Marcel was trying to strangle me.

I pointed at Daniel's head, and Kali gave me a nasty little smile that made it pretty apparent she was all for leaving him there soaking in his own plasma. I shook my head.

"Whatcha want to do with the twenty-timing womanizer then, white girl?" she said as she stifled a yawn.

I could totally tell it was a fake yawn, that she was just trying to "show me" how disinterested she was in Daniel's fate, but I knew it was all a front. She was without a doubt the poster girl for the bitter, jealous ex-girlfriend who was seething inside for revenge. But

I owed the guy one—probably two, actually—so I was gonna make damn sure any revenge she got was at a much later date, and without my involvement.

Squatting down beside him, I picked up the cup, ready for it to singe my fingers, but all the fire had been burned out of it. I slid the cup into the cool water and filled its body to the brim. Next, I crawled over to where Daniel lay sprawled in the sand and lifted his head onto my lap, smearing blood down my pant leg. (Now the pants matched the top.)

"Head, or mouth?" I squeaked, unsure of where to administer the water. *"It's* supposed *to help."*

Kali started to shrug, but I glared at her. Instead, she put her hands on her hips and sighed.

"The head. You wanna give him all your powers, you pour it down his throat."

"Huh?" I croaked.

"It's what gives you your powers, dipwad," Kali said, rolling her eyes. I still didn't understand. Kali stuck out her hip and shook her head at my stupidity.

"You fulfilled your tasks. You're Death now, you dumb white girl."

"I am?" This was unbelievable. I had to make sure. *"I'm* Death*?"*

"Yep." Kali giggled, suddenly finding the whole thing *hilarious.* "You be The Man."

Uh-oh. If Kali thinks I drank from the cup and that made me Death, then . . .

"I'm not Death," I whispered. *"He is."* I pointed over to Marcel, and Kali's eyes nearly bugged out of her head. *"I gave* him *the cup first."*

"You *what*?" Kali demanded, her lips pursed in fear.

"I let him drink out of the cup first," I stammered,

my throat on fire while a little bud of fear blossomed in the pit of my stomach.

"You're just lucky he wasn't at full power yet, or he would've killed your ass, white girl," Kali hissed at me. "You better drink that water now, or I'm not responsible for what I'm gonna do to you."

I looked down at the cup, not sure that I wanted this. In fact, I was *pretty sure* this was the opposite of what I wanted, actually. I had no interest in running the family business. Being the overlord of Death just did *not* appeal. Yet here I was, faced with the ultimate decision—one I'd *thought* I'd made back at Sea Verge when I accepted my mother's proposition but really hadn't. I'd just done what everyone else *wanted* me to do so I didn't have to make any decisions for myself . . .

I lifted the cup to my lips and drank.

The water was like a balm to my aching throat. I could feel it lubricating all the sore places where Marcel's hands had—and hadn't—been. I looked up, and Kali smiled at me.

"Congratulations, white girl. Now you're one of us."

Those eight little words did nothing but put the fear of God in me, no matter how well-intentioned they'd been. I felt a strange stirring inside my gut, and when I looked down at Daniel's prone face resting in my lap, my heart gave a lurch. Not with love, or lust . . . but with pity. He was going to die. My body was so attuned to the ebb and flow of life that I could feel it in my every fiber.

Instinctively, I knew how to remedy Daniel's situation.

"You're not going to die, Daniel," I said with such firmness that the lifeblood—which had been freely flowing out of Daniel's head up until that very moment—was immediately sucked back inside the wound with such fierceness that it made a *slurping* sound. I watched, fascinated, while the large gash in his skull knitted back together right before my eyes. Daniel's eyes fluttered open, and he grinned at me . . . Then he closed his eyes as I commanded his body to fall into a deep, restful sleep.

The whole thing was totally insane.

The whole thing was totally amazing.

I had never commanded anybody to do *anything*, and here I was in charge of the whole kit and caboodle of Life and Death.

I looked up at Kali, and her eyes were shining with pride like she was my mother or something. I guess having the power to forestall Death was kind of an impressive thing, especially when that power belonged to someone like me who was such a screwup in the normal world.

"I have to go tell Persephone and Wodin that you completed your tasks. You gonna be okay down here in Hell on your own, white girl?" Kali asked tentatively.

I nodded, but I wasn't really listening to her. I was so consumed by the feeling of power that now resided inside me that I probably would've agreed to *anything* the Hindu Goddess said.

In fact, I wasn't even really watching as Kali, her body shaded by the shadow of the sickly palm tree, waded into the pool of water and disappeared, the surface of the water instantly calming as if she had never entered its embrace at all.

I found that I was content to sit in silence and contemplate my existence, to feel the thread of power running through me, and know I could call it out to do my bidding anytime I wanted.

"You're alive," a dreamy voice said. I turned my head to find Marcel sitting up, rubbing the back of his skull, a pained expression on his handsome face. "I didn't kill you, after all."

Intellectually, I knew I should've been scared of the guy. The fact that he'd tried to kill me normally would've had me putting, like, a hundred million miles between us, but now somehow I couldn't get all that excited about him.

"Nope," I said. "You didn't kill me."

"Damn, you drank the water, didn't you," he said, shaking his head sadly. It wasn't really a question, but more of a statement . . . or maybe a *judgment*.

"I drank the water," I said calmly. "*I'm* Death now, not you."

He gave me a funny look, but didn't say anything. We sat like that, each lost in their own thoughts for quite a while, before I finally said:

"Who are you anyway?"

He gave me a crooked grin—his teeth were still shiny white—and said:

"You really don't know, do you?"

I shook my head.

"Oh, the irony . . ." he said, his words trailing off into a humorless laugh.

His tone kind of pissed me off. Jeez, it wasn't like I got an e-mail every time they added a new addition to *The Encyclopedia of Supernatural Beings*. How the heck was I supposed to know *anything* about nonhuman existence when I'd been living out in the human world for, like, practically *ever*?

"I am the two hundred and fifth incarnation of Yamatanka," Marcel said, interrupting my thoughts as he offered me his hand. I just looked at it. There was no way josé *I* was gonna touch *him* because I could literally taste all the bad vibes he was shooting in my direction. Marcel snorted, dropping his hand . . . and any pretense of being a "new friend."

"But you, Calliope Reaper-Jones? You can call me by my lesser-known title . . . *the Ender of Death*."

"No way? *The Ender of Death?*" I said loudly. "You're joking, right?"

Marcel shook his head firmly.

"I assure you that I am *not* joking. I *am* the two hundred and fifth incarnation of Yamatanka, the Ender of Death."

I giggled, and Marcel looked offended.

"Excuse me, do you have any idea who you're talking to—" he began, but I cut him off.

"That's so terrible." I giggled, finally understanding what he'd meant about the "irony" of the situation. Here I was face-to-face with the one being that could destroy me, and he had been the one to make my ascension to Death actually happen—what a riot!

Something suddenly occurred to me:

"Hey, you drank the water, too! How can the Ender of Death be allowed to do that? Wouldn't that make *you*, like, Death, and the total *opposite* of yourself?" I demanded.

He shook his head.

"It doesn't work that way. I was under an enchantment that only my mortal enemy could break. *You* had to give me—of your own free will—the water that brought you to your power in order for my curse to be ended," Marcel said wearily.

"But why me?" I demanded again.

"*Death* is your birthright."

"But what about him?" I said, gesturing to Daniel, who was snoring peacefully in the sand. "*You* kept telling me the water would cure him—and Death is his birthright, too, if what the Devil says is true about him being the next one in line for the job. So, why let *either* of us near that stupid water?"

The crazy thing was, given half a chance, I really *would've* given the water to Daniel first, and then Marcel really would've been dealing with him instead of me.

Wait a minute, I thought to myself. *That's the answer. Marcel would be dealing with him,* not *me. And he never meant to deal with* either *of us!*

"You didn't want me to give that water to Daniel at all," I snorted. "That was a trick to make me fill the cup and give it to *you*! You knew *he* would bleed to death and be out of the running. Plus, you thought *I'd* be a much easier mark anyway. You figured you could kill me *before* I drank any of the water, and then there'd be no Death anymore, at least for a while. Presto, Endo—you could take a vacation!"

Marcel looked sheepish.

"Well, that turned out pretty badly for you," I said, giving him the evil eye. I wasn't just some stupid mortal girl wannabe anymore. I was *Death*—and I did *not* like being trifled with.

Without even realizing what I was doing, I found myself crouched right in front of Marcel, my hands around *his* throat, squeezing for all I was worth—and my stock had gone up *a lot* since I'd drunk that water and accepted my birthright.

"*Pwease . . .*" he gurgled. "*I nee to tell you zomething . . .*"

I relaxed the pressure on his voice box. As much as I was enjoying revenge, I didn't want to be careless. If he had something *important* to impart before his death . . .

"Please," he stammered, *"let me go."*

"Why?" I said, not feeling the least bit in a forgiving mood.

"Because," he said as he gasped for air, *"there's something you don't know."*

"I don't think there's *anything* I need to know from *you.* Once you're dead, I'll wait for the two hundredth and sixth incarnation of Yamatanka—and kill him, too," I replied happily. *"Then the two hundredth and seventh, and the two hundredth and eighth . . ."*

This Death stuff was more fun than a shopping spree at Saks, or a full week's relaxation at the Golden Door. I didn't know *why* I hadn't been more accepting of my heritage before. What the hell was I thinking, wanting to be a mortal human being? I must've been crazy.

"Pwease," he gurgled, his face turning bright red as I increased the pressure on his trachea again. *"Lizzen to me . . . if you eba want to zee your father again."*

Damn, he said the magic words.

I instantly released him, and he fell, coughing, to the ground. I watched as the blood flooded back into his face, wishing that instead of him gasping like a codfish in the sand, he were lying as dead and cold as a doorknob.

"I will spare your life—but only for today—*if* you tell me where my father is," I said in a detached voice, not wanting him to know exactly how much I wanted to find my father and sister. I didn't want him to think he had any more leverage than he already did.

"I . . ." Marcel croaked just as he was consumed by a coughing fit and had to stop.

"Go on," I offered helpfully when he was done hacking. Crossing my arms across my chest, I gave him the most intense stare I could muster, and willed him to get on with his story without coughing up a lung.

Marcel—probably just to piss me off and prolong my curiosity to the breaking point—coughed a few more times, then nodded, ready to save his neck with his tongue.

"*You* are the only one with a birthright," he stammered as the livid imprint of my fingertips emerged like a scarlet necklet around his throat.

"He," Marcel continued, pointing at Daniel's prone body, "and one other that you have not met yet have a claim to the job. But *you* are the only one with the true birthright."

"I don't understand. You told me you knew where my father was, and now you're just babbling on about 'birthrights' and 'claims to the job'? This is bullshit—" I said, advancing toward him angrily with my hands clasped into two hard fists.

But Marcel was much quicker than I'd expected, and he shot across the sand on his belly, sliding into the water like a seal. If the guy hadn't been my mortal enemy—one who had just tried to strangle me in cold blood—well, I *might've* been kind of impressed with the guy's prowess.

"Figure it out for yourself, if you're not too stupid!" he called back to me, a grimace on his face as he slipped under the water and, with one hard kick of his feet, was gone. Even with all my amazing new powers, I was helpless to do anything but stand there and watch the bastard disappear to parts unknown.

Crap, I thought to myself. *I'm not any closer to finding my father, I just let my mortal enemy escape,* and *I'm still stuck in Hell!*

The old-Callie part of me wanted to sit down and cry, but the other, newer part of my personality whispered something *very* interesting into my brain. It told me that there *was* a way out of Hell . . .

And that was when I realized *exactly* what the pool of water in front of me was:

That sucker is a wormhole.

twenty-four

The old me would've taken Daniel into the wormhole with me, gone back to New York, found a safe place to drop him off—preferably a hospital or an Urgent Care Clinic—and then hung around in the waiting room to make sure he wasn't the proud owner of a concussion, a laceration, or a slight decapitation.

Instead, the new me—the *Death* me—dragged his body under the palm tree, ostensibly for shade, and gave him a nice pat on the head by way of a good-bye. Thus with my guilt satisfied, I waded into the water without a second thought about his health—or lack thereof.

I'd spent my whole life second-guessing, double-checking, and "just making sure" everything I did was done the "right" way, so it was kind of nice to let the new voice inside my brain tell me what to do.

And it is telling me to get my butt in gear, I thought to myself. *So I better get a move on.*

When I was waste deep in the pool, I pinched my nose with my fingers and shut my eyes tight against the oncoming influx of water. I took a deep breath, then let my whole body slide underneath the cool wetness. It took only a moment for the wormhole to swallow me up in its vortex, then shoot me out into the ether.

I had never been able to direct where I was going when I was in a wormhole before, but now I found that it was disgustingly easy to control my direction, and after a few seconds I was at my destination, my feet firmly on solid ground—without any of the crazy nausea or headaches that usually accompanied my wormhole-traveling experiences.

I had never been to this place before, but I hadn't had any trouble imagining what it would look like: *The Psychical Bureau of Investigations is just as nondescript and boring as I figured it would be.*

Trying to keep my initial appearance under the radar, I'd gotten the wormhole to drop me off near the revolving front door of the building, so that it looked like I was just any other poor sap who had trudged in off the street. The only guard on duty was quietly nursing a Styrofoam cup of coffee at the front desk. He gave me a curious glance as I spun around inside the revolving doorway one more time than was necessary before disembarking—I'd always had a penchant for the stupid things, and it had driven my parents crazy. I was the only kid in Newport known for causing revolving-door traffic jams.

Because it was so early in the morning, there was no one else waiting as I finally slipped out the door and stepped into the large, fluorescently lit lobby. There appeared to be no ceiling—just empty space that seemed to go on indefinitely, but that was the only "magical"-feeling thing in the place. The rest of the lobby was decorated in a mix of taupe linoleum, eggshell paint, and brown beige furniture. The long panels of glass tha made up the front wall let a little bit of natural light inside, but other than that, it was dim and unappealing. I bet whoever'd designed it was *known* for their "institutional" work.

The place was *so* dreary that I found myself wanting to slit a couple of throats just to add a bit of color to all the brown on taupe on white—*yuck!*

Looking up at the large, gold-rimmed clock hanging on the wall above the lonely guard's head, I saw that the minute hand was pointed at three and the hour hand was firmly wedged in between the five and six.

So, it's only 5:15, I thought to myself happily. *I have the whole morning to find out where they're keeping Jarvis,* and *to make the stupid detective who took him sorry that he ever drew a breath, period.*

"May I help you, ma'am?"

Startled, I looked away from the clock and down into the warm eyes of the guard who had just spoken to me. I was immediately reminded of an old bloodhound. His face was a mass of wrinkles topped with a thatch of white hair. His eyes drooped kindly, so that you instantly felt he was your friend, and that he was more than ready to listen to whatever problems ailed you—*and* to try to help you fix them.

I opened my mouth to tell him exactly why I was there, and what I wanted to do to that stupid Detective Davenport, but something inside my brain told me to hold my tongue, that the time for truth was *not* upon us . . . so I decided to keep my big trap shut.

"I'm here to inquire about a prisoner that you're holding in Purgatory," I began, putting on my patented "innocent face."

"A prisoner?" he said, one eyebrow cocked curiously at me.

"Yes, I was told that you had arrested a friend of mine. And that he was here. In Purgatory."

The old guard scratched his head.

"I don't rightly know what you're talking about, ma'am," he said finally. "We don't *put* people in Purgatory. Not these days. And you can't even get there from here anymore. Not since the use of Purgatory was outlawed anyway."

Not liking what he was saying at all, I decided he was being all dodgy in order to put me off the scent. Obviously, the Psychical Bureau of Investigations held their prisoners in Purgatory, and this place reeked of magic, so the boring old lobby *had* to be a front for all the covert things going on behind the bureau's "closed doors." Why else would they have chosen such a hideous color palette for their lobby if *not* to bore the people waiting in it into comas? That way no one was awake enough to ask any penetrating questions!

"Look, buddy," I said, putting away my Miss Innocent Face and glaring at him, "I want you to go and fetch Detective Davenport. And I don't care *what* kind of bullshit excuse you're cooking up in that bloodhound head of yours right now; just go get the waste of a human being out here so I don't eviscerate you where you stand."

I smiled, revealing my shiny white teeth threateningly, the way a dog would when it was really pissed off. It occurred to me that I could probably just flash the guard to death with all the pearly whiteness I was packing—I knew the Crest White Strips I used with religious precision would come in handy someday—but I supposed I needed the old guard alive, not dead . . . at least for now.

"Uhm, we don't have a detective named Davenport working here," the old guard said finally. "And we don't keep prisoners here—that's no lie. They go downtown now."

"This isn't downtown," I said, feeling like I was in a very warped version of *The Twilight Zone*.

"No, ma'am," he said, shaking his head. "This is *uptown*."

Shit, I thought to myself, *I guess I* haven't *mastered the art of the wormhole yet.*

"Okay, fine. I *may* be uptown, but that other part is a bald-faced lie. I know for a fact that you have a Detective Davenport working on my father's kidnapping case—so there!"

The old guard took out a pad of paper and pulled a pen from behind his ear. He licked his index finger with his tongue and used the wet tip to flip the cover on the pad.

"And your father is . . . ?"

"My father is Death . . . like, *duh*," I said, exasperated. Did I have to explain *everything* to the man?

The old guard started to write something down on his pad, but then he stopped and looked up at me quizzically.

"And your father has been kidnapped? Well, now."

"Days ago," I replied angrily. "Don't you keep up with current events? Or do you, like this lobby, live in circa 1984?"

"Look, ma'am, there's no need to be aggressive. Now, I hate to be the bearer of bad news, but there has been *no* report of Death going missing in action. And since you seem like a nice young woman, I'm sure I can get someone from the Mind Bending Squad to come up and explain—"

I slammed my fists down hard on his desk, gouging two large craters into its wooden surface. The old guard stared at me, uncertain as to how to proceed. I doubted he'd ever dealt with something like me before—all nice and cute on the outside, *but crunchy-mean on the inside.*

"Ma'am, you're going to force me to have to call for backup—"

"I don't care *who* you call; just get me Detective Davenport so I can give him a piece of my mind," I nearly yelled at the guard. I bet you a dollar that if someone had checked my blood pressure right there and then, it would've burst the cuff—I was that on edge. After all, the old guard was *not* supposed to flout my authority like this. He was *supposed* to do what I said, no questions asked. Instead, the guy was getting all uppity on me, threatening to call for backup or, even *worse*, sic the Mind Bending Squad on me!

I gave him one last chance to redeem himself—even though I was feeling about as charitable as the Grinch. In fact, I was starting to feel *downright homicidal* toward the old guy the longer I was in his company.

"Go and get Detective Davenport, or I will not be responsible for what I am going to do to you."

"Ma'am, I *can't* get someone who doesn't work here—"

Without even realizing I was doing it, I lifted my arm and pointed my right index finger at his chest.

"Then you're dead."

He opened his mouth to protest, but no words came out, just a loud hissing sound. I watched, disinterested, as his soul sailed out from between his lips and formed a cloud around his head. His eyes bulged in their sockets, and then he keeled over, his body draped across the desk, his arms splayed out like Jesus on the cross. The cup of coffee he'd been drinking fell forward with him, the thick, brackish liquid escaping its cup and cascading down the front of the desk and onto the floor near my feet.

As I took a step back to avoid the rushing coffee onslaught, I felt a hand on my shoulder, and I turned around to find a thin, skeletal man in a long black trench coat standing behind me. His eyes were like two burning holes, and his teeth were long and came to very fine points. He did *not* look like the kinda guy you wanted to meet in a dark alley, late at night, all by yourself.

"We'll take it from here, ma'am," he said, his voice as shrill as fingernails on a chalkboard. He lifted his hand from my skin, and my flesh sizzled where it had been touched.

A short, squat woman in a long, flowing black dress came to stand beside the skeletal man. Her face was hidden behind a black veil so I couldn't see what the heck she looked like, but whatever was behind there was totally giving me the creeps without even *having* to see it.

The cloud around the old guard's head was starting to separate, bits of it trailing off in different directions, but as I watched, the squat woman pulled a jar of something that looked like amber-colored honey from her pocket and twisted off the lid, holding it out for the cloud to sense. Instantly, the cloud re-formed and headed like a homing pigeon for whatever was in the jar.

Without a moment's hesitation, the skeletal man lifted up a butterfly net he'd pulled out of nowhere an swooped down on the unsuspecting cloud. There was a soft rustling sound, and then the cloud was gone, lost inside the net.

The skeletal man tipped his tall, black top hat at me, and the woman curtsied.

"Long live the reign of the New Death!" they said in unison before disappearing without another word and leaving me alone with the old guard's dead body.

Well, that was efficient, I thought, my eyes itching to look away from the corpse but totally drawn to it at the same time.

I stared at the pinched old face with its thatch of white hair and hound-dog eyes—and suddenly, the realization of what I'd done hit me so hard I almost collapsed.

My knees seemed to give out on me first, and I slid forward, my hands like claws, grasping for purchase on the desktop so I didn't end up on the floor—and soaked in coffee. I was able to remain upright—just barely—but now I was so low to the ground that I was eye level with the corpse's face. I turned my head away, and the tears poured thick and fast down my cheeks, like someone had broken my internal taps and was trying to flood me out.

I couldn't stop crying, my breath catching in my throat in great, heaving sobs.

I don't want to be Death. I never asked for this! The whole thing I just experienced was so *not as much fun as shopping at Saks or spending a day at the Golden Door!*

It sucked!

I felt like some alien force had taken over my life, and no matter what *I* wanted, this force was gonna make me do *its* bidding instead. Like, for example, *I* wanted to slam my head into the desk and make the nasty creature that was curled up inside my brain climb out, but it was no use—the sucker was here to stay.

I mean, even as I was *thinking* all these things, the little voice was directing me to get up and get the show on the road.

I climbed back up to my feet, my eyes still averted from the dead body I had helped to create, then started for the bank of elevators that led to the inner sanctum of the Psychical Bureau of Investigations.

I pressed the call button and waited as the elevators vied to see which one would reach me first. It wasn't even close. The elevator in the middle—the one directly in front of me—whooshed like a speed demon down the numbered floors until it came to a shuddering halt at the lobby. It slid open invitingly, and I stepped inside its plush red velvet and brass button–covered interior.

I looked over at the long row of thick, brass buttons that stood at attention on the thin, golden plaque in front of me. There were so many to choose from that for a moment I felt like a little kid and almost pressed them all at once just to see what would happen, but luckily, reason reinstated itself and I punched the topmost button—the one marked PENTHOUSE—instead.

The doors slid shut with a whisper, and I waited for the elevator to begin its ascent to the top, but nothing happened. The elevator just sat there, slightly swaying, but totally *not* going anywhere.

"C'mon," I said, punching the Penthouse button angrily with my index finger—if the thing wasn't going *up*, then I wanted *out*.

Suddenly, there was a loud *hiccup*, and then, like

someone had clipped its wings, the elevator began to free-fall like a bullet down a gun barrel . . . with me screaming my lungs out the whole ride.

we hit the bottom of the elevator shaft with a thud. Even though intellectually I knew we'd been falling way too long for us to be anywhere near the elevator's *original* end point, I was still holding out hope that there'd been some mistake, that I hadn't *actually* been shipped right back to my least favorite place in the whole universe.

But when the elevator chimed our arrival and the doors slid open, I finally had to accept the fact that I really *was* back in—you guessed it—*Hell.*

Well, this bites, I thought miserably to myself as I stepped out of the elevator, finding myself in the middle of a lush, tropical forest. Other than the extremely long elevator ride I'd just suffered through, the only reason I knew this place belonged to Hell was because it was so incredibly hot outside. I mean, it was *sweltering*—hotter even than the desert I'd left barely twenty minutes before.

I vaguely remembered someone once saying that it only *seemed* hotter in tropical climes because of the humidity. Well, they were full of crap—this place didn't just *seem* fifty degrees hotter; it *was* fifty degrees hotter. My skin was already covered in a thick sheen of sweat, and a cloud of nasty little gnatlike bugs were attacking every exposed part of my person, desperate to scarf down as much of my blood as possible before I could slap them away.

My head jerked up, instantly watchful, as I heard a loud rustling in the foliage to my right. I had no idea what kind of evil monsters inhabited this jungle—other than the hateful vampire gnats—but I hadn't come this far to get disemboweled by some mutant anteater creature.

It was only then that I remembered my true nature, and with that remembrance came the dissolution of all my fears. The buggers just instantly dropped away—dead as all the gnats I'd been able to get my hands on. I knew it didn't matter what kind of beast came for my head now that I was the anthropomorphic version of *Death*. I would dispatch it before it could get anywhere near me. Enough said.

This idea made me laugh, and the laugh was so heinous, so evil and cruel, that it nearly froze the blood in my veins. I hated that laugh and all it stood for.

I hate me. And I hate what I have become.

After a few minutes of fumbling my way through the thick jungle undergrowth, branches grabbing at my ass and leaves tickling my nose, I realized that I had totally missed the path. I clomped my way back through the underbrush and sighed when I was back on solid earth again, no more long tendrils of plant life clutching at my skin.

The path was long and narrow, winding its way through the jungle like a giant slalom course that went on farther than my eye could see. Since I still didn't know how to open a wormhole on my own—and my Death sense told me only where I could *find* one—I was stuck. All I could do was follow my version of the Yellow Brick Road and hope I came to the Emerald City without running into too much trouble.

As I set off down the narrow path, sweat pouring from my face and body, I made a promise to myself: I was *not* going to use my Death powers again, no matter what the little voice in my head said. I would not dispatch another soul—and that included any gnats I couldn't kill with my own two hands—until I knew what the hell I was doing.

With that decided, I let out a sigh of relief. I might have no idea *where* or *what* I was, but as long as I could keep that promise to myself, then the world wasn't such a terrifying place after all. I mean, looking on the bright side of things . . . if I could handle being the incarnation of Death on Earth, then what *couldn't* I handle, right?

There was only one thing niggling at the back of my brain, one question that I didn't have the answer to:

Why the hell am I back in Hell?

twenty-five

I walked for what seemed like an eternity before I came to the end of the jungle. I had suspected that the end was fast approaching only about ten minutes before it actually happened—primarily because the foliage had begun to thin *just* as the path had started to widen.

I hadn't seen another living soul—other than my constant companions, the gnats—the whole trip, and I had been looking. I tried to make as much noise as I could while I walked so that anything lurking out in the trees or undergrowth would know I was coming and get the hell out of my way.

I can't kill what I can't see, I wisely surmised.

I could feel the voice in my head aching to kill something, but I found that if I could keep up a constant barrage of singing, the voice would get annoyed and go away—at least for a little while. So, desperately grasping for songs that I knew the lyrics to, I made my way through the whole Beatles canon, and then when I got *really* desperate, I dusted off the Spice Girls and

Depeche Mode. I think the real "knock your socks off" number was my warbling, off-key rendition of Gloria Gaynor's "I Will Survive," which was so horrible that it made *even* Death want to take a vacation from my head.

It is weird the caliber of song that comes to one's mind when one is wandering through the jungles of Hell all by one's lonely, I philosophized. *I don't even much like the Spice Girls.*

Anyway, when I reached the end of the jungle, I stopped and looked around, uncertain of where to go next. It wasn't like the jungle had gradually faded into the next landscape. In fact, it was quite the opposite. Where the jungle ended there was only a sheer drop-off that seemed to stretch on into infinity.

And part of me—the one that itched to push *all* the buttons in the elevator—wanted to throw myself *into* that gaping chasm . . . but luckily, I restrained myself.

I don't know what it was about mountainsides and cliffs that made me want to fling my body off their ledges, but ever since I was a little kid, I had been obsessed with what it would feel like to do just that. I had a very vivid memory of being in the car, driving with my mother, and looking out the passenger seat into the swirling mass of the Rhode Island Sound. I remember rolling down the car window to feel the cold wind on my face, but really what I wanted was to get even *closer* to the edge.

The next thing I knew I was unsnapping my seat belt and reaching for the door handle. My mother must've had a heart attack when she realized what I was doing, but instead of screaming at me—which would have just encouraged me to make the leap—she quietly grabbed the collar of my shirt and yanked me over into her lap, the car door slamming shut almost as soon as I had gotten it open. (Yes, I wouldn't have died if I fell—but maternal instinct is strong, no matter what.)

I don't think my mother ever forgot my near escape from the cliff because, after that, she watched me like a hawk whenever we went anywhere near the sea. What she didn't realize was that it wasn't the sea that had so enthralled me: *It was the edge.*

"Welcome to end of Hell, Calliope," a voice called behind me.

I whirled around so quickly it made my teeth ache, and I saw *Daniel* standing at the edge of the jungle. He was wearing a clean white T-shirt and a pair of tight black jeans, and he looked pretty damn delicious.

Too bad I want to rip his throat out, I thought miserably.

"What're you doing here?" I asked as I casually made my way closer to the edge so I could get a better look at what lay at its bottom—and keep a safer distance between the two of us.

I didn't *want* to hurt Daniel. I *liked* Daniel. So why was I itching for his blood?

"I was waiting for you. The boss had you summoned, if you hadn't already realized." *Aha! So that is why I'm back in Hell,* I thought to myself. *Boy, that Devil is a sneaky little bastard.*

"You look nice," Daniel added as he moved closer to where I was standing, his eyes locked onto my face. It was totally crazy, but I was starting to feel that surreal sexual heat I'd experienced the first two times I'd met him—*what the heck is that all about? I thought we already cleared that up eons ago—jeez!*

"Thanks . . . I guess," I replied, my armpits starting

to sweat as Daniel came to stand beside me, his fingers only inches from mine. God, just being *near* him was intoxicating.

Wait a minute, I thought. *I don't look nice. I'm a mess.* It dawned on me what he was doing! He was trying to work his weird sexual mojo on me again. He seemed oblivious to the fact that I had been immune to his charms the last few times we were together, but I guess he was under the impression that "no" didn't *always* have to mean . . . well, "no."

"Not interested," I lied, sidestepping away from him, but he was quicker than me, reaching out and grabbing my hand. I felt an electric charge race through my skin, my body beginning to change its mind about Daniel's level of attractiveness. I was starting to feel *much* more positively charged toward him.

"Daniel, this is probably not a good idea—"

"I saved your life; you saved mine. I think we can put pleasantries aside."

"These aren't pleasantries—" I started to say, but my words were silenced by his lips firmly pressing against mine. He tasted terrible again, and I was totally *not* into it—*and* that was when the ugly little voice inside my head decided to make itself known. Suddenly, I was pushing Daniel away from me—shoving him away, actually—and I found my right hand lifting of its own accord, the index finger reaching out to place itself in the hollow of Daniel's solar plexus.

"*Die,*" I whispered, my lips still hot and bruised from Daniel's earwax-tasting mouth.

I waited for him to start shrieking, for his eyes to roll up into his head, for Death to sneak up behind him and suck him dry until he was a mere husk of flesh and bone.

Instead, absolutely nothing happened—other than Daniel started laughing like a hyena at me.

"Die!" I yelled again, my finger itching to take his life, not understanding why his life was rebelling against the inevitable.

"I don't understand! You should be dead," I screamed at him.

And then the strangest thing happened: Daniel's whole body began to smoke. I watched as his skin turned a dark brown, and large, liquid-filled blisters formed on every bit of his exposed flesh. He looked—and stank—like he was being set on fire from the inside out.

"What the—" I said, stepping back as his flesh began to slough off in wide swatches, leaving behind a sheath of new, pinkish skin. Daniel, still laughing like he was totally immune to the pain of being burned alive, reached up and started to pull off any of the old burned skin that remained, throwing it to the ground like it was refuse.

"Your skin," I said. "That's disgusting!"

"It's not mine," he said as he ripped the last of the dead flesh from around his mouth and smiled up at me. What he said was true. It wasn't Daniel I was looking at anymore. This was a new man entirely—one with a penchant for Keith Richards's old wardrobe.

"Who are you?" I whispered as I stared up at the handsome stranger. He was taller than Daniel, with a mane of thick, curling pitch-black hair, and pale pink skin that was becoming a startling shade of snow white. He had a wide, cruel mouth and the darkest, blackest eyes I had ever seen. He leered at me, his lean, well-built body moving closer and closer until I had to step back away from him—and closer to the edge of Hell.

"I'm the Devil, Calliope. I can take whatever form I want; I can control anyone"—*hmmm, like a rheumy old guard with hound-dog eyes*—"and the hysterically funny thing is: You can't kill me. Or anyone else down here in Hell . . . because—"

He giggled here, and it was the creepiest sound in the whole world.

"Because they're already dead, *Death*. Completely outside of your dominion."

Well, I guess my theory about just killing anything that attacks me down in Hell is shot to shit, I thought dryly.

"Wait a minute," I said, my mind whirling. "So you *made* me kill that old guard?" I was starting to feel all shaky inside again as I thought of the poor old man I'd cheated out of his life.

"You were after me, Calliope: the one who was controlling him. That little voice inside your brain wants *my head* on a plate."

"Really? 'Cause that makes me feel a *whole* lot better . . . *not*."

"SILENCE!" the Devil screamed, and I took another step closer to the edge because he was so terrifying.

"I don't know what your game is, Calliope Reaper-Jones, but you will not disobey me now that you are in my realm."

"What do you want?" I said.

He gave me a nasty little smile that made me shrink inside my skin—*not* a pleasant feeling.

"I want you to pledge Death to me. I want you on my team for eternity." He began to pace in front of me, one eye locked on my face, almost holding me in place with its intensity, the other eye rolling around his head like a marble. I guess *this* was how the man did his "power" thinking—even if it *was* a very odd-looking way to get one's thoughts in order.

"Look, it's like real estate, Calliope. I'm the head honcho, the one with his name on all the signs. You're the minion, the little guy that sits at all my open houses, fields questions you don't really know the answers to, and then refers all the buyers back to me. *Capiche?*"

Am I hearing this correctly? Is the Devil really *referring to himself as a real estate agent?*

"Excuse me, I don't mean to be a pest, but why real estate? That just seems like a strange choice, you know?" I finished, then held my breath, waiting for him to scream at me again.

"That's actually a very good question, Callie—may I call you Callie?" the Devil said, scratching his chin thoughtfully. I nodded.

I mean, who the hell am I to tell the Prince of Darkness that he can't call me anything he damn well pleases?

"I think managing Hell is *just like* running a real estate company. In fact, I can think of *nothing* more fitting."

"Really?" I offered, encouraging him to continue.

"All the rush to wealth on someone else's dime, and then the reckoning in the guise of foreclosure. All those families constantly moving in and out of properties . . . just like the ebb and flow of life and death. And me, running the show behind the show." He sighed happily at the thought. "Me controlling the purse strings of salvation."

He giggled to himself, then turned both eyes in my direction, serious again.

"You can't talk your way out of this one, Callie. There's no appeasing the Devil, no 'get out of jail free' card," he said, running his hand languidly through his thick hair. "But I do have to admit that you were a *much* worthier opponent than your father gave you credit for."

"*What?*" I said. That got my attention. Up until then I'd been kinda bored.

The Devil grinned eagerly at me, excited by my interest.

"What do you mean, 'I'm a much worthier opponent than my father gave me credit for'?" I demanded. "Tell me what you mean!"

The Devil sighed and cocked his head, appraising me.

"If I must, I must," he began. "You do understand the Death lineage, don't you?"

I shook my head. The Devil looked at me like I was some kind of mutant thing in a test tube that should've been thrown out a long time ago.

"When Old High and Mighty upstairs created the job of *Death*, it was decided that there would only be *one* successor in any given generation, and that successor would be so human, so split between Good and Evil, that the balance between the two would be kept in check."

"That's my father," I said. The Devil nodded.

"But then there was the backup plan," he continued. "This was my own personal idea—one that I almost had to *force* the stupid Board of Death to ratify, the stinkers. This plan called for there to be *two possibilities* who could vie for the job of *Death* should the true successor—the one with the birthright—be unable to fulfill the job. One of the possibilities would be from the good side of the tracks, and the other . . . well, the other would be one of *my* minions."

"Daniel," I said under my breath.

"Precisely! Oh, you do catch on fast," he said, smiling.

"Go on," I said. "Tell me about my father."

"Your father rescinded your birthright."

"What?" I said uncertainly.

"You're the one with the birthright, Cal. Your father thought you weren't up to the job, so he asked for the Board to step in and relieve you of the future position."

It was like the Devil had punched me in the stomach. I felt the air whoosh out of my lungs, and I totally couldn't breathe. The world turned a funny, dark color, and I could hear my heart thudding sluggishly in my ears. I couldn't believe what the Devil had just said. My father had *rescinded* my birthright—a birthright that I didn't even know I had had—because he thought I wasn't worthy of the job?

"How did he know *I* was the one?" I asked, my voice like glue in my mouth.

The Devil clapped his hands together excitedly. He was becoming more and more comfortable with me, showing me exactly what kind of a creep he *really* was: a sexy, dirty, nasty, jerkoid one.

"When you were a little girl, you were the one who found Yamatanka stuck inside that nasty little Frenchman, Marcel, who was stuck out in the desert where your father left him to rot."

"My father did that to him?" I managed to get out. I couldn't believe Father would do something so horrible to someone, regardless of who they were. I mean, I didn't like the guy any more than my father probably did, but I would *never* tie him to a palm tree with a little string and leave him there all by himself to rot.

Or would I?

Actually, on second thought, this *was* Marcel we were talking about. The guy who tried to kill me after I'd totally been nice enough to set him free? Maybe my father wasn't so far off the mark, after all.

The Devil, a cruel smile on his handsome face, waggled his finger at me like I was a small child.

"Of course your father did, silly girl! It was the only way to keep *the Ender of Death* where he could see him, and also, as it turned out, it was a marvelous way to monitor the advent of 'the one with the birthright.' *You*, as the story goes."

"Uh-huh," I said, wishing he wouldn't digress so much, that he'd finish the story and put me out of my misery.

"Of course, all of this showed the supernatural world that *you* were the true successor."

"Look, it was a stupid accident. I was playing hide-and-seek—"

"Yes, I remember," the Devil interrupted. "You *did* hide-and-seek your way right into Hell that afternoon."

"Why me?" I almost wailed. I was still reeling from Father's betrayal. I wanted to know *why* the universe had decided to screw with my life so badly.

But the Devil didn't have my answer.

"Who knows why you were chosen? I surely don't," he said. "But I *do* know what you're going to do for me right now."

"Yeah, what's that?" I said, not liking his tone one little bit.

"You're going to bind yourself to my will for eternity."

I glared at him. He was so full of himself that it made me sick to look at him.

"And if I don't?" I said.

He looked at me sadly.

"I was afraid you'd say that."

The Devil shook his head and began to walk toward me. He was lithe as a cat. His long, toned body moved with such grace that it was impossible to keep my eyes off him. He truly was a sexual predator of the highest degree. It made me wonder how much time I'd really spent with him when I thought I was dealing with his protégé. That thought made me actually sick.

"That's precisely why I brought you here, in fact. Now I really *am* going to have to go and fetch Daniel—that was a nasty blow I gave him to the back of the head, wasn't it—but so effective. I need to start prepping him for his new job since his predecessor was such an abysmal failure."

"Please don't," I said, but the Devil ignored my words.

"I have one piece of advice for you. When you fall? Don't look down. It'll just freak you out."

"Why?" I said, trying to remain calm, even though I was scared out of my wits.

"Because. Hell is bottomless, silly."

And with that he reached out and shoved me so hard with his long, tapered fingers that I didn't even feel my feet leave the ground.

you know how I said I was obsessed with the edge, that I'd *always* wanted to pitch myself into the horizon and see what happened? Well, I just want to say here and now *that I was frickin' crazy! What idiot in their right mind throws themselves off a bloody cliff?*

* * *

the devil was right. I should've kept my eyes closed. When you stare into nothingness and nothingness stares back at you, it's a pretty horrible feeling.

As I fell, I only seemed to pick up speed, so that the longer I was in free fall, the faster the nothingness swooshed past me. It was very jarring and disconcerting . . . and totally and completely *sad.* Here I was, in the prime of my life, and I would never get to eat an ice cream cone again. I would never get to explain to Clio that I was really the *good guy* in the story. I would never get to buy another pair of skinny jeans, or go to the gym and drop twelve pounds so I could fit into a perfect Marc Jacob's size zero.

But then, like a miracle, the *opposite* of the sad and endless free-fall existence I'd imagined for myself happened. After I'd totally prepared myself to spend the rest of my immortal eternity racing toward nothing, my body a bullet with no body to embed itself in—

I unexpectedly found *something.*

And that something . . . was God.

twenty-six

"Calliope Reaper-Jones, can you hear me?"

It was the weird voice from the beach, the one that reminded me of RuPaul. The one that had made sure I got my Sea Foam.

"Yeah!" I yelled back, the sound of my own voice flying back into my face as I continued my race toward the bottom of nothingness.

"Do you trust me?"

Do I trust the voice? I can't even tell what gender it *is, let alone whether or not I'm supposed to, in all good conscience, trust it.*

I decided not to answer—even though it *had* gotten me the Sea Foam—and the voice stayed mum, which made me think it was just a fluke, something I had probably *thought* I had heard because I was scared and lonely and wanted a friend.

Wait a minute—if I was gonna be chillin' in a bottomless pit at the edge of Hell for, like, eternity, why didn't I just accept any weird voice that I may or may not have heard, and say thank you for the company?

I really should stop feeling so negative about my fate. At least the terrible Death voice had shut up after its last run-in with the Devil—thank God for small favors.

"If I tell you what I am, will you trust me?" the voice said, startling me.

There it is again, I thought, *my friendly copilot in the long trip to the bottom of the bottomless pit of Hell.*

I seemed to be getting loopier and loopier as the seconds passed. I was gonna be nuttier than a fruitcake soon.

"Maybe!" I yelled.

There was a pause, and I really wasn't sure the voice was going to speak again, but—as if to confirm my insanity—it did.

"I am that I am."

It took a moment to process what the voice was saying.

"Are you saying that you're God?" I screamed, my body hurtling faster and faster through the nothingness. "Is *that* what you're saying?!"

"It is," the voice said.

"Why should I believe you? If what you're saying is true, then you're the one that gave me that stupid birthright in the first place! You're the reason I'm in this crazy mess!"

My voice was getting hoarse from screaming at God. It was definitely *not* the way I ever saw myself conversing with the Creator of All Things, but I was really starting to get upset about the compromising position I'd been put into.

"I only gave you the opportunity *to get yourself into this mess,"* God said in its sexy, yet *sexless* voice.

"Oh, that's *free will* you're talking about!" I spat back at God. I knew where *this* conversation was going. It was going right to the place where everyone could point their finger at me and say, "The whole thing's your own fault, Calliope Reaper-Jones."

There was a long silence, and then I swear I heard God trying not to laugh at me.

"That *is free will, Calliope Reaper-Jones."*

See, I thought miserably, *right on the money with that one!*

"All right," I said, "you win."

So God had pulled the trump card—I *had* gotten myself into the whole crazy mess. It wasn't like I was *forced* to say yes to my mother and Father McGee. I hadn't been *forced* to tell the Devil "no."

I hadn't been forced—coerced and guilt-tripped, maybe, but never *forced*—to do *anything.*

"God?" I said.

"Yes, Calliope Reaper-Jones."

"I don't want to be Death anymore."

"I know, my dear, but sometimes you can't always get what you want."

I really hated the fact that God had just quoted the Stones at me—even if the sentiment was right on the mark.

Damn it, my eyes were tired of crying, and I was sick of my heart hurting. I wanted to go back to my crappy little Battery Park City apartment in New York and crawl into bed so I could pull the covers over my head . . . and just disappear.

"You have to finish what you started, Calliope," God said.

Okay, I knew God was right, but it sucked that I had to admit it—so I hedged for a little bit longer.

"How can I finish anything when I'm lost in a bottomless pit at the edge of Hell!" I yelled up at God.

"Oh, honey," God said, laughing. *"That's the easy part."*

there was only silence.

I had stopped falling a long time before, but I hadn't had the nerve to open my eyes and see where I was. I was terrified I'd be back in the deserts of Hell, my leg tied to a palm tree with a loop of charmed translucent nylon.

Finally, after I gave myself a good stiff talking-to, I steeled my heart for utter disappointment and opened my eyes.

I was sitting on the topmost step of a long, intricately carved temple stairway. Below me lay the remains of what was once Indra's glorious soundstage. Now the stage looked like a heinous battle had taken place there only moments before. The once beautiful backdrops were in tatters, the scenery in shreds, the stairs torched . . . even the utility closet we'd used for a hiding place was a scattered mess of brooms and buckets.

What the hell happened here? I thought to myself.

I stood up and surveyed the space, looking for survivors.

It took me only a minute to see that there were none.

The Gopi were all dead, their bodies ripped open like stuffed animals, their entrails strewn around the painted scenery as if they were sacrificial garlands. It made me want to cry again, but I stuffed the feeling down deep into my gut, determined not to let emotion control me any longer.

I looked through the remains for any sign of Indra,

but the only thing I found was a pair of bloodied tap shoes underneath a fallen flat. I guess whoever had done this had either killed him and taken his body with them, or . . . Well, the thought of Indra as someone's prisoner wasn't a pretty picture, either.

"Poor Gopi," I said, and even though they had totally tried to kick my ass, I truly did mourn their passing. It looked like they had been loyal bodyguards right up until the end.

I jumped off the stairs, careful not to step on anybody's intestinal tract, and made my way over to the camera. I wondered if Indra had been able to record his final battle on film, but when I got there, I saw that someone had ripped the film out of its delicate case, ruining whatever had been captured on it forever—dancing girls or bloodshed, I had no idea which.

"This sucks," I said under my breath.

"I know it."

I whirled around, my heart hammering in my chest, but gave a sigh of relief when I realized who it was.

"Kali, hi," I said, then: "This really, *really* sucks."

She nodded. She was standing by the utility closet, still in the same outfit she'd been wearing the last time I saw her. Her beautiful dark eyes were stricken with sorrow as she took in the scene that surrounded us. She may not have loved the Gopi, but she felt the same way I did: Their deaths were a waste.

"What in the world happened here, white girl?" she said, shaking her head. She didn't look at me, just surveyed the destruction. I could tell that she wanted me to confirm that I'd had nothing to do with the massacre—and for once I could honestly say that *this* wasn't my fault.

"I don't know. I just got here myself."

She stepped over a fallen rack of saris, blood caking their shimmering sequins like paint, and came to stand beside me. Together, we tallied the damage.

"God sent me here," I said finally. She started at my words, her eyes curious yet a bit fearful at the same time.

I don't know *why* I blurted the words out like that, but I guess there was something about having a religious experience that left you kind of shell-shocked.

"You *saw* it?" she asked, her eyes wide. I liked how she called God an "it." I mean, that was exactly what I would've done, since the Creator of All Things that *I'd* spoken to was definitely of the "sexless" persuasion—which meant any gender that said *they* were made in God's image was full of shit.

"I *heard* it," I said. "It spoke to me twice, but the first time I had no idea who it was." Jeez, I felt like I was in high school talking about a boy I liked or something.

Kali nodded like she believed what I was saying, but for all she knew, I could've been hallucinating the whole thing.

"God doesn't personally intervene very often," she said. "In fact, I've never met anyone that's seen—*or heard*—from the Creator. At least in this century."

"Lucky me," I said bitterly.

She glared at me, her large eyes flashing. She really didn't like me pooh-poohing my fifteen minutes with God.

"Yes, lucky you."

I didn't know how to explain to Kali that, yes, maybe it *was* a great honor to meet God, or the Creator, or whatever "it" called itself these days, but right then I would've sold my firstborn to be a normal girl with a life span of sixty-five to seventy years and no knowledge whatsoever of the Afterlife.

"Look, Kali, God sent me here for a reason. I don't know what it is, but it must have something to do with this place or the Gopi—"

Kali looked down at her hands.

"I made a mistake, Callie." It was the first time she had used my real name: not "white girl" or "dipwad" or "bitch." I supposed that meant we were making some kind of progress in our tentative friendship. At least, *I* was gonna take the usage of my real name as a step in the right direction.

She stared down at her cuticles as she chose her next words carefully.

"I let you think you owed me a favor for coming down and helping you with Indra's movie," she continued. "I was gonna hold it over your head and make you do all kinds of embarrassing, ridiculous things just because I could."

If it hadn't been so obvious what a hard time she was having simply *telling* me how silly and selfish she'd been, I would've made her rue the day she'd ever set eyes on me. But since having to apologize to me *period* was such a major-league blow to her ego, I decided that *that* would be punishment enough without making her feel any worse.

"We were lovers once, but not for many, many centuries," she began, as if that explained everything.

"Okay," I said uncertainly. "Go on."

"You see, because of this, Indra felt very close to me," she continued, "and for a long time he had begged me to come to him; he said there was something he *needed* to tell me. But I was very angry with him—*for reasons that do not concern* anyone *else*—and I didn't go to him, nor would I allow him to come to me. So he used you to *make* me listen, and what I heard, I didn't want to believe . . . so I pretended to not hear at all."

I reached out and took Kali's hand, giving it a squeeze. This was really, really hard for her and I wanted her to know that no matter what she said next, she was my friend—probably my only one in the supernatural community—but a friend, nonetheless.

"Oh, Callie," she wailed, "in the memories I showed you, Indra let me see that he had never defeated Vritra. And he has lived with the fear and guilt for so many years—"

"Drowning his pain in drink?" I offered. She turned to look at me, surprised. Did she think I was *blind*? C'mon, how many times did the man pull the stupid flask out of his pocket just while *I* was looking at him?

I think it was pretty obvious the man had a problem—*whatever* ambrosia of the Gods' concoction he was drinking.

"Yes, that's right. He is addicted to Soma, and *that's* why I've been so angry with him. You saw in the memories how strong and beautiful he once was, and to let himself become only half a man . . . It made me so terribly angry with him," she finished, her eyes sad.

"Yeah, about that whole 'let's thrust Callie into Indra's memory so she can see Vritra's beautiful human corpse castle' thing. Let me just pause right here, so I can give you an extra-special *thanks* for that one. And when I say *thanks*, I really mean, *how insane are you to do that to me?*"

Kali grinned sheepishly at me.

"Sorry about that, but Indra wanted you to see . . . and then *you* asked, so what could I do?"

"I don't care. You *still* should be groveling at my feet," I countered.

"Not gonna happen," she said. "So don't even go there."

"Fine," I replied. "I never *did* see past Indra being captured by Vritra's mud men. Tell me what he showed you . . . and what you were *supposed* to show me.'

Kali sighed, not wanting to think about the fact that she hadn't done as she was told and shown me *all* of Indra's memories.

"You have to understand that after I saw the truth, I couldn't bear for you, or anyone else, to know it," she whispered, pleading for me to understand.

I didn't know what to say. I might've done the same thing had I been in her situation, so who was I to judge? Instead, I nodded for her to continue.

"He was captured by Vritra—*and instead of dying as befits a hero*—the dipwad made a deal with the slimy demon. He would tell the world that he had vanquished him with Sea Foam, and for *that* he would have his life."

"Okay, so he wanted to live. I can't blame him for that," I said. "But did he say *why* Vritra wanted the supernatural world to think he was dead?"

Kali shrugged unhappily, her bottom lip stuck out like a child's.

"He didn't know, white girl. It was the only thing the demon asked of him, so I suppose he didn't think it was wise to press him for information," she said defensively. Jeez, without fail, every time I thought Kali and I were becoming friends, she got all bitchy on me.

"And this was the *only* part of the memory you didn't show me?" I asked, checking to make sure she wasn't holding out on me.

She nodded, and then suddenly her face fell.

"I was Indra's undoing! If I had shown you what he wanted you to see, you could have saved him," she sniffled, gesturing at the carnage with her hand, her lips trembling like this was something she had created—which she obviously hadn't, no matter how guilty she felt.

"You didn't do this," I said. "There's something else going on here, something Indra didn't tell you about. Why else would he have the Gopi bodyguards at his beck and call? Why the bad disguise? He used *me* to call *you* because this way it would be a secret that the two of you had spoken. The guy was scared. That much I would bet a million bucks on."

"You really think so?" Kali said hopefully, her dark eyes looking happier than they had since I'd first thrown an *Elle* at her head. "You really, really, *really* think so?"

"Did I or did I *not* just say I'd bet a million bucks on it?" I said, looking heavenward. *So help me, if the Hindu Goddess of Destruction does* not *stop being all whiny on me . . .*

"Well, what do we do now?" Kali asked uncertainly as we stood there surrounded by enough blood and gore to fill twenty B horror movies.

Suddenly, there was a loud *crunching* sound behind us.

"It's coming from the closet," Kali said through clenched teeth. "We're gonna have to kill it, white girl. You up for it?"

I nodded, not sure *what* the hell I'd just agreed to. But Kali was right. Whatever had killed the Gopi was still in the closet, and we *would* have to defeat it with only our bare fists for weapons.

I felt like Dwayne Johnson on estrogen, and the sensation was kind of cool.

Kali let out a war cry as the door to the utility closet flew open and something large and black flew out at us.

"Wait a minute!" I screamed as I grabbed Kali by the arm and nearly yanked her off her feet. I knew that big black thing, and there was no way in hell I was gonna let Kali hurt it!

"Runt!" I nearly shrieked with joy as my hellhound puppy made a running leap right over Kali and into my open arms. I grabbed on to Cerberus's pup—*my* pup because there was no way josé I was ever giving her back now—and held the beast to my chest like my life depended on it. The feel of her heart drumming double time in her rib cage, and the smell of her stinky dog fur, was heavenly.

"Callie," Clio yelled as she came out of the utility room at a run, her long teenage legs sprinting toward me as fast as they could carry her. In two seconds flat I had my dog and my little sister smashed into a giant three-way bear hug—one of my patented ones—and all of us were crying and giggling like a bunch of two-year-olds.

"I'm sorry, Cal," Clio said, her voice raw and warbly. "I should've believed you, and I didn't!"

"It's okay," I said, squeezing her even tighter to me. "I shouldn't have been such a pussy. I should've stood up for myself."

"All right, white girls, you guys better *stop* cryin' and *start* explaining," Kali said from where she sat, a very safe distance from all the sisterly affection.

We both turned to stare at her. I had forgotten she was even there—which only made her madder. Clio and I both started snickering when we saw the pinched, put-upon look on her face.

"If you don't stop it right now, I am *so* out of here," she said, giving me one of her trademark "I'm gonna kick your ass" looks.

I nodded, realizing the time for a reunion was *not* among the Gopi carnage.

"Clio," I said, letting her pull away from me finally, "how did you guys find me?"

She smiled. "Oh, that was easy. *He* showed us."

She turned back to the utility closet and pointed to where Daniel stood, his back against the wall, a large janitor's broom lying at his feet.

He gave me a weak smile.

"Hey, Callie, I thought you might be needing this—"

He held out something small and silver for me to see as he took another tentative step forward.

"Don't you dare, you monster," I yelled at him, pushing Clio behind my back protectively. "I won't let you hurt a hair on her head!"

"Callie, you don't understand—"

"I know who you are, *Daniel*. Now stay away from me!" But then *something*, some small piece of trivia, niggled at my brain.

Hadn't the Devil said it is his own *presence that brings out the killing side of Death? So, if this is the Devil, and not Daniel, then why is the little voice inside my head not screaming for blood?*

"You figured it out," Daniel said happily, his face relaxing into a real smile for the first time since I'd seen him last. "I'm not really allowed to talk about it, you know? So it makes explaining kind of hard."

I nodded. I was really starting to hate all this magic

stuff. I liked honesty, and it seemed like *honesty* was something the supernatural world took for granted.

"So you're really *you*," I said, even though his answer was only a formality. I had all the proof I needed inside me.

"What's going on?" Clio said, her hand wrapped around Runt's leash.

"Nothing," I replied, giving her a reassuring smile.

When my eyes caught Kali's, she just shook her head reproachfully at me. I didn't know what her deal with Daniel was, but I had a funny feeling the Devil had been using his "shape-shifting" trick to bamboozle unsuspecting women (and Goddesses) for quite a while—with poor Daniel as his scapegoat.

"I'll explain later," I offered, but she rolled her eyes and snorted under her breath.

"It has to do with the Devil."

This caught Kali's attention, but I shook my head and mouthed the word "later."

While I had been trying to appease Kali, Daniel had closed the gap between us.

"The Cup of Jamshid," Daniel said, offering it to me with both hands. "You left it back in Hell after you saved my life."

"You saved his life," Kali said. I shook my head, letting her know I *really would* explain everything later.

"Thanks," I said, giving him a sheepish smile. "Sorry I left you there, but Death seemed to have bigger fish to fry."

"Hey, no worries," he said, smiling, and for the first time I felt myself *really, truly* attracted to him just like we were a *real boy* and a *real girl*—not two people caught up in a supernatural whirlwind of craziness.

"Why would you do this for me?" I said, giving him a searching look. I dropped my eyes as soon as I encountered his equally intense gaze in return.

"Because you saved my life, Calliope Reaper-Jones, when by all rights you should have been feasting on my soul."

twenty-seven

"Aw, shucks, it was nothing." I shrugged as I took the silvery cup from his hands.

The burning sensation I'd felt when I first touched the magical object was gone, replaced now by the warm weight of something magical that was ready to do my bidding.

"How did you find us?" I said as I literally had to drag my eyes away from the cup, its magical force was calling out to me so fiercely.

"The Cup of Jamshid showed us," Clio said. At the mention of its name, the thing began to glow a bright silvery white color, and I could feel the thrum of life inside it, like there was a heart welded right into the metal.

"Thank you for all of this," I said to Daniel as I gave his hand a squeeze. It was pretty hysterical to watch the man blush. The real Daniel was so the *opposite* of the Devil.

"Oh, give me a break," Kali said. "This isn't the Love Boat, for Christ's sake."

"Shut up, Indian Princess," I said tartly, not even looking in her direction. After a few seconds, Daniel broke the weird connection between us by clearing his throat.

"Uhm, remember how you drank the paralysis potion back in the desert—" he began.

"You drank *paralysis potion*?" Clio said. I gave her a look, and she closed her mouth.

"Well, I kept wondering how anyone could possibly know where you were at any given time, let alone pinpoint your *exact location* so they could feed you a magic potion . . ."

"Uh-huh," I said impatiently.

"There had to be a trick to it. And the only charm I could think of that could do it was—"

"A homing spell!" Clio said excitedly.

"Precisely," Daniel said, giving Clio a wink.

"But who would put a homing spell on white girl here?" Kali said, totally not buying Daniel's scenario.

"Yeah, who would want to put a homing spell on me *other than to kill me, paralyze me, or otherwise render me incapable of completing my tasks*," I said sarcastically. The point seemed to be taken because Kali backed off, letting Daniel and Clio continue.

"It's a totally hard-core spell, so it would have to be someone really well versed in magical theory," Clio said, her cute forehead scrunched up with thought.

"So *great*, that could be anyone," I said miserably. Everyone was pretty quiet after that. I guess I'd sort of put a damper on the proceedings with my injection of *reality*.

"Look, we may not know their name, but we *do* know

their magical signature," Daniel offered, breaking the silence. "And because of that, we can sever the connection."

"We can?" I said hopefully.

"It's easy as pie, Cal," Clio said as she held out her hands, giving them a shake before placing them on my shoulders. It took only about two seconds after her touch for a sharp, jarring pain to shoot up both my arms.

"Ow!" I screeched. "Stop it! That hurts!"

Clio dropped her hands and looked down at my arms . . . *where a handcuff-shaped circlet of bright purple glowed warningly from around both wrists.*

"Well, I guess that answers the first question." I sighed. "Now we know who did this to me. It was that stupid wannabe detective from the Psychical Bureau of Investigations."

"The one that kidnapped Jarvis?"

"The very one," I said as I handed Daniel the Cup of Jamshid, then lifted my wrists up in the air for a little attention. "Would someone please take them off me?"

"Let me do it," Kali said, pushing her way past Clio, who was already reaching out to try to take the spell off me. Under Kali's breath, I heard her say:

"Easy as pie my ass . . ."

And then she grabbed my wrists.

"ARRRGGHHHH!"

I watched in horror as her hands caught fire, turning a succession of painful-looking red and brown colors before she got smart and dropped my arms, letting them slam painfully into my sides. Luckily, it hadn't all been in vain. When I looked down, the purple circlets were gone.

Yay, I'm free! I thought to myself. *Thank* you, *God.*

"That bloody hurt!" Kali wailed as she glared at my wrists with such intense hatred that I kinda feared for their lives—that is, if wrists *had* lives.

"Well, I guess that's *that*," I said as I listened to Kali trying not to moan with pain as she nursed her damaged hands.

"So what do we do now?" Clio said, looking from me to Daniel.

I really wanted to give my sister some amazing, well-thought-out answer. Some new, wonderful idea that would put us right on the road to finding our father and going home, but my only problem with all that was—

I wasn't anyone's fearless leader. I couldn't come up with some crack plan right out of my ass. I was just some *girl* who worked in the home and garden sector, and had a cruddy dating track record.

But apparently I was still one of the honored few in our universe that was on speaking terms with God because I didn't have to wait very long for some help from above.

"Why's the cup glowing like that?" I said, my eyes instantly drawn over to the silvery object in Daniel's hands. Not waiting for anyone to reply to my rhetorical question, I nimbly plucked the cup from his fingers and looked inside it.

I would've bet my one good pair of Jimmy Choo's that the cup had been *empty* when I was holding it not two minutes before, but now, to my utter surprise, it was completely full of a shimmering, mercurial substance that glowed like lightning as it leapt and burbled in its container.

"What the—" I started to say, but my attention was caught by the startlingly clear image of my father's face suspended in the depths of the liquid. His eyes were closed, and the skin of his face so pinched and ashen that it made me sick—he looked *awful*, no, *worse* than awful.

I wanted to look away—I mean, what kid wants to see their parent looking like a semiconscious corpse—but I couldn't, even when I felt Clio's hand on my shoulder.

"What do you see?" she asked. "What is it?"

I shook my head, waiting for the image to clear, but instead it changed.

"Oh, no," I breathed as I realized what I was looking at now. "This can't be. It doesn't make any sense."

But then, suddenly, it *all* started to make a *whole lot of sense*—more sense than I ever wanted to think about, actually. The pieces were starting to fall into place, and the picture was not looking like it was gonna be a very pretty one.

From the beginning, I hadn't been able to put my finger on *why* someone would want to kidnap my father, sister, and the other company Executives. It seemed like a totally pointless exercise in making a quick buck. After all, my father and sister were immortal, and if I were a gambling woman, I'd have bet most of the other company Executives were, too, so Death wasn't really on the table here.

At best, the kidnappers would make their demands while hiding their victims away for a while to keep everyone on tenterhooks, and then when they'd gotten whatever ransom they wanted, they'd let their hostages go.

Only, I was starting to suspect that ransoming "hostages" had never been this kidnapper's intention. I mean, didn't the word "hostage" kind of imply that there was something someone wanted in exchange for the victim's safe return? And strangely enough, in this case, *no one* ever brought up the existence of a ransom note. Period.

So, either the kidnapper's plan was never to let anyone go, or maybe—just maybe—the plan was for *no one* to know that a kidnapping had ever taken place at all.

That was what the Devil had been trying to tell me when he'd been picking my brains through the old guard at the Psychical Bureau of Investigations: No one had ever reported the kidnapping to the authorities, *so why the Hell was one of their agents investigating the case?*

The question I now had to ask myself was: Who benefited the *most* from having Father out of the way?

If I hadn't been me, and I didn't know all the things I know about myself—like I was a quasinormal girl who didn't have *any* aspirations toward usurping her father's position as the Grim Reaper—then I probably would've had to put myself at the top of the list of people who benefited from his "disappearance."

Someone out there had gone to a lot of pains to discredit me by putting a buttload of money in my bank account, then spreading the story that I'd accepted said money as payment from the Devil to do away with my father and the others. No wonder the King of Hell wasn't a happy camper—that put just as much blame on him as on me.

I decided that even though I really, *really* disliked the Devil, this kind of gave him an alibi. Yes, he would benefit—and he would try to spin whatever he could in his favor—but he wasn't the kidnapper. It would've taken entirely too much effort on his part, and frankly, it wasn't his style.

I had to lump Daniel in with the Devil. The guy *was* his protégé—whatever that entailed—and probably wasn't allowed to come up with big, fancy kidnapping plans all by himself anyway.

I wanted to clear my family at one fell swoop, but I didn't have enough information to rule them out. My mother and Father McGee had been very persistent about dragging me—kicking and screaming—into all of this insanity, but they both *did* seem genuinely worried about Father and Thalia.

I had no problem vouching for Clio—c'mon, if you didn't know your kid sister, then who *did* you know? She and Runt were as innocent as newborn babies, as far as I was concerned.

And Jarvis saved my life. Enough said.

That left Indra—who was probably lying dismembered somewhere—and the *mystery man*: the infamous Detective Davenport, who wasn't a detective at all.

I didn't know anything else about the guy—except that I hated his guts and would fry him like a fish the next time I saw him—but he was fast becoming my primary suspect. He was obviously a liar who knew entirely too much about the kidnapping situation to be only an innocent player in the game. He was the one who'd had the most opportunity to spread the bullshit story about me taking bribes, he was the jerkoid who'd kidnapped Jarvis, he was the one who'd put some sort of magical tracking device on my wrists when he'd cuffed me, and that meant he was the bastard who'd sent that poisoned Midori Sour to me—*ruining* the beauty of that frosty beverage forever in my mind. The only thing that I couldn't figure out was how the heck this jerkoid detective had gotten himself mixed up with Indra's arch nemesis, Vritra.

You remember Vritra . . . the scary serpent creature

that owned the disgusting *human corpse* castle? The very *castle* in which—if the Cup of Jamshid could be believed—my father and the other hostages were being held against their will?

I gave my band of merry men and women—Daniel, Clio, Kali, and Runt—the best explanation I could muster as to what I'd seen in the cup. I don't think you can ever *really* give a good description of something as heinous as Vritra's castle, but I tried. Needless to say, I only ended up making *myself* a little sick since I was the wussiest member of my little crew. All Clio wanted to know was *how* they got the bodies to stick to the walls of the castle.

I didn't have the heart to tell her that the corpses *were* the walls.

The next order of business was to figure out how in the world we were gonna *get* to Vritra's castle. The last time I'd been there, it had been through Indra's memories, so I was really hoping Kali could send us back the same way.

"Look," I said coaxingly, "I know your hands hurt—"

"You're damn right they bloody well hurt!"

"But we really need you to take us to the first place in Indra's memory. If you can get us to that *pavilion* . . ."

I could see that Kali was so *not* feeling her Girl Scout best, but she nodded her head in assent anyway, making me feel like the case for our friendship wasn't lost, after all.

"All right, I can do that, white girl, but I don't know *where* the stupid castle is. You're the only one who's been there."

"It's why Indra needed you, Kali," I said. "You weren't his downfall; you were his savior. You gave me the map to Vritra's castle in Indra's memories. And because of that, once we're there, I can find the place blindfolded. It's like Indra's legacy or something."

"Legacy-schmegacy," she snorted. "We'll see, white girl. We'll see."

I really didn't want Clio and Runt to go with us into Vritra's realm, but no matter what I did, Clio was one step ahead of me. The girl *was* the smartest one in our family for good reason.

"You want me to tell Mom?" she threatened, pulling out her BlackBerry.

"Does that thing really work out here?" I asked, incredulous.

"You wanna find out?" she said.

"Nope."

Our last order of business before we left Indra's soundstage was to try to give the Gopis a proper burial. None of us could stomach leaving them there, soaking in their own viscera like that. Daniel suggested we set the soundstage on fire, but I didn't have the heart to do it.

Finally, it was Kali who had the best idea of all.

"You know, the Gopi are just lying here, doing nothing for nobody," she offered, pursing her lips. "You could just resurrect them."

"Resurrect them?" Did I just hear what I *thought* I'd heard—she wanted me to bring the Gopi *back* from the dead? Was that really such a wise idea?

"You are Death, aren't you?" she said, goading me into it.

She's right. I am *Death,* I thought to myself, *so why not put any powers I still have to good use.*

I promptly called every single one of the Gopi back into being. The only problem was that they'd been dead a little too long to return to a normal state of existence. From afar, the Gopi looked *okay*, but if you got up close and personal in their business . . . well, that was another story. A number of the ladies were missing body parts or had co-opted body parts that didn't quite fit. There were a few missing eyeballs and teeth—and one headless Gopi who couldn't stop walking into the staircases and knocking herself out.

It was hard to believe that these were the same beautiful women I'd envied as they twirled like dervishes for Indra's camera. Now they were little more than walking zombies with broken fingernails, in tattered saris.

"Ladies," I called, and they slowly turned to face me.

Seriously, as I surveyed the crowd, I kept imagining I was staring at the extras rejects from the "Thriller" music video. All we needed was Vincent Price, and we'd be ready to go.

"I know that I have no right to ask *anything* of you," I continued, "but we plan on going to fight the evil Vritra—"

"VRITRA . . . ?" they muttered as one—which was pretty freaky.

"Yes, we're going to fight Vritra—"

"VRITRA . . . ?" they said again. Daniel reached over and grasped my forearm.

"I don't know if it's such a good idea to use the word 'Vritra,' Callie," he whispered. "You seem to be agitating them."

He was right. They *had* started to repeat the name among themselves, and the sound of their bitterness was only building with each passing second.

"Why don't you come with us?" I said to the assemblage. "Let's go kick some *Vritra* ass!"

"Vritra . . . Vritra . . . VRITRA . . . VRITRA . . ." they continued to chant until the word was like a mantra shared between their brains.

"Let's go!" I said, turning to Kali, who was totally getting freaked-out by the weird Gopi behavior.

"*I* can totally kick their asses, but they're giving *me* the willies right now," Kali said, her eyes unblinking. Even Runt was smart enough not to bark while the Gopi were around. I had a feeling that if they couldn't get a little Vritra blood, they'd probably settle for any blood at all.

"Give me your hand, white girl—and the rest of you, hold on to a piece of her shirt," Kali yelled over the drone of the Gopi chanting.

"What about them!" I said, indicating the Gopi.

"They don't need my help," she said, shaking her head, her eyes wide. I turned my head and saw why Kali was looking a little overwhelmed.

The Gopi were eating each other.

Not really chowing down, not tearing flesh, nor drawing blood . . . Instead, they were swallowing each other *whole.* One would unhinge her jaw the way a snake did when it was about to consume its dinner, and her partner would climb inside. This went on and on, Gopi consuming Gopi, until only three were left—one of them being the headless Gopi—and then two . . . and then finally only the headless Gopi remained as her last sister with a head unhinged her own jaw and ate herself.

"They may look like they're eating one another," Kali continued, "but as each one is consumed, they are actually being transported into the next realm so they can find Indra and fulfill their mission to protect him. Only the last one will remain trapped on this plane."

I kind of felt sorry for the poor, headless Gopi as she wandered pathetically around the soundstage, but I forgot her plight the moment Kali began to squeeze my hand, and I felt all the little bones inside my skin begin to break into a million pieces.

And then I was gone.

twenty-eight

I looked in the mirror and once again I was Indra: all tall and lithe and with a well-muscled body and a regal face and an extremely large . . . Hmm, I wondered if I'd get a chance to give the package a test-drive this time? But then I blinked, and sadly, *I* was the only person staring back at me in the mirror's reflection.

It was getting dark in Vritra's realm. And that meant all the bad things would be coming out to play soon.

Daniel stood behind me, his hand holding on to the bottom of my tank top, dangerously close to my, ahem, derriere. Clio, Runt's leash looped in her belt, was holding on to my shoulder.

"Did you just have a penis?" she said, her eyes flaring. "Like maybe Indra's penis?"

I ignored her.

"Where's Kali?"

Daniel shook his head, his eyes taking in the glorious profusion of tent that surrounded us.

"I don't think she could come with us. I felt her trying

to cross over, but it wasn't happening," Daniel said. "I think she was more than a map, Callie. I think she was the only conduit by which we could cross over into this realm."

"That's so cool," Clio said, and Runt barked.

"I wish she was here," I said, shivering. Daniel caught my eye, his own eyes full of worry.

"Me, too."

There was a familiar chanting sound just outside the tent, and we all ran to the side just in time to see the Gopi as they marched, en masse, across the desert toward Vritra's castle. They looked better here, more alive, but it was kind of hard to tell really because they were so far away.

"Well, I never thought I'd say this, but seeing a whole army of living-dead Indian milkmaids crossing the desert floor to slay a sea serpent *is* kinda comforting," I said.

Daniel snorted.

I turned to Clio, who was admiring herself in the mirror. She caught my eye, and gave me a reassuring smile.

"Look, Clio, I think you're aces, and that's why if anything happened to you, I'd shoot myself—" I began.

"I know," she said, cutting me off. "You want me to stay *here*." She indicated the tent, and I nodded happily. I couldn't believe my luck. My headstrong little sister was *actually* gonna do what I told her to!

"Bite me, Callie."

I knew it was too good to be true.

"Crap, okay, just do what Daniel or I tell you to and keep your mouth shut. I've been here before and you haven't so—"

"Whatever," she said dismissively.

"I mean it," I said firmly.

"Fine."

"Okay, then let's get out of here," I said, and headed for the sand. I was still holding the cup in my hand when I noticed that for the first time ever it was freezing cold to the touch. I didn't know what it meant, but I didn't think it was a good thing.

"The cup's like a block of ice," I whispered to Daniel as the three of us and Runt clomped through the sand, following the trail of footsteps the Gopi left behind. I hadn't had to use my memory once since we'd gotten here—thank God for small miracles—because I couldn't have found the *pavilion* again, let alone the corpse castle.

"What's it mean?" he asked, and I shrugged. *I have no idea; that's why I'm asking you,* I thought to myself.

Out of nowhere Runt started barking like Cujo, and Clio had to throw all her body weight into yanking Runt back by the halter or the puppy would've run off into the darkening twilight.

"What is it?" I called up to her, but Clio didn't answer. It took Daniel and me a minute to catch up to her, but when we did, I saw why she was being so quiet.

We'd reached Vritra's castle. And we were late. The battle had already begun.

The castle stood in all its villainous horror just like I remembered it. There were still too many eyes to count, too many blackened tongues protruding from lacerated mouths, eviscerated entrails plastered together, cracked bones rammed in place. It made me sick to look at it.

I looked over at Clio again, and I could see the enormity of the evilness of the place filling her imagination with a hundred thousand nightmares.

"It's built out of people, Callie. You said it was a

castle . . . but it's really a mausoleum." She stumbled over her words as she spoke, and right then I would've given up shopping for the rest of my life if I could've only peeled away this image from my sister's brain forever.

But I couldn't.

"I think you're right, Clio," I said, squeezing her arm. "It's anything *but* a castle."

I looked over at Daniel, but he was too busy surveying the fighting to pay much attention to what the castle was made of.

"The Gopi are winning," he said, pointing to where one of the Gopi was slaughtering a brigade of scarlet and black armored soldiers.

These were the very soldiers that Indra had defeated so deftly with his double-headed scepter the last time I was here. It made me remember that they were just the first—and easiest—defense that Vritra had protecting his castle of bodies.

"There's more where they came from," I said. "Just wait."

It didn't take the Gopi long to destroy the first wave of soldiers. Once all the infantrymen had been killed, the Gopi stood around poking at the dead bodies, waiting for whatever was going to happen next.

From where we stood—which was as far away as I could convince Clio and Daniel to stand from the action—we could still here the faint chant of the word "Vritra" as it was carried through the air toward us.

"This is creepy," Clio said, rubbing Runt's head more for her own comfort than for giving Runt the scratchies.

"Just wait," I repeated. It was going to be *very* interesting to see what Clio and Daniel did once the goop monsters reared their ugly heads.

We didn't have to wait long.

The earth began to shake, knocking some of the less-well-put-together Gopi onto the ground. The others who were able to retain their balance looked up at the sky, their eyes locked on something that we couldn't see—but that *I* could remember.

"What's going on?!" Clio shrieked as she grabbed my hand, terrified. She shrieked again as a loud belching sound filled the air and the stench of poop and burning hair assailed our nostrils.

"Ew!" Clio wailed, covering her nose. I looked over and saw that Daniel was doing the same thing.

The smell is even worse than I remember.

"Just wait," I said—it was fast becoming my mantra. Suddenly, the sky was lit up with fire as the giant masses of black goop sailed through the air like cannon balls and splatted thick and gooey onto the ground, taking out chunks of earth—and any Gopi not quick enough to get out of the way.

Runt started barking again, but this time Clio was so focused on the goop balls flying through the air that she wasn't quick enough to stop the puppy from yanking her leash free and running helter-skelter right into all the action.

"Runt!" Clio screamed as she instinctively took off after the hellhound, completely forgetting the insanity that was going on all around her.

"Clio! Come back!" I yelled, but I was too far behind for them to hear me.

All I could do was watch in horror as Clio, her eyes pinned to Runt's retreating back, tripped on a fallen piece of armor . . . *and sailed headfirst into one of the glistening blobs of black goop.*

"Clio!" I screamed as the goop ball swallowed her whole. I took off again, dodging fallen soldiers, attack Gopi, and black goop balls, until I reached Clio's side. The only part of her body that was still visible was her left arm, which stuck out from the goop at a weird angle.

"Damn it," I cried, plunging my hands into the viscous, gluelike stuff and pulling at my baby sister's arm. The more I pulled, the less she budged—but the more I got myself entangled in the goop. It seemed like hours that I fought for my sister, but it could have been only seconds because when I looked back to where I'd left Daniel, he was still quite a distance away from us and running pretty damn fast.

"Daniel!" I shouted, willing him to reach me before I was subsumed, but there wasn't enough time. Too soon, I felt the goop overwhelm me, and then I was sucked down into a black, hazy world—one from which I was afraid that I would never escape.

The last thing I remembered as I was sucked down into unconsciousness was clutching the Cup of Jamshid so tightly in my hand that it felt like my fingers were going to freeze off.

"callie?"

It was Clio's voice, sounding small and scared. I opened one eye and didn't see anything but darkness, so I shut it again.

"Callie," she said again, shaking me. The girl was persistent—I'd give her that. I cracked both eyes open this time, and that was when I saw Clio, her whole person covered in black glop, sitting next to me, holding the severely tarnished Cup of Jamshid in her lap.

"The cup," I said, my voice a whisper.

"I had to pry it out of your hand," Clio said, wiping her nose with the back of her hand but just smearing more goop onto her face.

"Where are we?" I said, sitting up, my back cracking as I lifted myself from the cold stone floor.

I could see that we were in some kind of massive feasting hall—there was a long wooden table in the center of the room, bits of meat and sauce drying to its top from the last meal, and this was facing a huge stone hearth that Clio and I and about twenty roast pigs could've fit into easily. All along the sides of the table were rough-hewn wooden chairs and candelabra with thick, dripping tallow candles that gave the room its only light except for the raging fire in the hearth.

The place reeked of sweat, unwashed bodies, and death. It seemed that the castle was just as unsettling on the *inside* as it was on the *outside*.

"Give me the cup," I said, holding out my hands. Clio deposited the poor blackened thing in my hands, and I held it up to the light so that I could see inside it.

"What do you see?" Clio asked.

I couldn't see a bloody thing. *Stupid cup,* I thought to myself as I threw it into the wall. It made a hollow *pinging* sound when it hit the stone, then clattered to the floor and lay still. Clio crawled over to the cup and gently picked it up.

"It's not the cup's fault, Callie."

I nodded. She handed it back to me, and I put it down, opting instead to stare at my goop-covered hands.

"I didn't see anything."

"You didn't?" Clio asked tentatively.

"Nothing."

She took a deep breath and let it out slowly through her nose.

"Okay," she tried. "What did you see before? Where in this place did you see Dad?"

I closed my eyes, trying desperately to remember, but all I could see was my father's ashen face and the way his eyelids fluttered once, then didn't move again.

"I don't know," I wailed.

"Well, we can't just sit here waiting to get eaten," Clio said finally as she took the cup and stood. "Let's go exploring."

"I don't want to," I said, pouting like a small child. Clio grabbed my arm and yanked on it, trying to force me to stand.

"Stop it," I said through gritted teeth.

"Not until you get up and stop feeling sorry for yourself," she said, pulling on my arm again.

"I said to stop it!" I slapped her hand away from me, and too late I realized that I'd hit her a lot harder than I'd meant to. She gasped at the sting of flesh on flesh, and then her eyes filled with tears. She dropped my arm and scuttled away from me.

"I really hate you sometimes, Calliope," she whispered, and then she took off. At first, I just watched her go, her long legs carrying her through one of the myriad of doorways that led in and out of the hall.

"Clio, wait!" I called, but my voice only seemed to get sucked up in the roar of the fire and the steady drip of tallow onto the floor.

Damn it, I thought as I stood up and marched over to the doorway Clio had gone through. But when I got there, I saw the door was padlocked shut.

That's weird, I thought. *I must've been mistaken.*

I tried every single door in the whole place—and every one of them was locked up tight as a drum. I had no idea what to do now. I'd lost my sister, and I was nowhere near finding my father.

I walked over to the hearth and sat down in front of it, letting the warmth penetrate my skin and sink into my bones. I closed my eyes and sat there, trying to collect my thoughts and calm my brain.

"Shit, shit, shit . . ." I moaned under my breath.

"Mistress Calliope?"

My eyes popped open, and I looked around frantically, trying to locate the sound of *Jarvis's voice.*

"Jarvis?" I hissed. "Is that you?"

I looked up *and saw the stairway hidden inside the heart of the hearth.*

"How do I get in there?" I said, but Jarvis didn't seem to have any ideas for me.

"I couldn't tell you, Miss Calliope. I've only ever seen *this* side of the hearth."

There were no buckets of water to put out the flames, no blanket to suffocate them with, so I sucked it up and made a running leap for the bottom step.

I was *really* hoping it would turn out to be magical fire—specifically a magical fire that didn't burn.

Magical fire, my ass.

I felt like one of those Yogis running across a bed of hot coals on bare feet, only I didn't have the luxury of being able to transcend my body and get my mind away from all the pain that fire can so lovingly wreak on delicate human skin.

"Ow!" I yelped as my foot found purchase on the last step of the stairway. I made a grab for the wrought-iron railing that encircled the winding staircase, but yanked my hand back when I realized it was superheated from being so near the fire.

"Yikes," I said under my breath, still feeling the bite of the iron rail and knowing it would probably leave a scar on my palm.

I pushed my body up the stairway, feeling the cool air from above as it hit my face and neck, offering me a bit of freedom from the heat. I reached a landing that I thought was the top of the stairs but was really only the bottom of another hearth. When I looked up again, I saw that the winding stairway actually continued upward, farther than I could see.

"Mistress Calliope!"

Sitting in the corner of a small room filled with large, rickety spindles—the Sewing Room, presumably—was Jarvis, a large, bloody gash streaked across his handsome cheek. He was tied to one of the decrepit spindles by a long length of that same nylon string my father had bound Monsieur D to the palm tree with. Jarvis and Monsieur D were both magically adept, I realized now, so the string must've possessed some kind of antimagical property.

Jarvis gave me a big, toothy grin. He looked *very* happy to see me.

"I decided that no one would ever come for me. That I would be bound here for the rest of my natural existence," he said, the giddiness he felt at seeing me—or just another friendly living being—evident in the tone of his voice.

"It's good to see you, too," I said, feeling a little choked up as I knelt down and gave the faun a hug. "Thank you for saving my life," I whispered in his ear.

I swear to God he blushed.

"How do I get you out of this mess?" I said, my fingers fumbling with the string. He shook his head.

"I can only be released by the magician that created the spell," he offered sadly.

"Screw that," I said, reaching for the string and snapping it in two. "I'm Death, and I can kill anything. Even a spell."

Jarvis looked at me, wide-eyed.

"You did it, didn't you? You completed the tasks!"

I nodded.

"I always knew you could do it!" he said, tears in his eyes.

Jarvis *believed* in me—and he was *proud* of me, too. Would wonders ever cease?

I grabbed his arm, helping the faun to stand, but I could see he was still sore from his struggle with the detective. I doubted he would be able to keep a very fast pace.

"Can you walk?" I asked, and he nodded, a determined look on his face. Suddenly, he saw the cup in my hand and gasped.

"You brought the Cup of Jamshid here? Are you out of your mind?" he nearly screeched at me.

"What?" I said, not understanding *why* he was getting all freaked-out about the stupid cup.

"You want to let the cup fall into the detective's hands? Do you know what that would mean?"

I shook my head. I loved Jarvis, but he really *could* be a bit tedious at times. I just hoped I wasn't going to get another supernatural history lesson.

"The Cup of Jamshid grants eternal life . . . ?" he said, doing that teacher thing where you make the class answer a question, expecting your students to chime in with the "because" part. I decided to humor him—after all, he had saved my life.

"And because it has the power over life and death, it would be a totally *bad* idea for some bad guy to control it," I said in a monotone. Jarvis looked surprised, but he nodded his head happily at what I was saying.

As much as the whole question-answer game was just *superfun*, I'd really started to worry about Clio and the rest of my family. We were gonna have to say hasta la vista to the Sewing Room and get our asses in gear if we were gonna do any people-rescuing.

"Let's get out of here," I said, taking Jarvis's hand and guiding him back to the hearth. Together, we stepped inside and started to climb.

The next landing we passed belonged to another empty room—this one a well-appointed, feminine-looking bedroom. The next two didn't grab our interest either—more bedrooms. It wasn't until we reached the fourth, and seemingly final, landing that we hit pay dirt.

"I think this is it," I whispered in Jarvis's ear as we had reached the topmost part of one of the turrets.

It was a grand, sweeping space with windows that looked out into the darkness of the surrounding night. It would have been a romantic place with all the stone and candles and beautiful views—as long as you were able to ignore the chains embedded into walls and the prisoners pinioned into them.

"Father!" I cried as I saw him, his body leaning forward, chains wrapped around his arms and torso and legs. He looked terrible, but when he heard my voice, he lifted his head up and blinked at me.

I handed Jarvis the cup and ran over to my father, holding him up so the pressure from the chains was lessened.

"Father, are you okay?"

He nodded, a small smile of mirth playing in the corners of his mouth. I guess he was right. It was kind of a *dumb* question.

"Jarvis and I are here to rescue you," I said, trying to sound more confident than I felt. I doubted seeing Jarvis and me, and realizing *we* were the "rescue party," really made him feel much better.

"Thank you, Calliope," my father said, his voice low and booming even though he must've been exhausted. "We have to free the others, too." He indicated with his head to where the rest of the Executives from the company lay chained to the walls, trapped in the same predicament.

As I counted the men and women chained here and there, I realized something funny: There weren't enough of them. I counted again, and still I got the same number. Someone was missing.

Someone really important.

"Where's Thalia?" I said, my voice scared.

"Why, I'm right here, Callie," a cold voice said behind me.

twenty-nine

My father's eyes were sad, sadder than I'd ever seen them before. It didn't take me long to understand—I wasn't a complete dummy. I took a step back from him and turned around.

"Thalia," I breathed, my eyes having a hard time accepting what I was seeing. My older sister, Thalia, tall and beautiful but with a cruel look etched on her fine-boned face, stood beside Jarvis, her hand grasping him painfully by the scruff of the neck. In her other hand, she held Clio in much the same way.

"Look who I found wandering in my castle," Thalia said, her voice like ice.

"Your castle?" I whispered.

She gave me a wicked smile, and Jarvis cringed.

"Of course it's my castle. Who else would it belong to? I *am* Vritra's new wife, after all."

I was aghast.

"You married that slimy serpent?"

She didn't take the bait; she only squeezed Clio's

neck harder, making her gasp with pain. I was incredulous. I couldn't believe Thalia'd done something so *stupid*—and was being such a bitch about it to boot.

"Leave them alone!" I said. "They're just a kid and a faun."

I got two nasty looks from Jarvis and Clio, but I didn't care. It was the truth, and if the truth would set them free, then screw them both.

"I'll let them go, if that's what you want, Callie," Thalia said as she marched over to one of the windows. Clio whimpered, and Jarvis closed his eyes.

"Wait!" I screamed. "Just wait a minute . . ."

She turned back around, still clutching her prey, her hands like talons. It was becoming very hard to reconcile this monstrous woman with the girl who had once been my sister.

"Tell me something, Thalia. Why did you do it?" This seemed to please my older sister—just like it did *anytime* anyone asked a supervillain in the movies to explain their dastardly plans. She slackened her grip on Jarvis's neck and licked her lips, eager to impart the details of her perfect crime to me.

"Calliope, you must know by now that you're the one with the *birthright*—you, the one who doesn't even *care* about the business. I slaved for Dad, I gave my lifeblood to that company, and the only thing they ever *gave* me was the Vice Presidency of Asia. *Asia . . . ? Come on!* What the hell was that? *Nothing!*"

"Asia's nice," I mumbled.

"Shut up, Callie. I'm talking right now."

I did as she said.

"Of course, it *is* the reason I met Vritra, so maybe you're right, Callie: Asia *is* nice."

I swallowed hard, trying to think of anything to keep her talking.

"And you two planed the whole thing *together*?" I said.

She nodded.

"Of course! And what a brilliant plan it was. We would kidnap the top echelon of Death, Inc., send the Board into an uproar, and then like magic I would appear—sadly, the only one to have escaped from the kidnapper's clutches. The Board would grant me the interim Presidency of Death, Inc., since I was the highest-level Executive left. Then unbeknownst to everyone else, Vritra and I would find the Cup of Jamshid, dispose of any other contenders for the position, and have the market cornered on Death. And no matter what the Board did, *we'd* have all the control!"

I stared at her. It really *was* a brilliant coproduction between two seriously twisted minds.

"That's terrible, Thalia, and really mean-spirited," I said. "How could you do it?"

"No, the question is: How could *you* come back and stick your nose into something that doesn't concern you? I would've laughed if anyone had even *suggested* that you would actually *try* to attempt those stupid tasks."

"Hey! I completed those tasks, you bitch!"

I saw the shift in her thinking right there and then. The *idea* that I might actually *be* Death had never even entered her brain. I could see her mind start working in overtime, reassessing the situation as quickly as it could—which, knowing Thalia, was pretty damn quick.

I knew I had only one chance to stop her before my modelicious-looking sister from Hell could think of something truly terrible to do to me.

"I'm sorry, Thalia. You're my sister, and I guess even though you're actually a horrible, evil creature underneath it all . . . I still love you. So, it kind of sucks to have to do this to you."

I raised my hand and pointed my index finger at her chest.

"Do it, Callie!" Clio screamed.

"Die," I whispered.

Now, I knew that Thalia was still immortal because she was part of my bloodline, but if I could set her on fire in an exact repeat of what happened with the Devil, then I would have the advantage.

I almost cried when Thalia's body erupted in flame.

"You bitch!" she shrieked as she dropped Jarvis and Clio, her body engulfed in a raging inferno.

The moment I saw that Clio and Jarvis were out of harm's way, I rushed Thalia, hitting her right in the stomach, the force of our collision sending us flying out the window, each of us clutching on to the other like a pair of tandem skydivers.

We hit the ground hard, both of us getting the air knocked out of our lungs.

"Damn, that hurt," I wheezed. But it didn't hurt *half* as bad as the kick to the head that Thalia gave me as she was clambering to her feet.

"You stupid bitch!" she screamed as she made another run for my head. This time I saw it coming and was able to roll out of the way, but not before I caught sight of her mangled face and hair. She wasn't regenerating as quickly as the Devil—and she wasn't in the middle of a shape-shift, either—so the damage was pretty bad. Her eyebrows and eyelashes were gone, and her nose was just a smidgen melted-looking. Her hair was black with soot and scorched almost to her scalp.

Yep, my evil sister looks like crap.

As she raced for me again, her fists balled and her teeth bared, I decided that I really didn't want to deal with her anymore. I was tired of her bad attitude and her evil-looking, lashless eyes.

"Gopi!" I screamed, hoping that there were at least a few of the ladies still in existence. "Gopi! This is Vritra's wife! She's *bad*!"

Thalia just stared at me, disbelieving.

"Are you insane? We killed all those Gopi—"

The first Gopi attacked from behind, slamming herself into Thalia, so that the two ended up in a heap on the ground.

"Well, I resurrected them," I said as I watched three more Gopi pile onto my sister. I had experienced a Gopi attack firsthand, so I decided that it would be *just fine* to leave Thalia in their capable—if half-dead—hands.

Like I'd been saying, I had bigger fish to fry.

"Vritra!" I screamed. *"Show yourself!"*

Sidestepping dismembered Gopi body parts, and what was left of the goop men, I felt just like Indra when he called out the nasty demon the last time I was here: *totally insane.*

You didn't *goad* the bad guy like that unless you had a plan, and I was *not* in possession of anything even *resembling* a plan.

When I reached the castle moat, I stopped and screamed again:

"VRITRA, SHOW YOURSELF!"

There was a low rumbling sound, and then Detective Davenport came striding out of the castle's drawbridge dragging Indra on a piece of chain behind him like a dog.

Oh, Lord, how stupid had I *been,* I thought to myself. I had never put together the truth.

Detective Davenport was *Vritra.*

"You called," the detective said. I saw that he had put on another nicely tailored men's suit and a pair of highly polished dress shoes to come out of his castle and meet me.

Talk about being Mr. Vanity, I thought disgustedly. The man was worse than Madonna when it came to costume changes. I really *was* afraid this whole experience was gonna put me off shopping for at least the next six months.

"We're gonna end this now," I said, my voice coming out firm and confident—score one for me.

But instead of shaking in his shoes and cowing before me, Davenport only laughed. And it was not a nice laugh.

"Don't you dare laugh all condescendingly at me, you jerkoid," I yelled, but this only made him laugh harder.

I didn't know how to shut the guy up permanently—even though I thought a knuckle sandwich would do just fine if I were given half an opportunity to serve it. I *could* try the "die" thing, but I had a feeling that he'd weather all the burning just fine. Other than that, I was at a complete and utter dead end.

"Have I stymied the great Queen of Death?" he said.

I had nothing. Not *one* idea that would allow me to slay Vritra and put everything back together the way it was before all this started. In truth, all I wanted was to be Dorothy and click my ruby red slippers together three times until I was home again, safely tucked in bed with a pint of Cherry Garcia.

But going home wasn't an option for me; I didn't know if it ever *really* had been. I was the daughter of Death—no, amend that; I wasn't the daughter of Death . . . *I was Death*—and as much as I whined about it, I was never going to escape it. I was never gonna be anything but what I was.

"No way have you stymied *this* white girl!" I yelled, preparing myself for utter annihilation by goading the detective just that little bit *more*. "You're nothing but a slimy little eel that the world should've gotten rid of eons ago!"

Davenport howled, rage glistening out of every pore, as he sized me up for attack.

I was at the point of no return. I was going to have to try my "die" routine and hope for the best. I closed my eyes, said a quick good-bye to all the people in my life that I loved: Jarvis and Clio and my mom and dad, Runt—

My thoughts were interrupted by a loud bark from inside the castle. Suddenly, I saw her. She was moving so fast she looked like a streak of midnight as she raced across the ground, her teeth pointed right at the detective's ankles.

"*Runt!*" I screamed as she made contact.

She was unstoppable, gripping his leg and shaking her head around to dig her teeth deeper into his flesh. All this to protect . . . *me*.

"Stupid dog!" he screamed, leaning back and kicking Runt hard in the side with his foot. She gave a heart-rending howl, and her body flew backward, limp.

"*Runt, no!*" I cried as I watched her disappear over the edge and into the moat.

"*Oh my God,*" I wailed. "*Please not my dog.*"

But she was gone.

I couldn't stop crying. My hatred for the creature in front of me was so great that I thought I was going to burst with it. I started to march toward him, my hands balled into the tightest fists I could manage. I felt a hand on my shoulder, and I tried to shake it off, but it grasped me so hard that I was forced to stop moving forward.

I turned on whoever was behind me, my eyes streaming and anger making my heart a hard ball of stone.

"Leave me alone!" I screamed, my rage palpable.

"I can't," Daniel said.

I shoved at him, trying to escape his grasp, pummeling him with all that I was worth, but he was too strong.

"I'm sorry, Callie," he said, his eyes wistful. "I can't let you do this."

He held me as tight as he could to keep me from abusing him, then leaned down and kissed me hard on the lips.

"Good-bye," he whispered as he broke the kiss and punched me firmly in the stomach. I fell forward, gasping for breath, the lack of oxygen making me see stars.

"I saved your life . . ." I wheezed.

"And I saved yours," he said, then walked away. I sat kneeling on the ground, clutching at my aching stomach. I watched him go, my heart reeling from the betrayal. I couldn't believe that I had misjudged him so badly.

He crossed the gap between the detective and where I lay in about twenty strides.

"I'm one of the other possibilities," I heard Daniel say as he held out his hand to Davenport. "I want to offer my services to you. With me at your side, we can claim the mantle of Death by birthright, and no one can contest it."

The detective looked uncertainly at Daniel. "You want to align yourself with me?"

"I do," Daniel replied. "Shall we shake on it?"

He stuck out his hand, and the detective stared at it.

"It's no trick," Daniel said, turning to look back at me. "She's less than nothing to me. I want to *be* Death."

This seemed to cinch it for the detective—the jerk. He took Daniel's hand, and they shook.

But not for long.

"Go to Hell," Daniel said, slamming his other hand into the side of the detective's head. He lost his balance, and they both pitched forward off the side of the drawbridge.

What the hell had just happened?

I barely had time to wonder at the insanity I had witnessed before there was a gut-wrenching earthquake, and the whole world seemed to go upside down.

Rising from the bottom of the moat was Vritra—in full serpent mode.

He was a hideous thing to behold as he thrust himself onto the ground and started sidewinding toward me. I quickly climbed to my feet, my stomach still aching, and started to run.

Right for Vritra.

I had forgotten something. Something I should've remembered a long time before this: *I have the Sea Foam.*

And I was gonna use it to kick the demon's ass.

But before I could reach the serpent, it stopped moving forward and instead began to shake itself like a giant cat. I looked farther down its body and saw that *Indra* had the monster by the tail and was pulling him away from me.

"Indra!" I screamed. "Wait, I have something for you!"

I didn't know how to transfer the Sea Foam to him manually, so I was gonna have to do it by magic.

I closed my eyes and *wished* with every ounce of my being that the Sea Foam would leave me and go over to him. My skin began to burn like it was being slathered in hot coals, but then the heat was gone, replaced with a shower of coolness that drenched me from the inside out.

When I opened my eyes, I knew the Sea Foam had left me.

Indra, still holding Vritra's tail with one hand, reached inside his tattered pants and pulled out his scepter.

"I am avenged," he yelled as he plunged the scepter into Vritra's neck. Then, he took Vritra's tail in both hands and leaned forward, sinking his teeth into the slimy scales. The demon howled in pain and rage and tried to turn back on itself to get at Indra, but it was no use; the scepter was in the way.

I watched, fascinated, as the Sea Foam raced out of Indra's body and injected itself into Vritra's skin, turning the giant demon tail a bright shade of gold.

It took only a few moments for the rest of his body to follow suit, each muted brown scale transmogrifying into a brilliant golden hue until the monster looked like a humongous, golden statue of itself. Then Indra pulled the scepter from Vritra's body, and the giant demon exploded, sending tiny shards of golden glass in every direction.

Indra smiled and gave me the thumbs-up—which I weakly returned. He looked as pleased as punch that he'd vanquished his mortal enemy—with a little help from his friends.

"Callie," Clio yelled as she and Jarvis led my father and the rest of the Death, Inc., Executives out of the castle and down the drawbridge. They all looked the worse for wear, but at least they were free and in one piece. Clio dropped our father's arm and ran over to me.

"We couldn't get them out of the chains with magic because they were spelled, but then I thought of summoning up some bolt cutters, and that totally did the trick," she said, extremely proud of herself. It turned out that sometimes the practical choice worked far better than magic *ever* could.

"Good job," I said, my voice catching in my throat as I ruffled her hair. She gave me a funny look.

"What's wrong, Cal?"

More than anything in the world, I didn't want to have to tell her about Runt and Daniel. Runt, who had saved my life more times than I could count, and Daniel . . . whose last lie saved us all. I still didn't understand why he'd done it, why he'd sacrificed himself for me. Maybe I never would. And the awful part was that I'd totally thought he was a traitor, right up until the very moment he'd pushed Vritra into the moat and forced him to take on his true form.

Oh, Daniel . . .

"Where's Runt?" Clio said, an edge of hysteria creeping into her voice. I couldn't answer, or I would've started crying again.

"Where's our dog!" she demanded, grabbing my arm and shaking it, trying to force me to speak.

"Clio . . ." I started to say, and then I heard something. It was very faint at first, and I put my finger to my mouth to shush her so that I could hear better.

If that's what I think it is . . .

"Do you hear that?" I said frantically. I pulled away from Clio's grasp and ran over to the side of the moat, crawling onto my belly so that I could see down.

I'd like to say that I believe in miracles . . . but this was almost too much.

Down inside the moat, on a piece of rock sticking out of the side of the dirt wall—the *only* such outcropping I could see in either direction—was Runt, standing on her hind legs and barking up a storm as she pawed at the sheer dirt wall. I don't know how the dog managed to land on the only safe piece of real estate down there, and frankly I don't care. The only thing that mattered to me and to Clio was that she was alive and very, *very* eager to get back onto safe ground.

"Someone help me get her up!" I called as I looked back to Clio. She ran over to my side and slithered onto her belly so that she could see over the edge, too.

"How did she get down there?" she asked me.

"It's a long story—"

"And I know. You'll tell me *all* about it later," Clio said. I nodded, glad that we finally had an understanding.

"So, how we gonna do this?" I said, looking down at Runt, who was whining pitifully. Clio gave me a devilish smile.

"Can you get some of the Gopi to come over here?"

with a little help from the last few remaining Gopi, we were able to get Runt out of the moat. It's very interesting what you can do with body parts when they're not attached to a body.

Jarvis, Indra, and Father stayed to help us with Runt, but the rest of the Executives hightailed it out of Vritra's realm as fast as the wormhole they conjured could take them. Not that I blamed them. The place *was* pretty horrible, and now that Vritra had been destroyed, the castle was starting to disintegrate, ravaged bodies falling every which way. It was pretty disgusting.

The Gopi had made short work of Thalia, wrapping her up in their tattered saris and presenting her to me like some kind of weirdo Christmas present. I hadn't wanted to offend them, so I'd just smiled and nodded as nicely as I could. I *did* notice the small star tattoo on Thalia's lower leg, and I instantly remembered the first time I saw it.

She'd come home from her first semester at college proudly brandishing her new tattoo at anyone who came into her sight. I'd been soooo jealous because Mother wouldn't even let me get my ears pierced, let alone have someone ink something permanently onto my skin. Thalia had spent the whole weekend lording it over me, and I had totally *detested* her for it.

It's funny the things we forget.

Well, I didn't know what was going to become of my sister, but I had a pretty good idea that she was *not* gonna be at Thanksgiving this year. After what she'd pulled, I didn't think that *Purgatory* was good enough for her. I mean, she *did* try to kill me, Father, a bunch of other innocent people—and she'd absolutely ruined Midori Sours for me.

Apparently, she'd committed a similar injustice to Father: at the Executive meeting where they'd all been kidnapped, they had drunk a toast in honor of Thalia's promotion to Vice President in Charge of Asia. Of course, they had no idea that they were actually toasting with a Brandy Alexander—paralysis cocktail—that she and Vritra had whipped up especially for the occasion.

I don't think my father or I would ever look at an alcoholic beverage in *quite* the same way. Nor did I think

I would ever look at my father's job in *quite* the same way, either.

As much as I *loved* my family, I was still so *not* ready to join the family business. The minute we'd pulled Runt up to safety, I'd been at Father's arm, begging to be released from my suffering. I wanted those Death powers—and that nasty little voice—out of my head, and I meant now.

"Callie," my father said, "we can only make the transference if we have the Cup of Jamshid."

"But we do!" I said. "Jarvis, get your butt over here—spit spot, on the double now!"

Jarvis didn't even bat an eyelash at my words, but came trotting over with the cup in hand. I took it from him and passed it to my father.

"But how did you—" my father began, but I cut him off.

"I gave it to Jarvis before Thalia came into the room."

Jarvis nodded. "And I put an invisibility spell on it the moment it came into my possession. Just to be on the safer of sides."

Father looked down at the cup, and once again it was a shiny, silvery color, all the tarnish completely gone. He handed me the cup, and I saw that it was full of liquid.

"Drink," he said, and I did. It was cool and tropical and left a coconut aftertaste on my lips. *Yummy.*

I handed the cup back to him, and he lifted it to his mouth, drinking deeply. As soon as the liquid touched his lips, his body began to glow, and all the grief and exhaustion of the past few days was lifted from his face and shoulders. I didn't need to be a magical rocket scientist to know that I was finally free of my burden.

"Why did you rescind my birthright?" I said suddenly. I didn't know where the words had come from, but there they were right there for everyone to hear.

I expected Father to be mad at me for being so blunt, but instead he laughed.

"You were a child, Calliope. You weren't ready for the job yet," he said soothingly. Jarvis nodded, backing him up.

"The Devil made that wormhole in the basement so that he could lure you to the Cup of Jamshid before you were of age. If your father hadn't asked the Board to rescind your birthright, you'd have been forced to take the job," Jarvis finished, pleased with himself.

"So, it *wasn't* because you didn't think I could handle the job," I asked.

He smiled fondly—no, cancel that—*proudly* at me.

"It was because I didn't want you to be forced to do something that you weren't ready for."

"Oh."

"Any more questions?" my father asked.

I nodded.

"Dad, can we go home now?"

epilogue

I sat at my desk in my old room at Sea Verge staring into one of those lighted makeup mirrors. I had had a real bitch of a time putting on the false eyelashes I'd bought at the drugstore that morning, but now that they were finally in place, I thought the effect was quite charming.

As I stared at my reflection, I found it hard to imagine that the silly young woman with the false eyelashes smiling back at me had ever been the Grim Reaper. But she had been, if only for a very few—yet very memorable—hours. Now, thank God, I was finally back to being my old, *normal* self.

Not that my life was ever gonna *really* be normal again. Since I was back in touch with my family, of course, it was expected that I'd show up for the obligatory holidays, family gatherings, etc., whether I wanted to or not. But strangely, I found that it wasn't as much of a hardship as I had once made it out to be. In fact, I guess I was kind of looking forward to Christmas with the Grim Reaper and family—as weird as that sounded coming from the girl who once upon a time placed a Forgetting Charm on herself so she'd never have to deal with said crazy family again.

I dabbed a touch of perfume behind both ears and thought about what had happened when I'd shown back up to work. I still hadn't asked Jarvis what excuse he'd given my boss about why I'd missed work, and frankly I didn't *want* to know. Whatever he'd said had made everyone behave very solicitously toward me, and *no one* had said a damn thing about "taking off too much time," or harassed me about "no paid vacation." I decided that I wasn't going to look a gift horse in the mouth.

I was startled out of my thoughts by a knock on the door, making me almost drop my precious bottle of Chanel No. 5 onto the floor.

"Crap," I said, fumbling with the bottle. "Come in!"

The door opened, and Clio stepped inside, Runt right behind her. She looked lovely in a fitted yellow silk dress, and high-heeled sandals that looked vaguely familiar.

"Are those mine?" I asked, pointing at her shoes.

"And if they are, what are you gonna do about it?" she replied tartly.

I shrugged.

"Nothing. They look good."

She blushed.

"Thanks. I wanted to let you know that the limo is here," she said.

"It is?" I shrieked, fumbling with the clasp at the back of my dress. I'd borrowed a vintage deep purple Halston from my mother's closet, and even though it looked amazing, it had been a bitch to put on.

"Here, let me help you," Clio said, coming over and easily doing up the clasp.

"It's harder when you're doing it backward," I said.

"Uh-huh."

I started hunting for my Manolos, but somehow they'd gotten shoved under the bed. I climbed to the floor—careful not to hurt the dress—and stuck my hand underneath the bed skirt like a vet birthing a baby cow.

"Go on down," I called. "I'll be there in a minute."

"Uhm, Callie," Clio said, and I looked up, surprised by her serious tone of voice. "I just wanted you to know that Daniel was a good guy. He didn't mean to punch you in the stomach . . . well, not really."

"Why're you telling me this now?" I asked as I found one of the shoes and dragged it out of its hiding place.

"Because you should know. He used the Cup of Jamshid to find me and Runt back here at Sea Verge. He said that you needed us, that I shouldn't believe *anything* bad anyone said about you. That you were the greatest person he had ever known—and he'd known *a lot* of people."

Runt came out from under the bed, the other shoe in her mouth. I took it from her, but didn't have the heart to put either of them on.

"Yeah? He said that?"

Clio nodded.

"He knew what the cup was, Callie. He could've used it to trick you and become Death himself . . . but he didn't. I don't know why. But he didn't."

I sat there in stunned silence. *Why had I never realized any of that before?*

"Well, I guess I better go down and make sure they don't leave without us," Clio said. She closed the door softly behind her, taking Runt and leaving me alone with my thoughts.

I had looked long and hard inside that moat, but I

had never found any trace of Daniel's body. I had wanted to think that he went straight up to Heaven—do not pass Go; do not collect two hundred dollars—and was right now playing an unending game of Parcheesi with God, but who knew?

Only Death.

Maybe someday I would work up the nerve to pull out his Death Record and see what really happened to him . . .

And who he really was.

But until then I didn't want to think about sad things that I had no control over.

I slipped my shoes on and stood up, admiring myself in the mirror. I thought I looked pretty damn good, even if I did say so myself.

Although I really wasn't one hundred percent *feeling* it, I put on a happy face and thought about how exciting it was to be going to my first Bollywood premiere. Indra had invited my whole family to the screening of his "Masterpiece" (his word, not mine), kind of as a thank-you for all the help we'd given him, I guess.

At first I *did* wonder if Kali had put him up to it, but then I decided that I really didn't care *what* the reason was. It was just kind of cool to be invited.

Period.

I knew that no matter what happened tonight, I was going to go to this thing, and I was going to *make* myself have a good time—*even if it killed me.*

I gave myself a quick wink in the mirror for courage, then I picked up my clutch bag. I flipped off the overhead light and closed my bedroom door firmly behind me as I headed down the stairs, following the gentle hum of conversation coming from the front hall. I could just make out Clio's voice intoning the words "Mr. Sex on a Stick."

Oh, brother, I mused, *here we go again.*

I had a funny feeling this premiere was gonna turn out to be a hell of a lot more *interesting* than I'd imagined.

I just hope the Gopi remembered to bring their heads.

Now on HBO®,
***True Blood*℠, the original series**
based on the Sookie Stackhouse novels
from

Charlaine Harris

DEAD UNTIL DARK

Sookie Stackhouse is a small-time cocktail waitress in small-town Louisiana. She's quiet, keeps to herself, and doesn't get out much. Not because she's not pretty. She is. It's just that, well, Sookie has this sort of "disability." She can read minds. And that doesn't make her too dateable. Then along comes Bill. He's tall, dark, handsome—and Sookie can't hear a word he's thinking, making him her perfect match.

But Bill has a disability of his own: He's a vampire with a bad reputation. He hangs with a seriously creepy crowd, all suspected of—big surprise—murder. And when one of Sookie's coworkers is killed, she fears she's next.

penguin.com

M336T0908

PO #: 0003177728